W9-AAI-959

**written and illustrated
by Ross Campbell**

**super special thanks to
Michelle Silva**

published by SLG Publishing
Dan Vado: President & Publisher
Jennifer de Guzman: Editor-In-Chief

www.slavelabor.com
www.shadoweyes.net

SLG Publishing
P.O. Box 26427
San Jose, CA 95159

First Printing: June 2010
ISBN: 978-1-59-362189-6

printed in Hong Kong.

SHADOW EYES

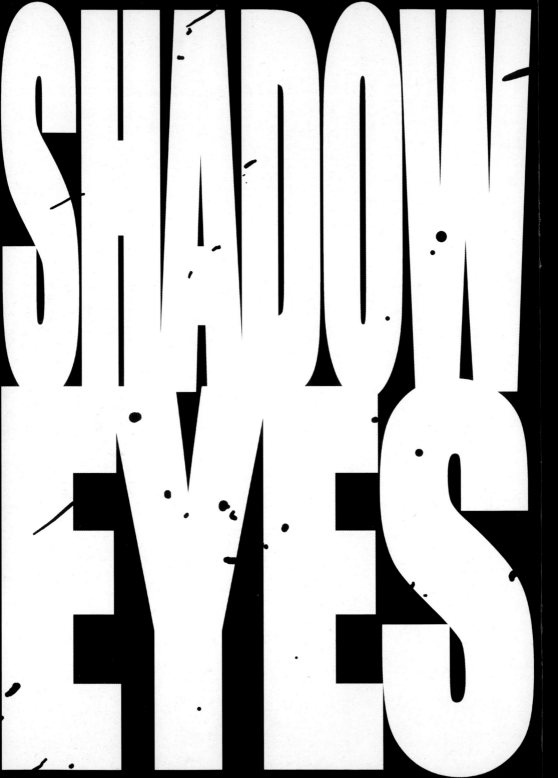

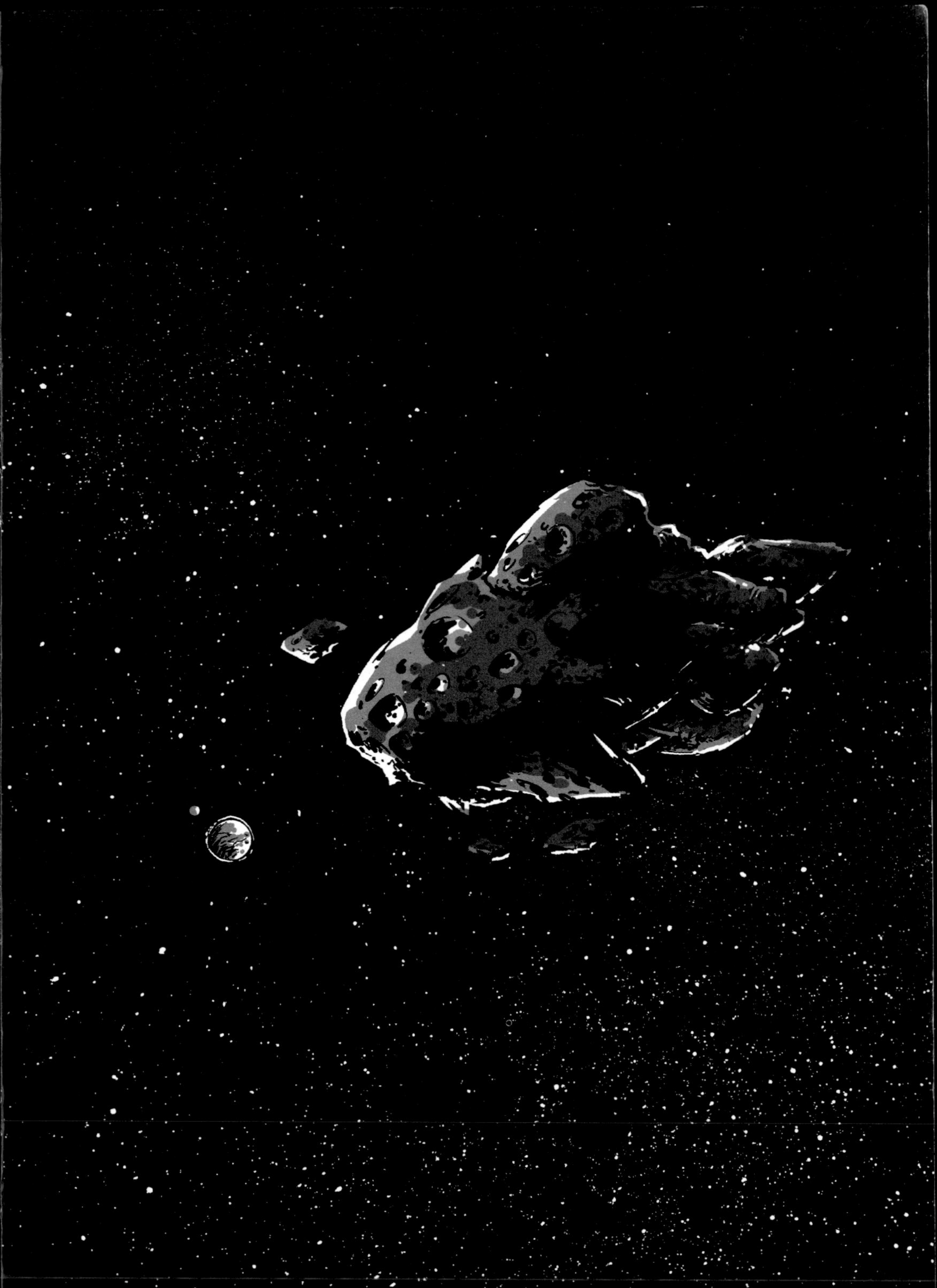

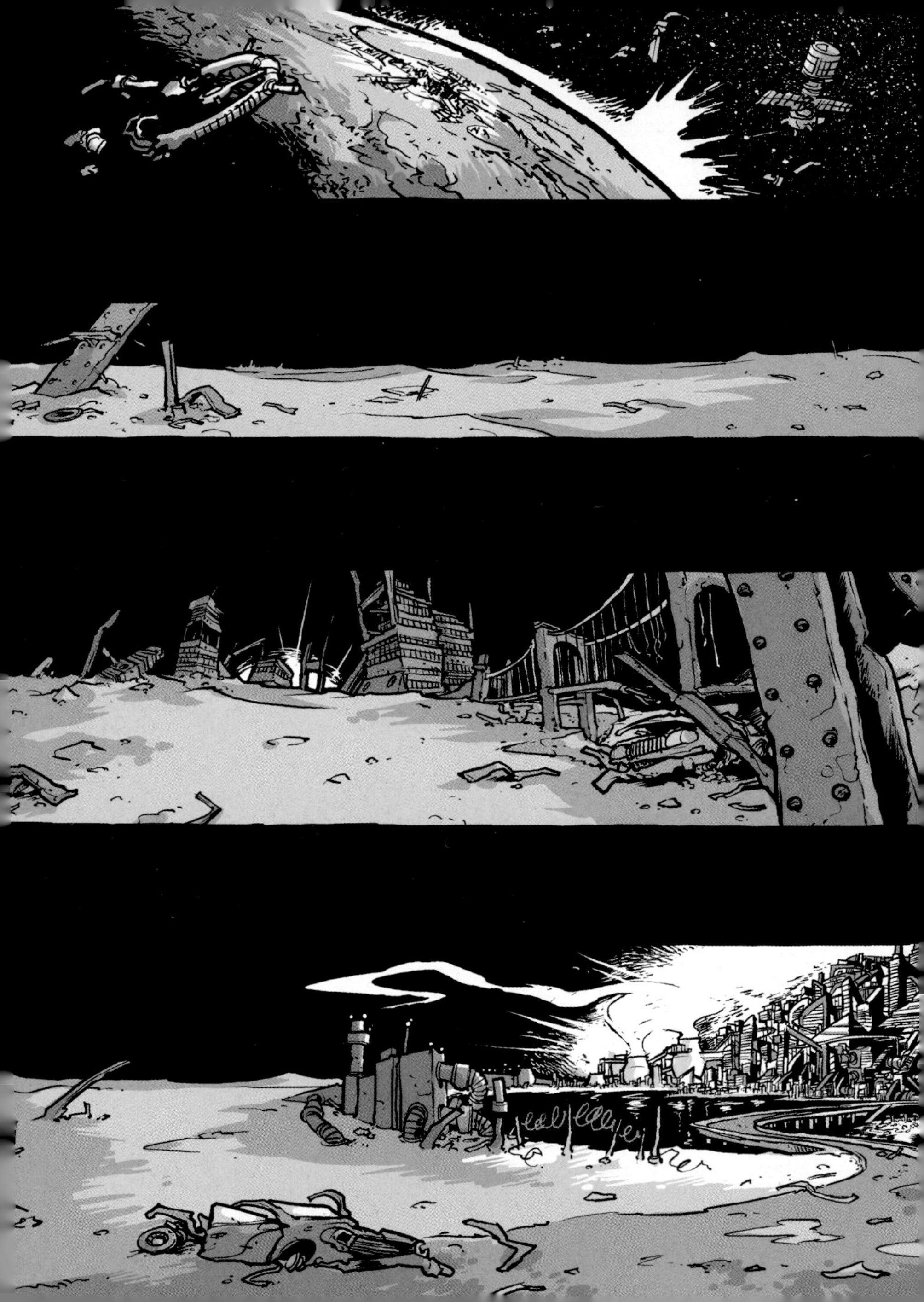

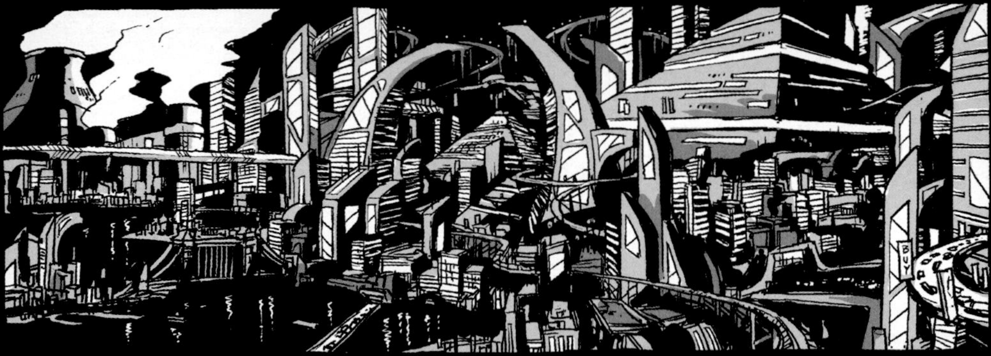
BUY

the city of Dranac.

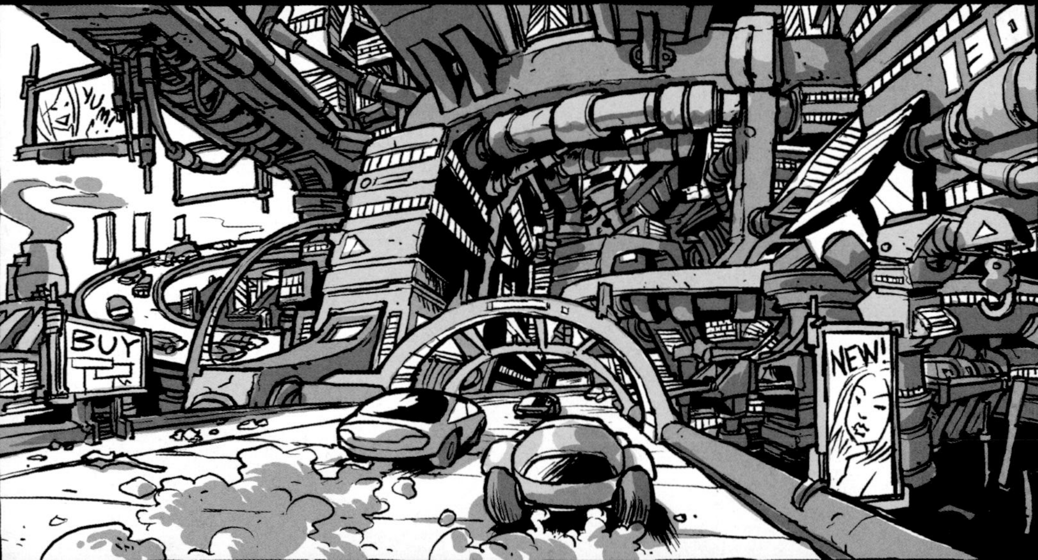
BUY
NEW!

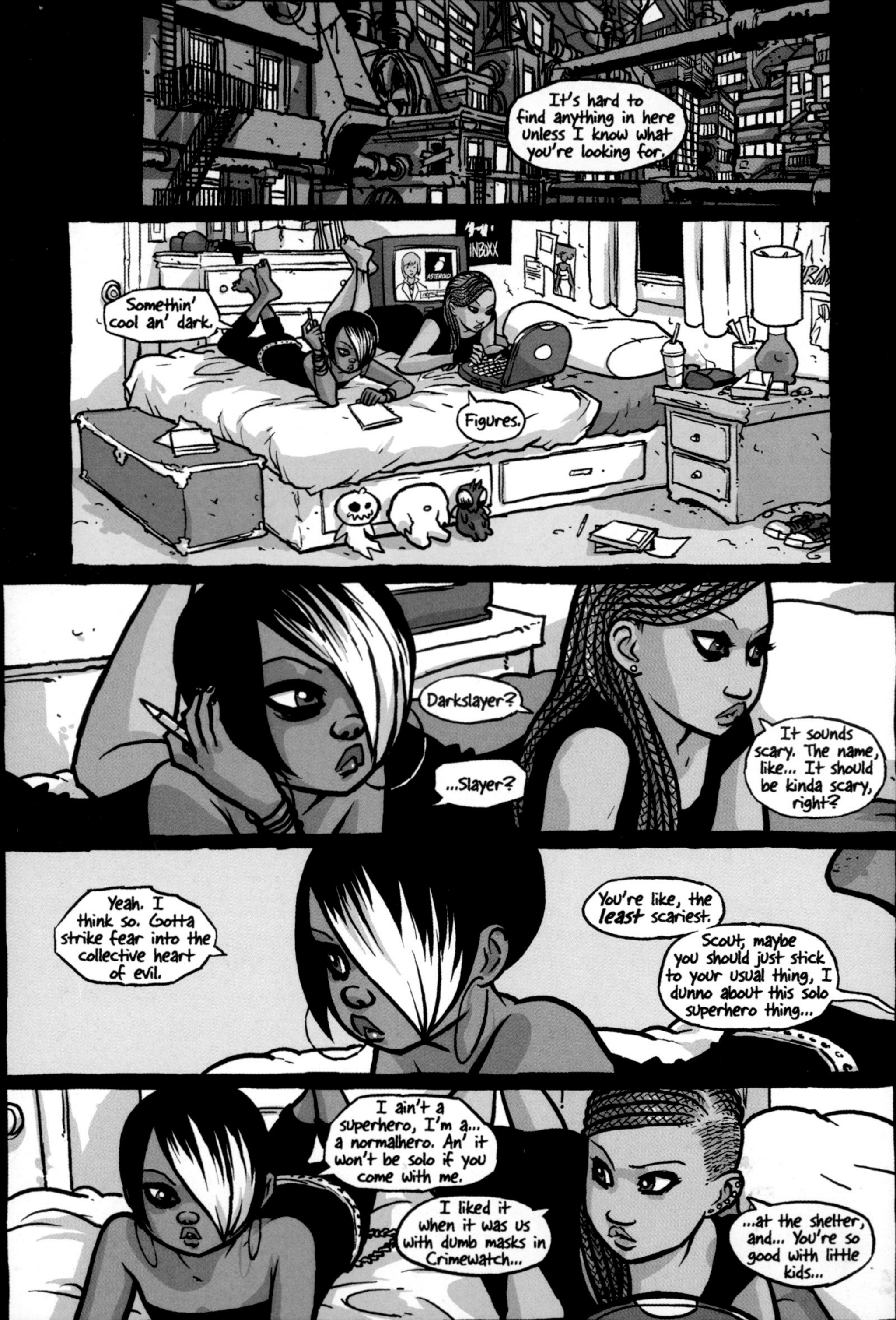
It's hard to find anything in here unless I know what you're looking for.
Somethin' cool an' dark.
INBOXX
ASTEROID
Figures.
Darkslayer?
...Slayer?
It sounds scary. The name, like... It should be kinda scary, right?
Yeah. I think so. Gotta strike fear into the collective heart of evil.
You're like, the *least* scariest.
Scout, maybe you should just stick to your usual thing, I dunno about this solo superhero thing...
I ain't a superhero, I'm a... a normalhero. An' it won't be solo if you come with me.
I liked it when it was us with dumb masks in Crimewatch...
...at the shelter, and... You're so good with little kids...

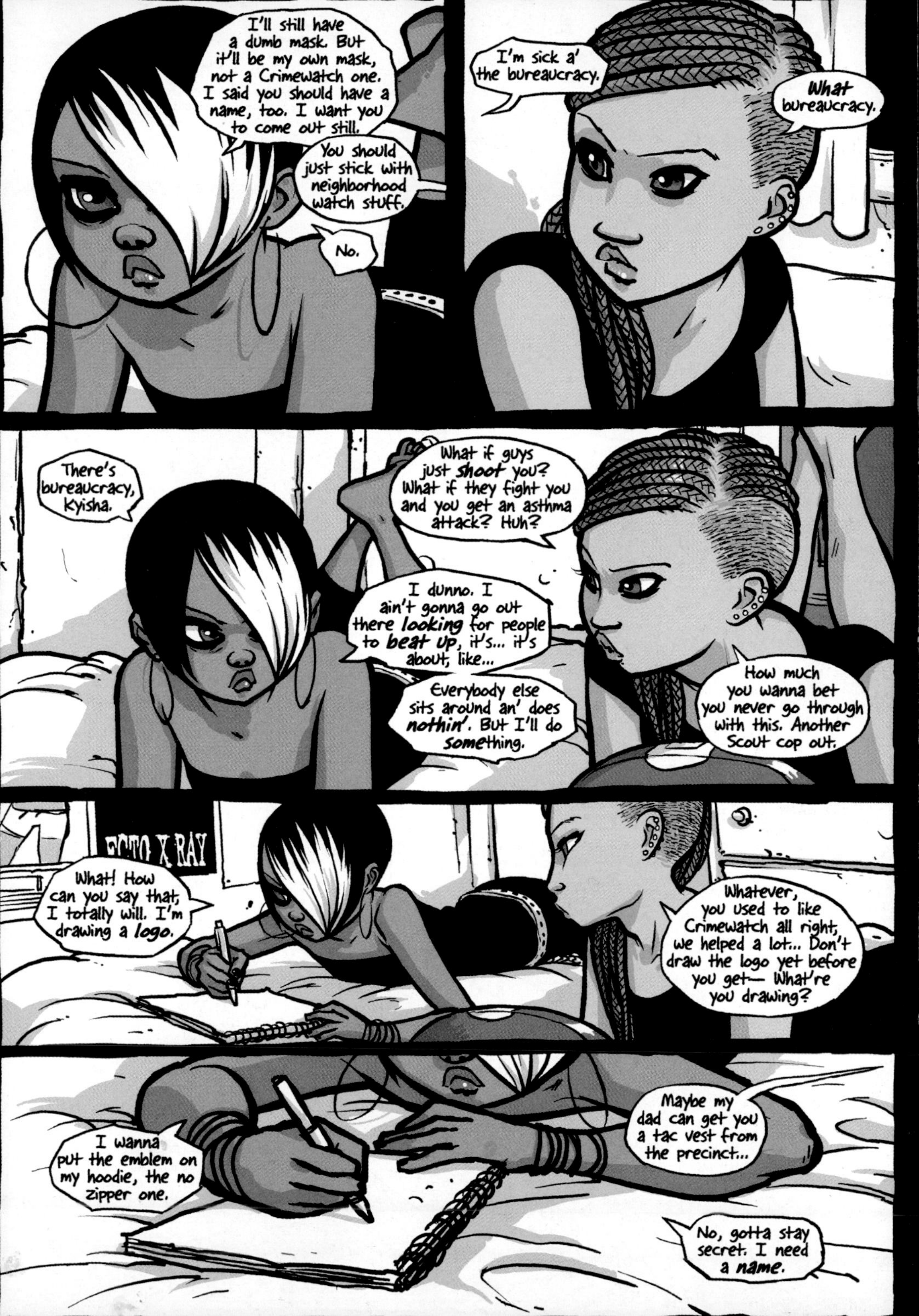

I'll still have a dumb mask. But it'll be my own mask, not a Crimewatch one. I said you should have a name, too. I want you to come out still.
You should just stick with neighborhood watch stuff.
No.
I'm sick a' the bureaucracy.
What bureaucracy.
There's bureaucracy, Kyisha.
What if guys just shoot you? What if they fight you and you get an asthma attack? Huh?
I dunno. I ain't gonna go out there looking for people to beat up, it's... it's about, like...
Everybody else sits around an' does nothin'. But I'll do something.
How much you wanna bet you never go through with this. Another Scout cop out.
ECTO X RAY
What! How can you say that, I totally will. I'm drawing a logo.
Whatever, you used to like Crimewatch all right, we helped a lot... Don't draw the logo yet before you get— What're you drawing?
I wanna put the emblem on my hoodie, the no zipper one.
Maybe my dad can get you a tac vest from the precinct...
No, gotta stay secret. I need a name.

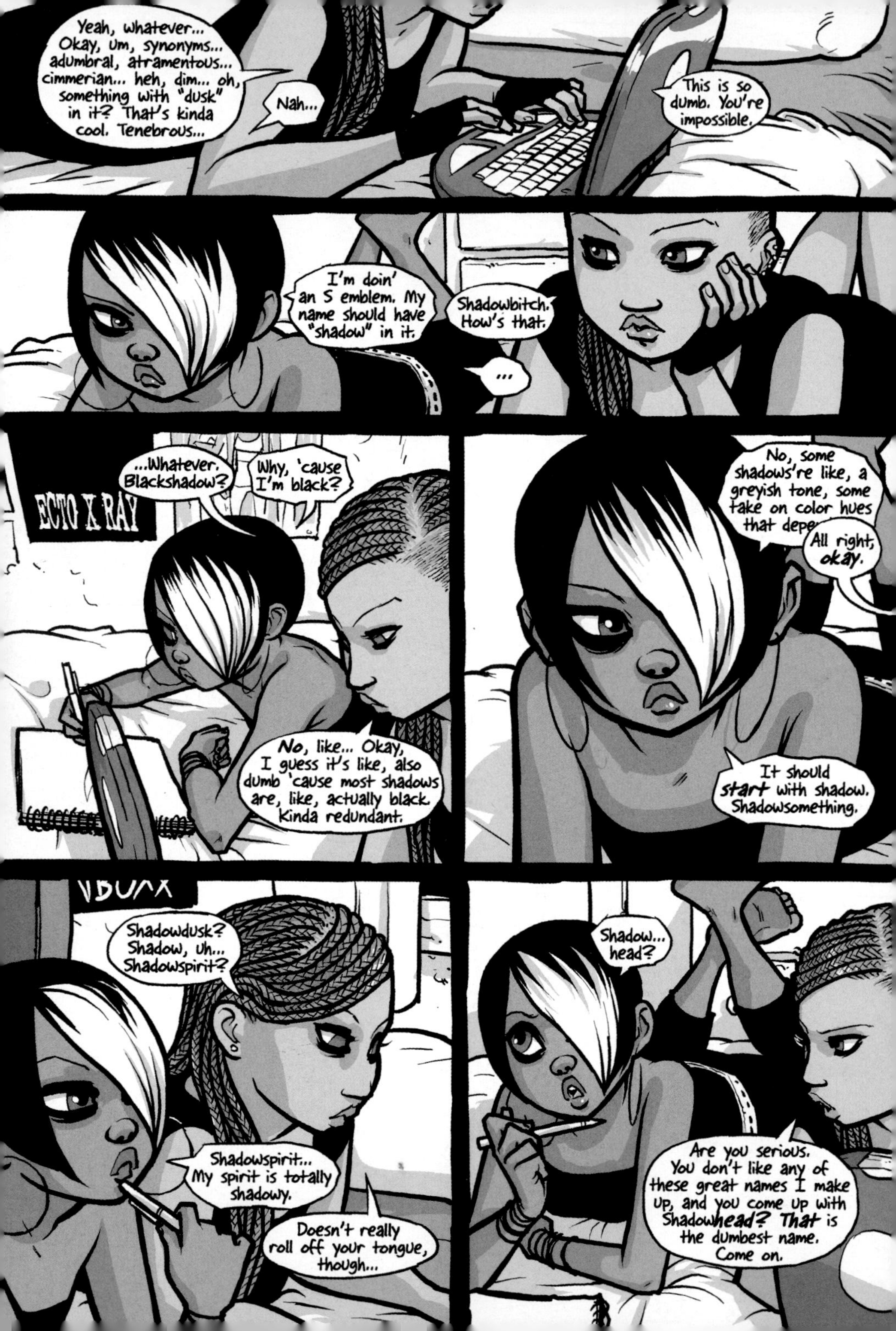

Yeah, whatever... Okay, um, synonyms... adumbral, atramentous... cimmerian... heh, dim... oh, something with "dusk" in it? That's kinda cool. Tenebrous...
Nah...
This is so dumb. You're impossible.
I'm doin' an S emblem. My name should have "shadow" in it.
Shadowbitch. How's that.
...
ECTO X RAY
...Whatever. Blackshadow?
Why, 'cause I'm black?
No, like... Okay, I guess it's like, also dumb 'cause most shadows are, like, actually black. Kinda redundant.
No, some shadows're like, a greyish tone, some take on color hues that depe—
All right, okay.
It should start with shadow. Shadowsomething.
Shadowdusk? Shadow, uh... Shadowspirit?
Shadowspirit... My spirit is totally shadowy.
Doesn't really roll off your tongue, though...
Shadow... head?
Are you serious. You don't like any of these great names I make up, and you come up with Shadowhead? That is the dumbest name. Come on.

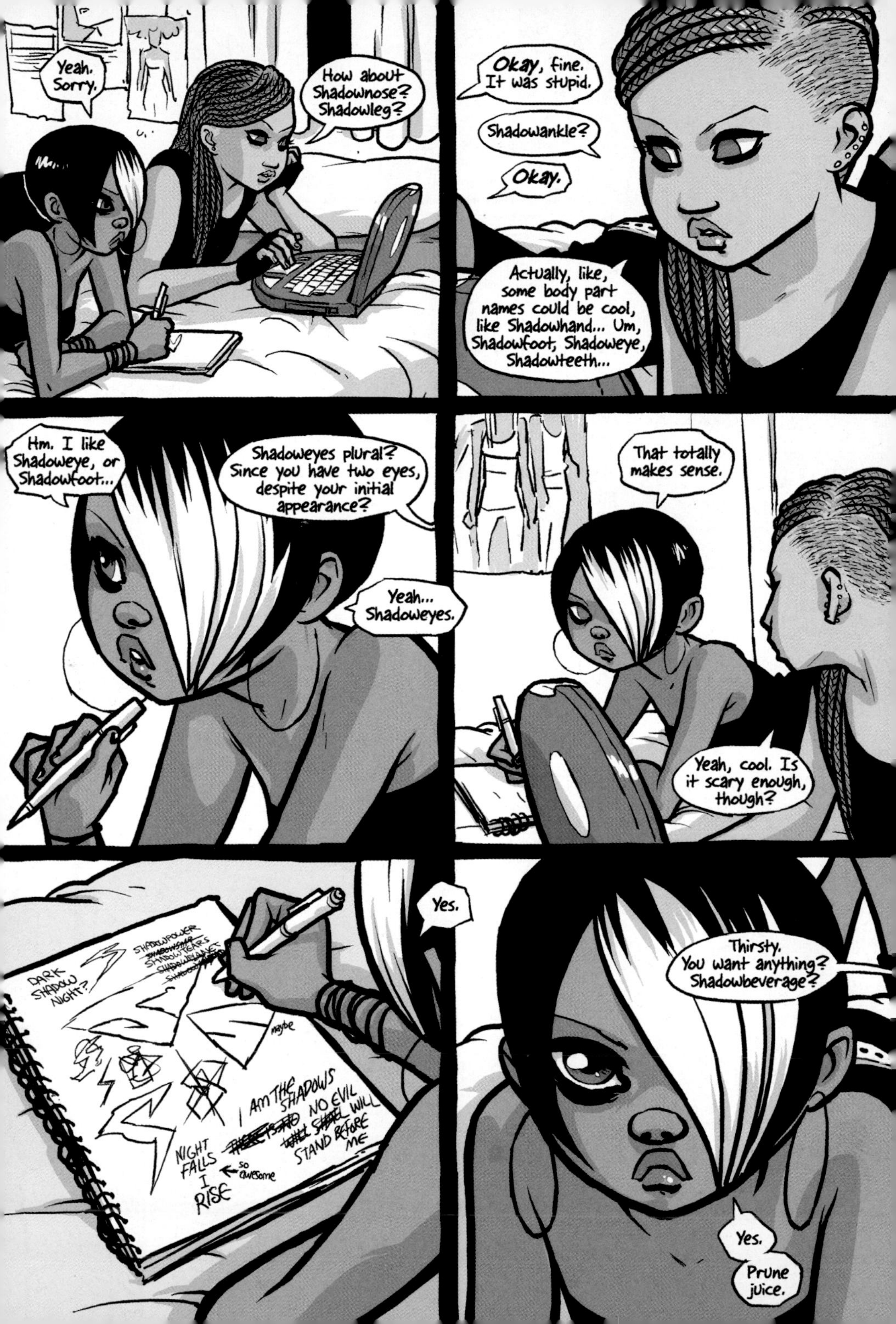
Yeah. Sorry.
How about Shadownose? Shadowleg?
Okay, fine. It was stupid.
Shadowankle?
Okay.
Actually, like, some body part names could be cool, like Shadowhand... Um, Shadowfoot, Shadoweye, Shadowteeth...
Hm. I like Shadoweye, or Shadowfoot...
Shadoweyes plural? Since you have two eyes, despite your initial appearance?
Yeah... Shadoweyes.
That totally makes sense.
Yeah, cool. Is it scary enough, though?
DARK SHADOW NIGHT?
SHADOWPOWER
SHADOWTEARS
maybe
I AM THE SHADOWS
NO EVIL WILL STAND BEFORE ME
NIGHT FALLS I RISE
so awesome
Yes.
Thirsty. You want anything? Shadowbeverage?
Yes.
Prune juice.

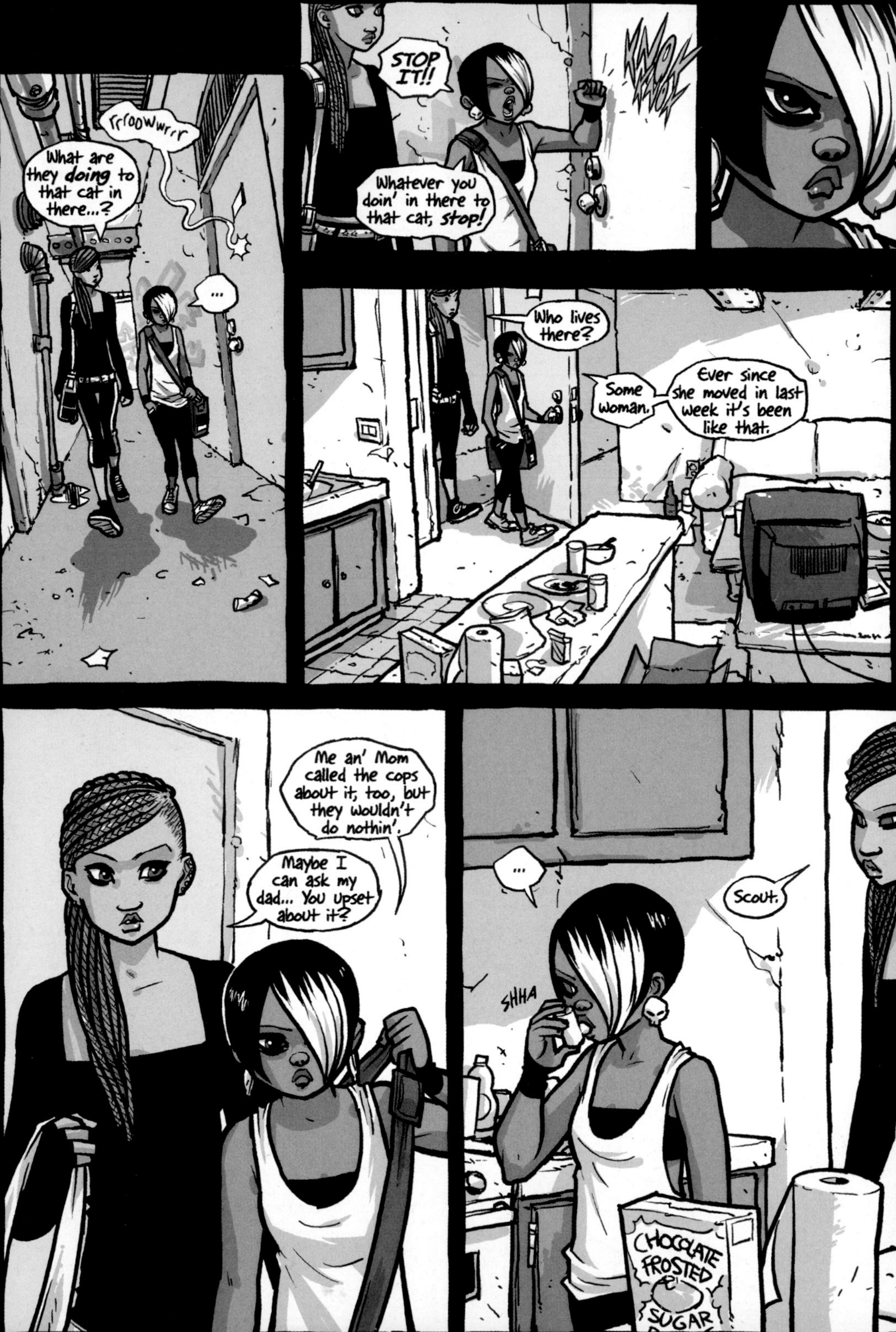

rrroowwrrr
What are they doing to that cat in there...?
...
STOP IT!!
Whatever you doin' in there to that cat, stop!
KNOCK KNOCK
Who lives there?
Some woman.
Ever since she moved in last week it's been like that.
Me an' Mom called the cops about it, too, but they wouldn't do nothin'.
Maybe I can ask my dad... You upset about it?
...
SHHA
Scout.
CHOCOLATE FROSTED SUGAR

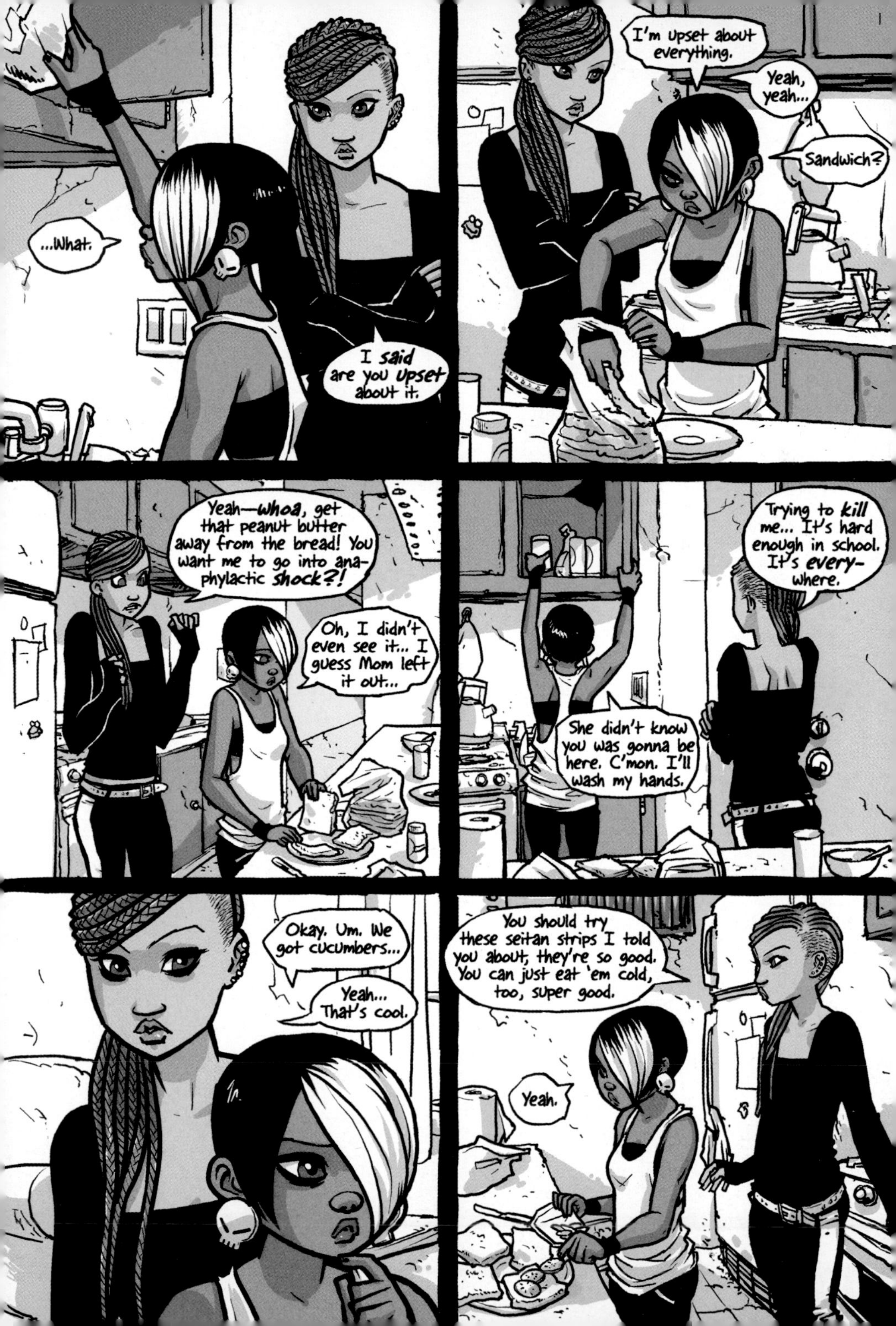
...What.
I said are you upset about it.
I'm upset about everything.
Yeah, yeah...
Sandwich?
Yeah—whoa, get that peanut butter away from the bread! You want me to go into anaphylactic shock?!
Oh, I didn't even see it... I guess Mom left it out...
Trying to kill me... It's hard enough in school. It's everywhere.
She didn't know you was gonna be here. C'mon. I'll wash my hands.
Okay. Um. We got cucumbers...
Yeah... That's cool.
You should try these seitan strips I told you about, they're so good. You can just eat 'em cold, too, super good.
Yeah.

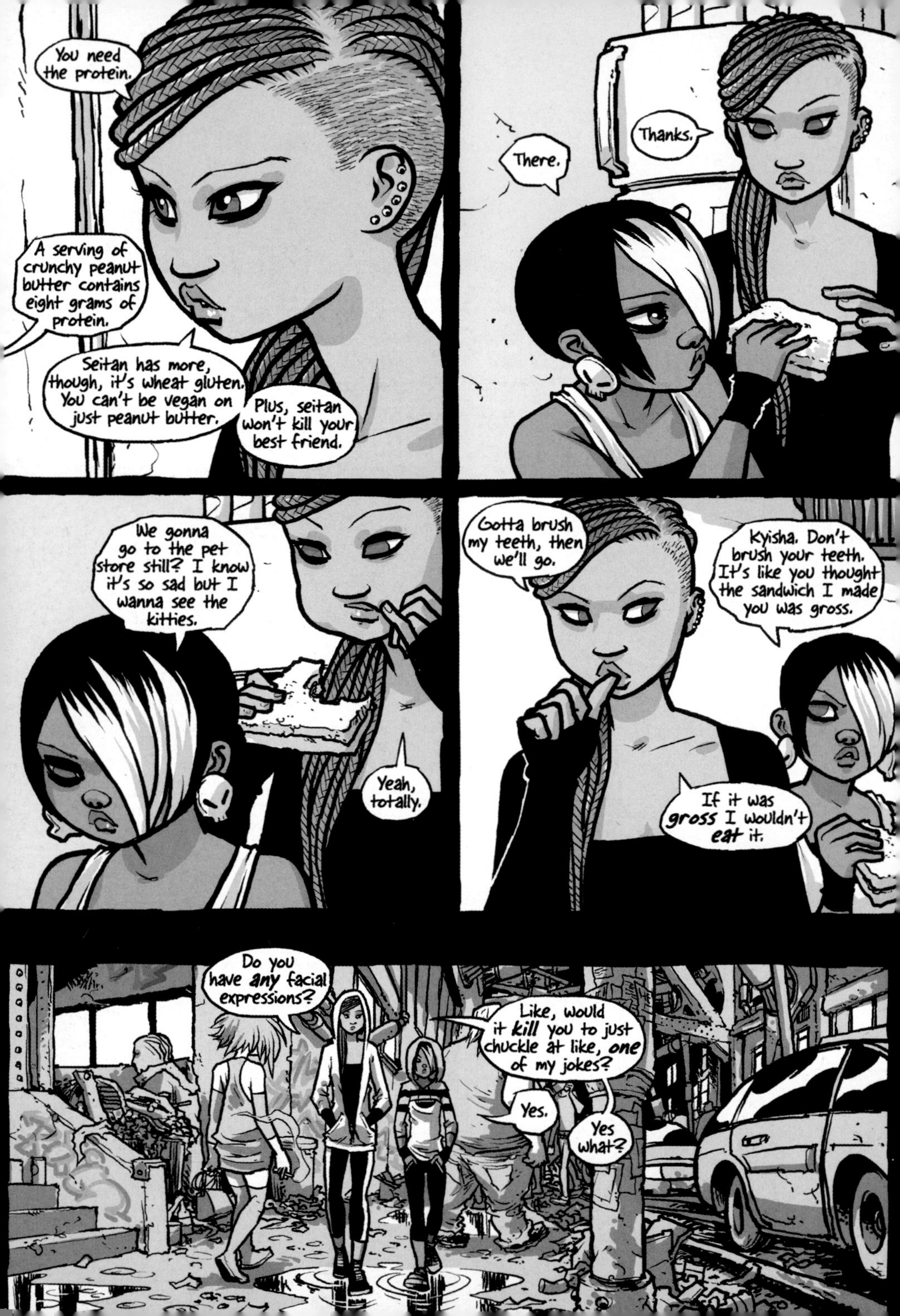
You need the protein.
A serving of crunchy peanut butter contains eight grams of protein.
Seitan has more, though, it's wheat gluten. You can't be vegan on just peanut butter.
Plus, seitan won't kill your best friend.
There.
Thanks.
We gonna go to the pet store still? I know it's so sad but I wanna see the kitties.
Yeah, totally.
Gotta brush my teeth, then we'll go.
Kyisha. Don't brush your teeth. It's like you thought the sandwich I made you was gross.
If it was **gross** I wouldn't **eat** it.
Do you have **any** facial expressions?
Like, would it **kill** you to just chuckle at like, **one** of my jokes?
Yes.
Yes what?

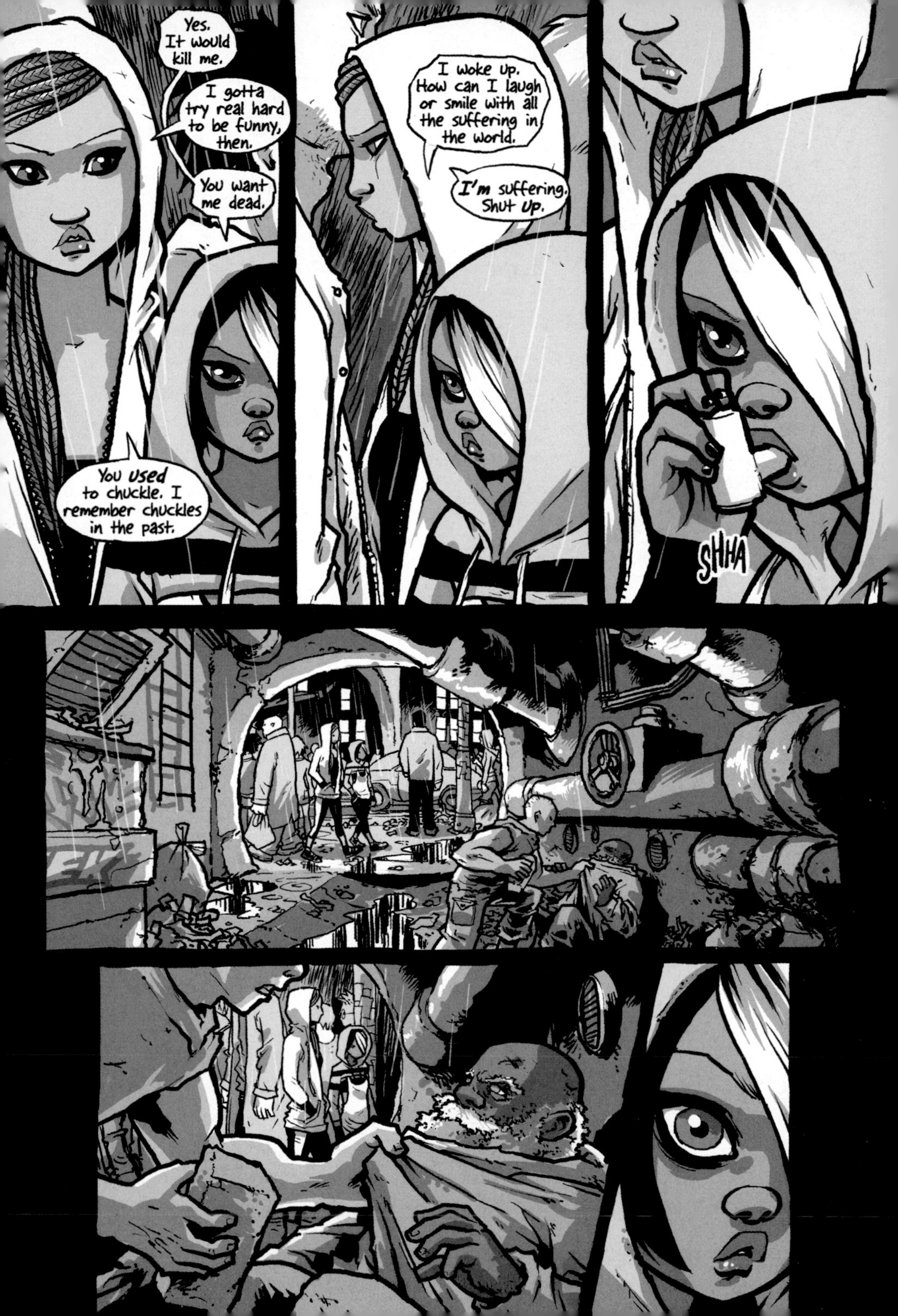
Yes. It would kill me.
I gotta try real hard to be funny, then.
You want me dead.
You used to chuckle. I remember chuckles in the past.
I woke up. How can I laugh or smile with all the suffering in the world.
I'm suffering. Shut up.
SHHA

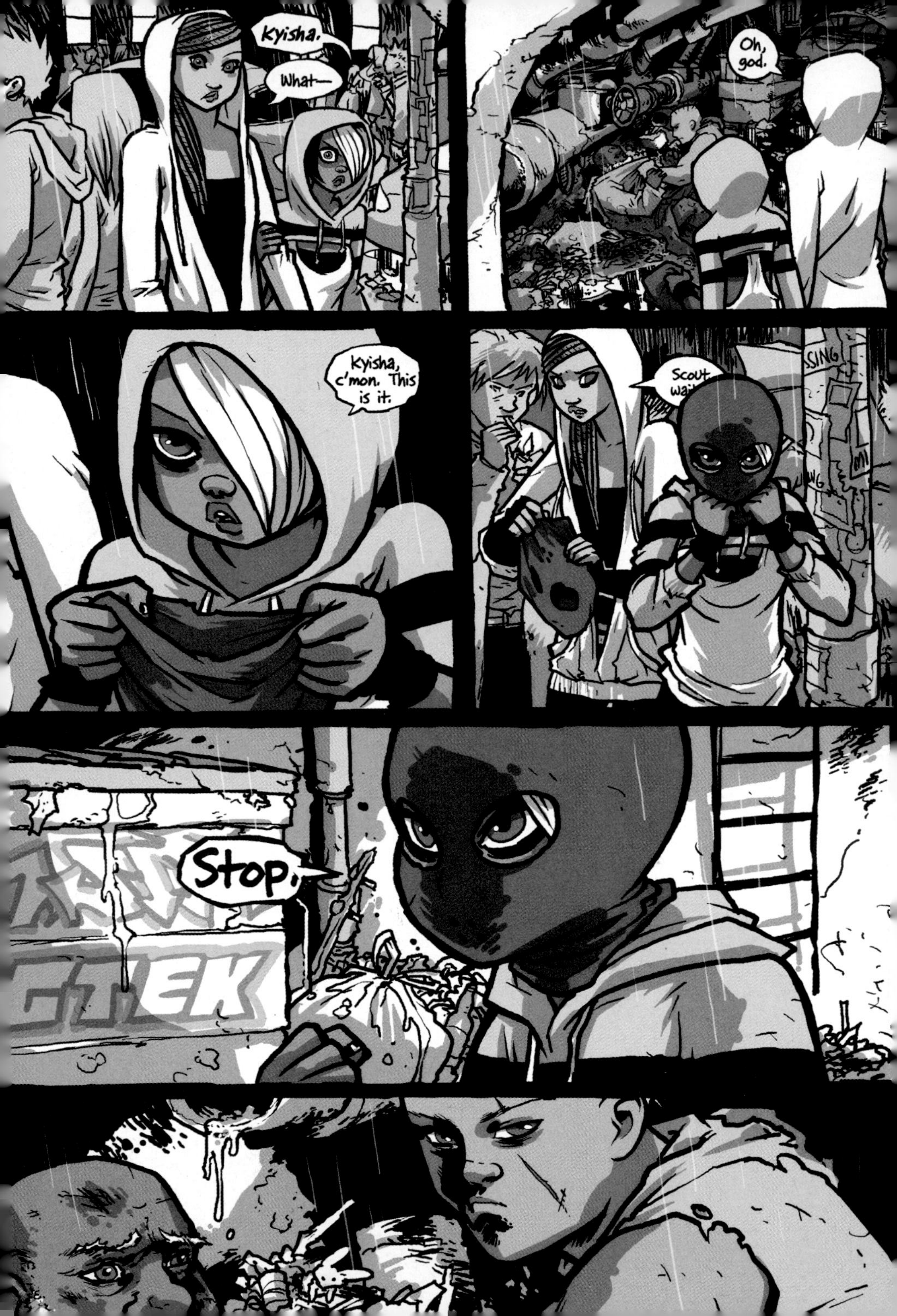
Kyisha.
What—
Oh, god.
Kyisha, c'mon. This is it.
Scout, wai
Stop.

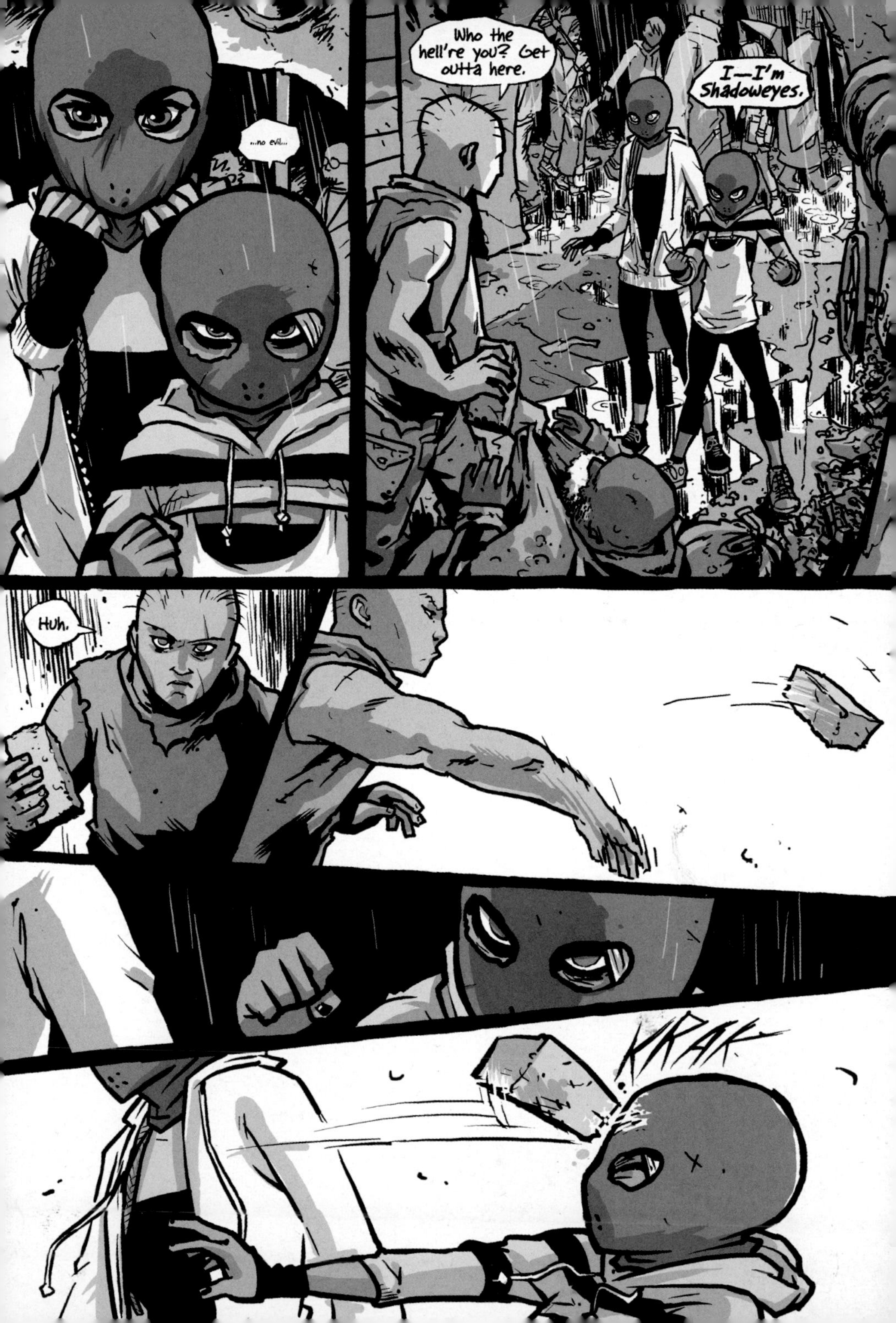
...no evil...
Who the hell're you? Get outta here.
I—I'm Shadoweyes.
Huh.
KRAK

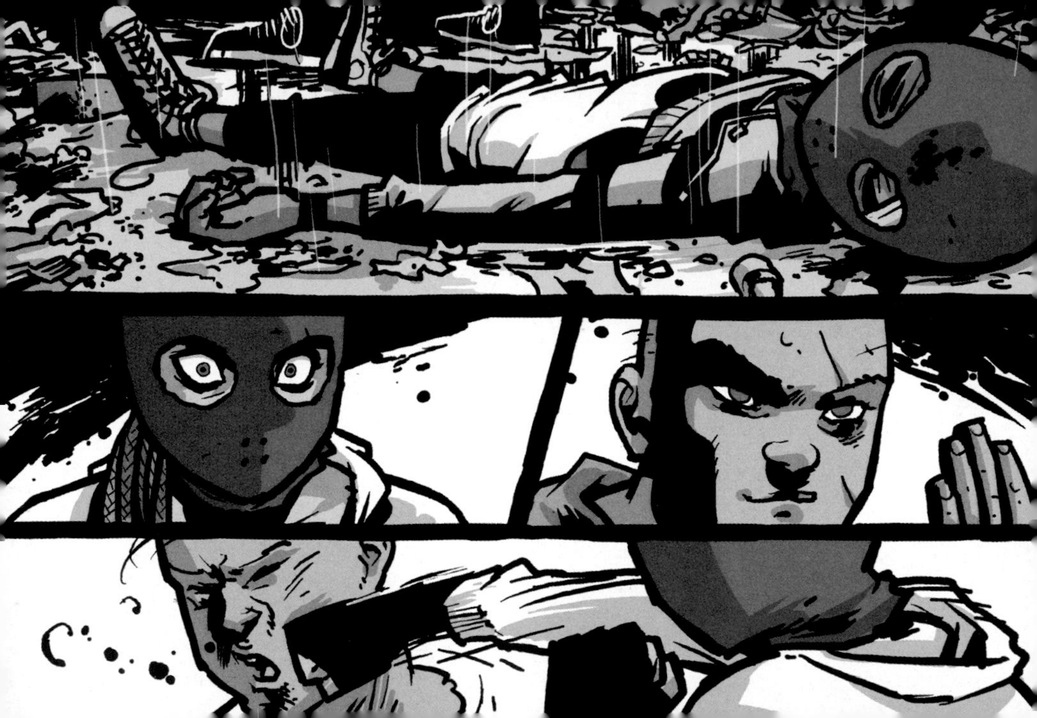

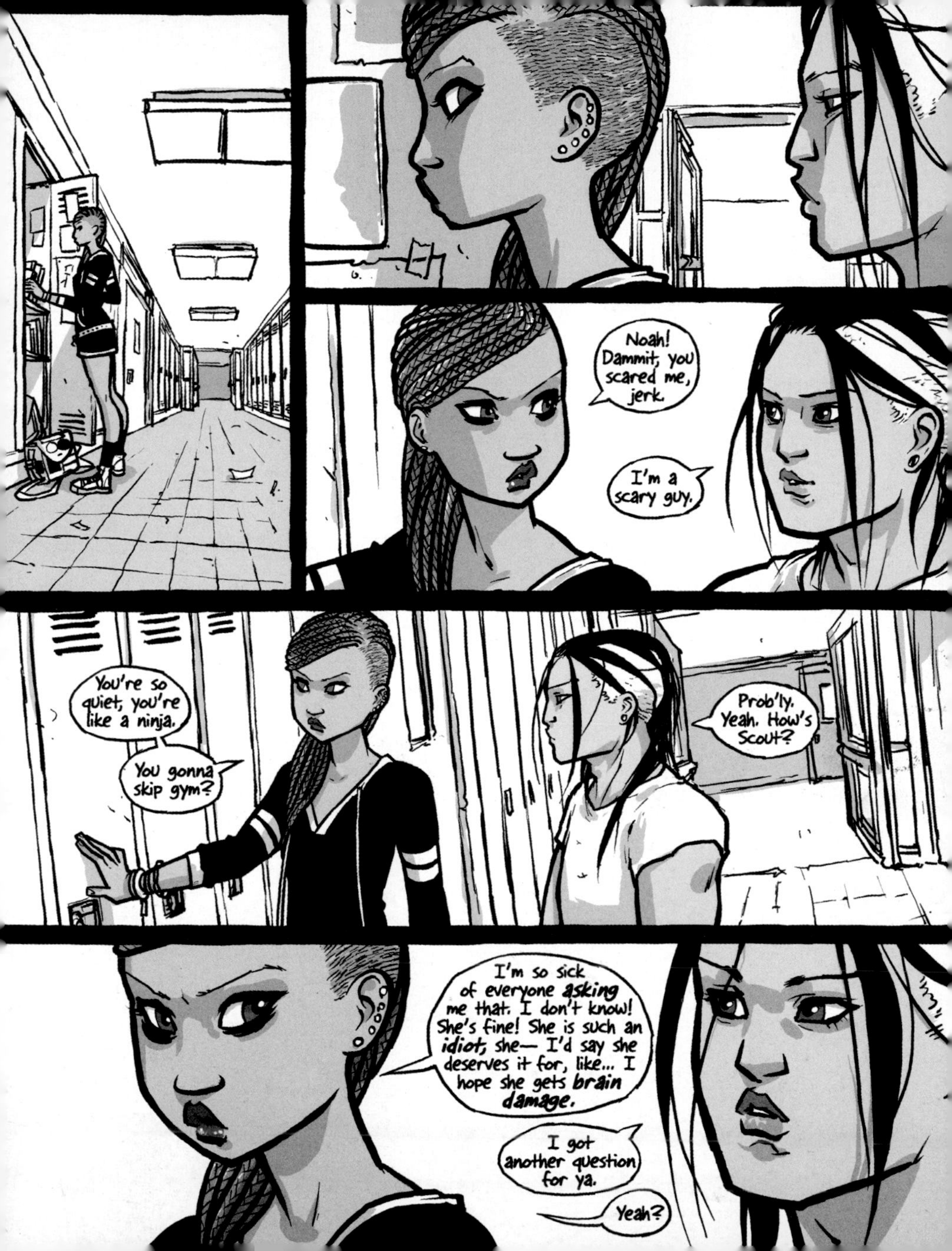

Noah! Dammit, you scared me, jerk.
I'm a scary guy.
You're so quiet, you're like a ninja.
You gonna skip gym?
Prob'ly. Yeah. How's Scout?
I'm so sick of everyone asking me that. I don't know! She's fine! She is such an idiot, she— I'd say she deserves it for, like... I hope she gets brain damage.
I got another question for ya.
Yeah?

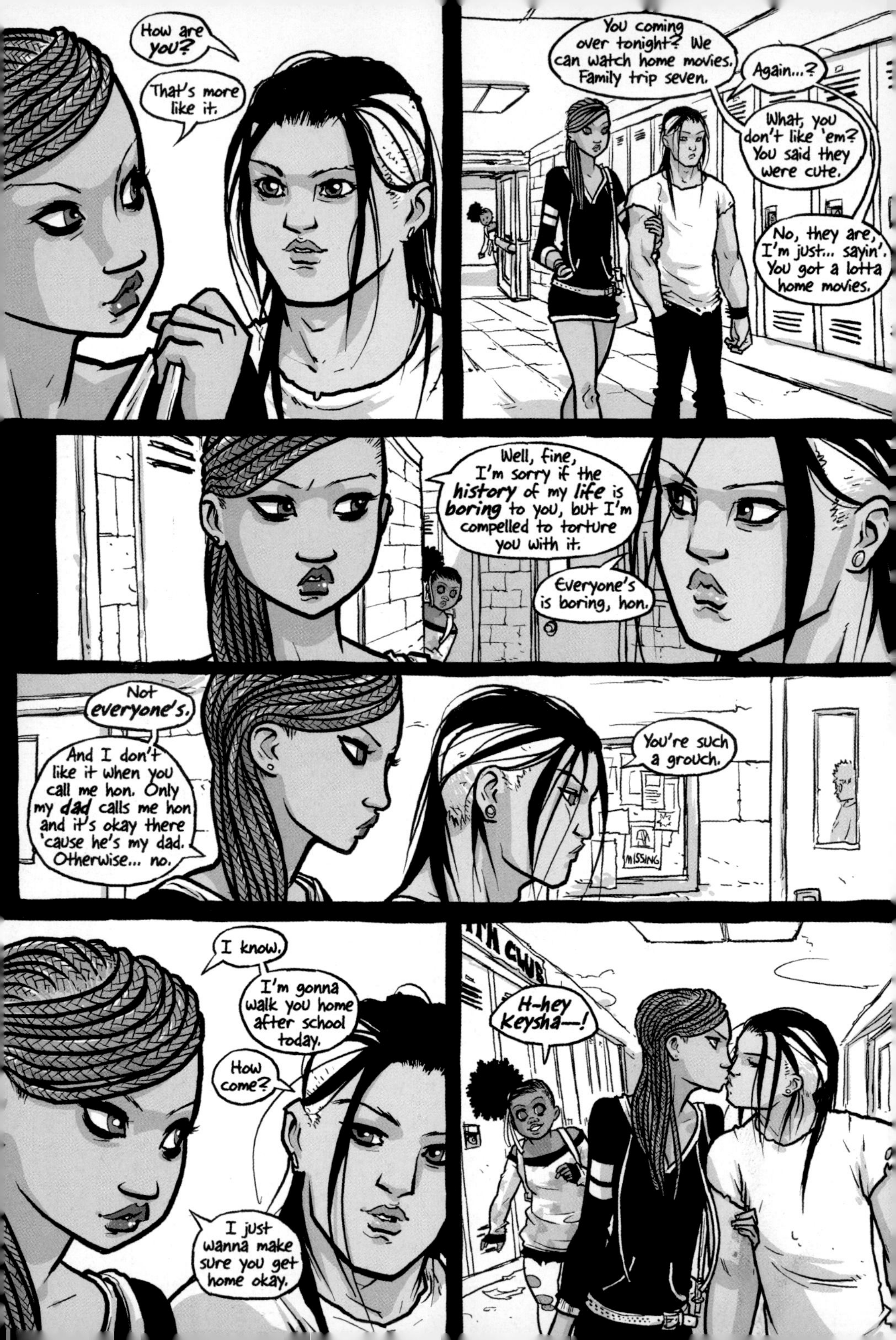
How are you?
That's more like it.
You coming over tonight? We can watch home movies. Family trip seven.
Again...?
What, you don't like 'em? You said they were cute.
No, they are, I'm just... sayin'. You got a lotta home movies.
Well, fine, I'm sorry if the history of my life is boring to you, but I'm compelled to torture you with it.
Everyone's is boring, hon.
Not everyone's.
And I don't like it when you call me hon. Only my dad calls me hon and it's okay there 'cause he's my dad. Otherwise... no.
You're such a grouch.
MISSING
I know.
I'm gonna walk you home after school today.
How come?
I just wanna make sure you get home okay.
H-hey Keysha—!

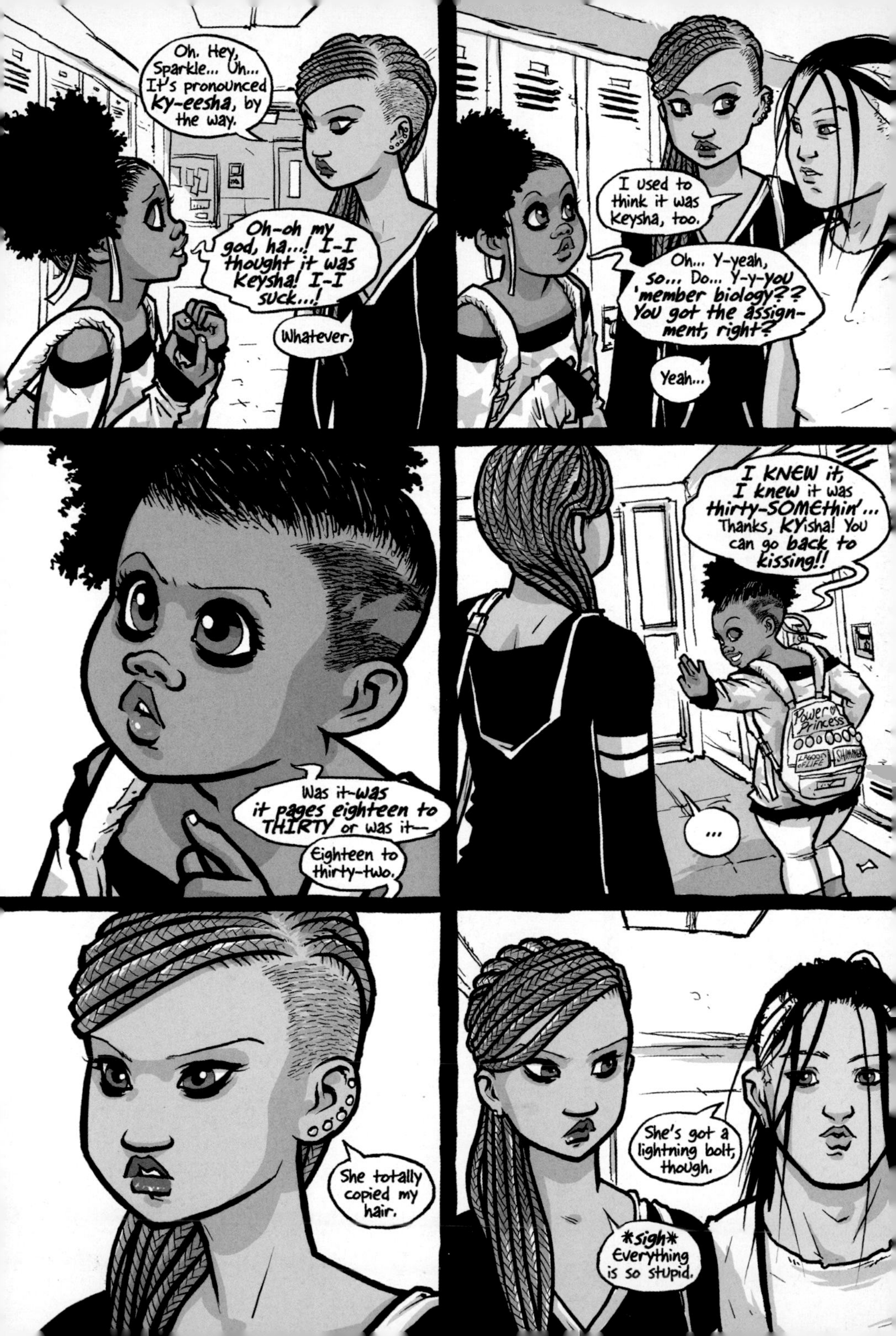
Oh. Hey, Sparkle... Uh... It's pronounced Ky-eesha, by the way.
Oh-oh my god, ha...! I-I thought it was Keysha! I-I suck...!
Whatever.
I used to think it was Keysha, too.
Oh... Y-yeah, so... Do... Y-y-you 'member biology?? You got the assignment, right?
Yeah...
Was it-was it pages eighteen to THIRTY or was it—
Eighteen to thirty-two.
I KNEW it, I knew it was thirty-SOMEthin'... Thanks, KYisha! You can go back to kissing!!
...
She totally copied my hair.
She's got a lightning bolt, though.
sigh Everything is so stupid.

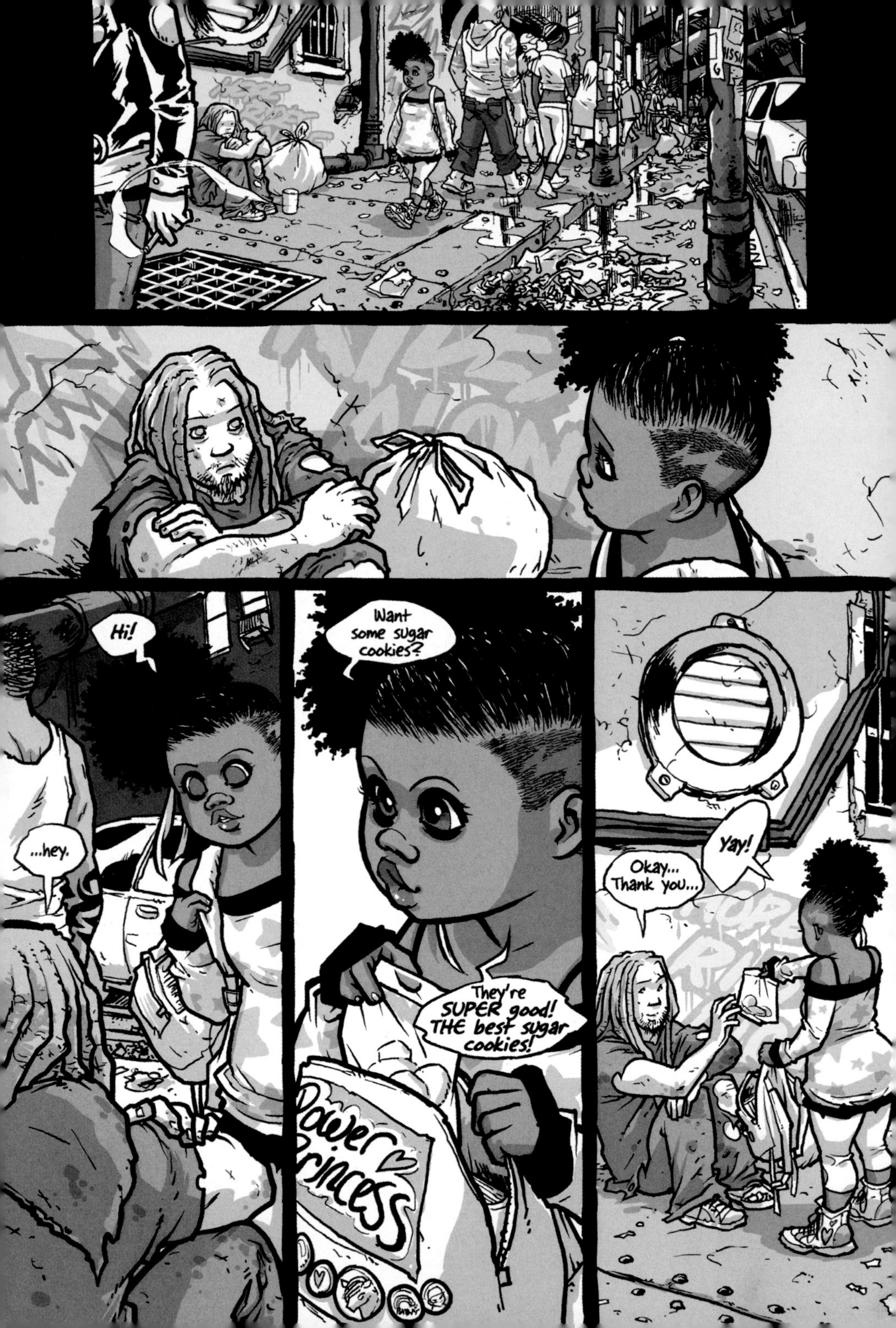
Hi!
...hey.
Want some sugar cookies?
They're SUPER good! THE best sugar cookies!
Okay... Thank you...
Yay!

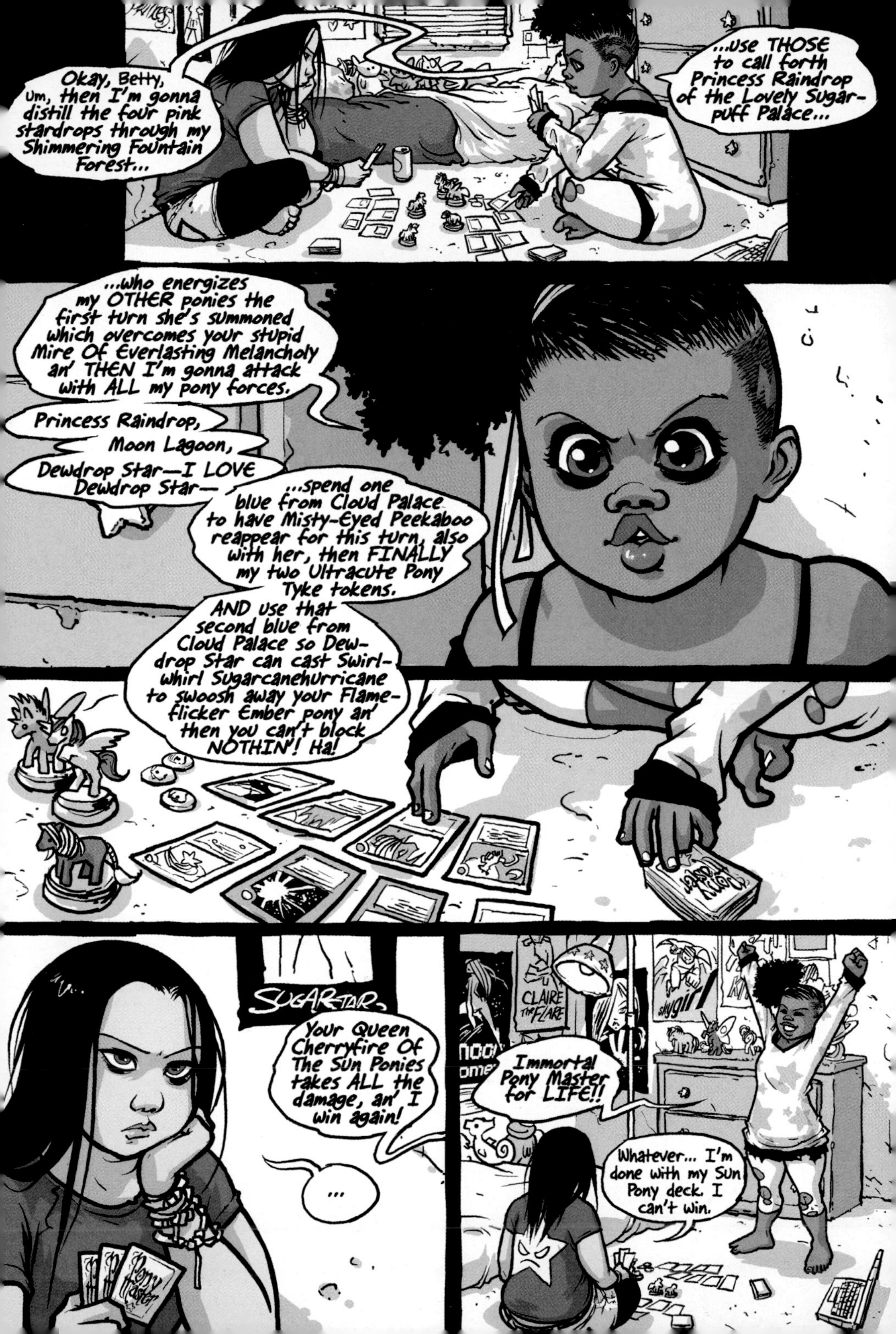
Okay, Betty, um, then I'm gonna distill the four pink stardrops through my Shimmering Fountain Forest...
...use THOSE to call forth Princess Raindrop of the Lovely Sugar-puff Palace...
...who energizes my OTHER ponies the first turn she's summoned which overcomes your stupid Mire Of Everlasting Melancholy an' THEN I'm gonna attack with ALL my pony forces.
Princess Raindrop,
Moon Lagoon,
Dewdrop Star—I LOVE Dewdrop Star—
...spend one blue from Cloud Palace to have Misty-Eyed Peekaboo reappear for this turn, also with her, then FINALLY my two Ultracute Pony Tyke tokens.
AND use that second blue from Cloud Palace so Dew-drop Star can cast Swirl-whirl Sugarcanehurricane to swoosh away your Flame-flicker Ember pony an' then you can't block NOTHIN'! Ha!
Pony Master
SUGARSTAR
Your Queen Cherryfire Of The Sun Ponies takes ALL the damage, an' I win again!
...
Pony Master
CLAIRE THE FLARE
skygirl
Immortal Pony Master for LIFE!!
Whatever... I'm done with my Sun Pony deck. I can't win.

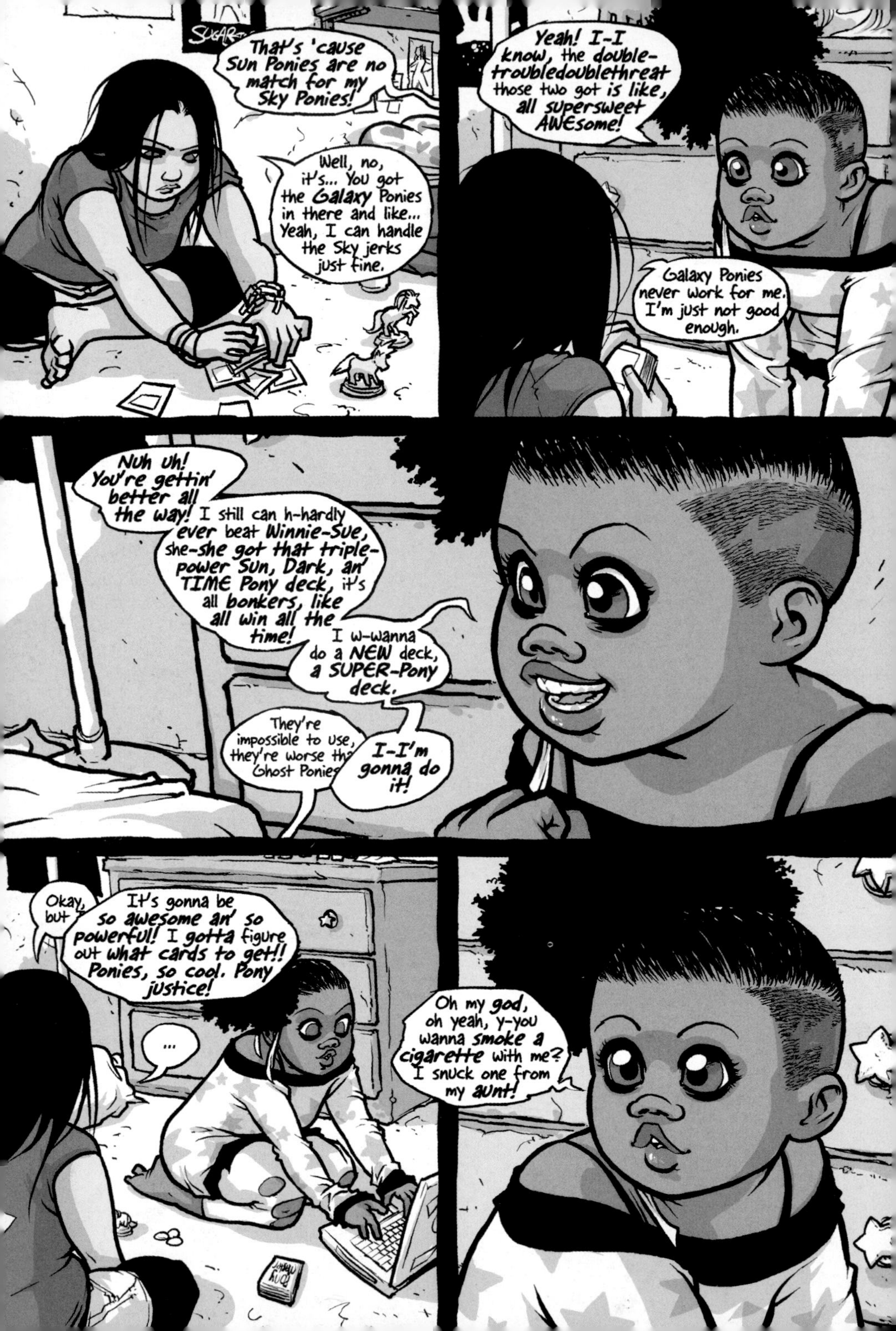
That's 'cause Sun Ponies are no match for my Sky Ponies!
Well, no, it's... You got the Galaxy Ponies in there and like... Yeah, I can handle the Sky jerks just fine.
Yeah! I-I know, the double-troubledoublethreat those two got is like, all supersweet AWEsome!
Galaxy Ponies never work for me. I'm just not good enough.
Nuh uh! You're gettin' better all the way! I still can h-hardly ever beat Winnie-Sue, she-she got that triple-power Sun, Dark, an' TIME Pony deck, it's all bonkers, like all win all the time!
I w-wanna do a NEW deck, a SUPER-Pony deck.
They're impossible to use, they're worse th Ghost Ponies
I-I'm gonna do it!
Okay, but
It's gonna be so awesome an' so powerful! I gotta figure out what cards to get!! Ponies, so cool. Pony justice!
...
Oh my god, oh yeah, y-you wanna smoke a cigarette with me? I snuck one from my aunt!

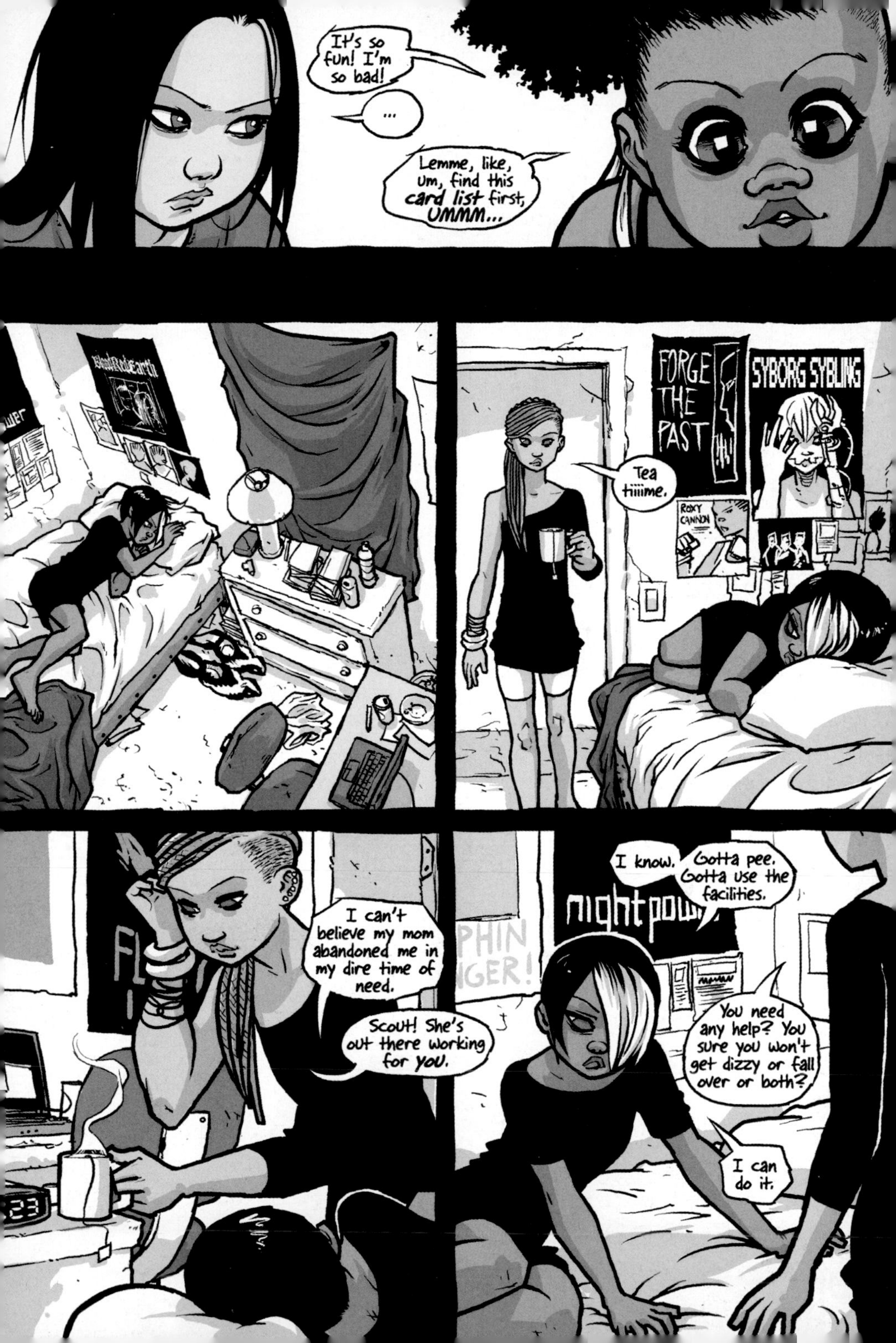

It's so fun! I'm so bad!
...
Lemme, like, um, find this card list first, UMMM...
bloodredearth
wer
FORGE THE PAST
SYBORG SYBLING
Tea tiiiime.
ROXY CANNON
I can't believe my mom abandoned me in my dire time of need.
Scout! She's out there working for you.
PHIN
GER!
nightpow
I know.
Gotta pee. Gotta use the facilities.
You need any help? You sure you won't get dizzy or fall over or both?
I can do it.

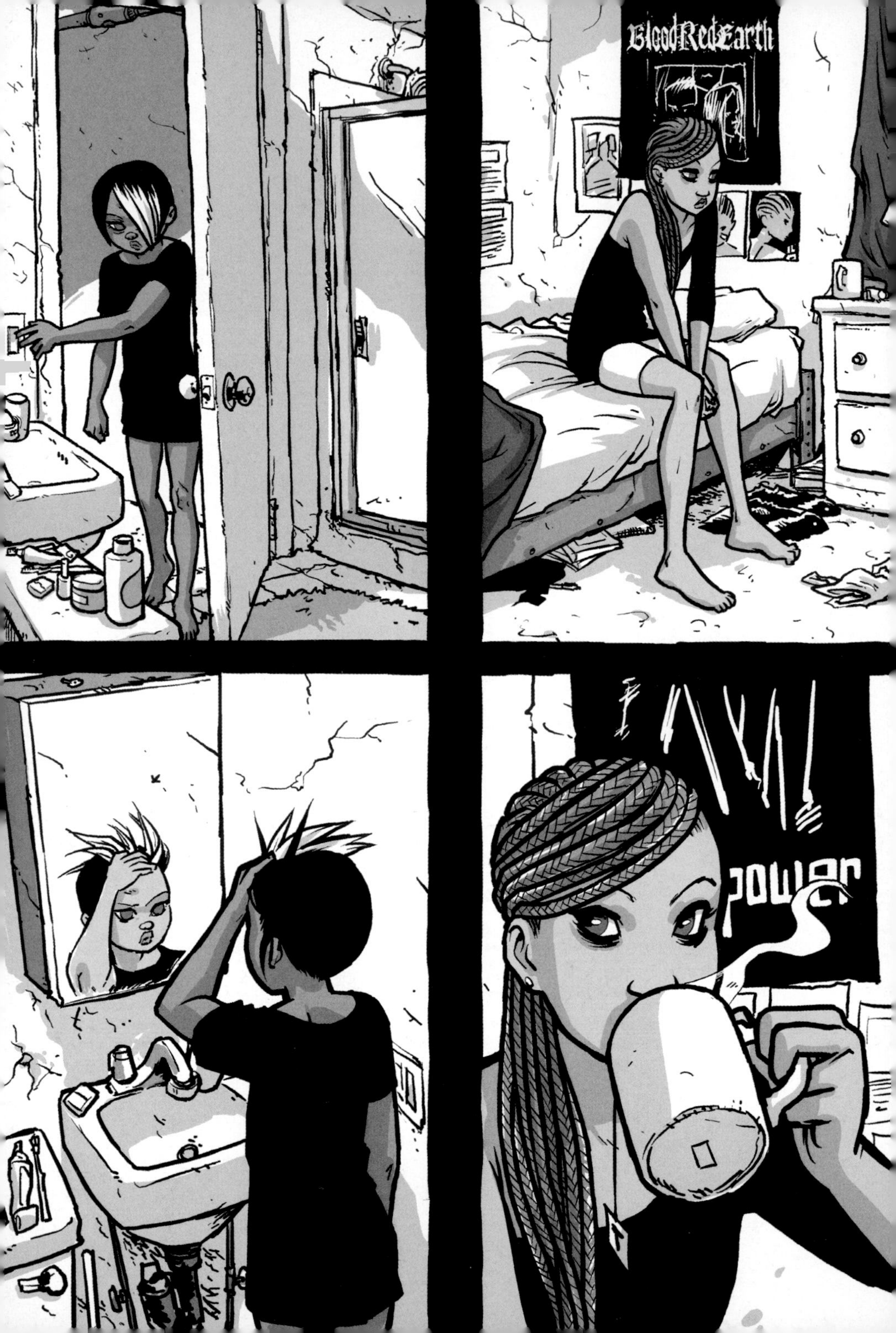
BloodRedEarth
power

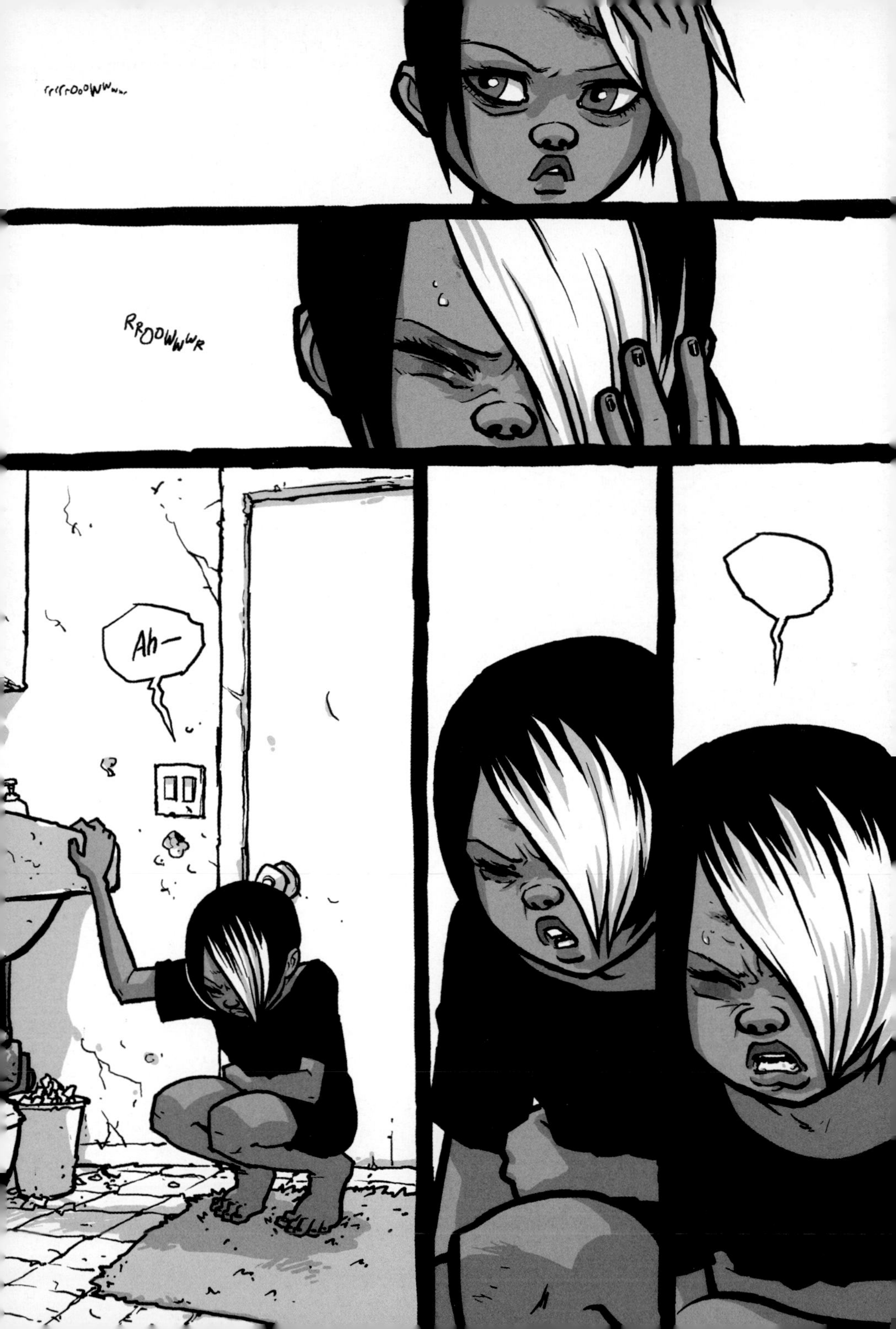
rrrrrOOOWWwwr
RROOWWWR
Ah—

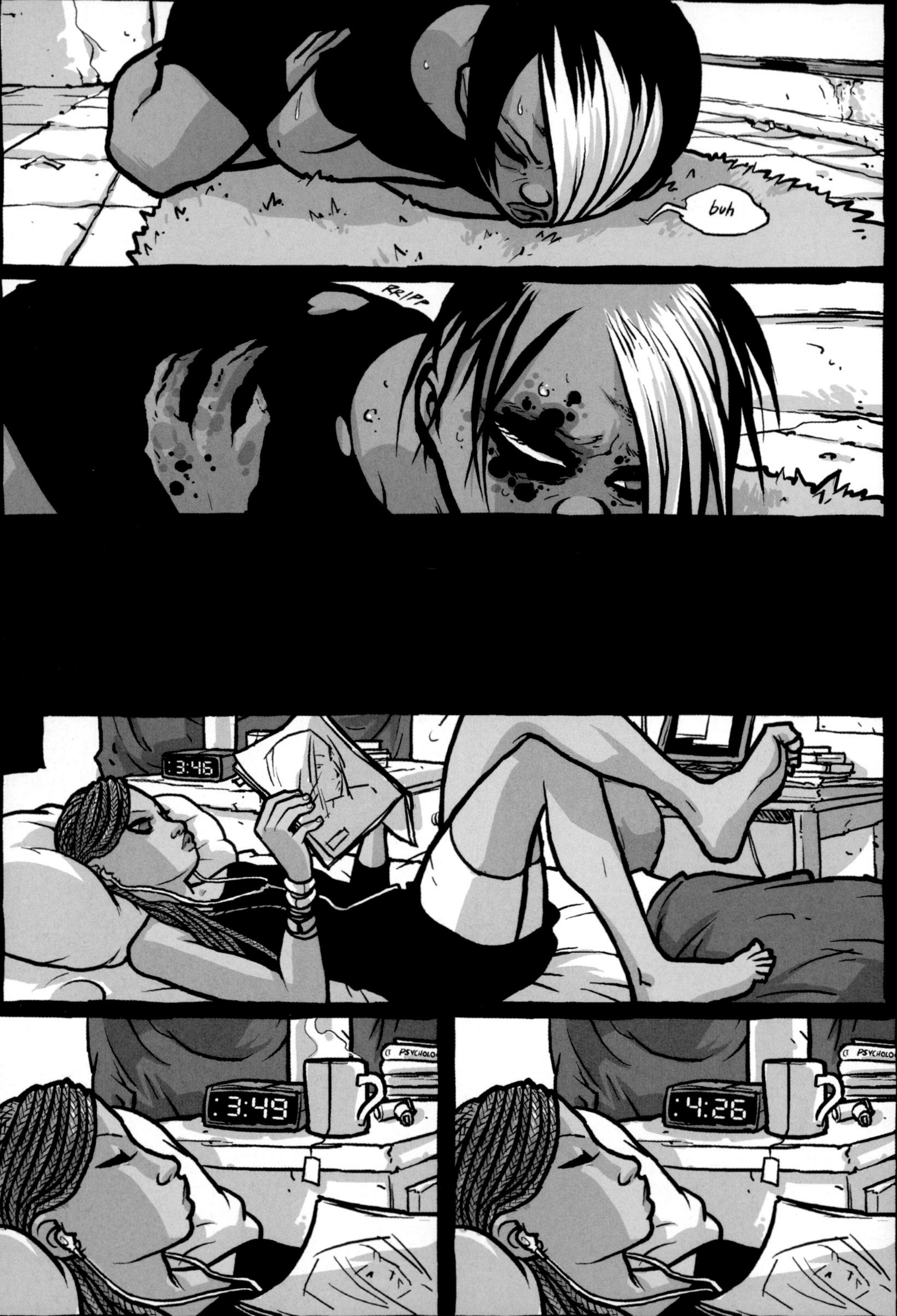
buh
RRIPP
3:46
PSYCHOLO
3:49
PSYCHOLO
4:26

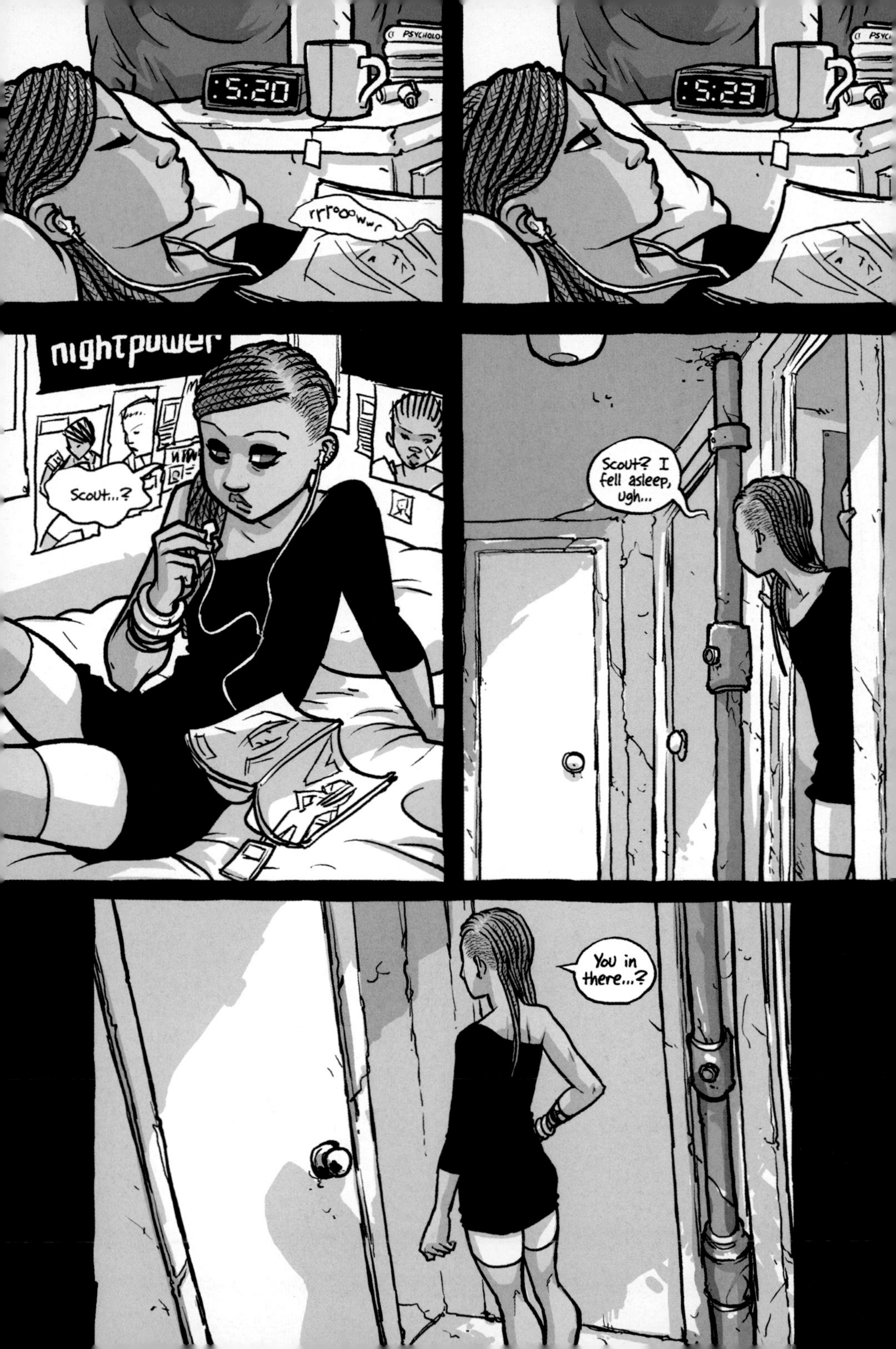
PSYCHOLO
5:20
rrrooowwr
PSY
5:23
nightpower
Scout...?
Scout? I fell asleep, ugh...
You in there...?

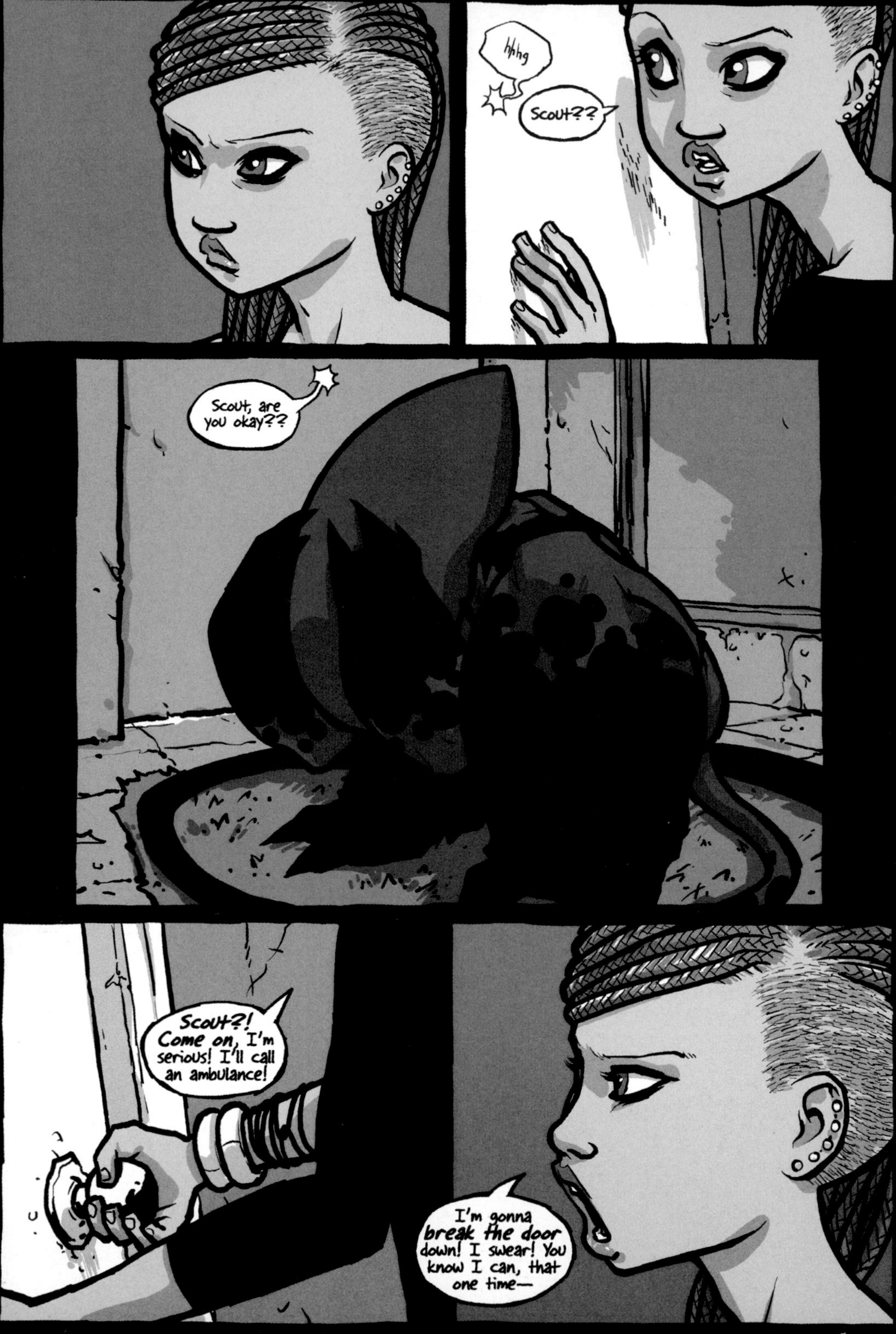
hhhg
Scout??
Scout, are you okay??
Scout?! Come on, I'm serious! I'll call an ambulance!
I'm gonna break the door down! I swear! You know I can, that one time—

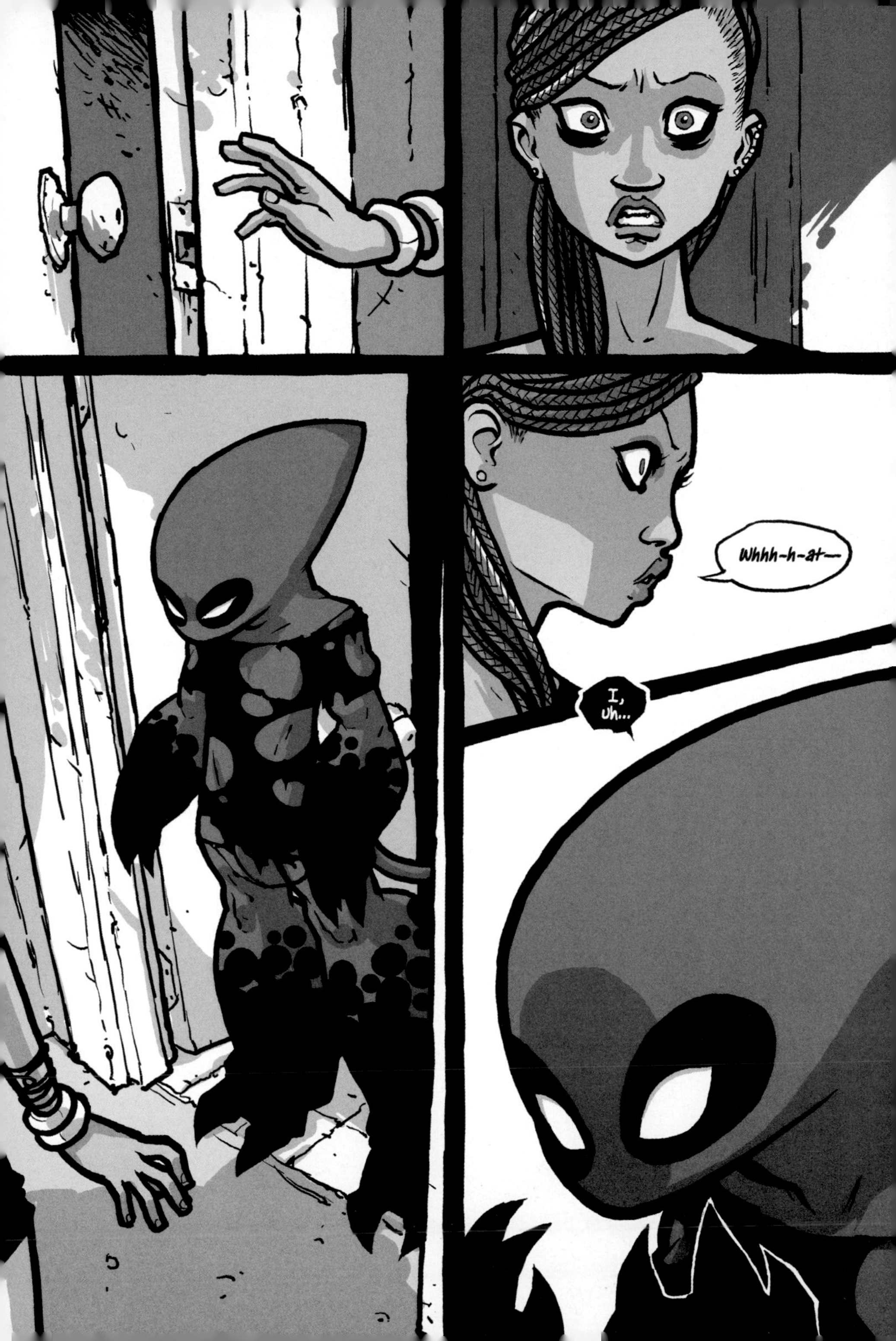
Whhh-h-at—
I, uh...

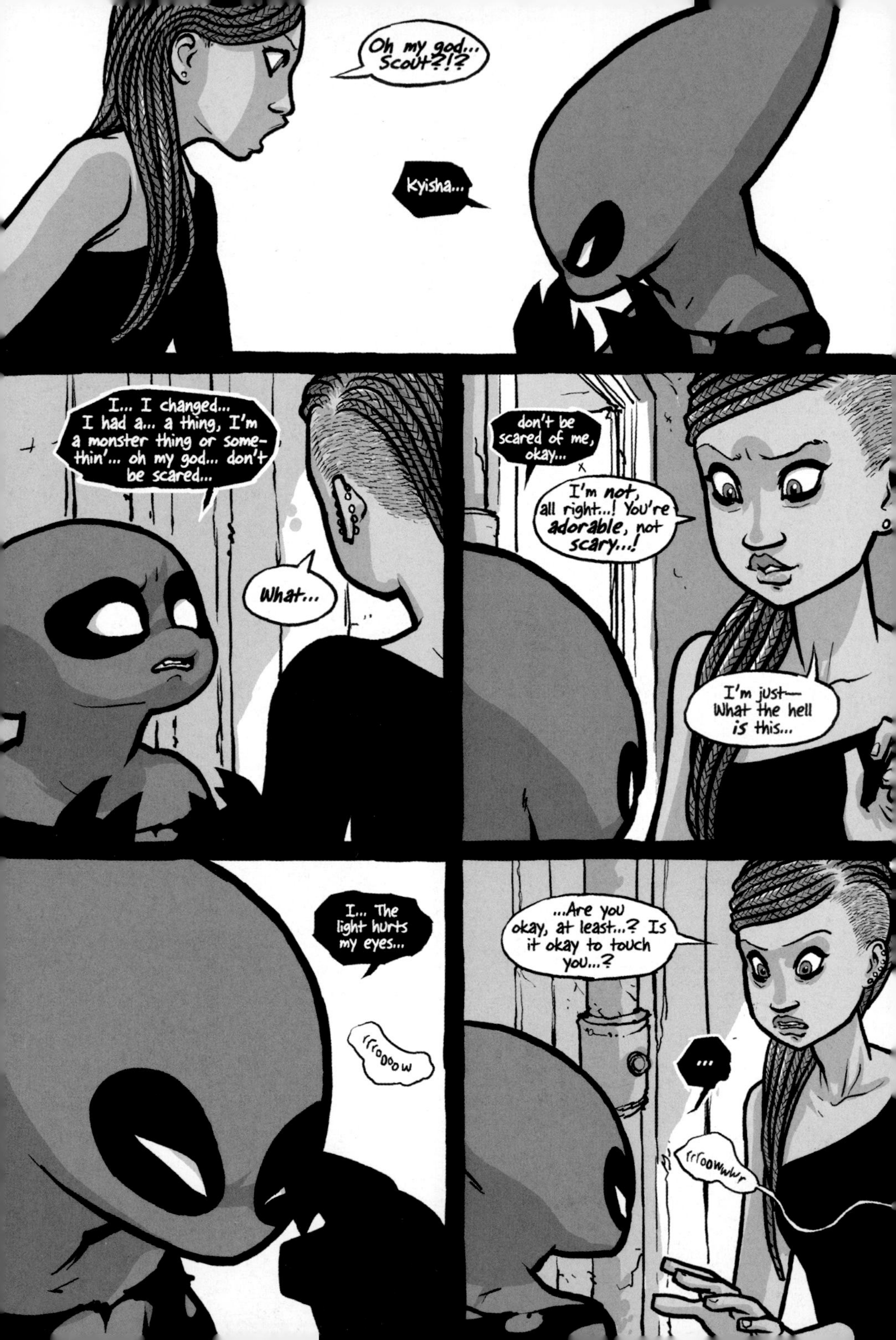
Oh my god... Scout?!?
Kyisha...
I... I changed... I had a... a thing, I'm a monster thing or some-thin'... oh my god... don't be scared...
What...
don't be scared of me, okay...
I'm not, all right...! You're adorable, not scary...!
I'm just— What the hell is this...
I... The light hurts my eyes...
rrroooow
...Are you okay, at least...? Is it okay to touch you...?
...
rrroowwwr

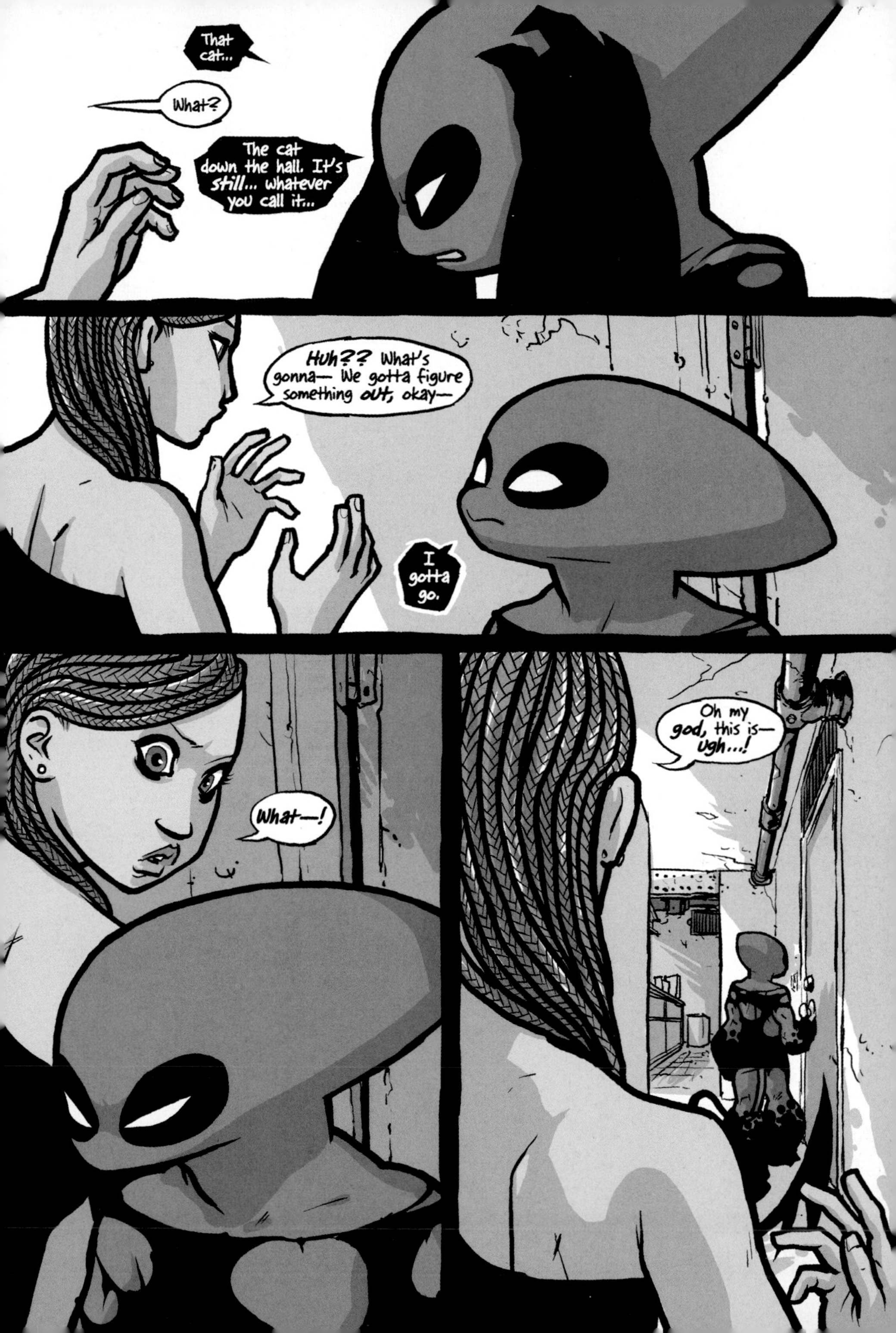
That cat...
What?
The cat down the hall. It's *still*... whatever you call it...
Huh?? What's gonna— We gotta figure something *out*, okay—
I gotta go.
What—!
Oh my *god*, this is— *ugh*...!

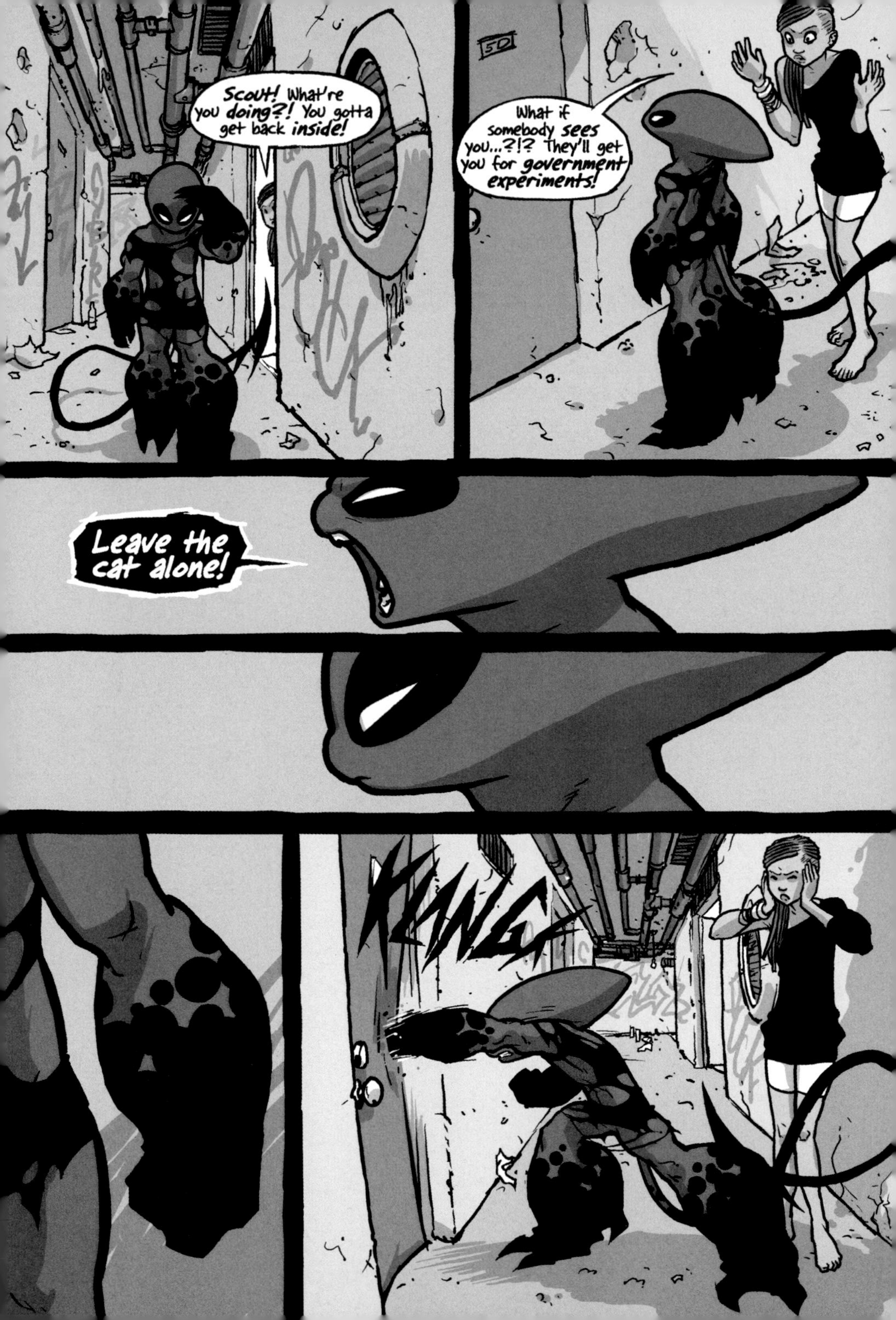
Scout! What're you doing?! You gotta get back inside!
What if somebody sees you...?!? They'll get you for government experiments!
Leave the cat alone!
KLANG!

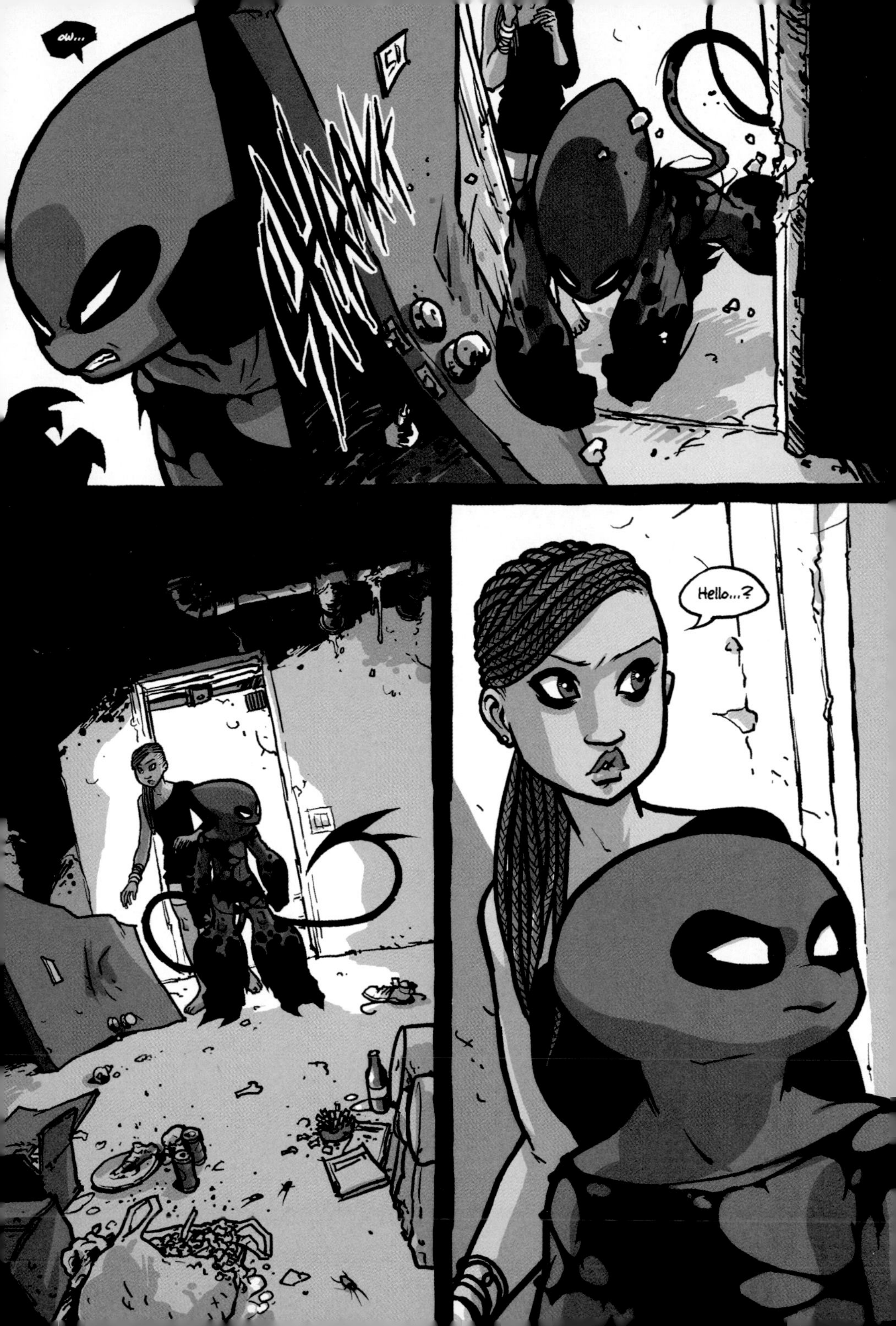
ow...
5D
Hello...?

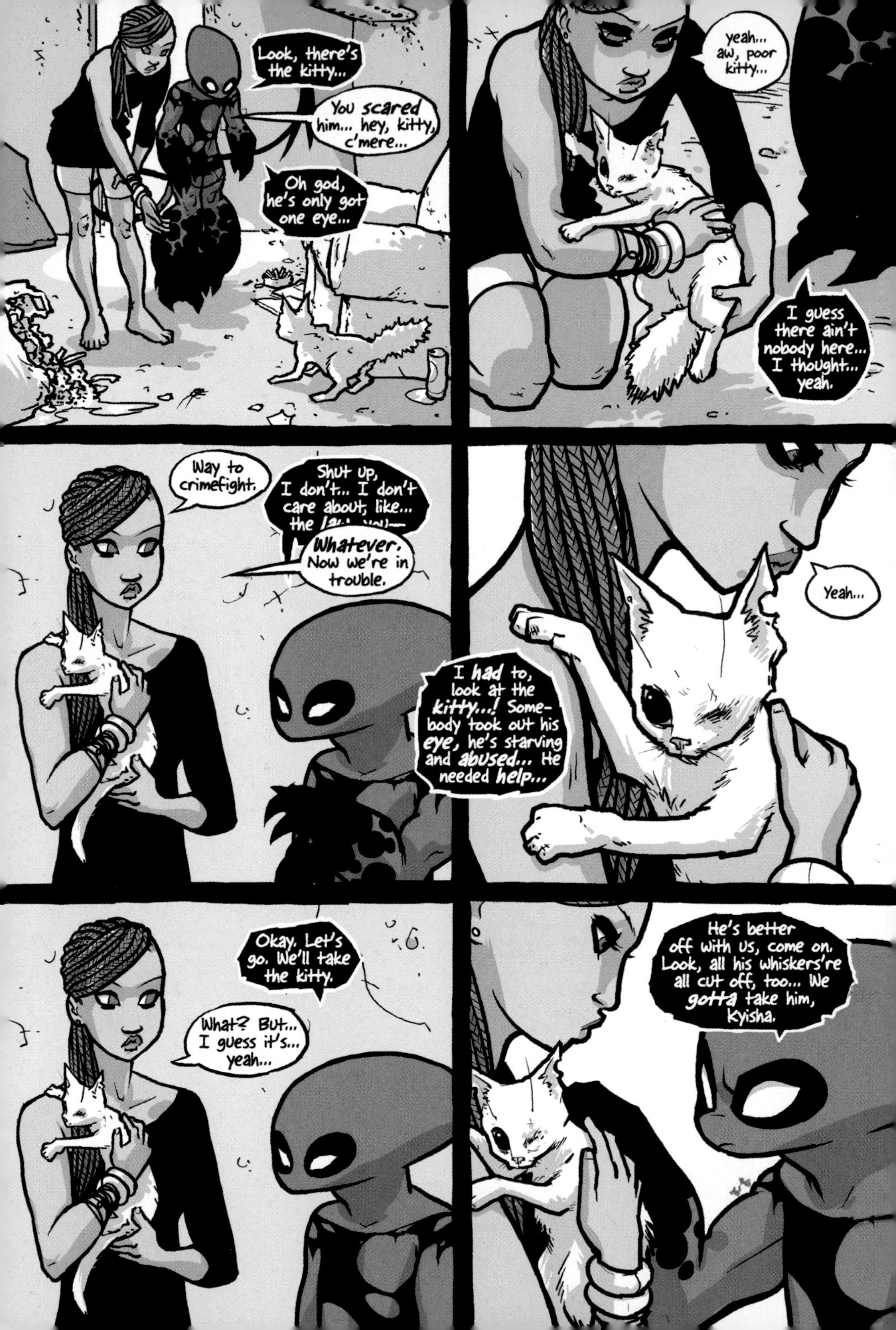
Look, there's the kitty...
You scared him... hey, kitty, c'mere...
Oh god, he's only got one eye...
yeah... aw, poor kitty...
I guess there ain't nobody here... I thought... yeah.
Way to crimefight.
Shut up, I don't... I don't care about, like... the
Whatever. Now we're in trouble.
I had to, look at the kitty...! Somebody took out his eye, he's starving and abused... He needed help...
Yeah...
Okay. Let's go. We'll take the kitty.
What? But... I guess it's... yeah...
He's better off with us, come on. Look, all his whiskers're all cut off, too... We gotta take him, Kyisha.

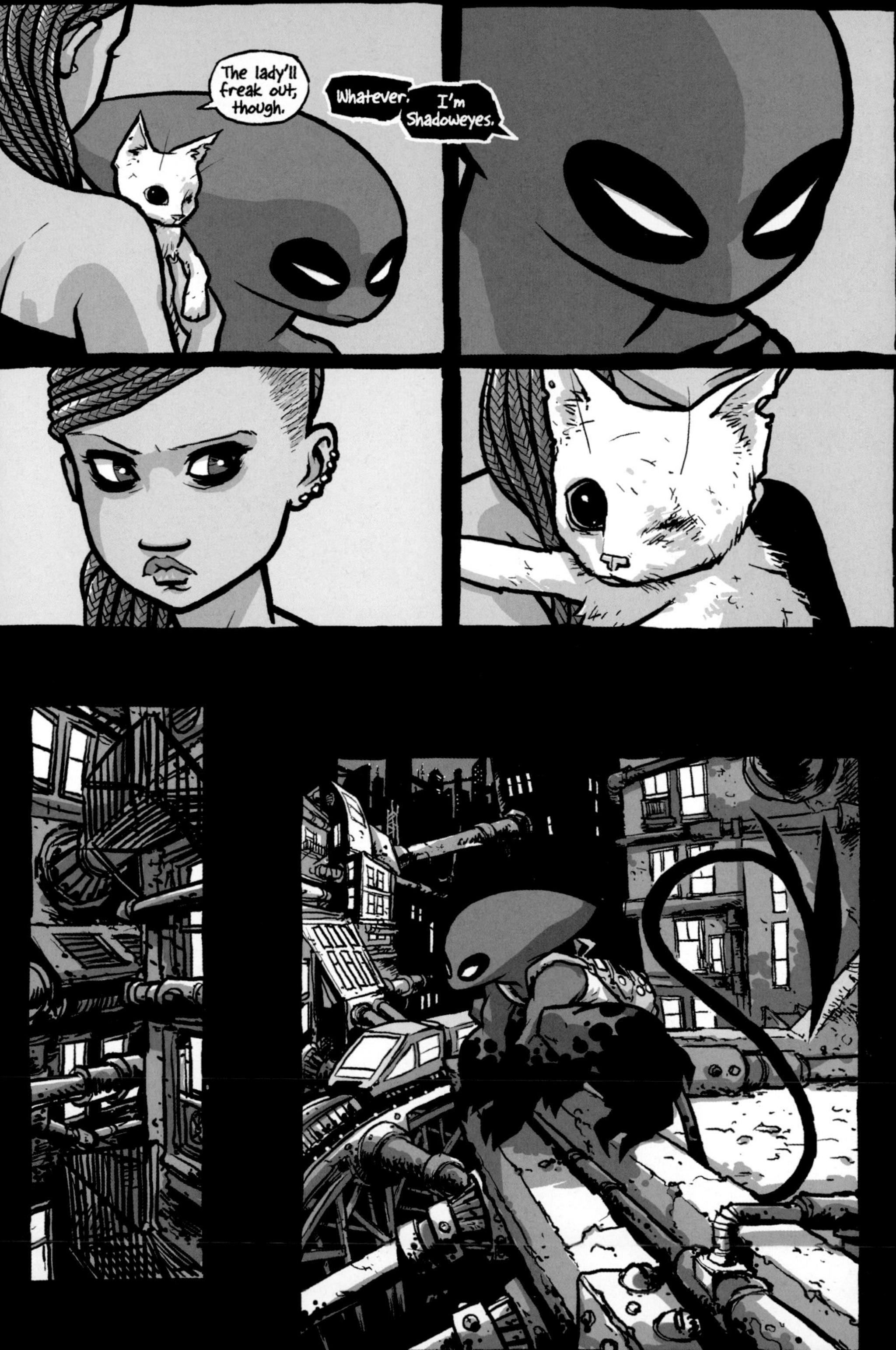

The lady'll freak out, though.
Whatever.
I'm Shadoweyes.

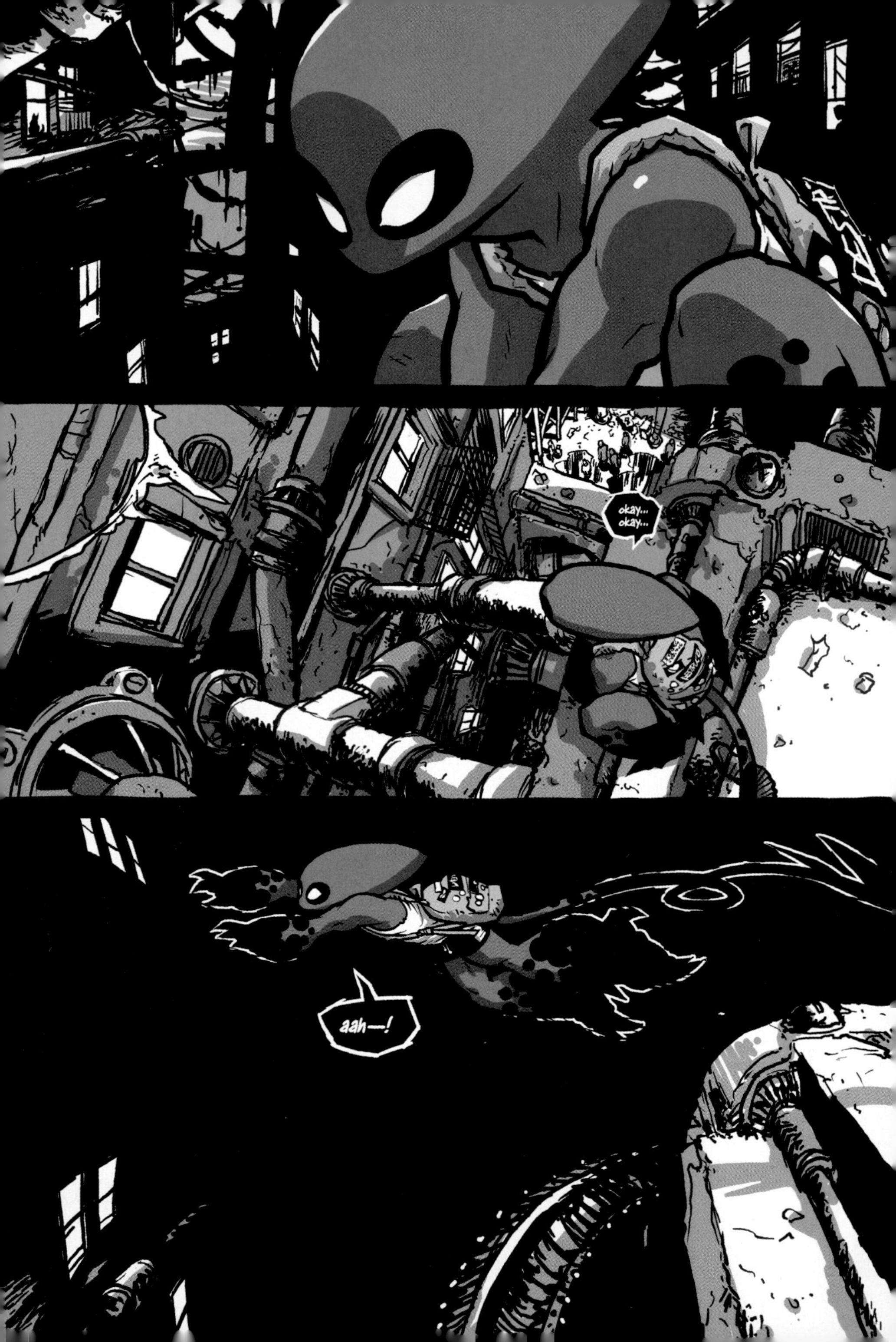
okay... okay...
aah—!

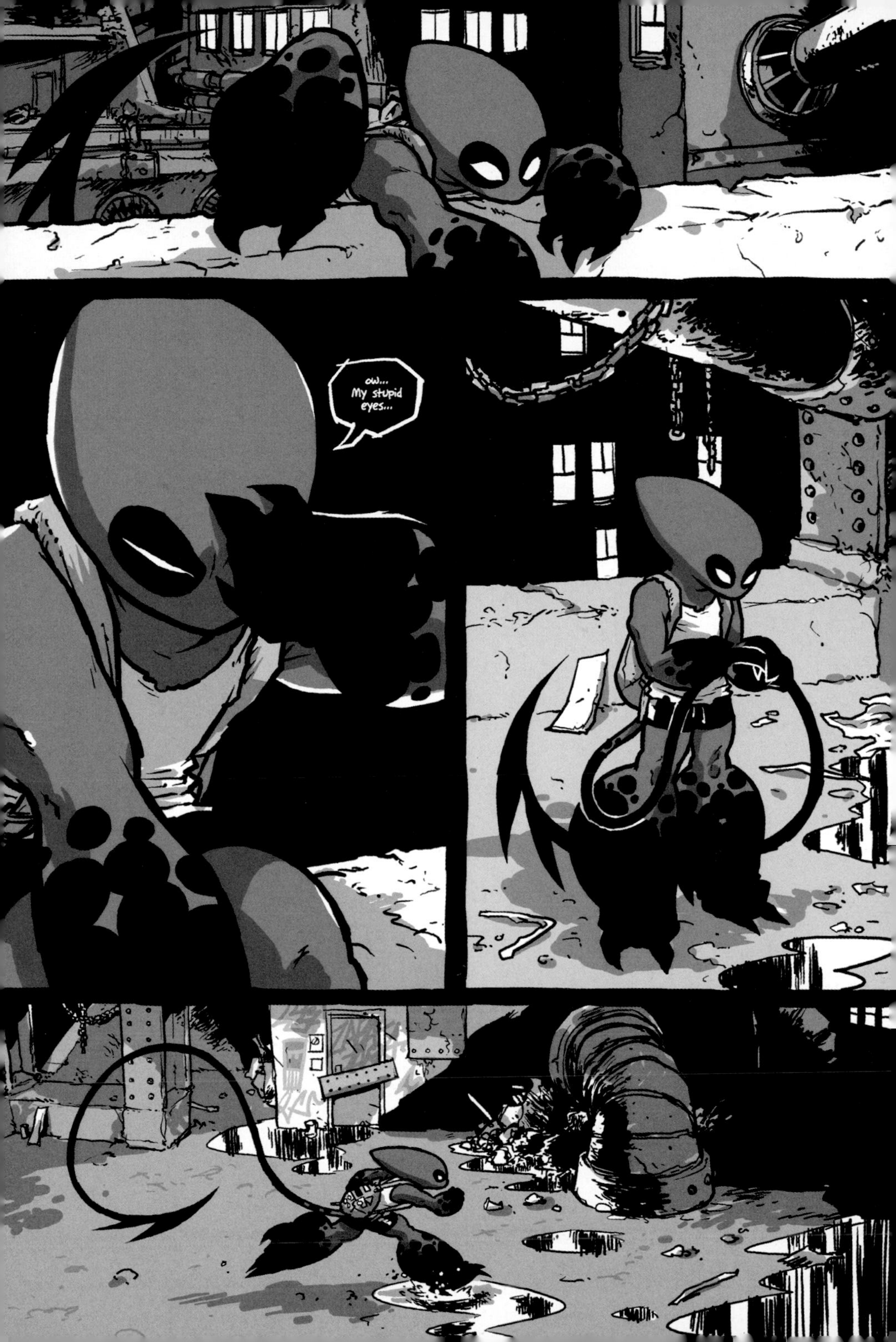
ow... My stupid eyes...

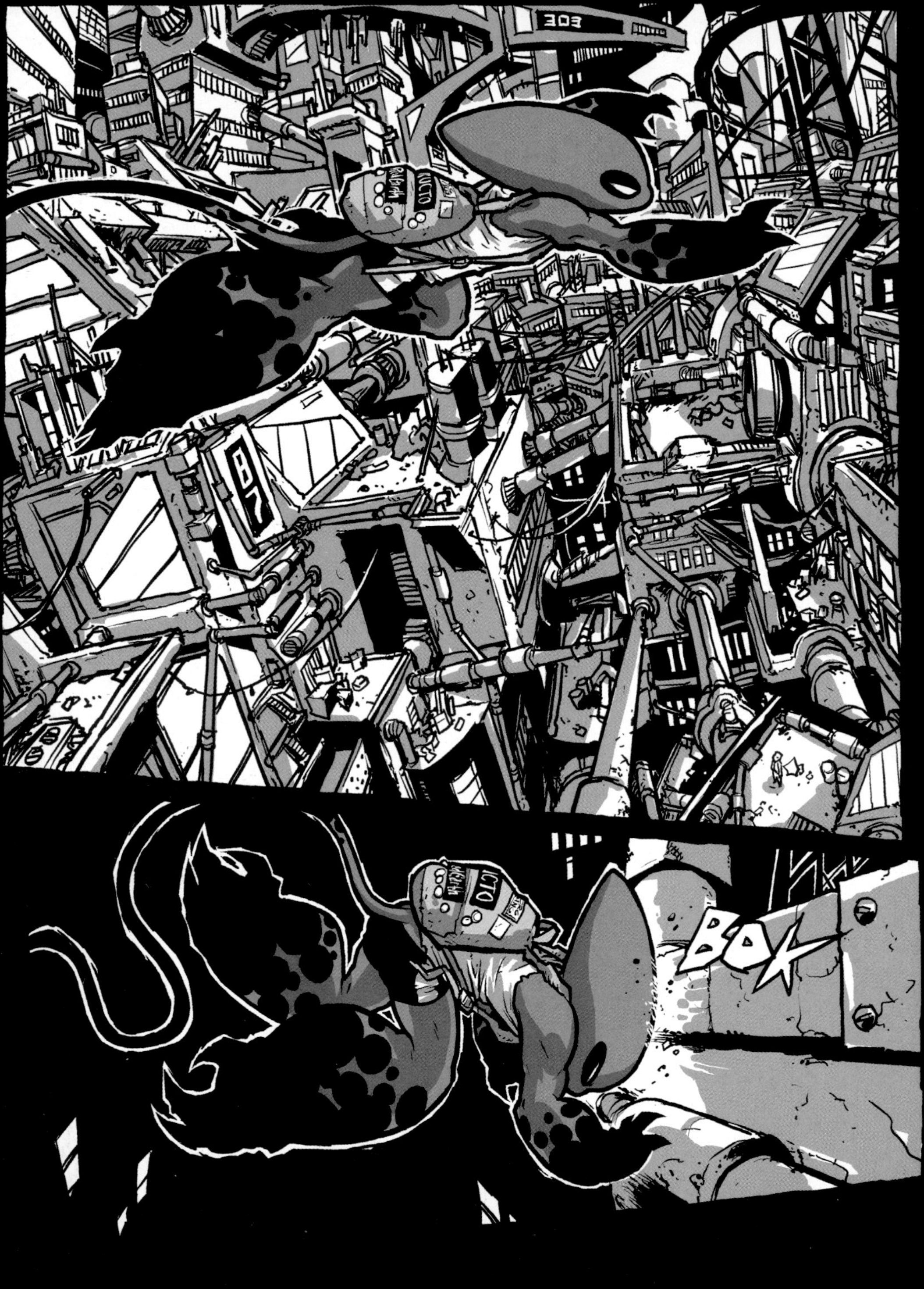
87
BOK

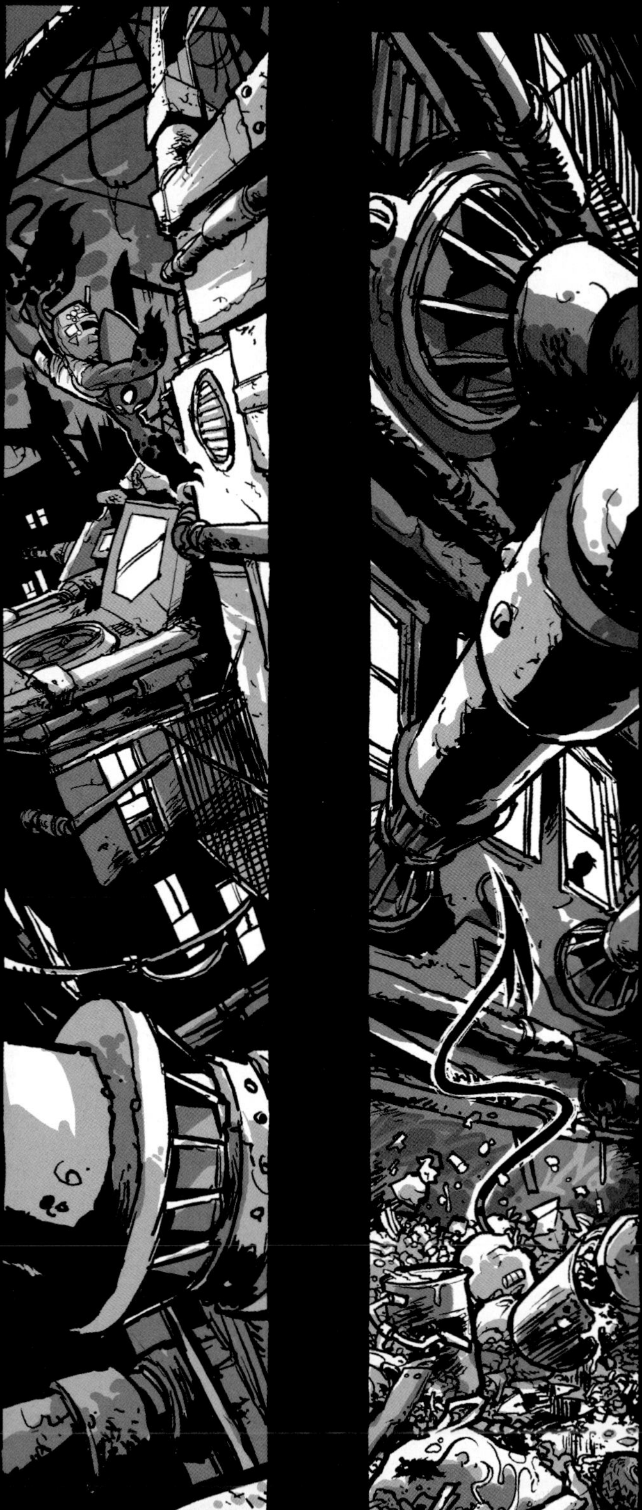

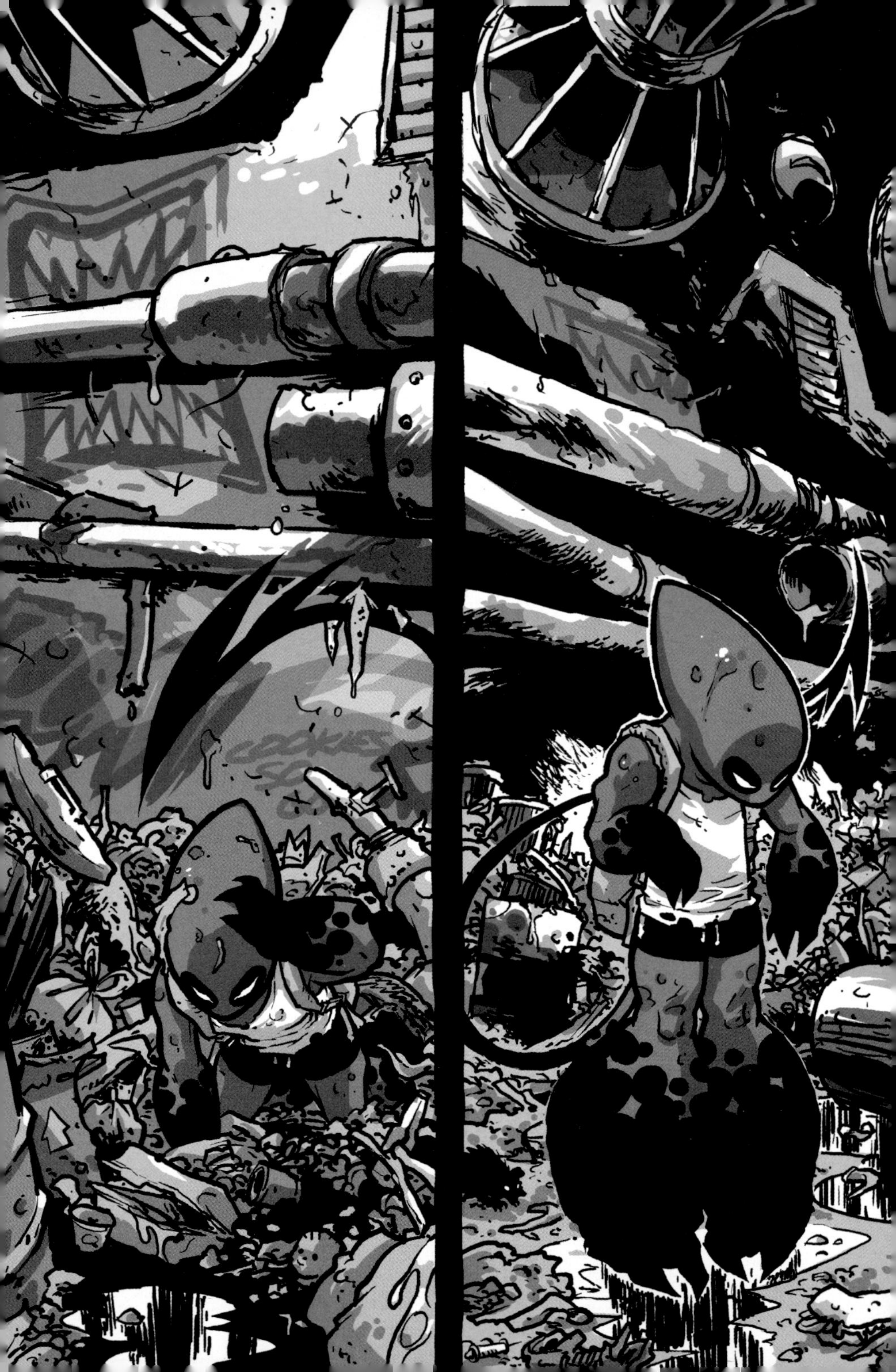

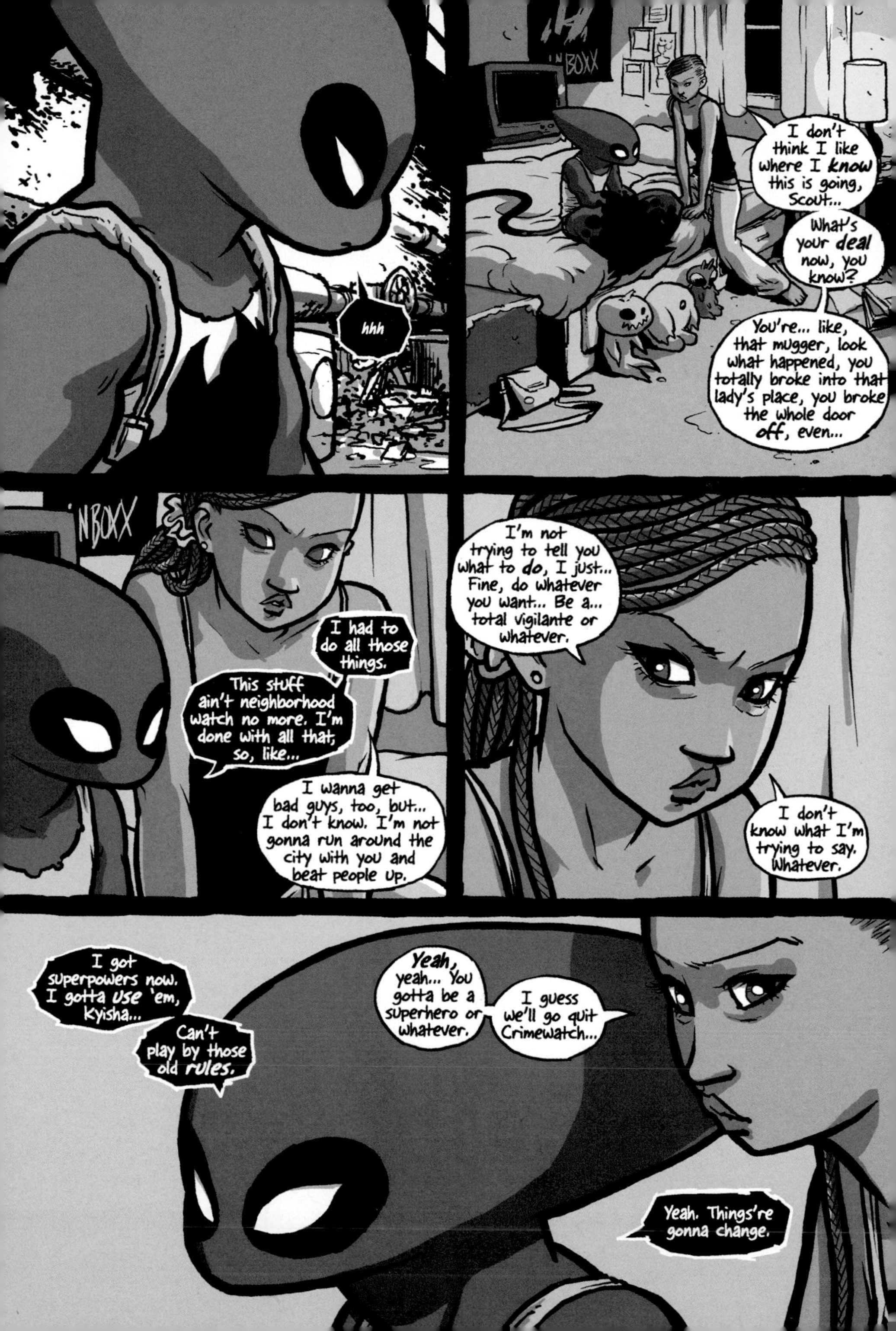
hhh
I don't think I like where I *know* this is going, Scout...
What's your *deal* now, you know?
You're... like, that mugger, look what happened, you totally broke into that lady's place, you broke the whole door *off*, even...
I had to do all those things.
This stuff ain't neighborhood watch no more. I'm done with all that, so, like...
I wanna get bad guys, too, but... I don't know. I'm not gonna run around the city with you and beat people up.
I'm not trying to tell you what to *do*, I just... Fine, do whatever you want... Be a... total vigilante or whatever.
I don't know what I'm trying to say. Whatever.
I got superpowers now. I gotta *use* 'em, Kyisha...
Can't play by those old *rules*.
Yeah, yeah... You gotta be a superhero or whatever.
I guess we'll go quit Crimewatch...
Yeah. Things're gonna change.

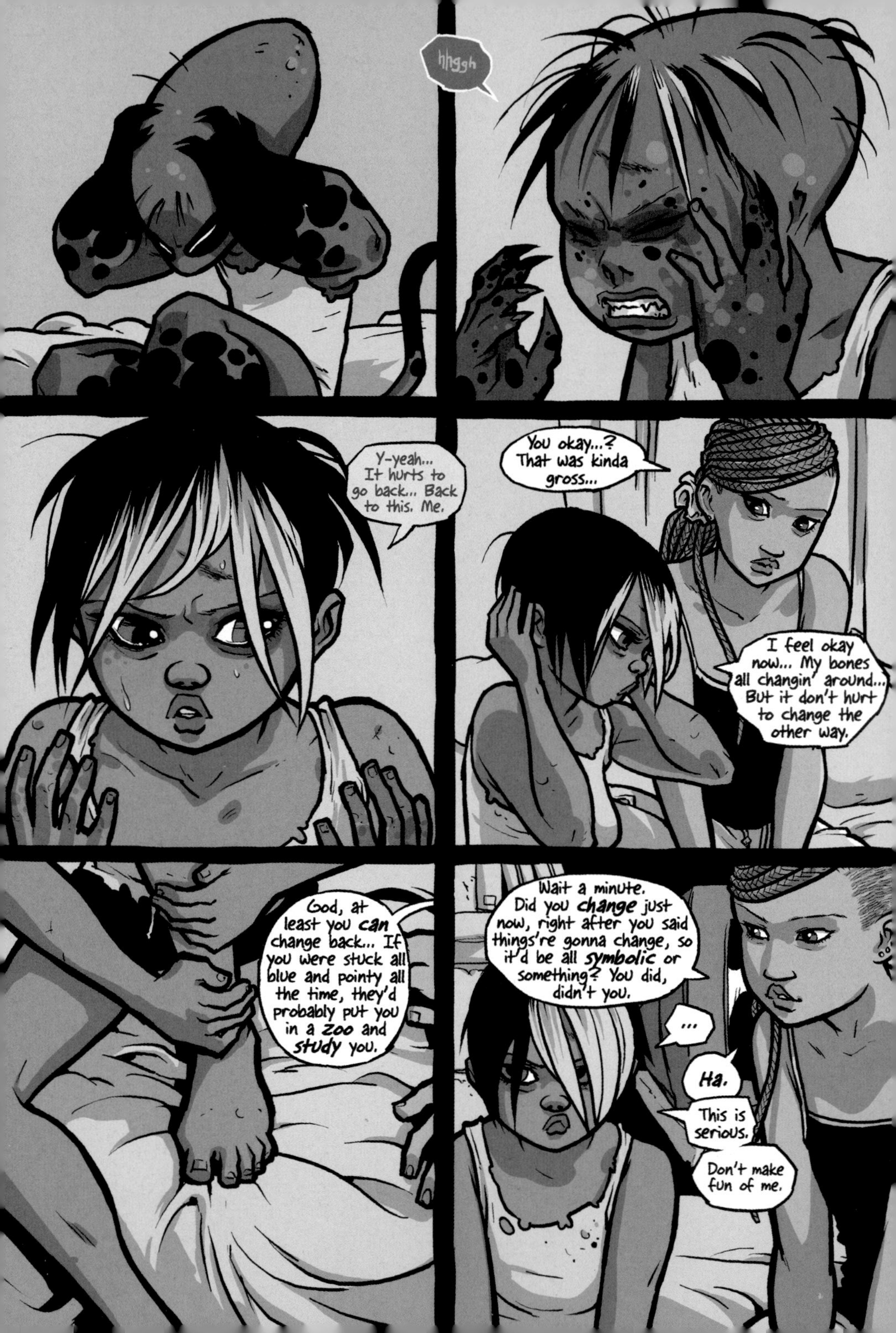
hhggh
Y-yeah... It hurts to go back... Back to this. Me.
You okay...? That was kinda gross...
I feel okay now... My bones all changin' around... But it don't hurt to change the other way.
God, at least you can change back... If you were stuck all blue and pointy all the time, they'd probably put you in a zoo and study you.
Wait a minute. Did you change just now, right after you said things're gonna change, so it'd be all symbolic or something? You did, didn't you.
...
Ha.
This is serious.
Don't make fun of me.

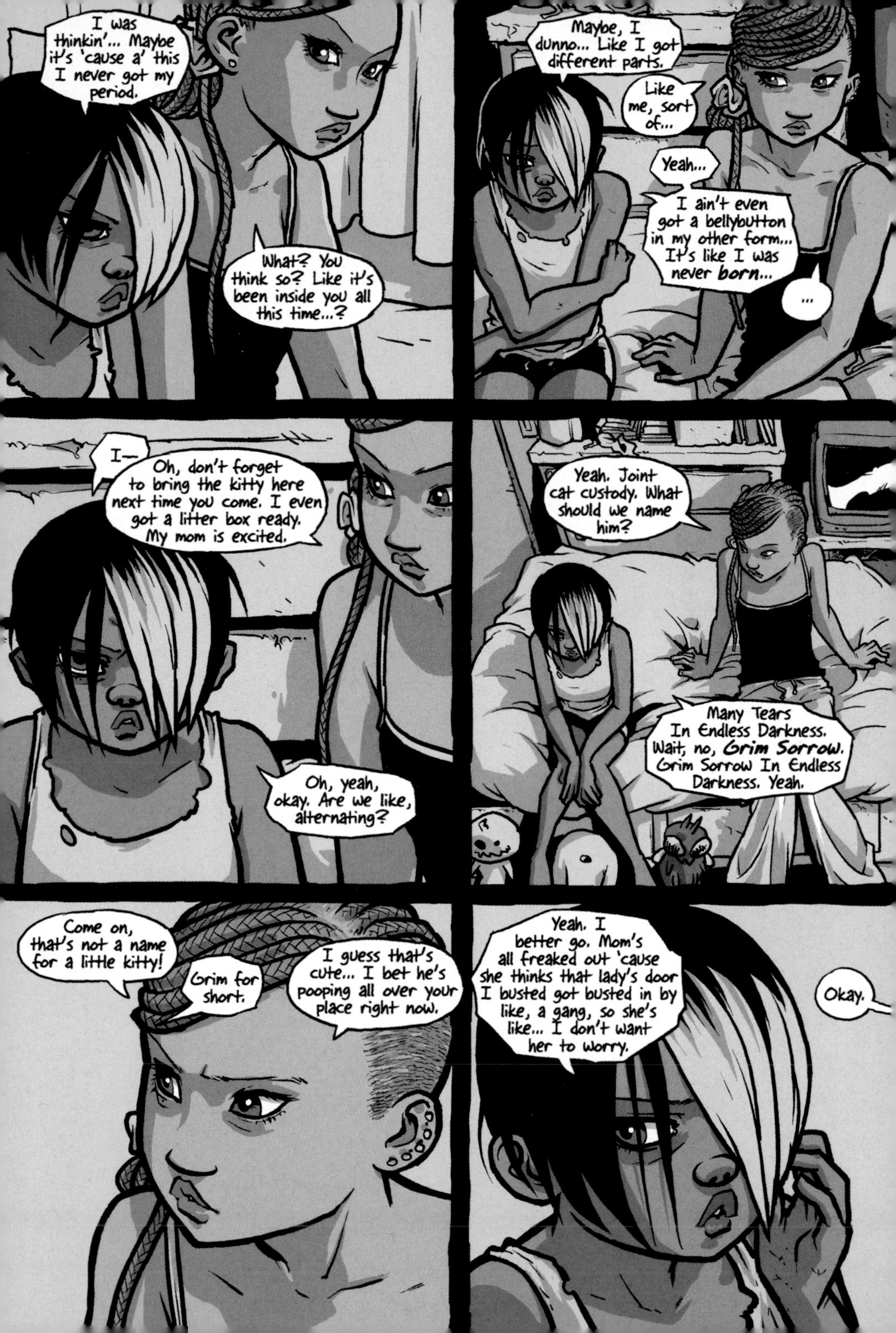
I was thinkin'... Maybe it's 'cause a' this I never got my period.
What? You think so? Like it's been inside you all this time...?
Maybe, I dunno... Like I got different parts.
Like me, sort of...
Yeah...
I ain't even got a bellybutton in my other form... It's like I was never **born**...
...
I—
Oh, don't forget to bring the kitty here next time you come. I even got a litter box ready. My mom is excited.
Oh, yeah, okay. Are we like, alternating?
Yeah. Joint cat custody. What should we name him?
Many Tears In Endless Darkness. Wait, no, **Grim Sorrow**. Grim Sorrow In Endless Darkness. Yeah.
Come on, that's not a name for a little kitty!
Grim for short.
I guess that's cute... I bet he's pooping all over your place right now.
Yeah. I better go. Mom's all freaked out 'cause she thinks that lady's door I busted got busted in by like, a gang, so she's like... I don't want her to worry.
Okay.

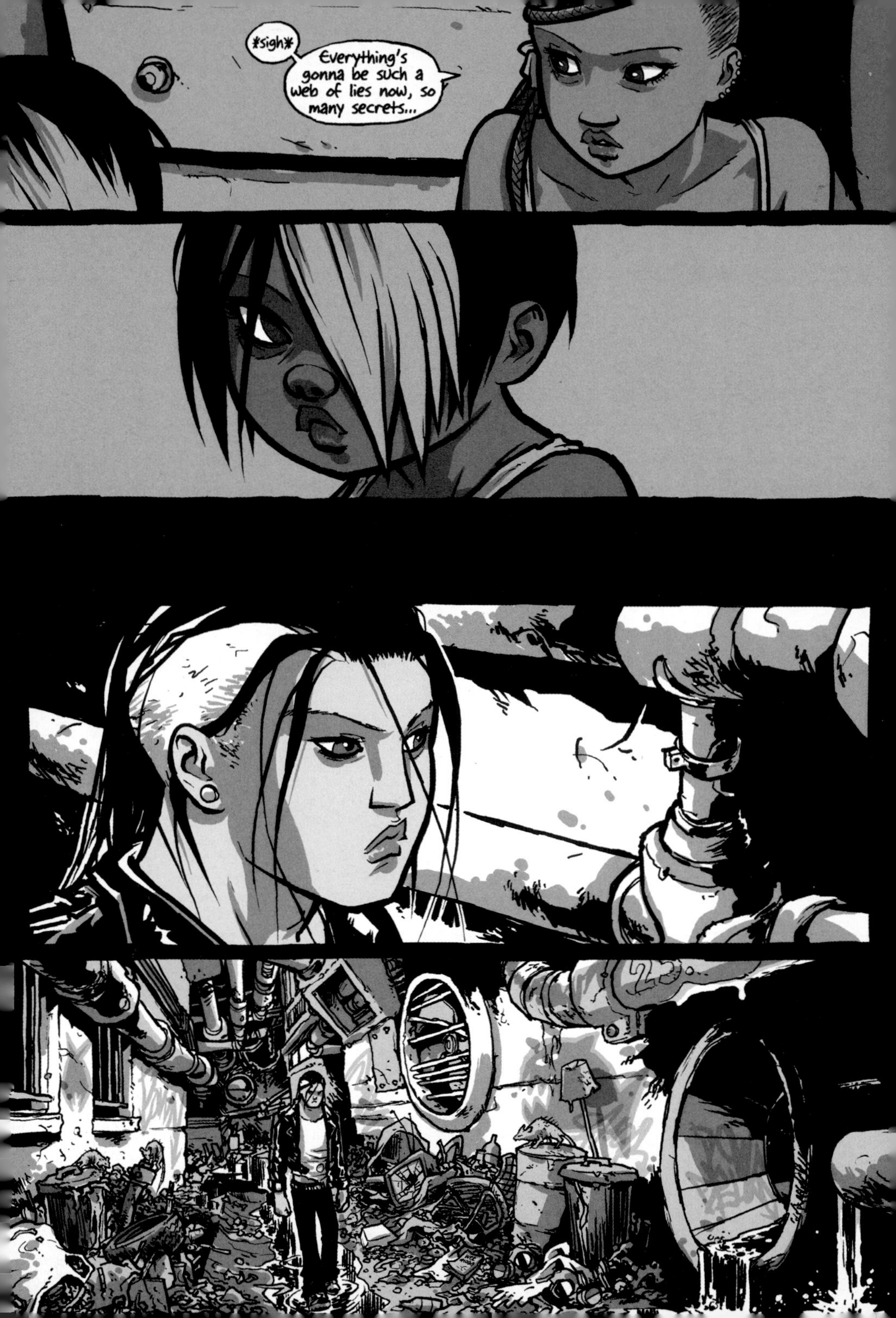
sigh
Everything's gonna be such a web of lies now, so many secrets...
23

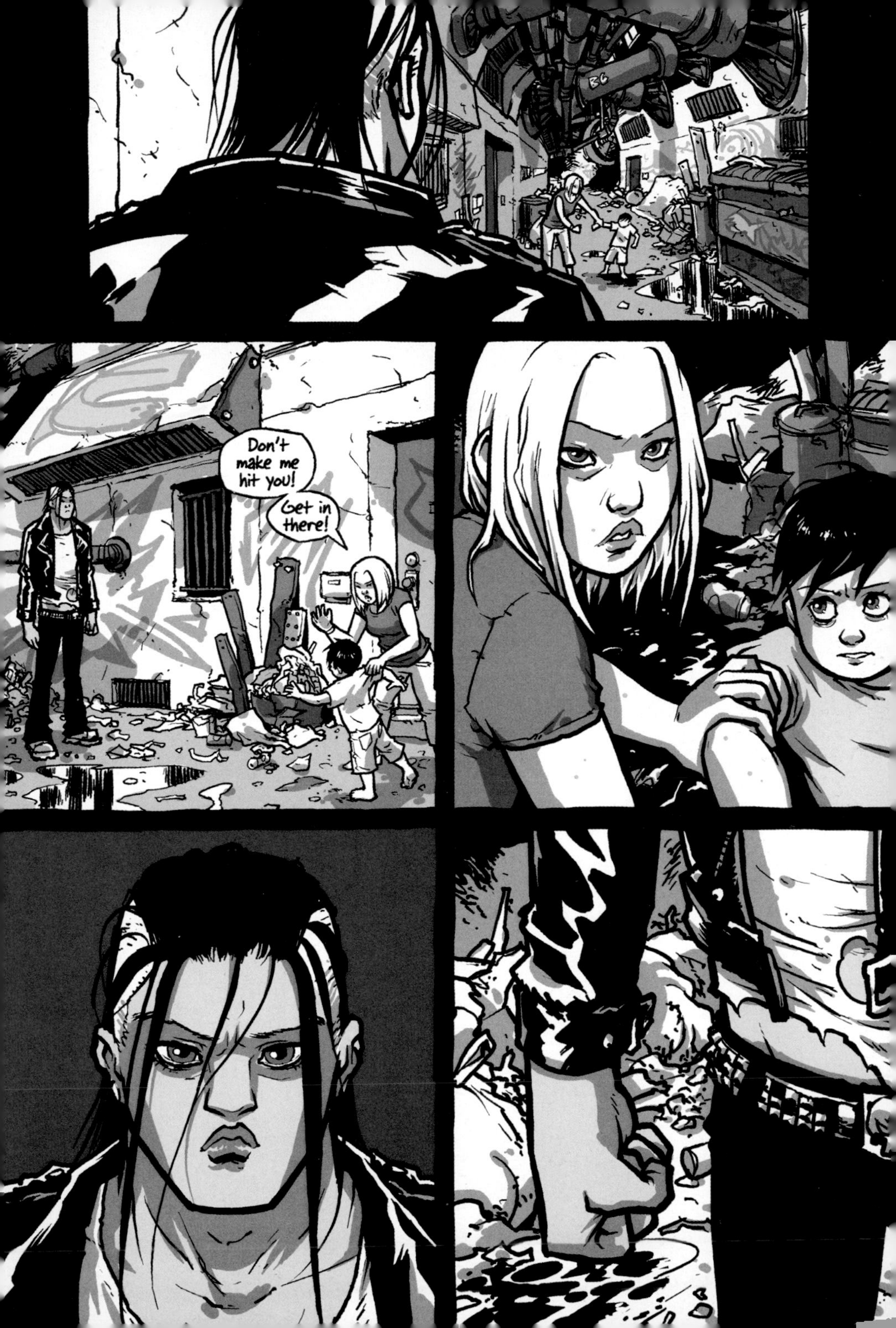
Don't make me hit you!
Get in there!

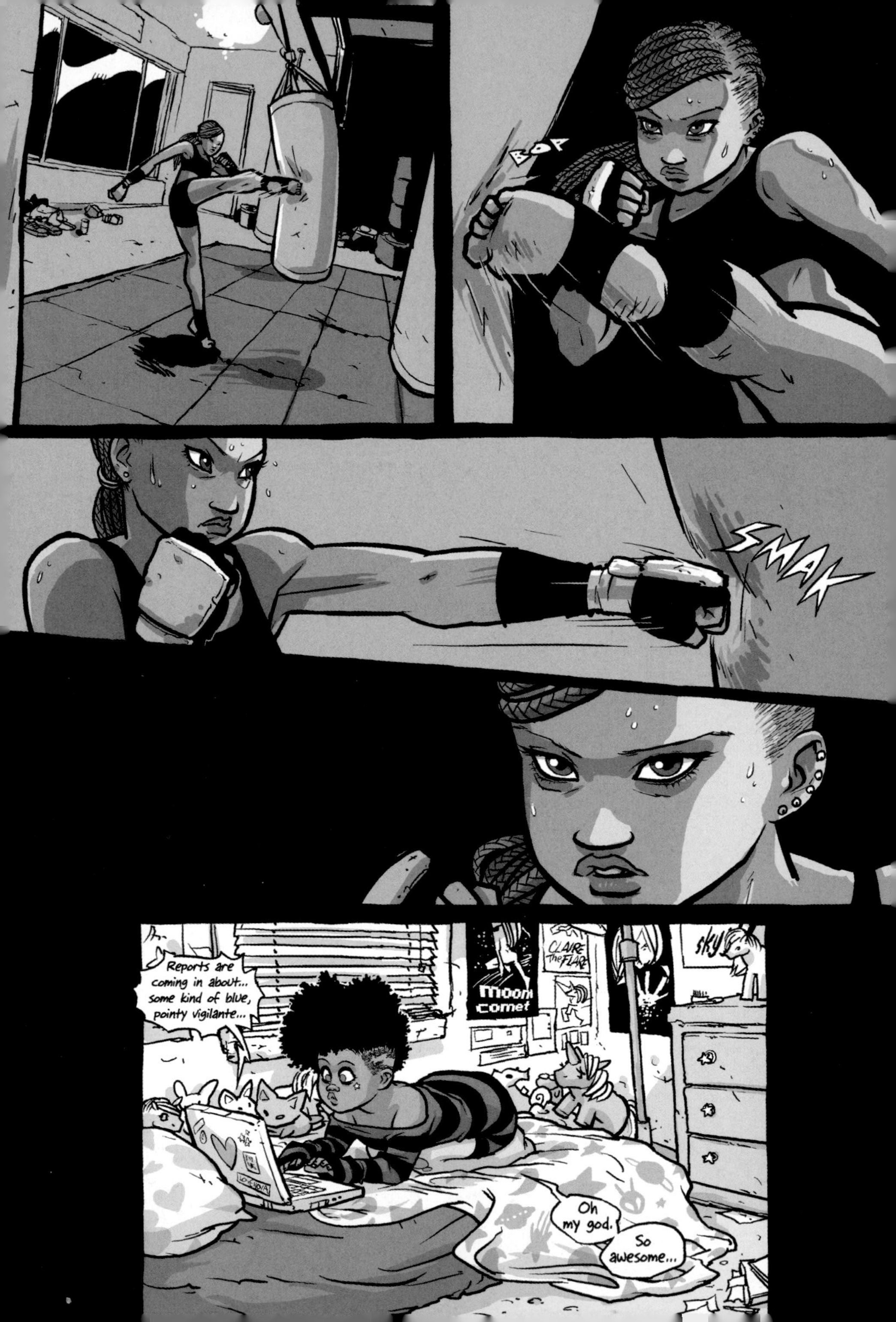
BOA
SMAK
Reports are coming in about... some kind of blue, pointy vigilante...
CLAIRE THE FLARE
sky
Moon comet
Oh my god.
So awesome...

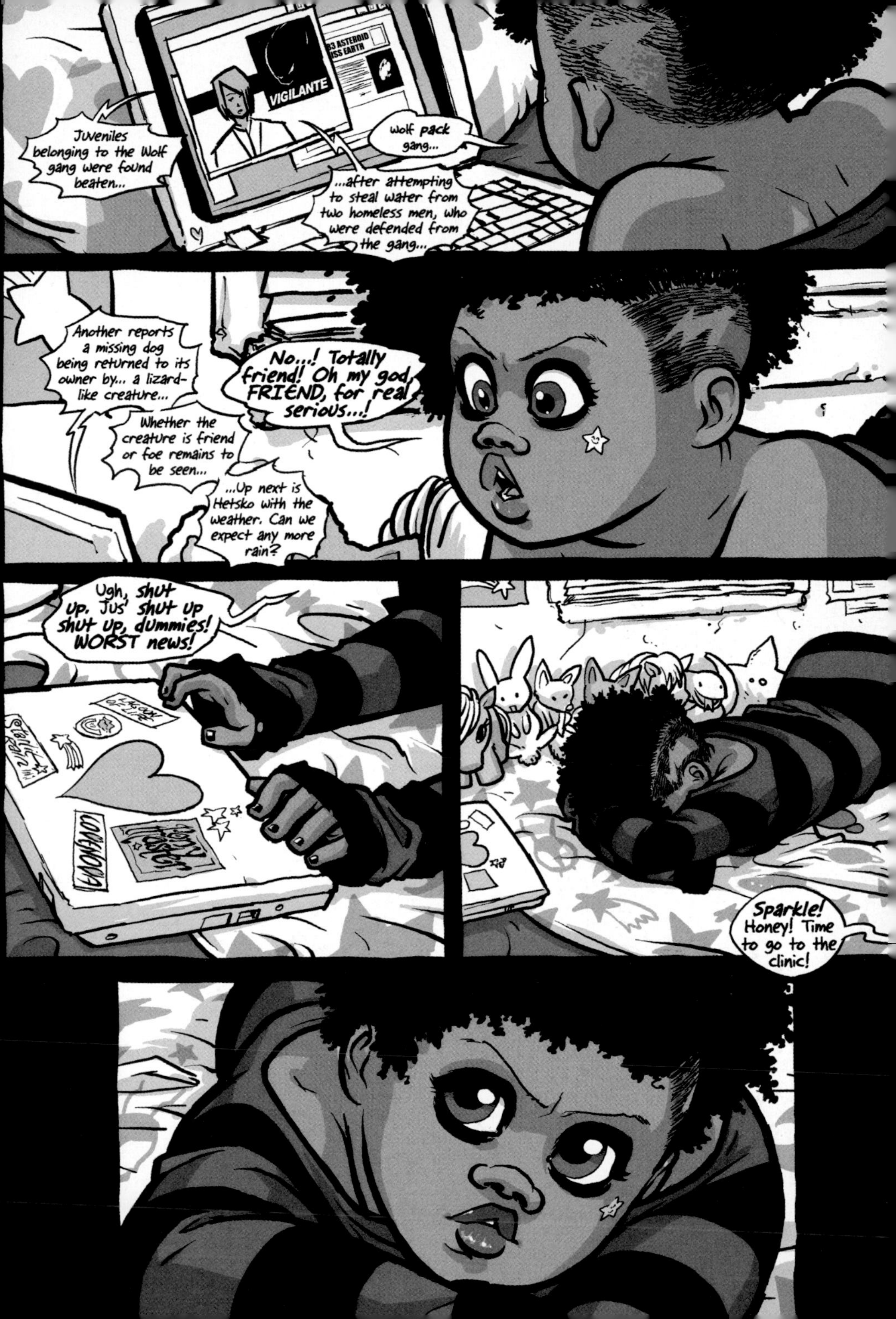
VIGILANTE
Juveniles belonging to the Wolf gang were found beaten...
Wolf pack gang...
...after attempting to steal water from two homeless men, who were defended from the gang...
Another reports a missing dog being returned to its owner by... a lizard-like creature...
No...! Totally friend! Oh my god, FRIEND, for real serious...!
Whether the creature is friend or foe remains to be seen...
...Up next is Hetsko with the weather. Can we expect any more rain?
Ugh, shut up. Jus' shut up shut up, dummies! WORST news!
Sparkle! Honey! Time to go to the clinic!

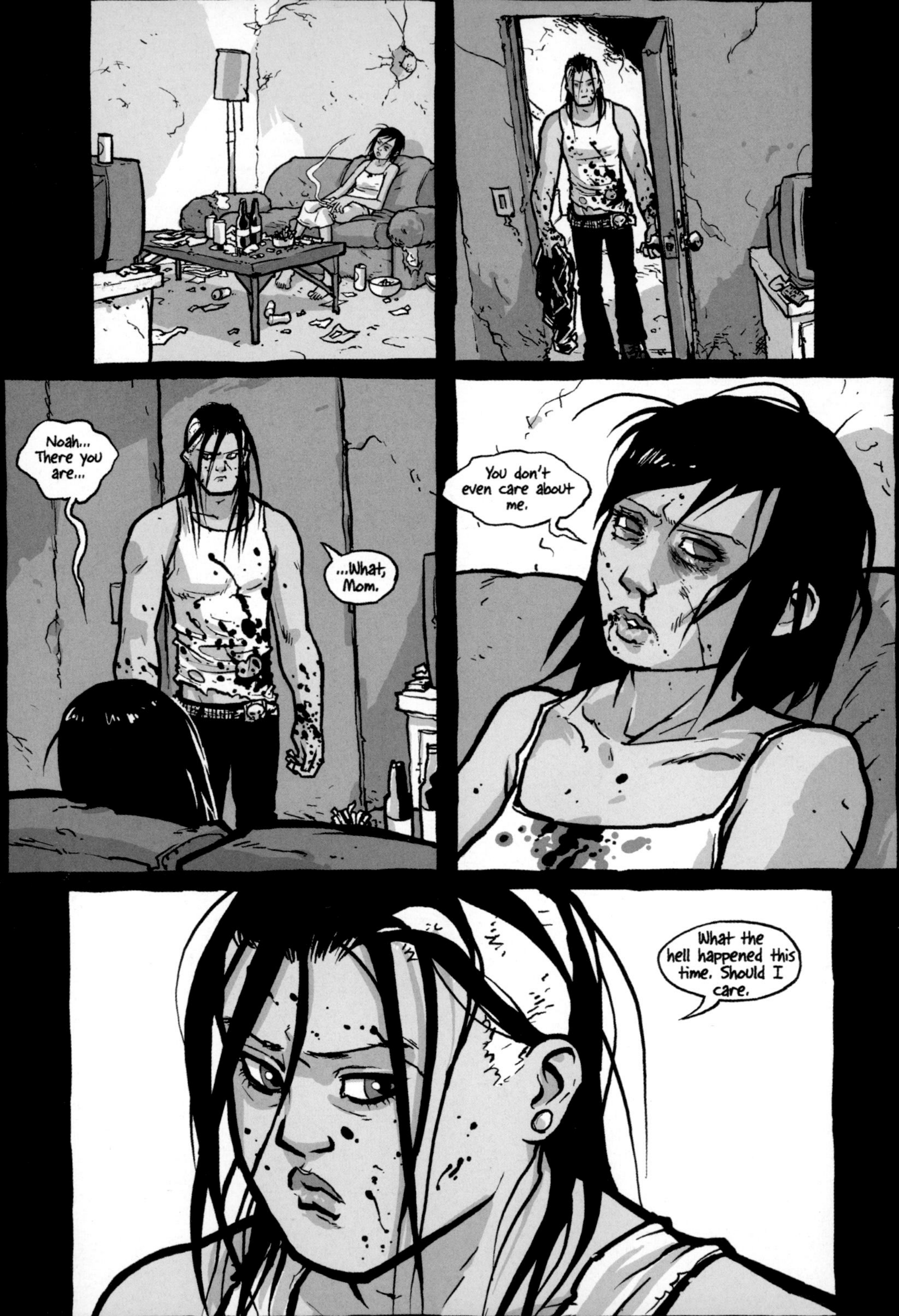
Noah... There you are...
...What, Mom.
You don't even care about me.
What the hell happened this time. Should I care.

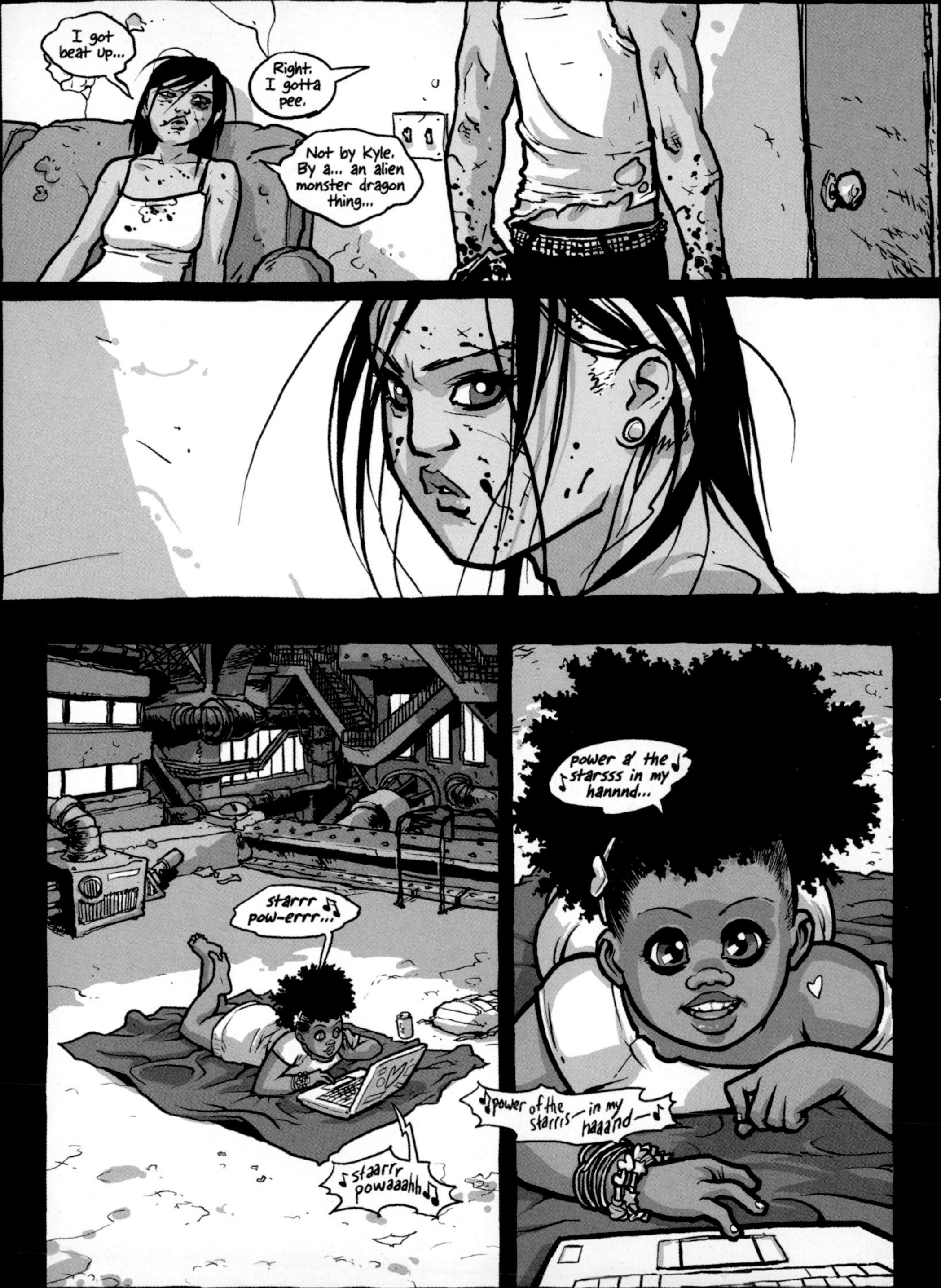

I got beat up...
Right. I gotta pee.
Not by Kyle. By a... an alien monster dragon thing...
starrr ♫ pow-errr...
♪ staarrr powaaahh ♫
power a' the ♪ starsss in my hannnd...
♪ power of the starrrs— in my haaand— ♪

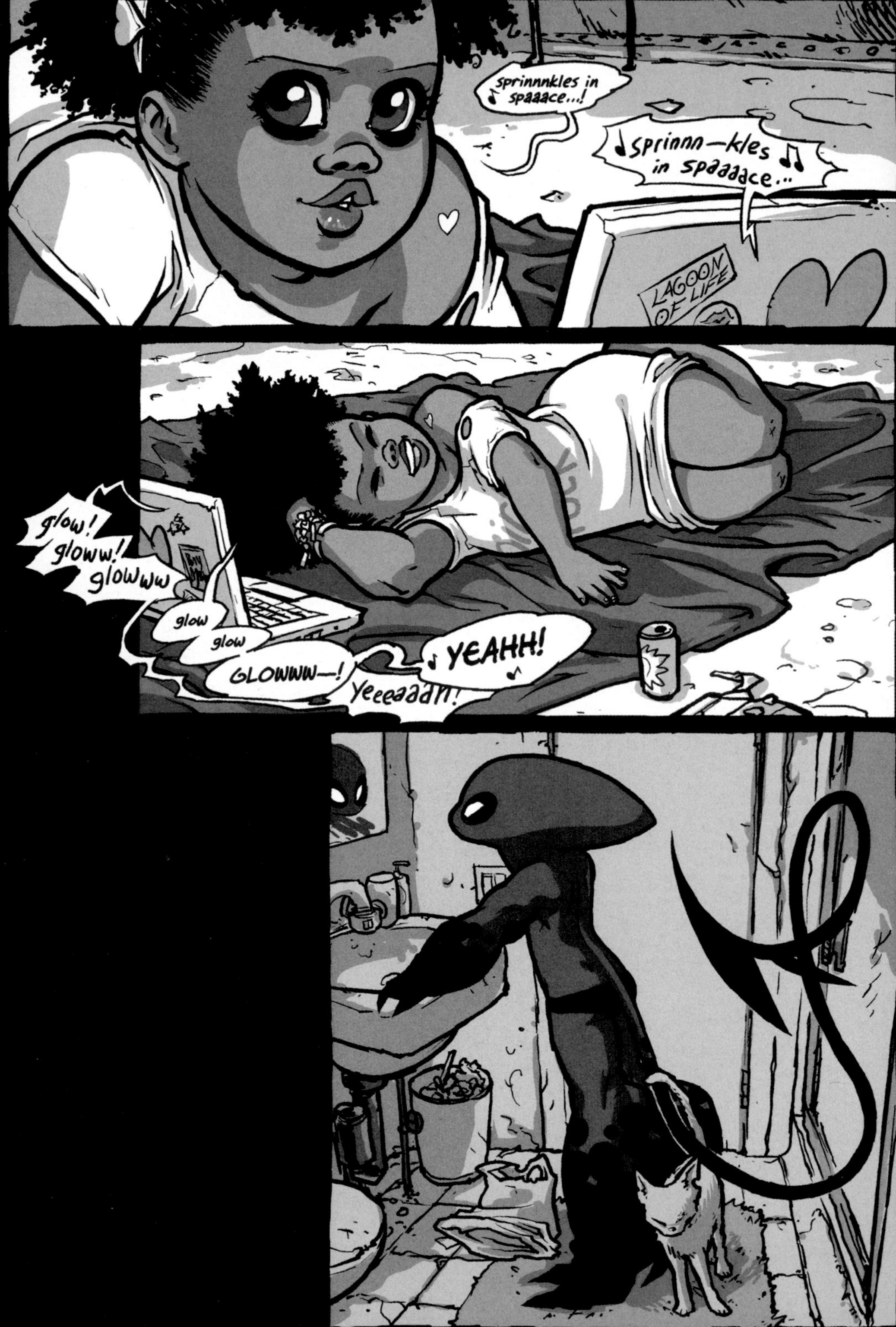
sprinnnkles in spaaace...!
sprinnn-kles in spaaaace...
LAGOON OF LIFE
glow! gloww! glowww
glow glow GLOWWW-!
YEAHH!
Yeeeaaah!

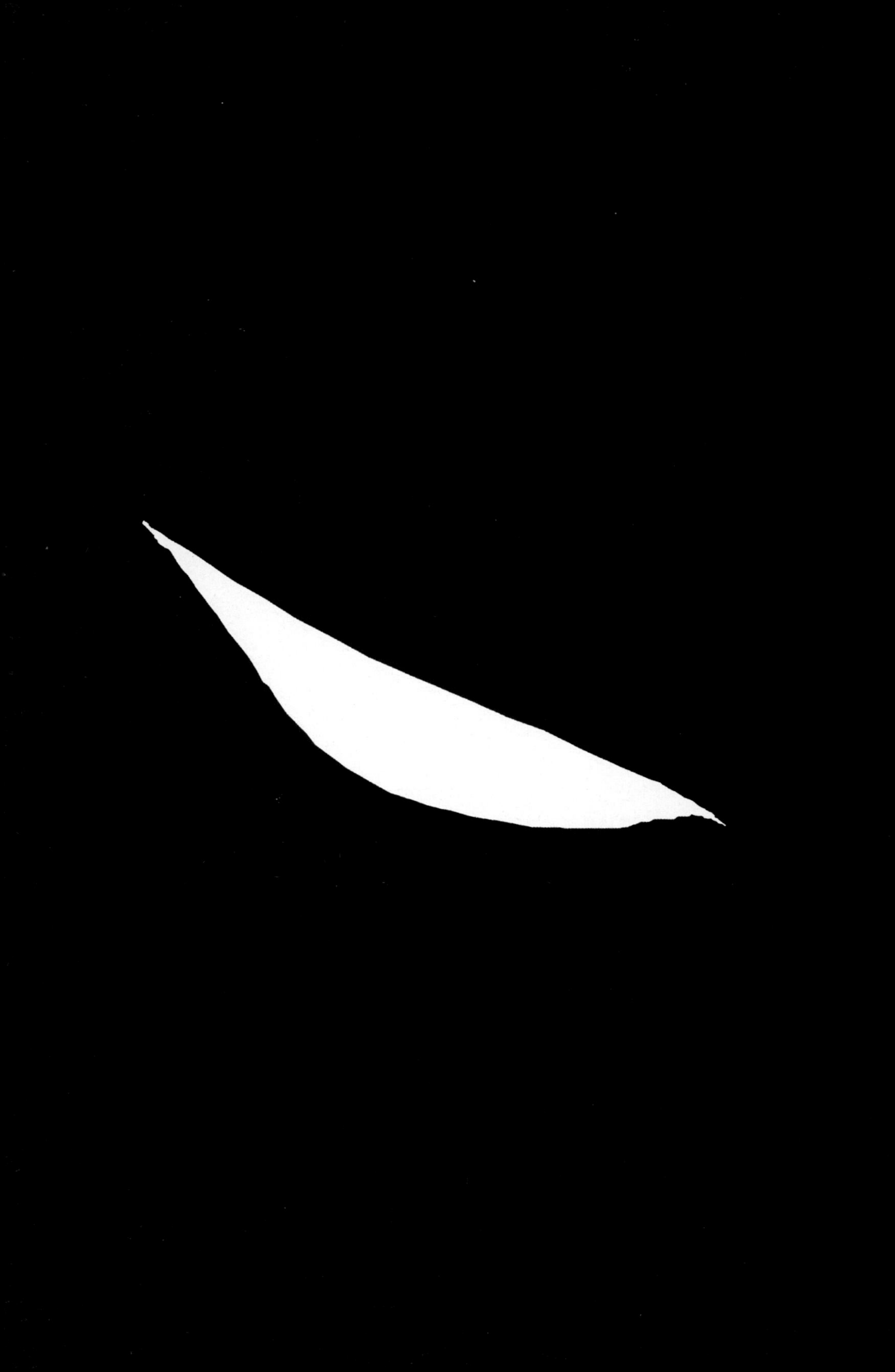

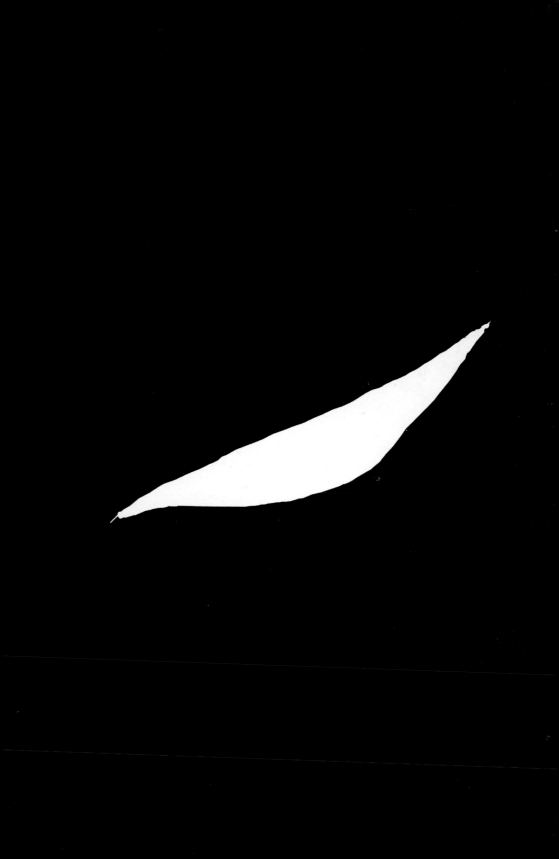

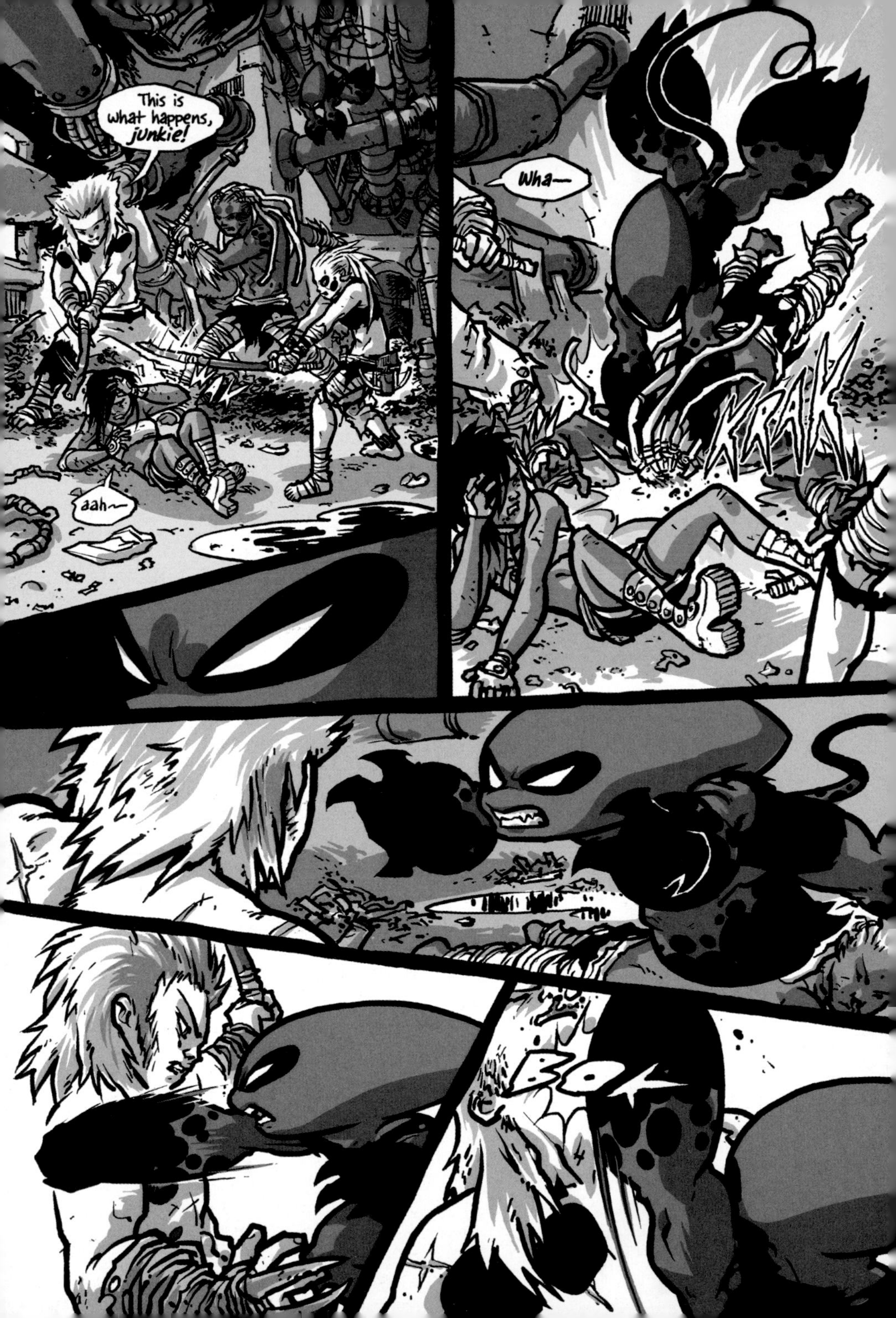
This is what happens, junkie!
aah—
Wha—
KRAK
BOK

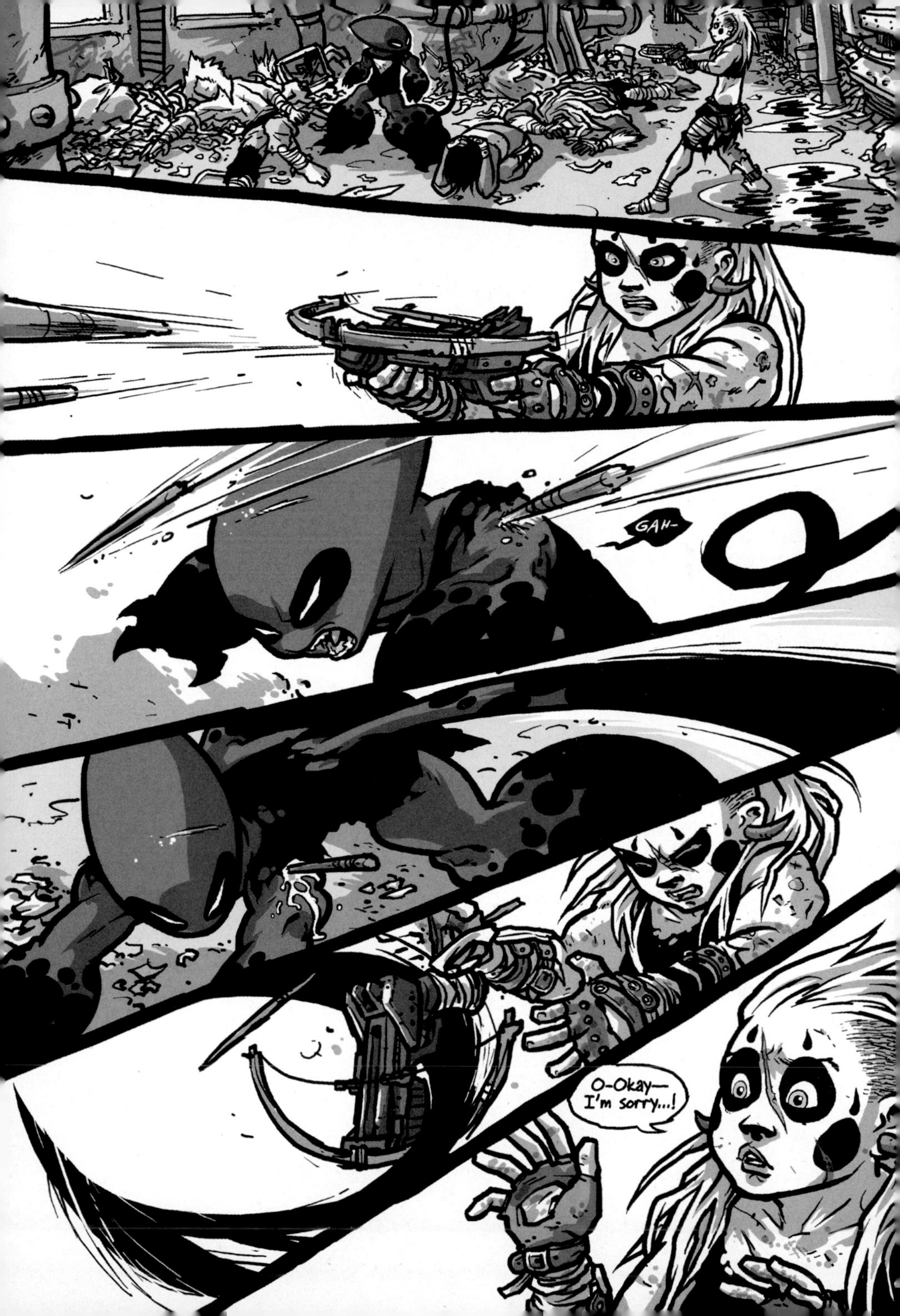
GAH-
O-Okay—
I'm sorry...!

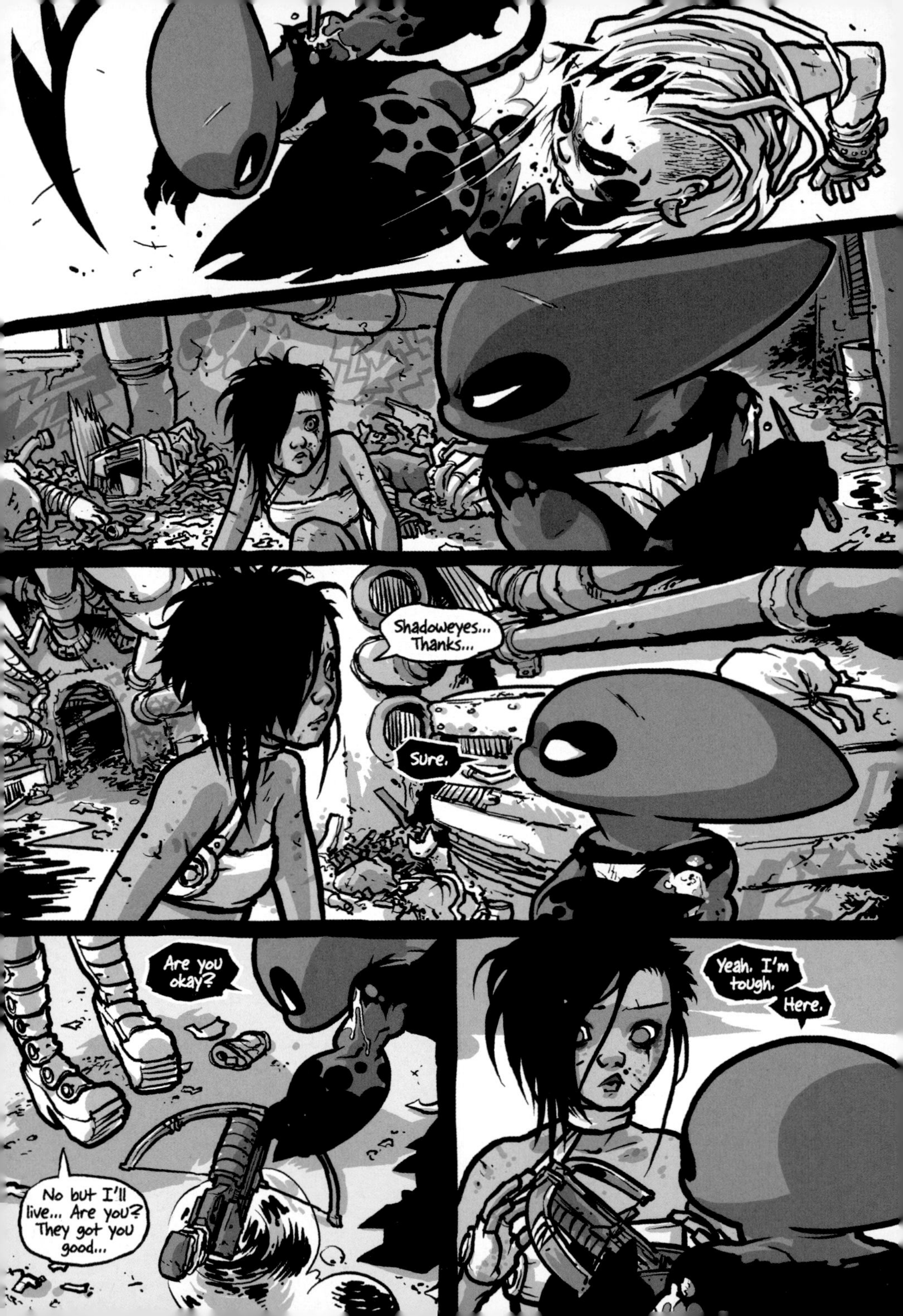
Shadoweyes... Thanks...
Sure.
Are you okay?
No but I'll live... Are you? They got you good...
Yeah. I'm tough.
Here.

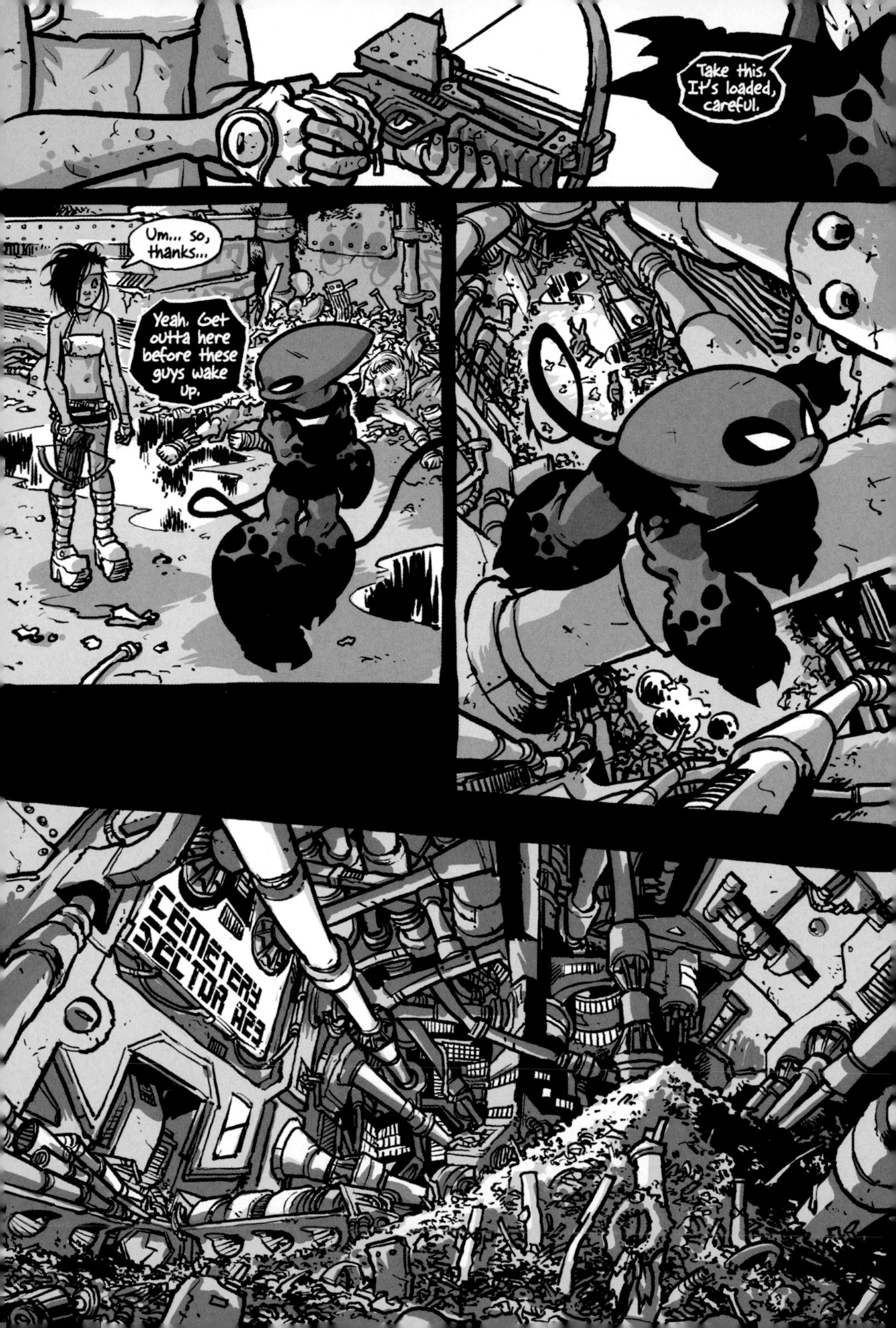
Take this. It's loaded, careful.
Um... so, thanks...
Yeah. Get outta here before these guys wake up.
CEMETERY SECTOR A23

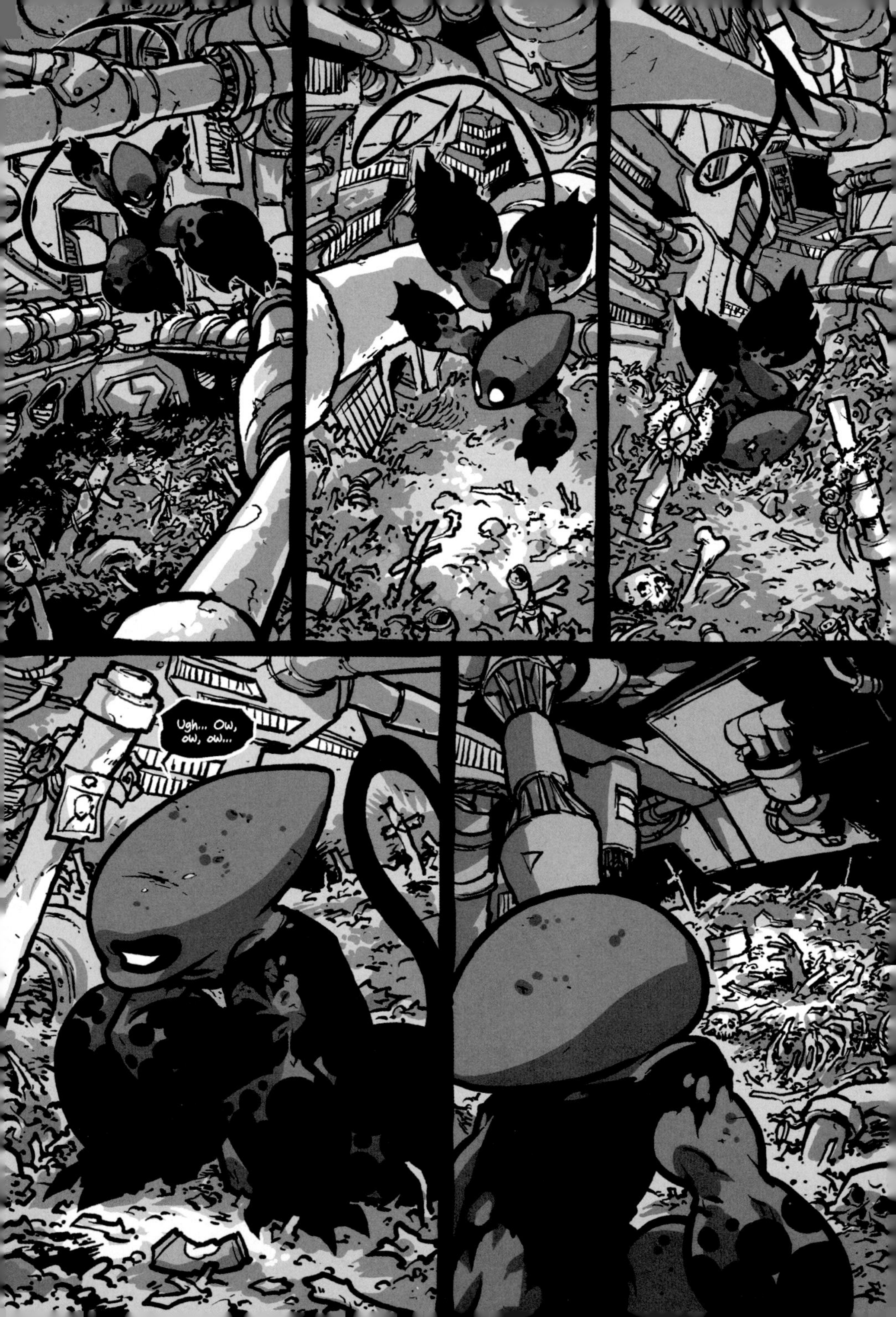
Ugh... Ow, ow, ow...

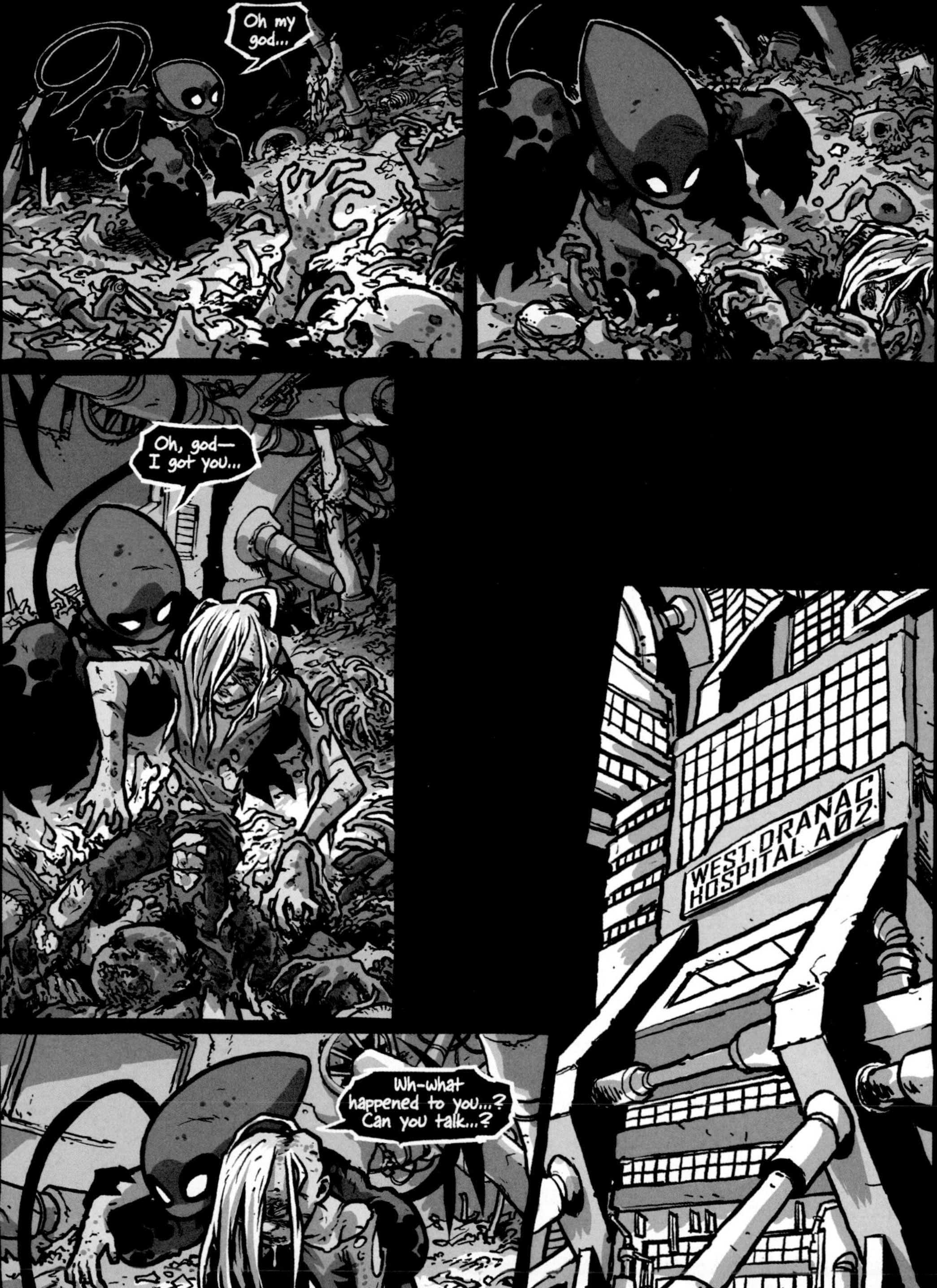
Oh my god...
Oh, god— I got you...
Wh-what happened to you...? Can you talk...?
WEST DRANAC HOSPITAL A02

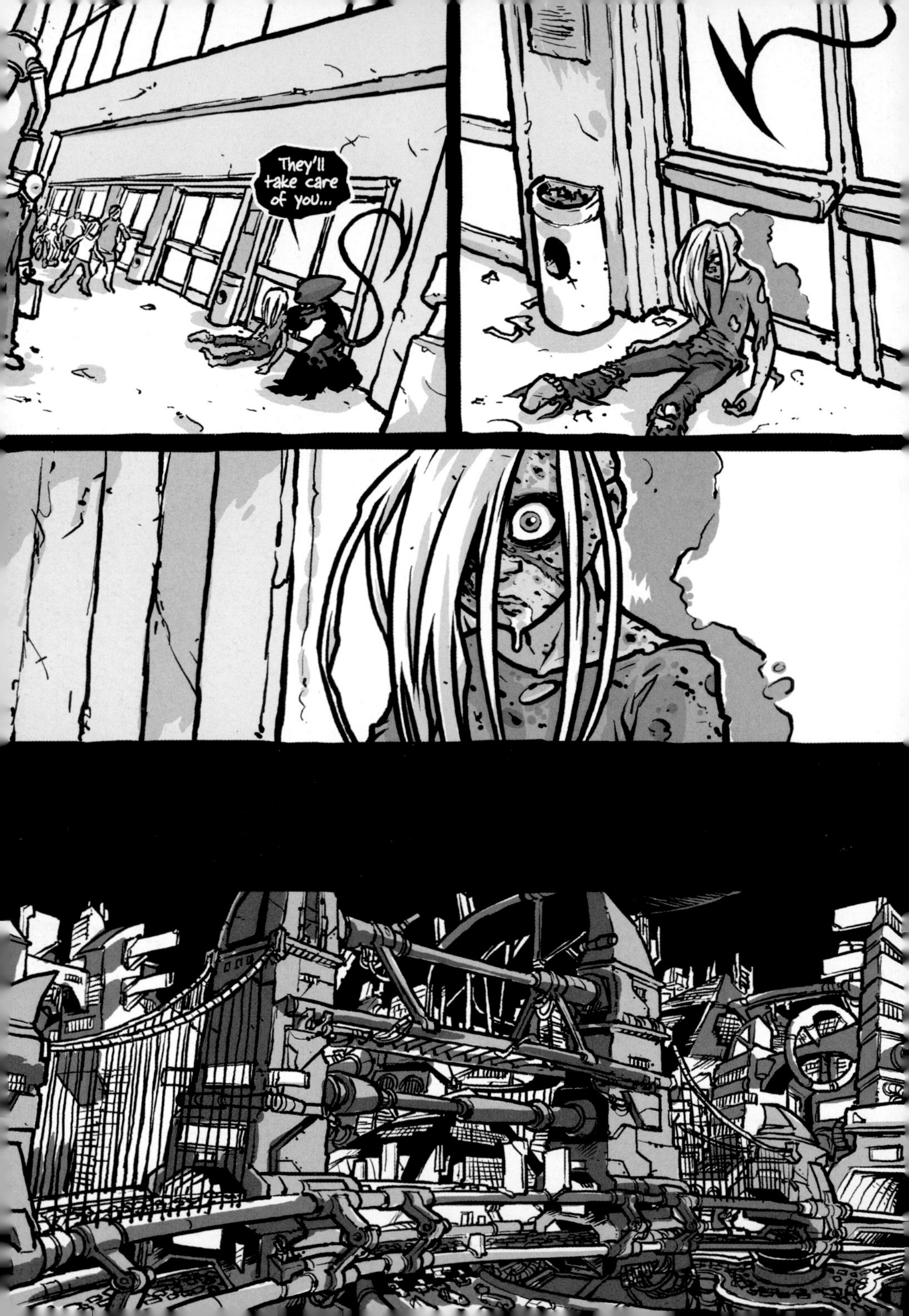
They'll take care of you...

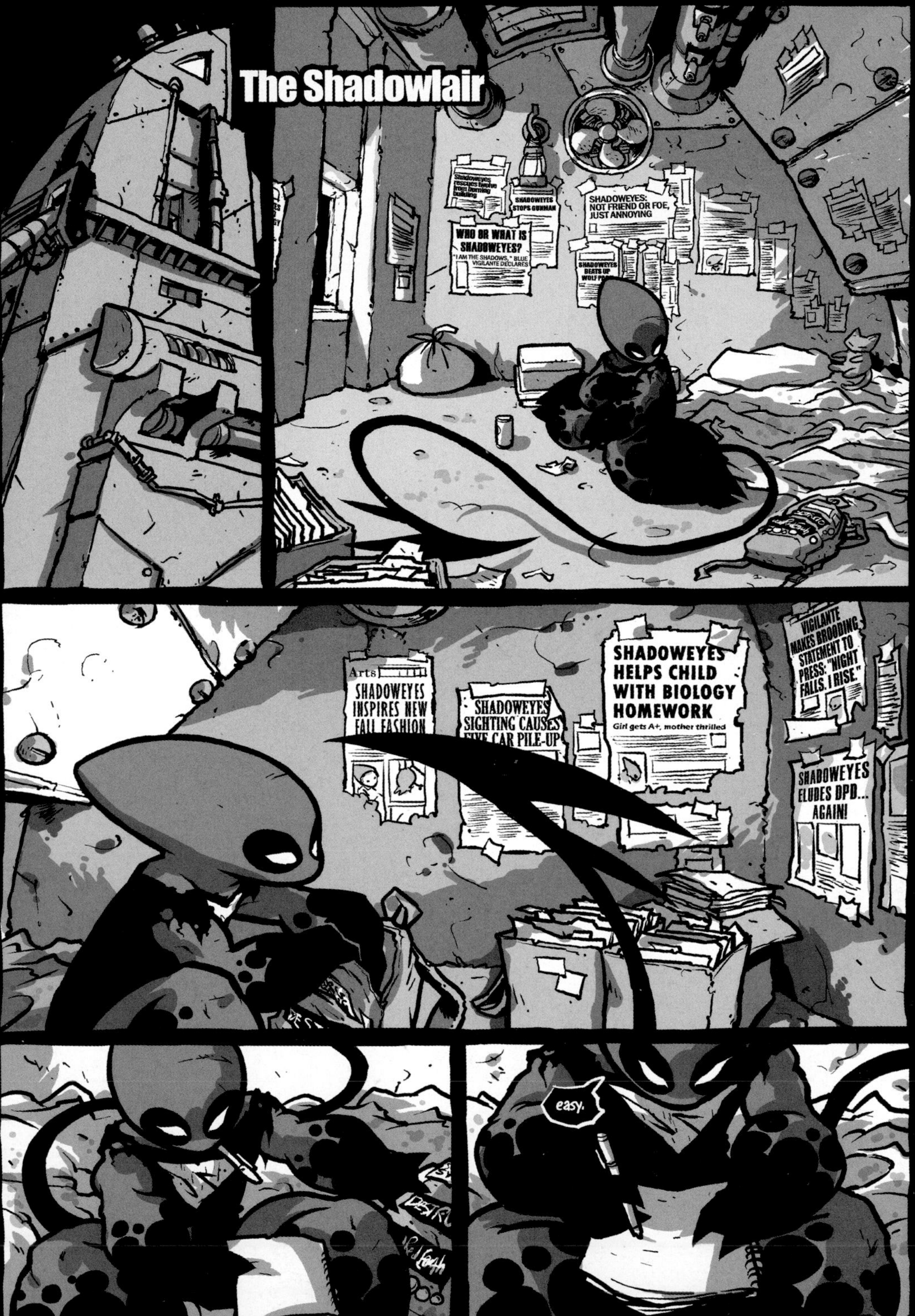
The Shadowlair
Shadoweyes rescues twelve from burning building
SHADOWEYES STOPS GUNMAN
SHADOWEYES: NOT FRIEND OR FOE, JUST ANNOYING
WHO OR WHAT IS SHADOWEYES?
"I AM THE SHADOWS," BLUE VIGILANTE DECLARES
Arts
SHADOWEYES INSPIRES NEW FALL FASHION
SHADOWEYES SIGHTING CAUSES FIVE CAR PILE-UP
SHADOWEYES HELPS CHILD WITH BIOLOGY HOMEWORK
Girl gets A+, mother thrilled
VIGILANTE MAKES BROODING STATEMENT TO PRESS: "NIGHT FALLS. I RISE."
SHADOWEYES ELUDES DPD... AGAIN!
easy.

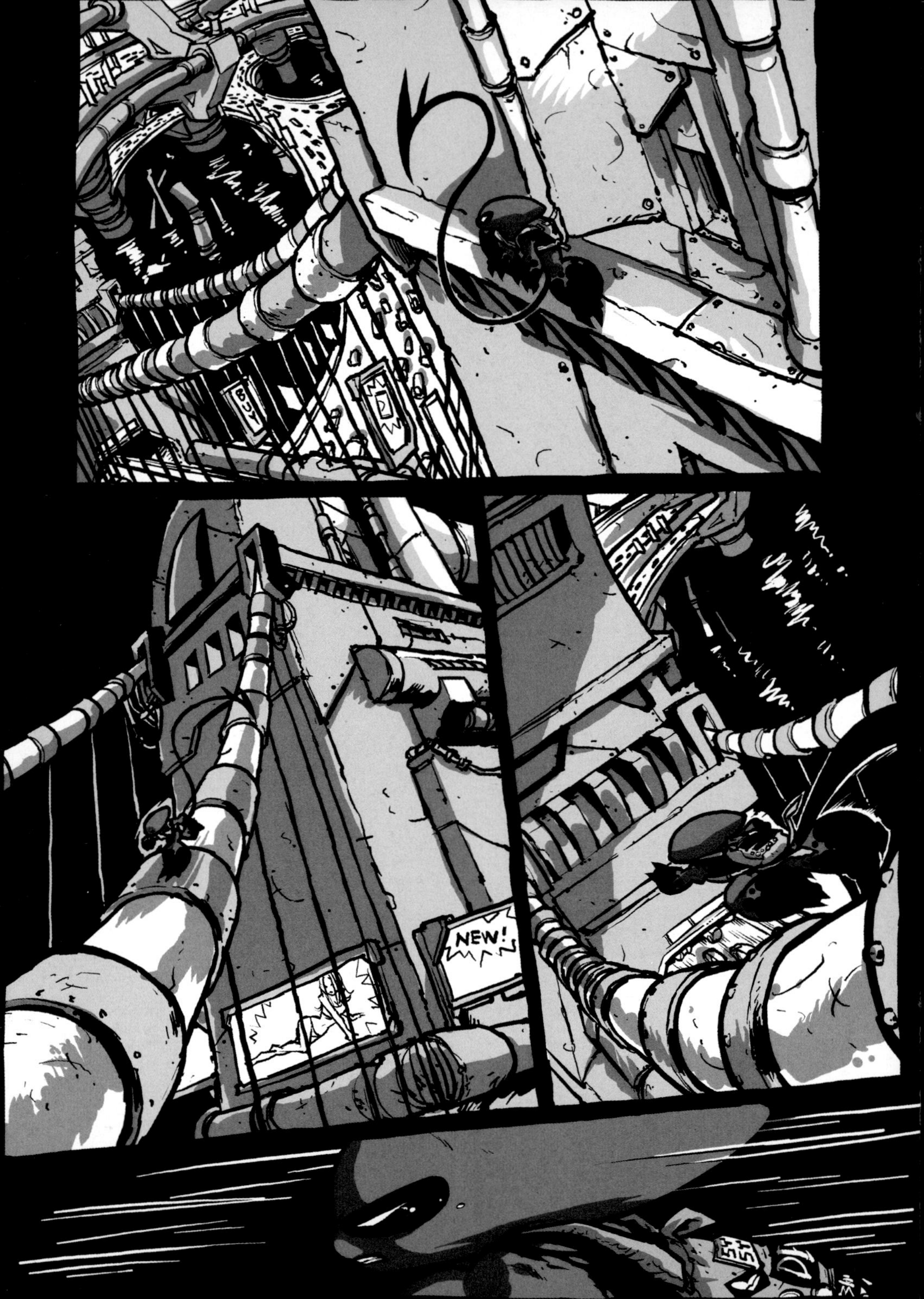
BUY
NEW!

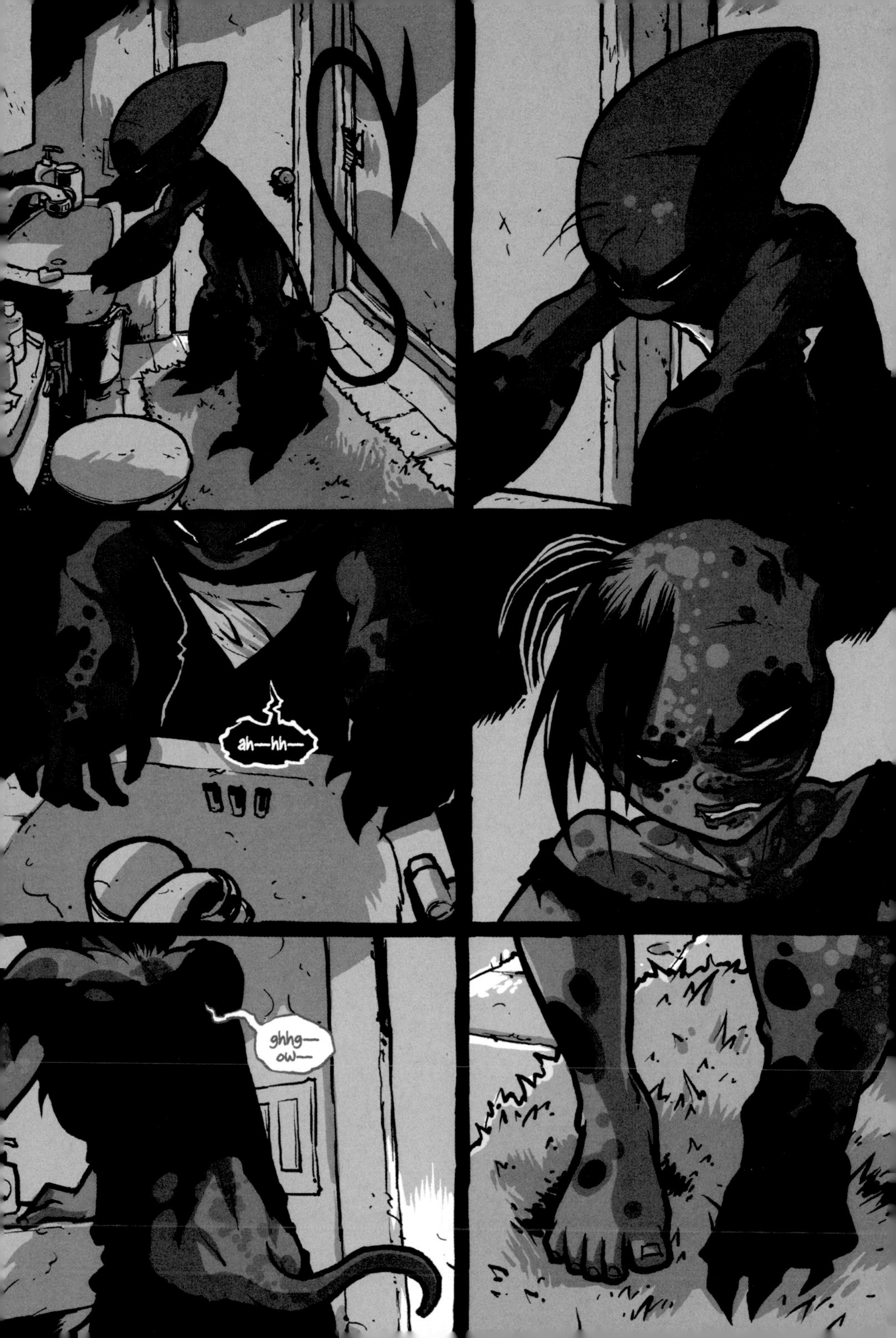
ah—hh—
ghhg—ow—

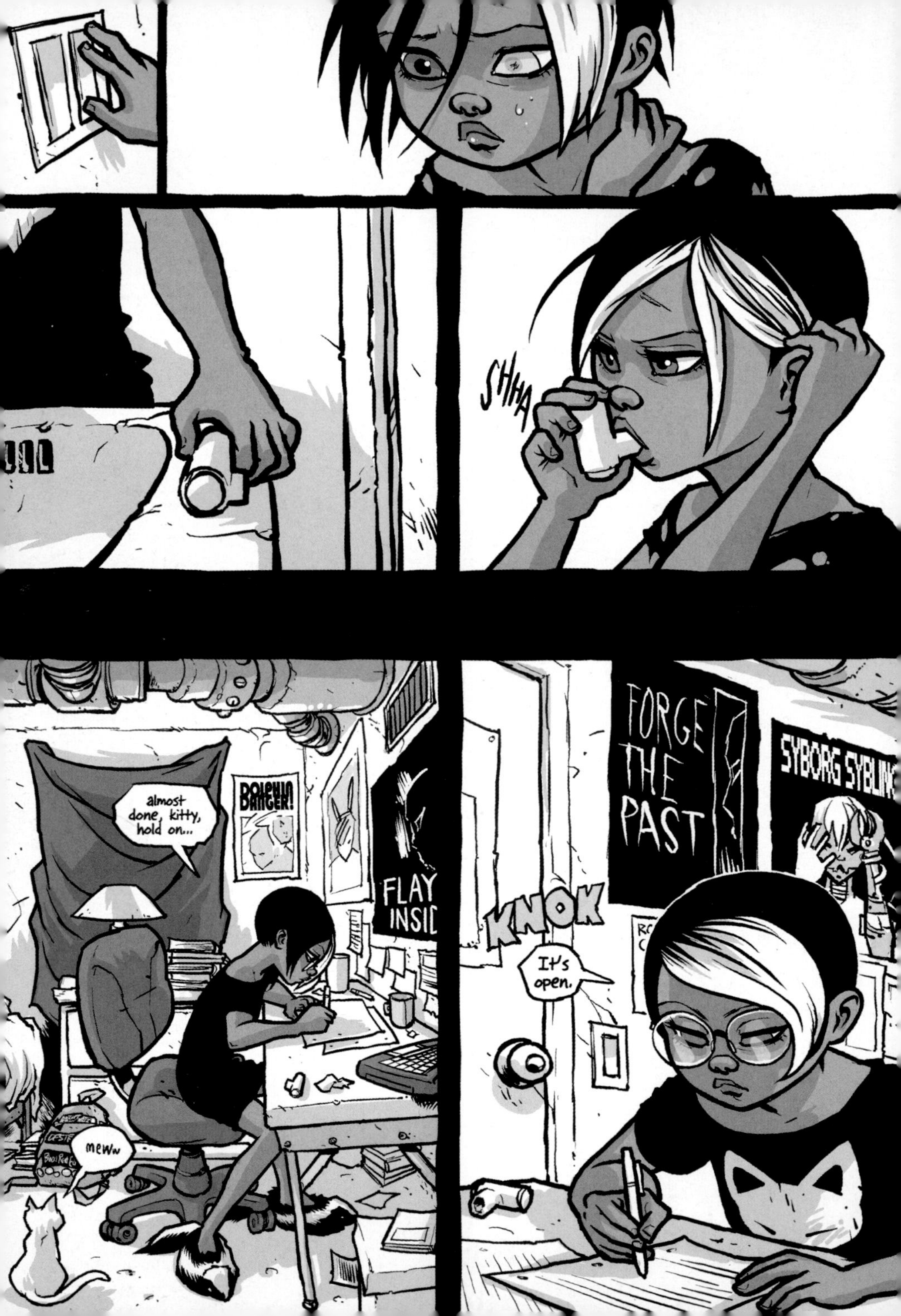
SHHA
DOLPHIN DANGER!
almost done, kitty, hold on...
mewww
FORGE THE PAST
KNOK
It's open.

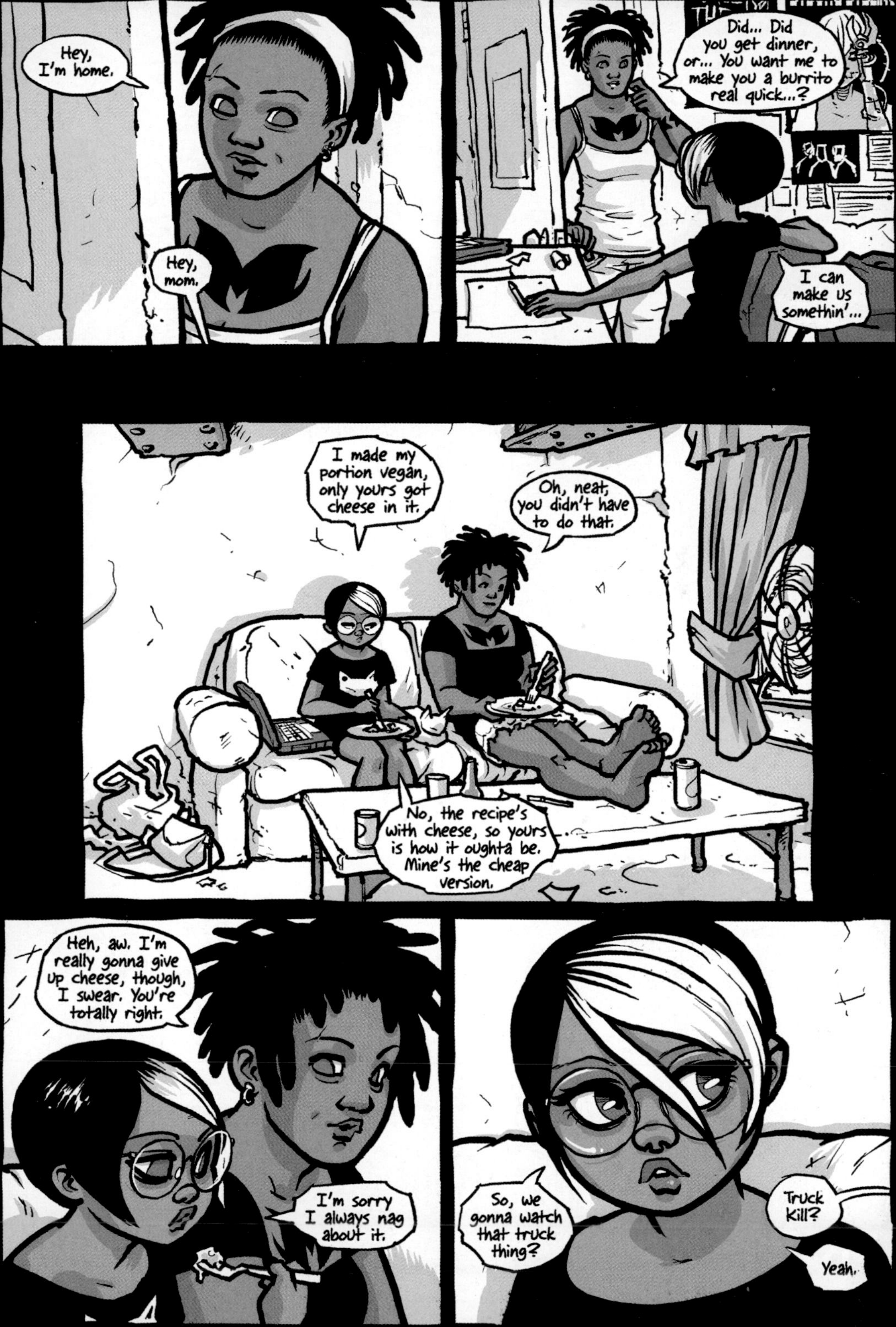
Hey, I'm home.
Hey, mom.
Did... Did you get dinner, or... You want me to make you a burrito real quick...?
I can make us somethin'...
I made my portion vegan, only yours got cheese in it.
Oh, neat, you didn't have to do that.
No, the recipe's with cheese, so yours is how it oughta be. Mine's the cheap version.
Heh, aw. I'm really gonna give up cheese, though, I swear. You're totally right.
I'm sorry I always nag about it.
So, we gonna watch that truck thing?
Truck Kill?
Yeah.

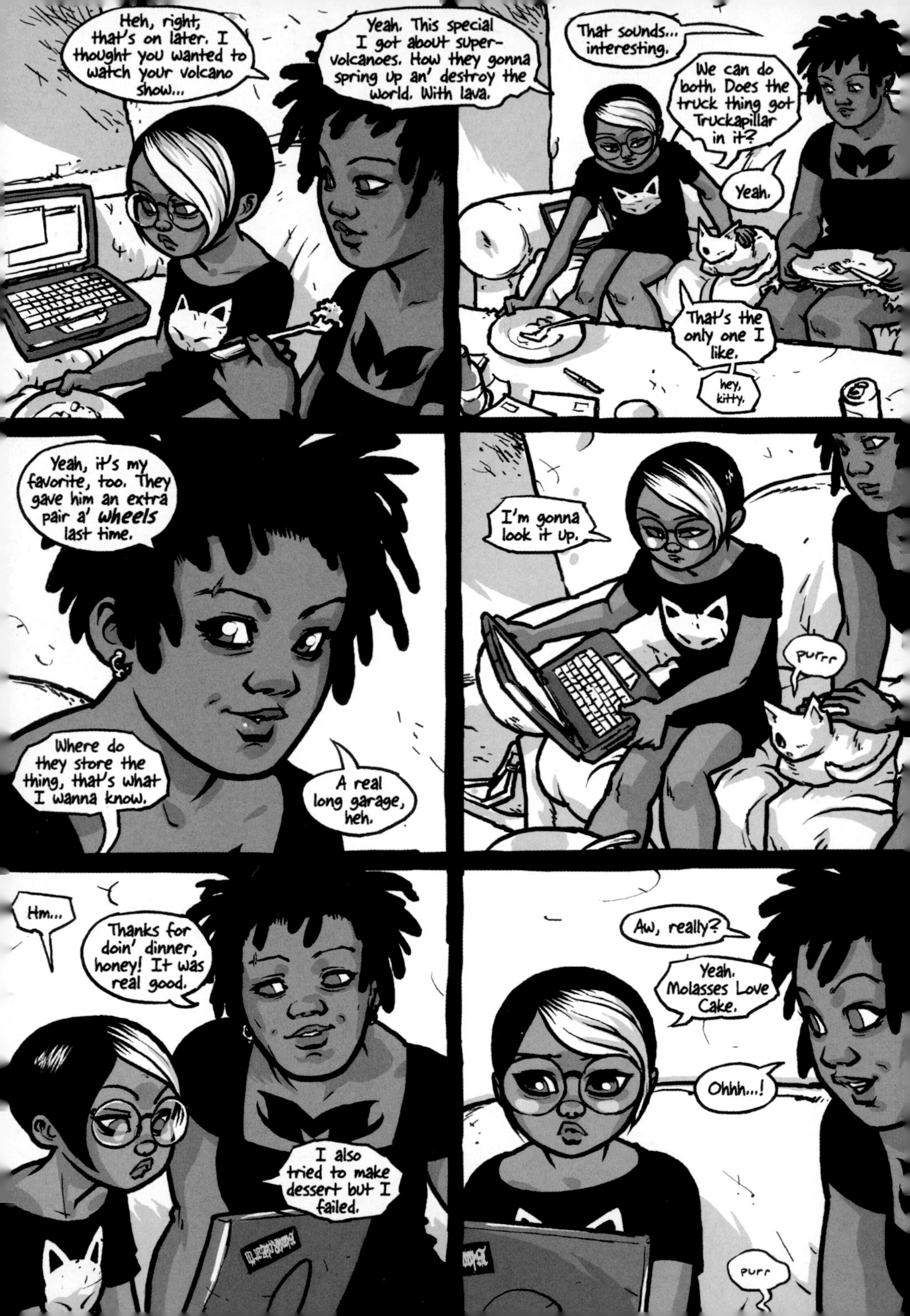
Heh, right, that's on later. I thought you wanted to watch your volcano show...
Yeah. This special I got about super-volcanoes. How they gonna spring up an' destroy the world. With lava.
That sounds... interesting.
We can do both. Does the truck thing got Truckapillar in it?
Yeah.
That's the only one I like.
hey, kitty.
Yeah, it's my favorite, too. They gave him an extra pair a' wheels last time.
Where do they store the thing, that's what I wanna know.
A real long garage, heh.
I'm gonna look it up.
purrr
Hm...
Thanks for doin' dinner, honey! It was real good.
I also tried to make dessert but I failed.
Aw, really?
Yeah. Molasses Love Cake.
Ohhh...!
purr

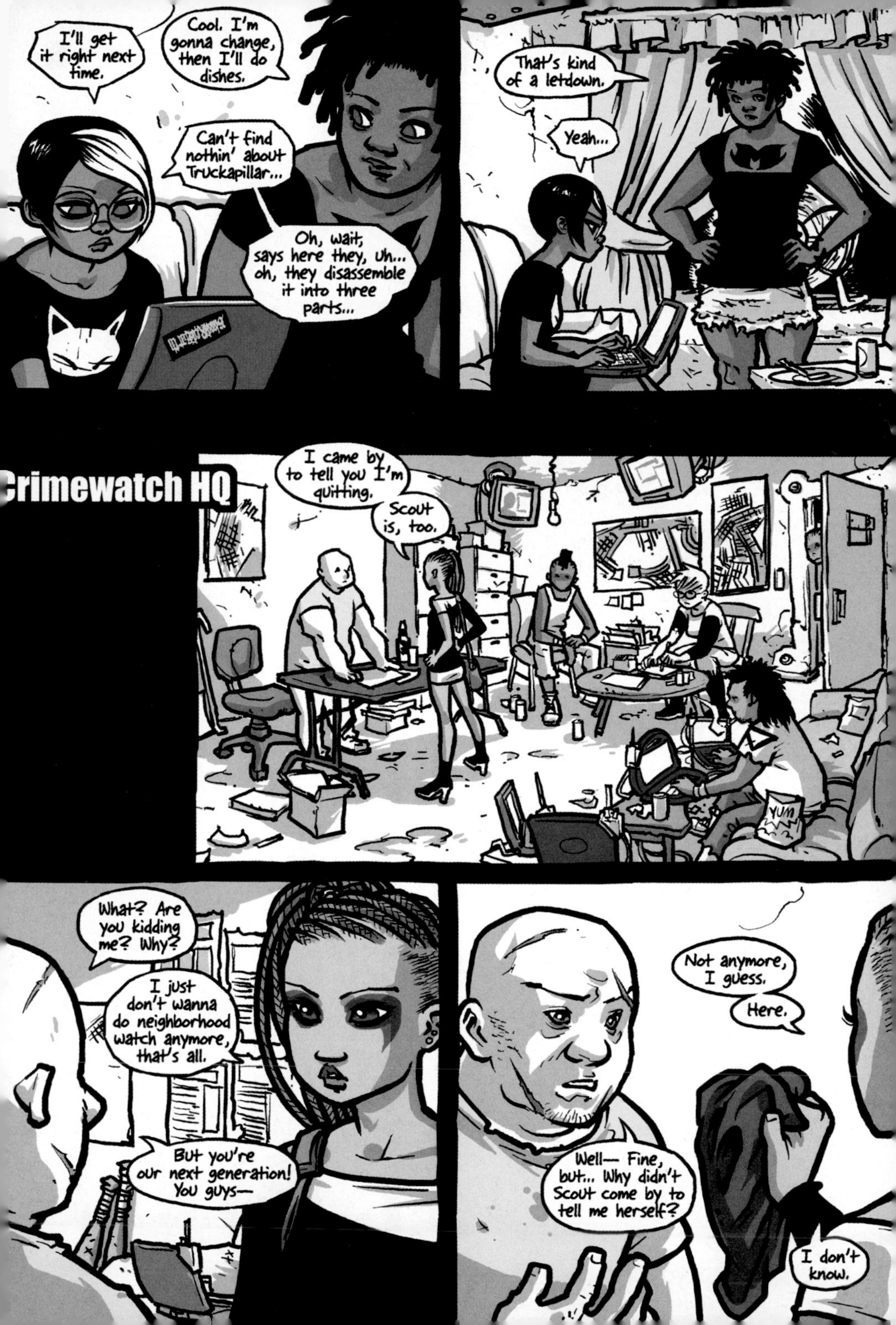
I'll get it right next time.
Cool. I'm gonna change, then I'll do dishes.
Can't find nothin' about Truckapillar...
Oh, wait, says here they, uh... oh, they disassemble it into three parts...
That's kind of a letdown.
Yeah...
Crimewatch HQ
I came by to tell you I'm quitting.
Scout is, too.
What? Are you kidding me? Why?
I just don't wanna do neighborhood watch anymore, that's all.
But you're our next generation! You guys—
Not anymore, I guess.
Here.
Well— Fine, but... Why didn't Scout come by to tell me herself?
I don't know.

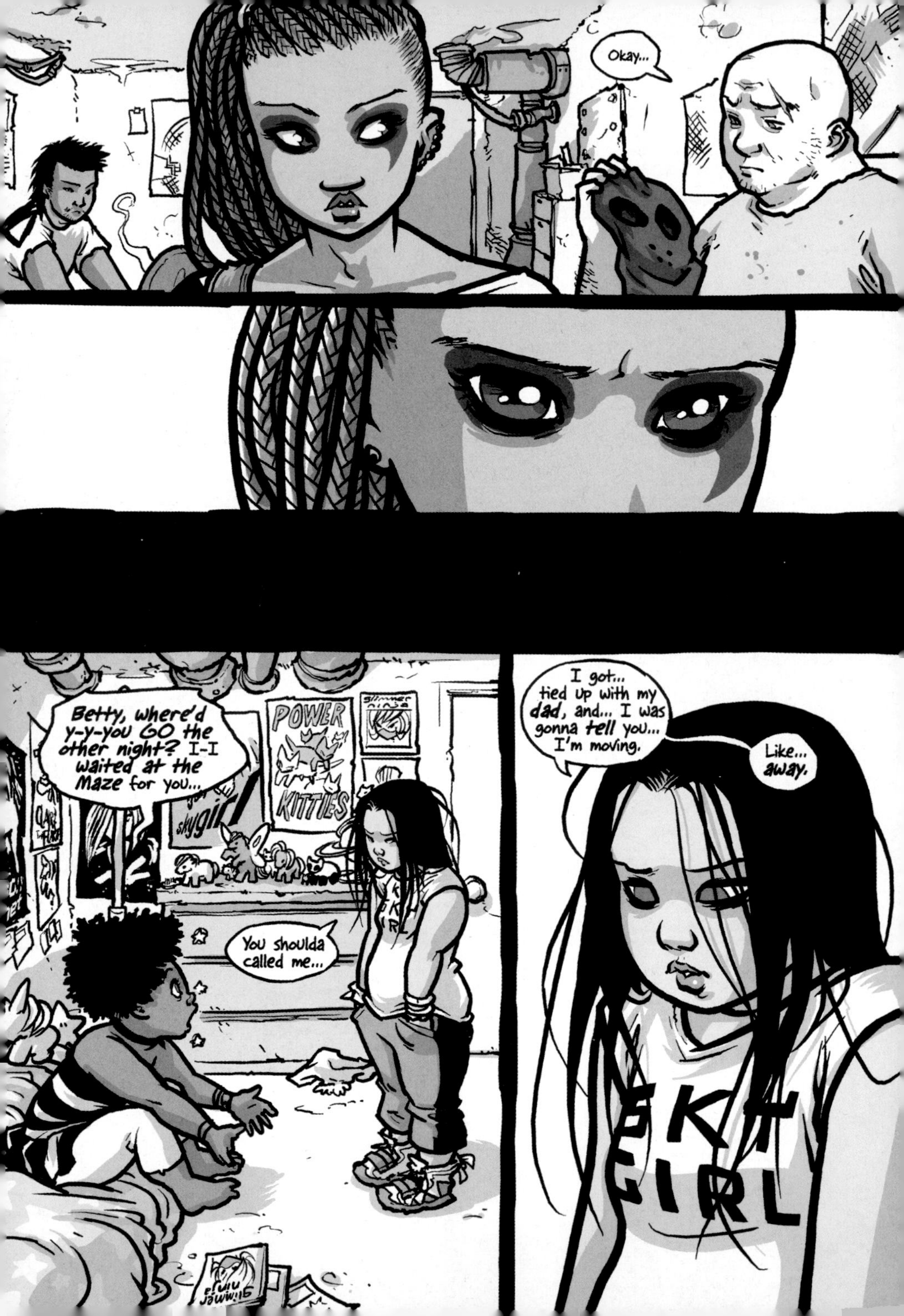
Okay...
Betty, where'd y-y-you GO the other night? I-I waited at the Maze for you...
POWER
KITTIES
You shoulda called me...
I got... tied up with my dad, and... I was gonna tell you... I'm moving.
Like... away.

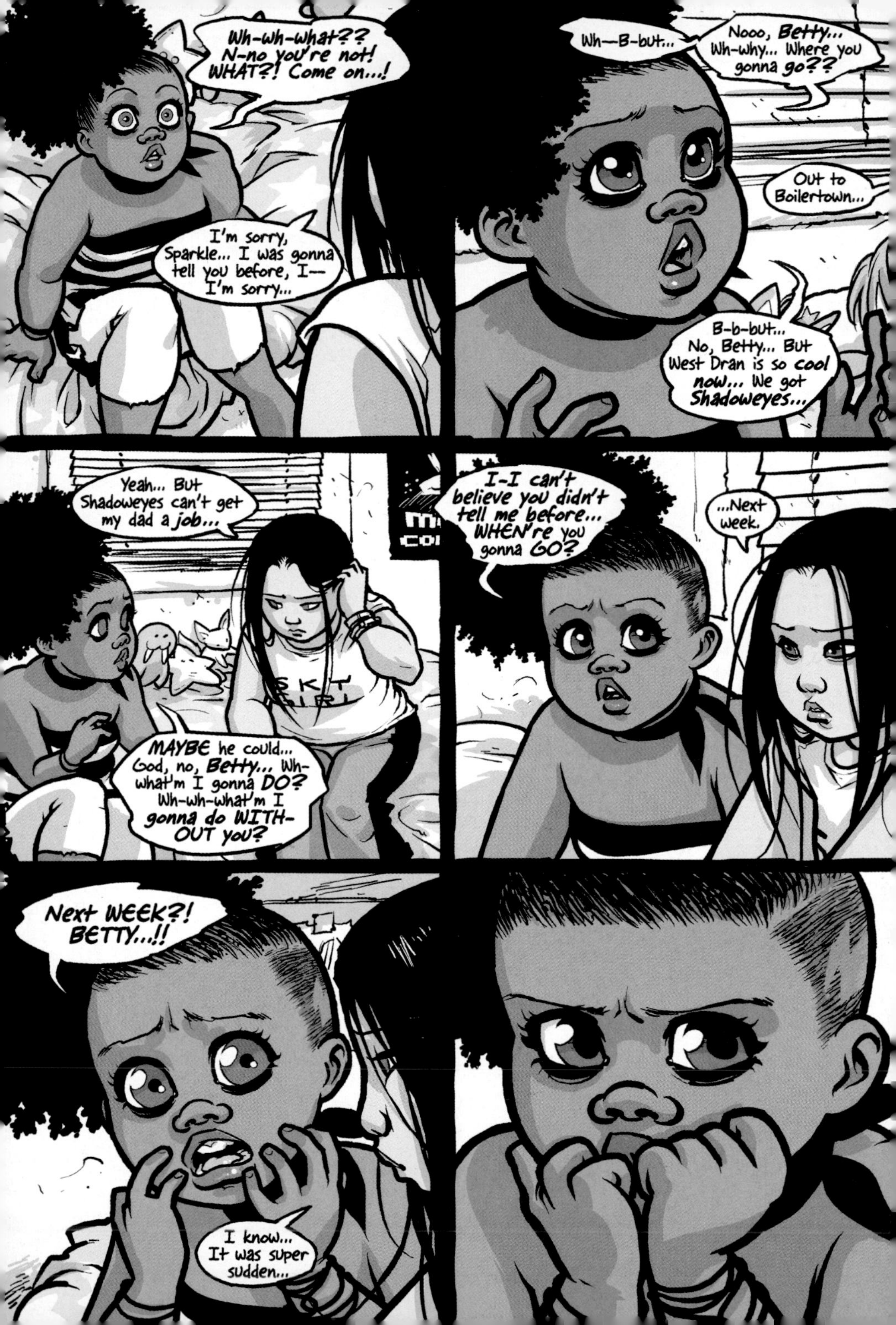
Wh-wh-what?? N-no you're not! WHAT?! Come on...!
I'm sorry, Sparkle... I was gonna tell you before, I-- I'm sorry...
Wh--B-but...
Nooo, Betty... Wh-why... Where you gonna go??
Out to Boilertown...
B-b-but... No, Betty... But West Dran is so cool now... We got Shadoweyes...
Yeah... But Shadoweyes can't get my dad a job...
MAYBE he could... God, no, Betty... Wh-what'm I gonna DO? Wh-wh-what'm I gonna do WITH-OUT you?
I-I can't believe you didn't tell me before... WHEN're you gonna GO?
...Next week.
Next WEEK?! BETTY...!!
I know... It was super sudden...

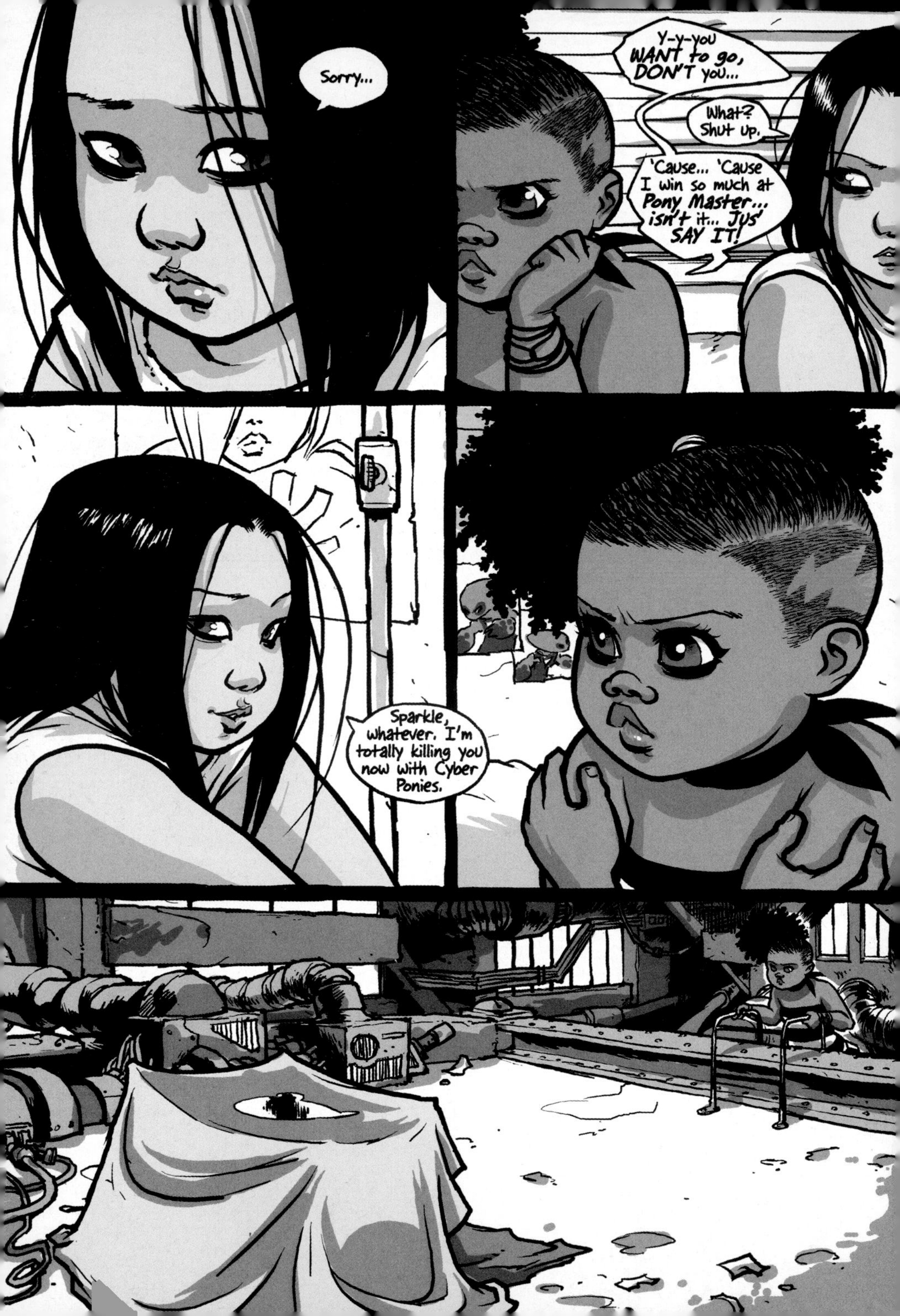
Sorry...
Y-y-you WANT to go, DON'T you...
What? Shut up.
'Cause... 'Cause I win so much at Pony Master... isn't it... Jus' SAY IT!
Sparkle, whatever. I'm totally killing you now with Cyber Ponies.

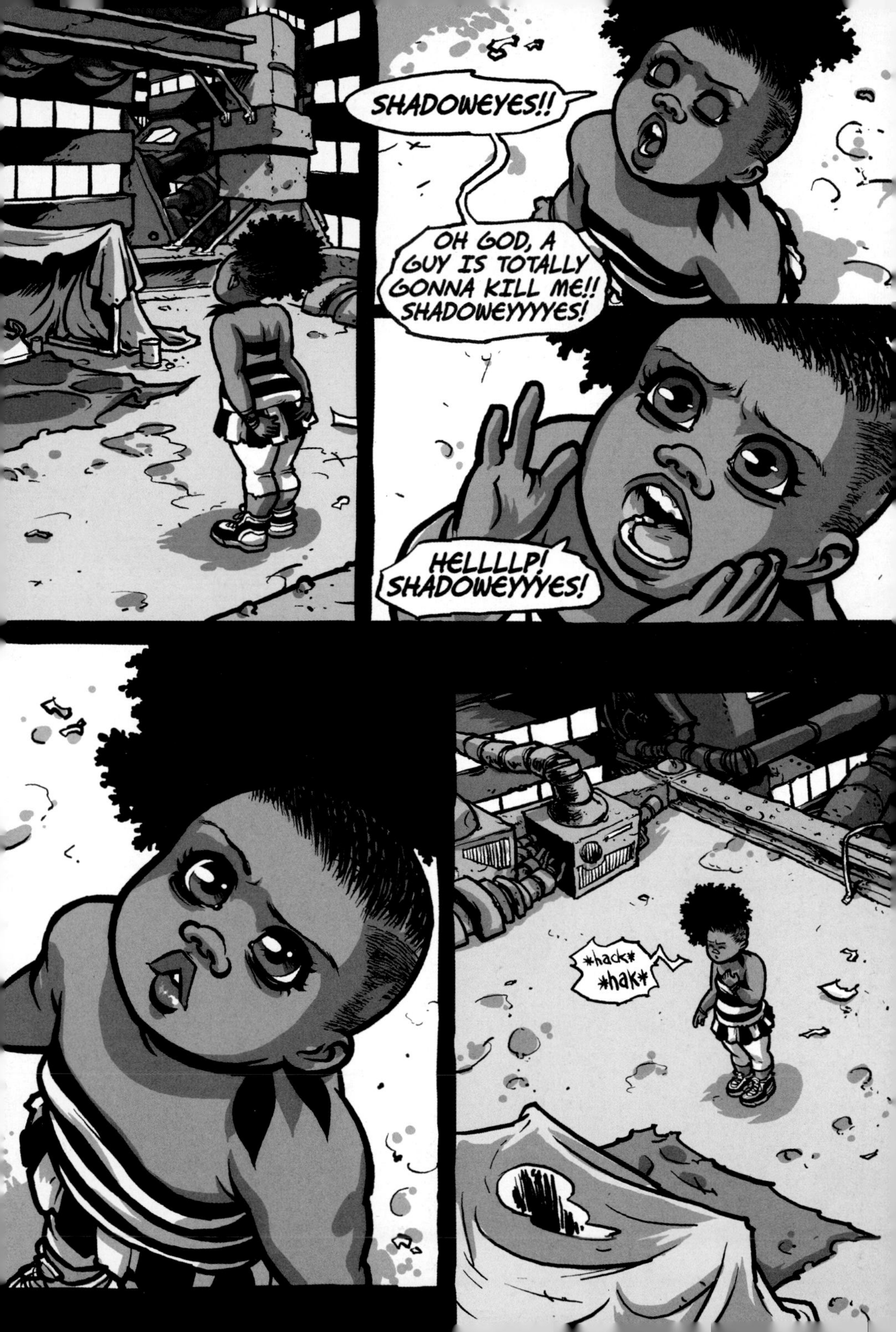
SHADOWEYES!!
OH GOD, A GUY IS TOTALLY GONNA KILL ME!! SHADOWEYYYYES!
HELLLLP! SHADOWEYYYES!
hack *hak*

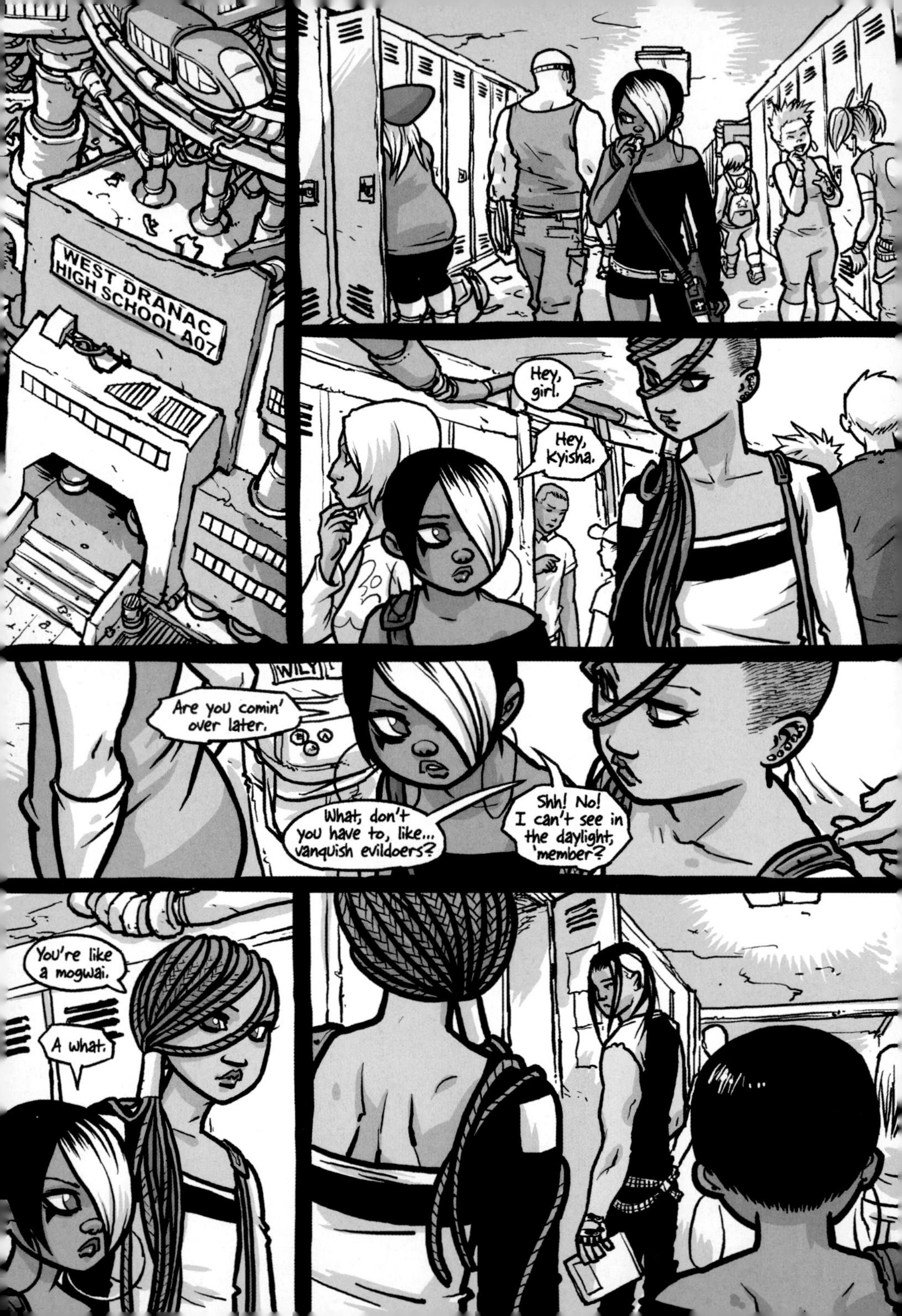
WEST DRANAC HIGH SCHOOL A07
Hey, girl.
Hey, Kyisha.
Are you comin' over later.
What, don't you have to, like... vanquish evildoers?
Shh! No! I can't see in the daylight, 'member?
You're like a mogwai.
A what.

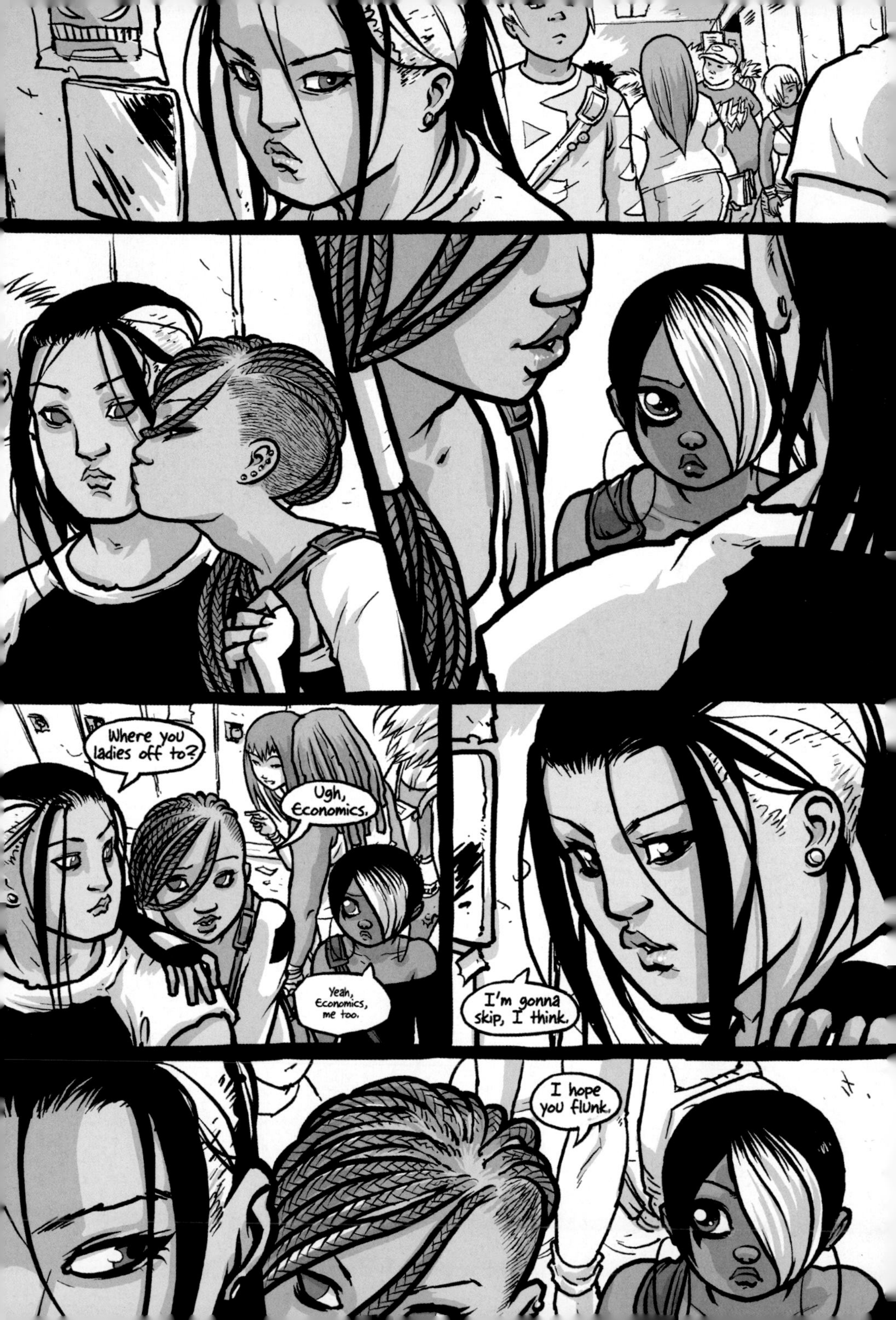

Where you ladies off to?
Ugh, Economics.
Yeah, Economics, me too.
I'm gonna skip, I think.
I hope you flunk.

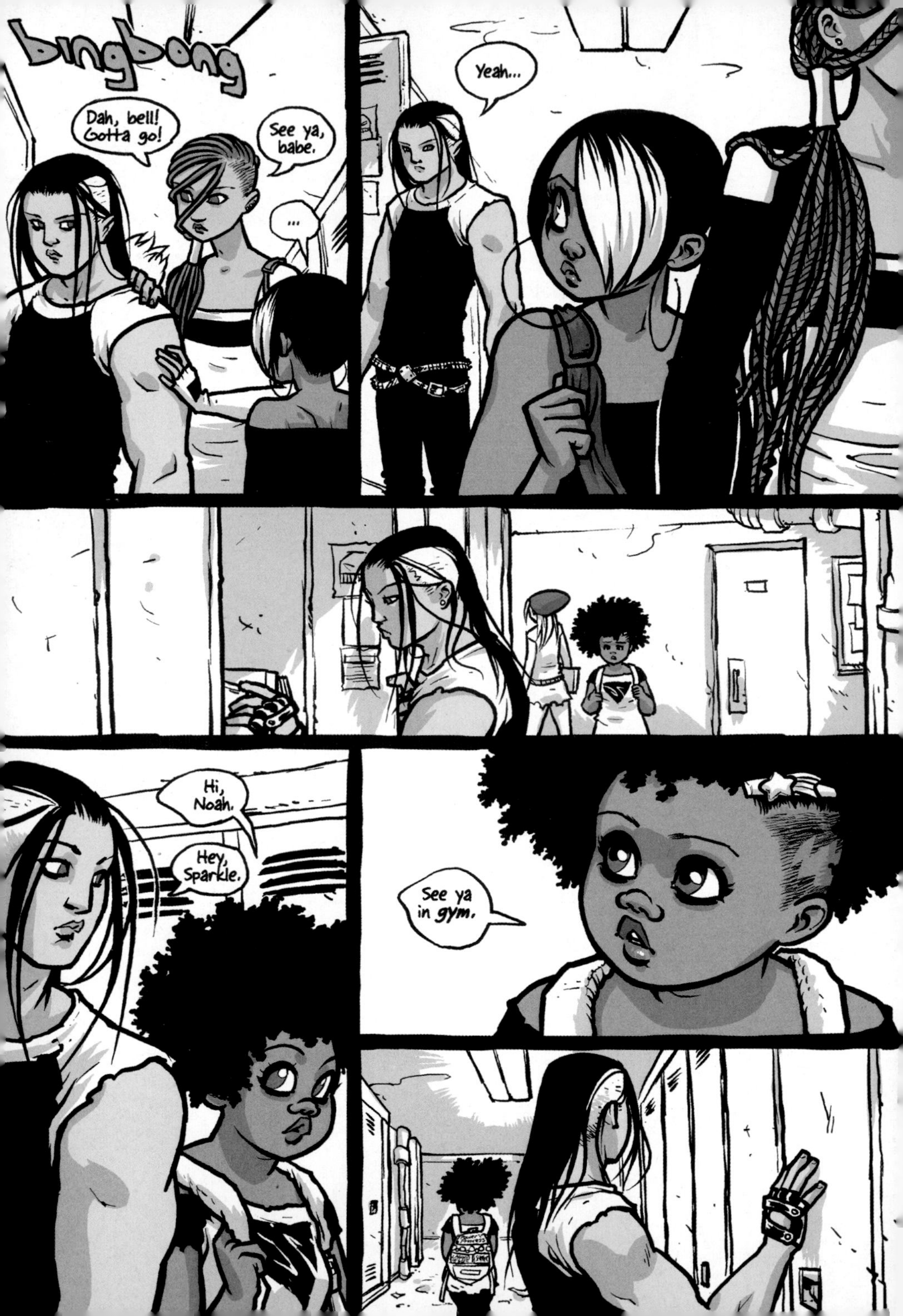
bingbong
Dah, bell! Gotta go!
See ya, babe.
...
Yeah...
Hi, Noah.
Hey, Sparkle.
See ya in gym.

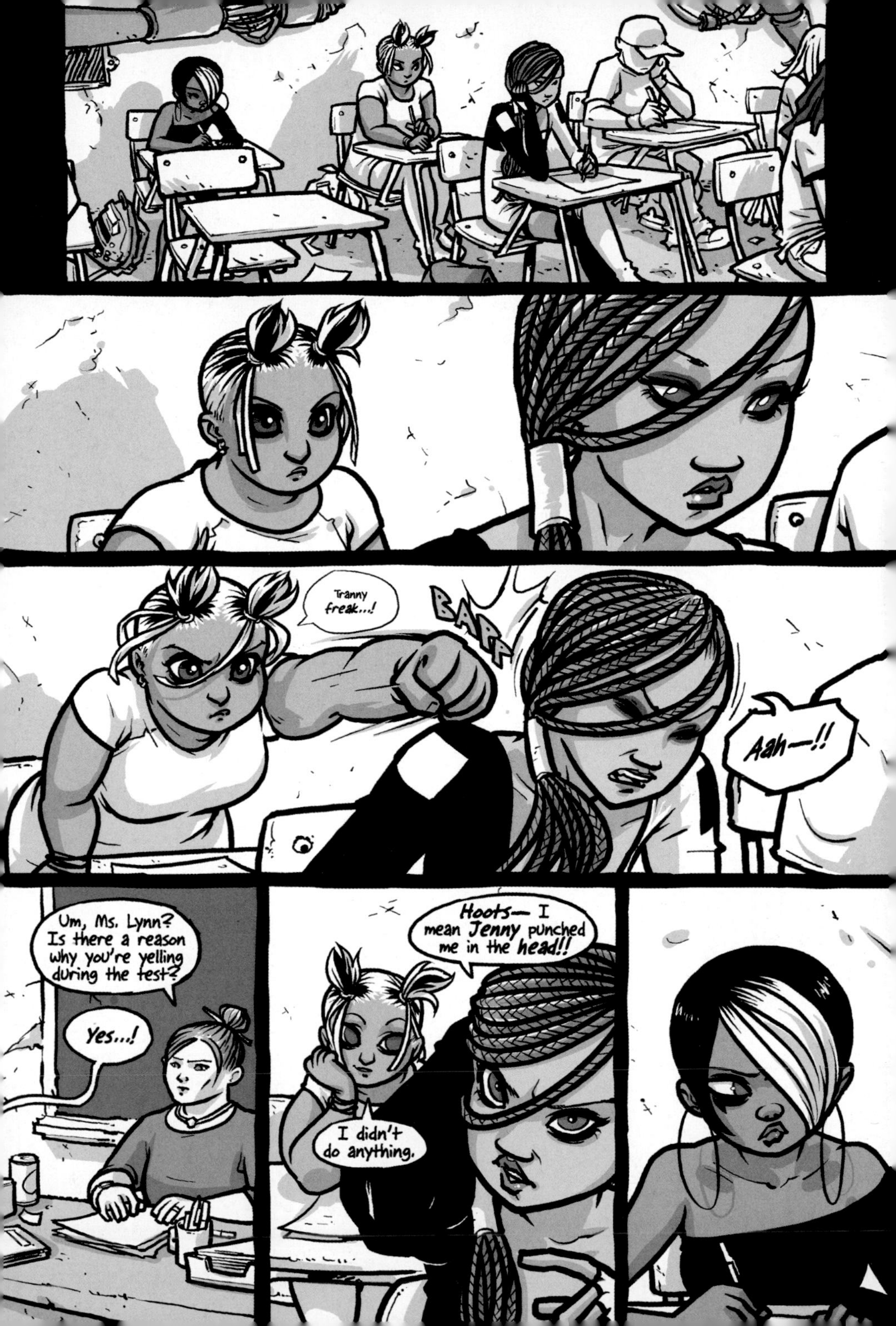
Tranny freak...!
BAPP
Aah—!!
Um, Ms. Lynn? Is there a reason why you're yelling during the test?
Yes...!
Hoots— I mean Jenny punched me in the head!!
I didn't do anything.

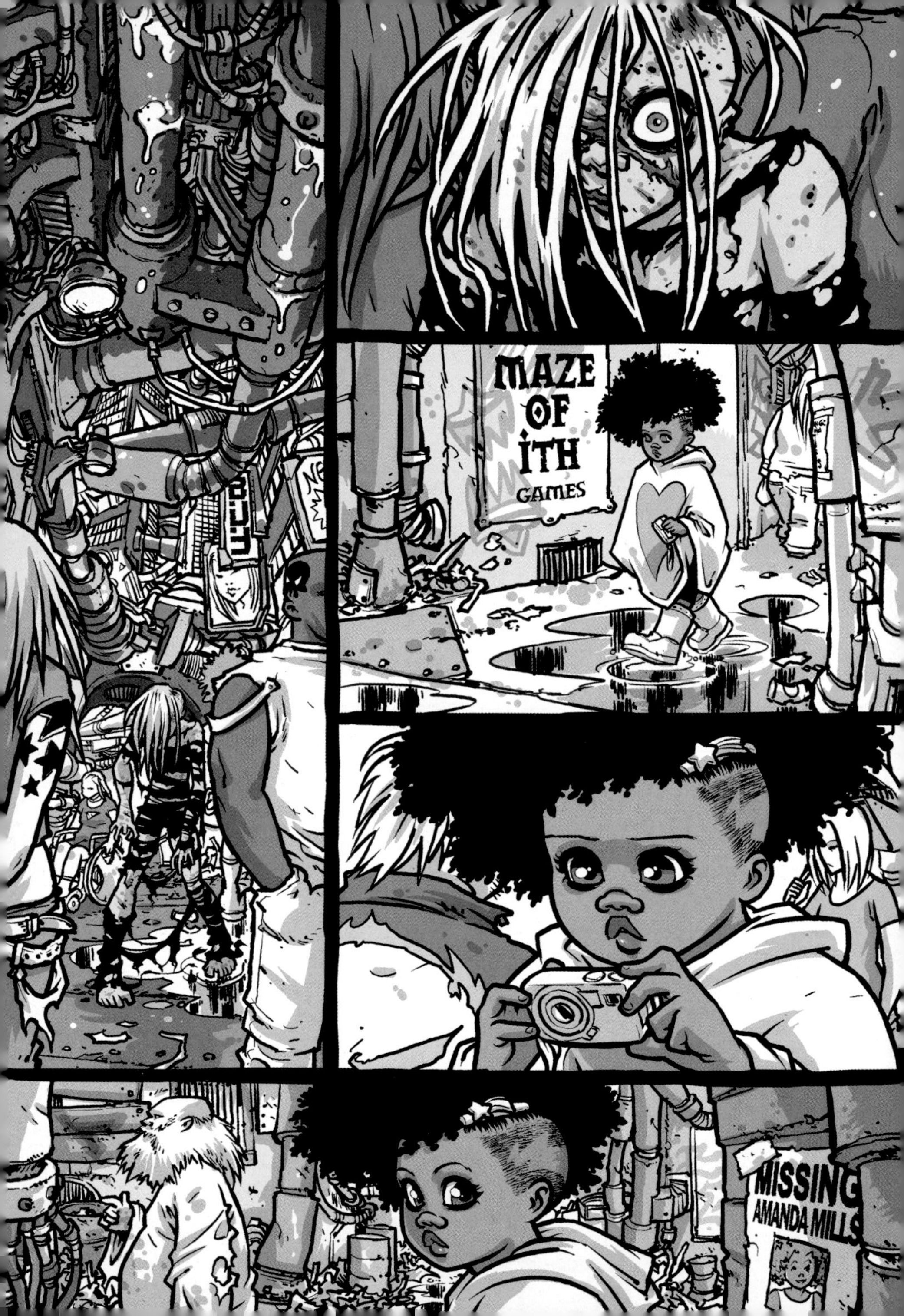
BUY
MAZE OF ITH GAMES
MISSING
AMANDA MILLS

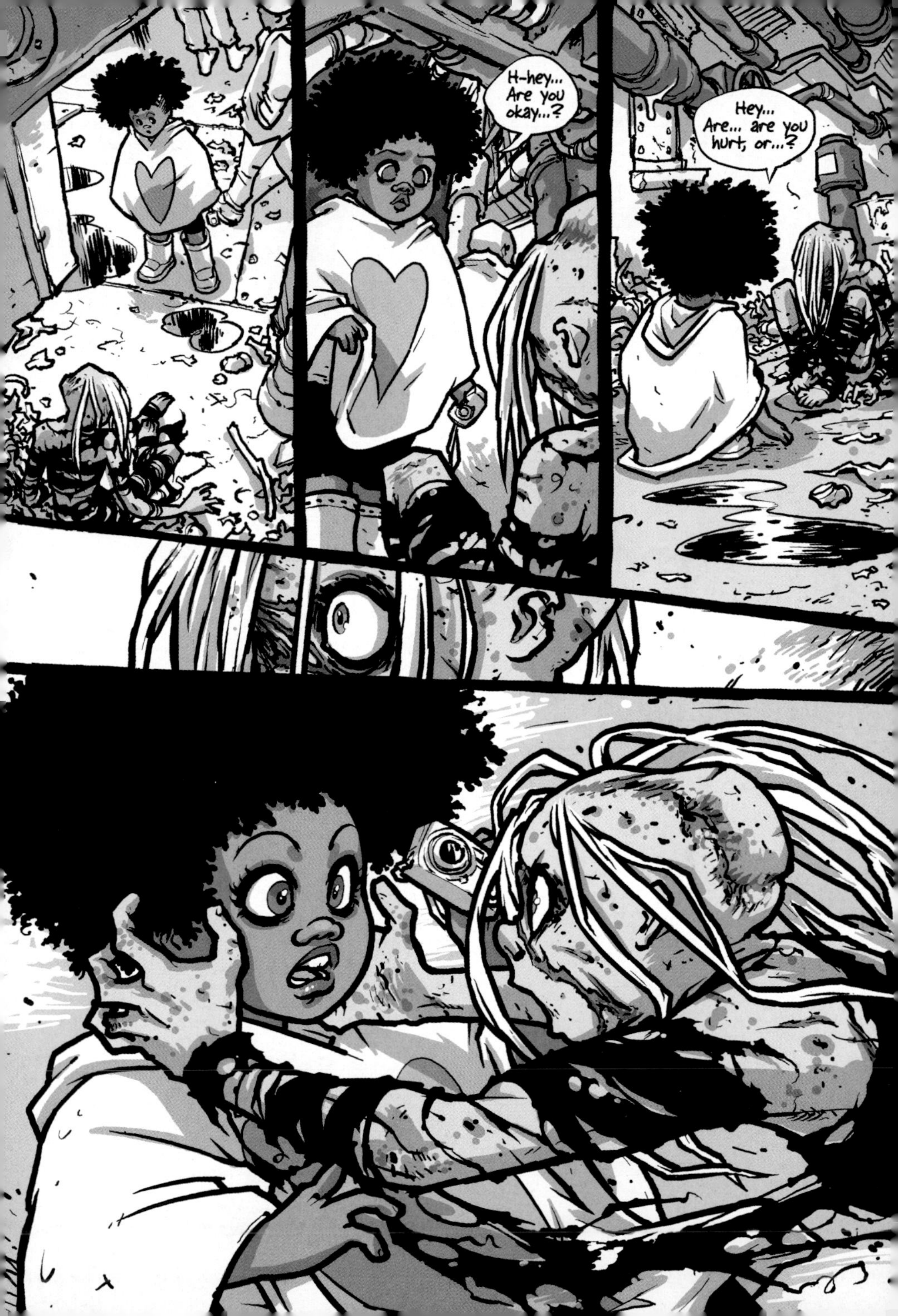
H-hey... Are you okay...?
Hey... Are... are you hurt, or...?

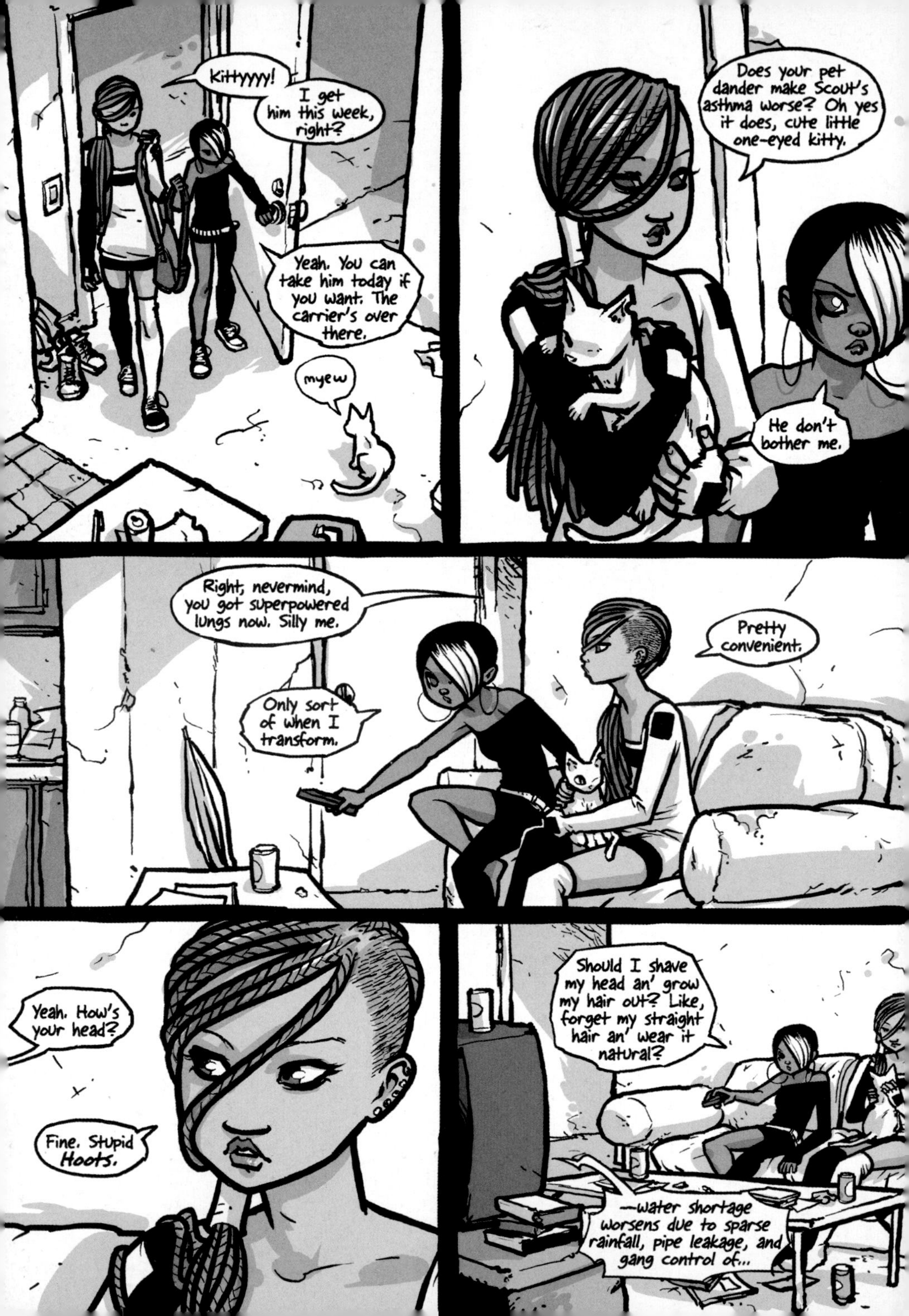
Kittyyyy!
I get him this week, right?
Yeah. You can take him today if you want. The carrier's over there.
myew
Does your pet dander make Scout's asthma worse? Oh yes it does, cute little one-eyed kitty.
He don't bother me.
Right, nevermind, you got superpowered lungs now. Silly me.
Only sort of when I transform.
Pretty convenient.
Yeah. How's your head?
Fine. Stupid Hoots.
Should I shave my head an' grow my hair out? Like, forget my straight hair an' wear it natural?
—water shortage worsens due to sparse rainfall, pipe leakage, and gang control of...

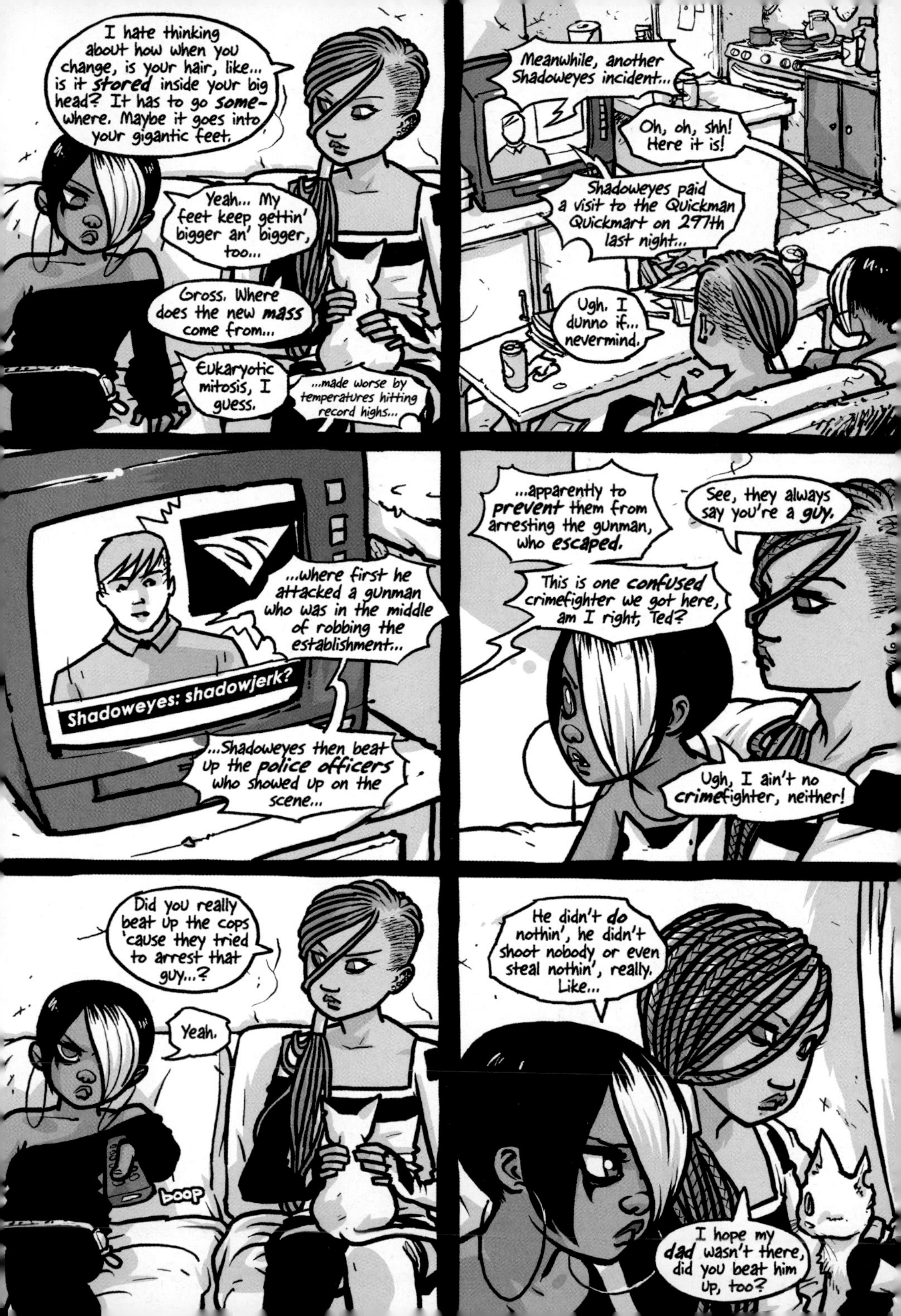
I hate thinking about how when you change, is your hair, like... is it stored inside your big head? It has to go some-where. Maybe it goes into your gigantic feet.
Yeah... My feet keep gettin' bigger an' bigger, too...
Gross. Where does the new mass come from...
Eukaryotic mitosis, I guess.
...made worse by temperatures hitting record highs...
Meanwhile, another Shadoweyes incident...
Oh, oh, shh! Here it is!
Shadoweyes paid a visit to the Quickman Quickmart on 297th last night...
Ugh. I dunno if... nevermind.
Shadoweyes: shadowjerk?
...where first he attacked a gunman who was in the middle of robbing the establishment...
...Shadoweyes then beat up the police officers who showed up on the scene...
...apparently to prevent them from arresting the gunman, who escaped.
See, they always say you're a guy.
This is one confused crimefighter we got here, am I right, Ted?
Ugh, I ain't no crimefighter, neither!
Did you really beat up the cops 'cause they tried to arrest that guy...?
Yeah.
boop
He didn't do nothin', he didn't shoot nobody or even steal nothin', really. Like...
I hope my dad wasn't there, did you beat him up, too?

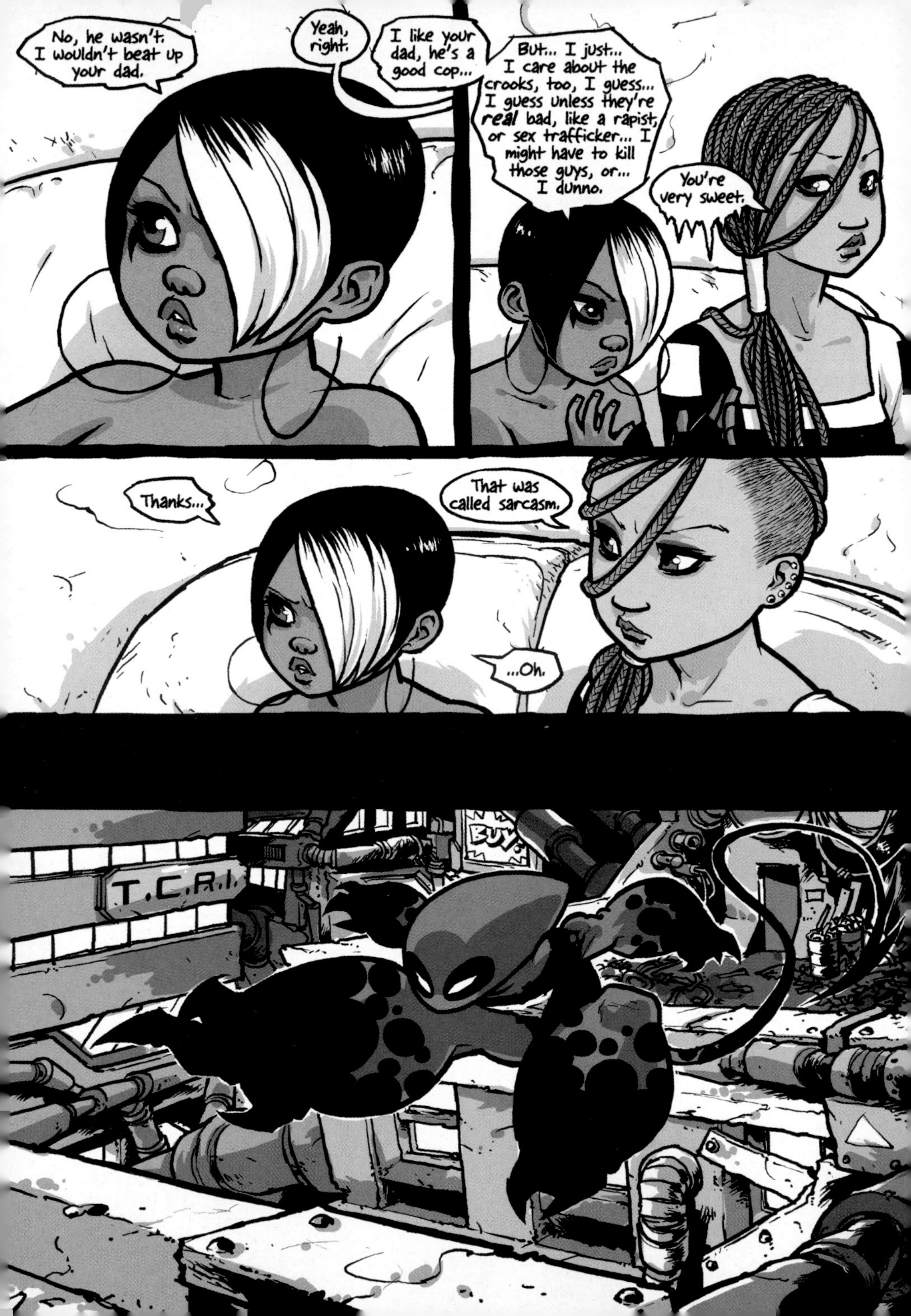
No, he wasn't. I wouldn't beat up your dad.
Yeah, right.
I like your dad, he's a good cop...
But... I just... I care about the crooks, too, I guess... I guess unless they're *real* bad, like a rapist, or sex trafficker... I might have to kill those guys, or... I dunno.
You're very sweet.
Thanks...
That was called sarcasm.
...Oh.
BUY
T.C.R.I.

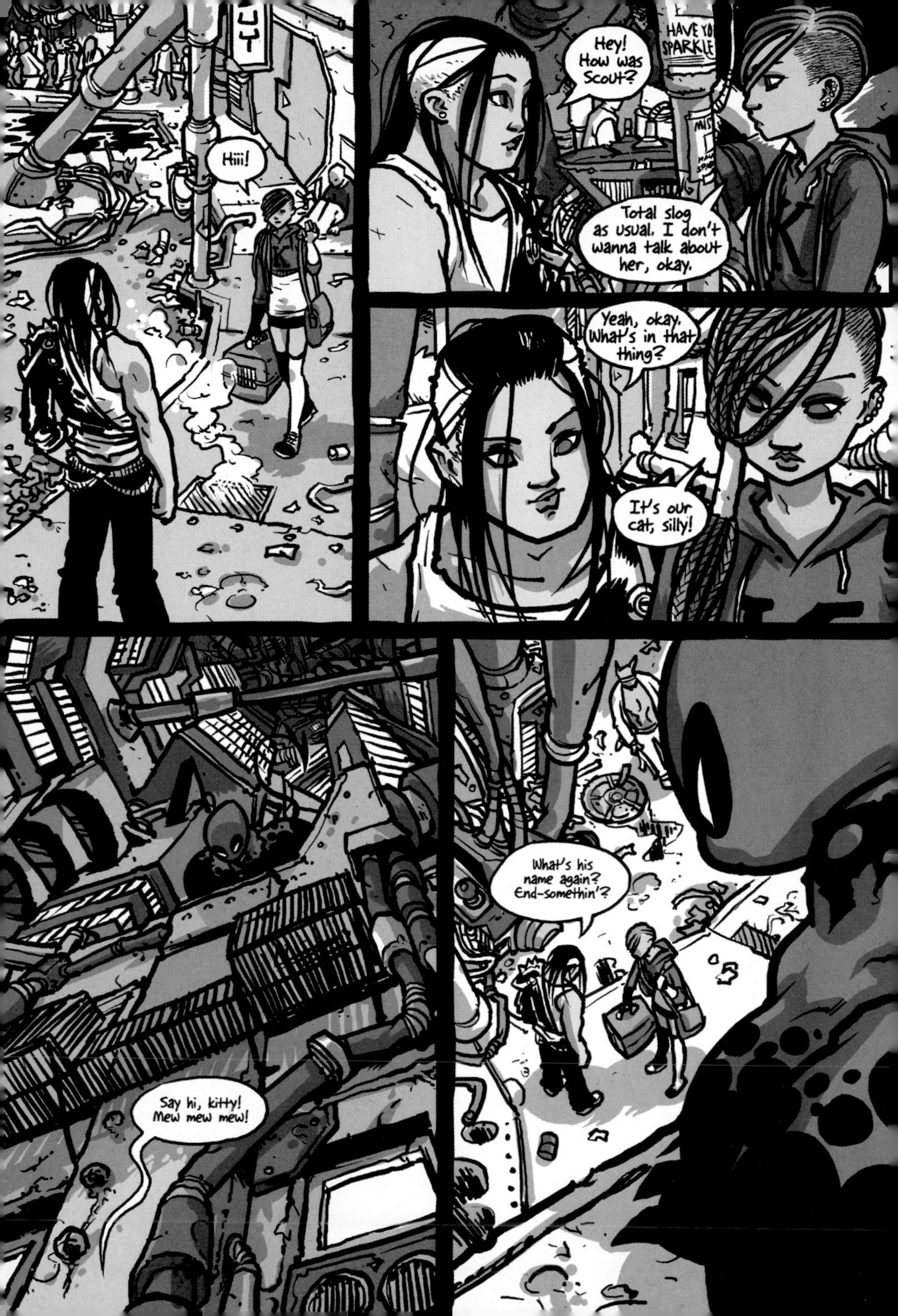
Hiii!
Hey! How was Scout?
Total slog as usual. I don't wanna talk about her, okay.
Yeah, okay. What's in that thing?
It's our cat, silly!
Say hi, kitty! Mew mew mew!
What's his name again? End-somethin'?

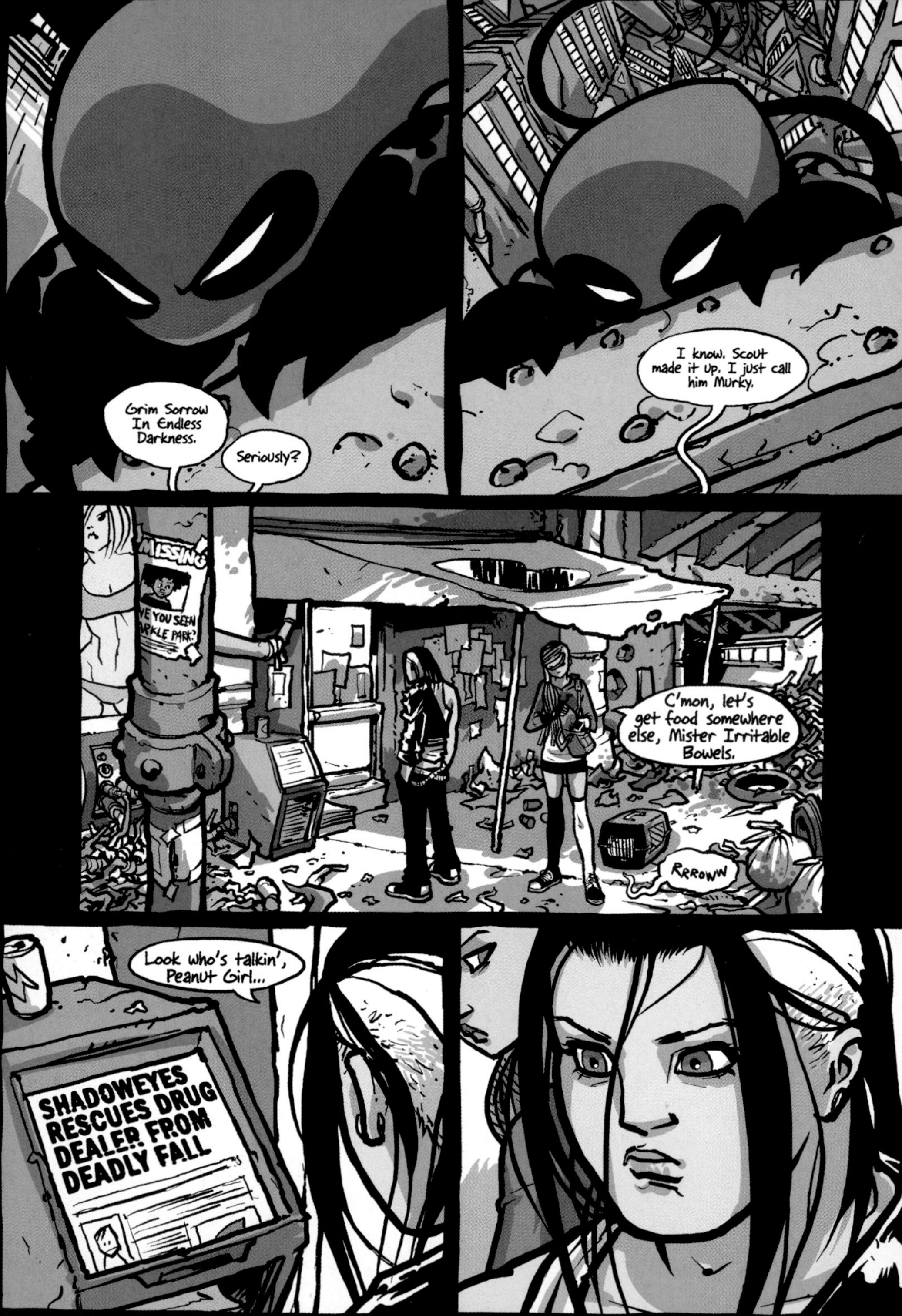
Grim Sorrow In Endless Darkness.
Seriously?
I know. Scout made it up. I just call him Murky.
MISSING
...VE YOU SEEN ...RKLE PARK?
C'mon, let's get food somewhere else, Mister Irritable Bowels.
RRROWW
Look who's talkin', Peanut Girl...
SHADOWEYES RESCUES DRUG DEALER FROM DEADLY FALL

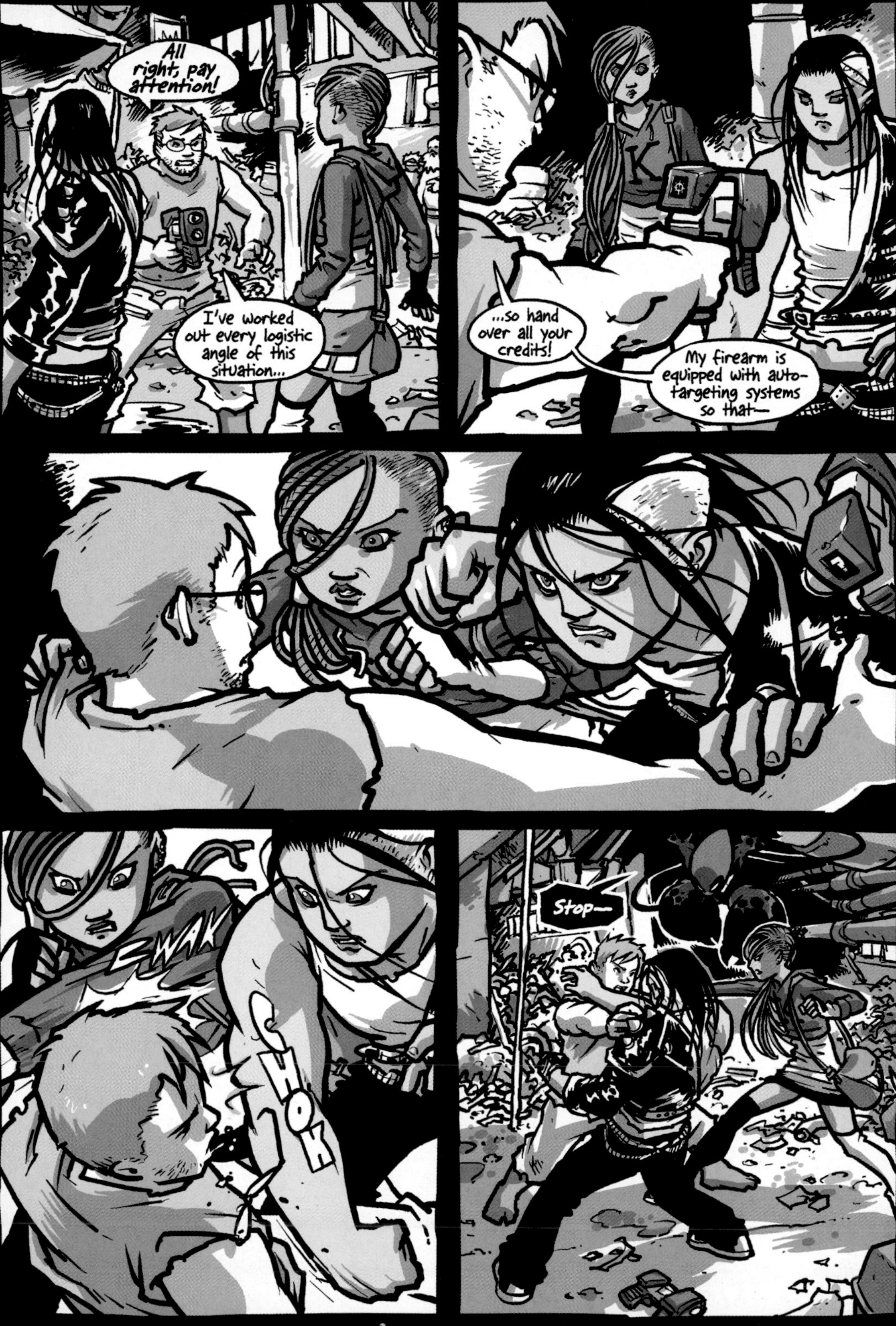
All right, pay attention!
I've worked out every logistic angle of this situation...
...so hand over all your credits!
My firearm is equipped with auto-targeting systems so that—
CHWAK
WHOK
Stop—

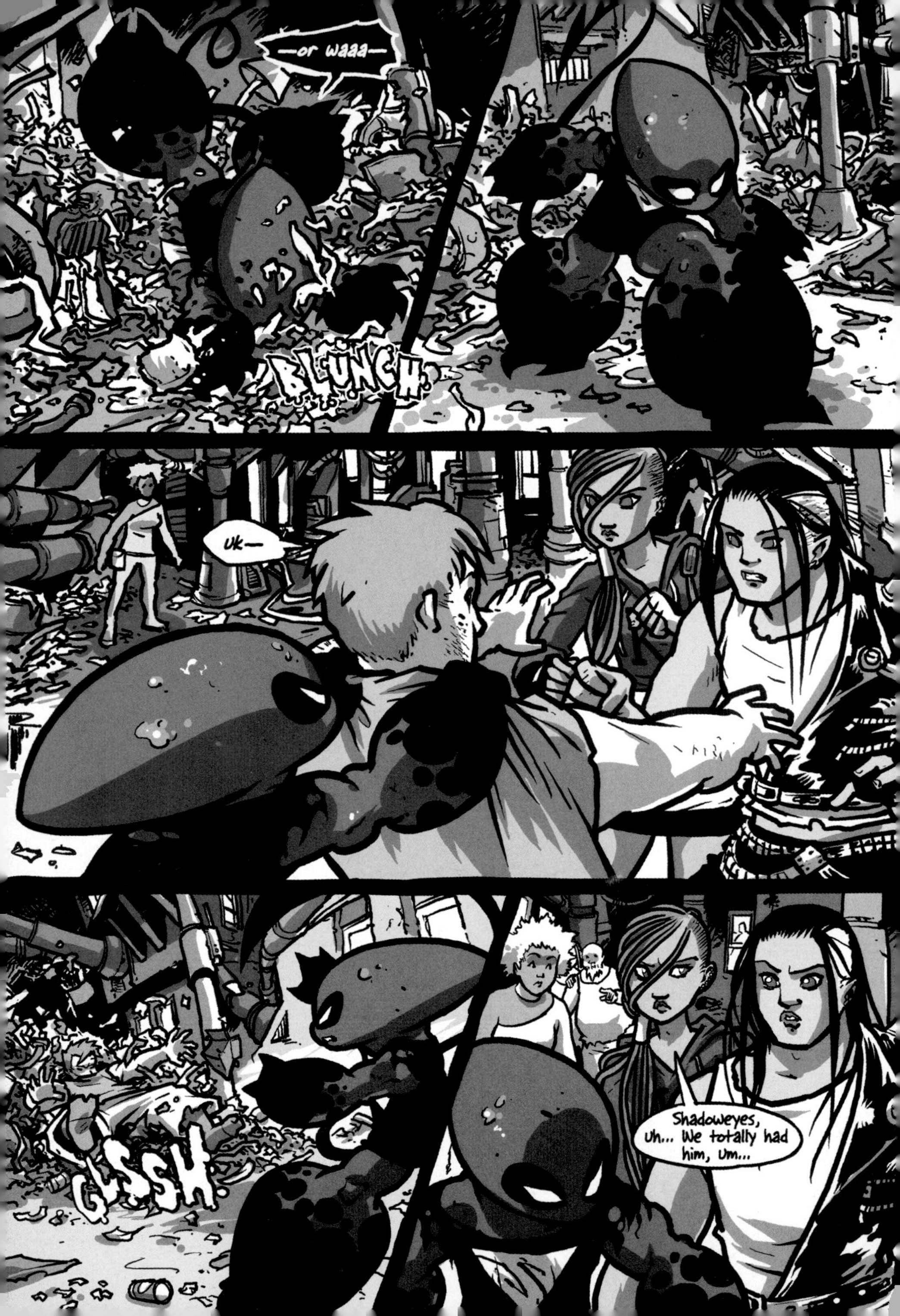
—or waaa—
BLUNCH
UK—
GSSH
Shadoweyes, Uh... We totally had him, Um...

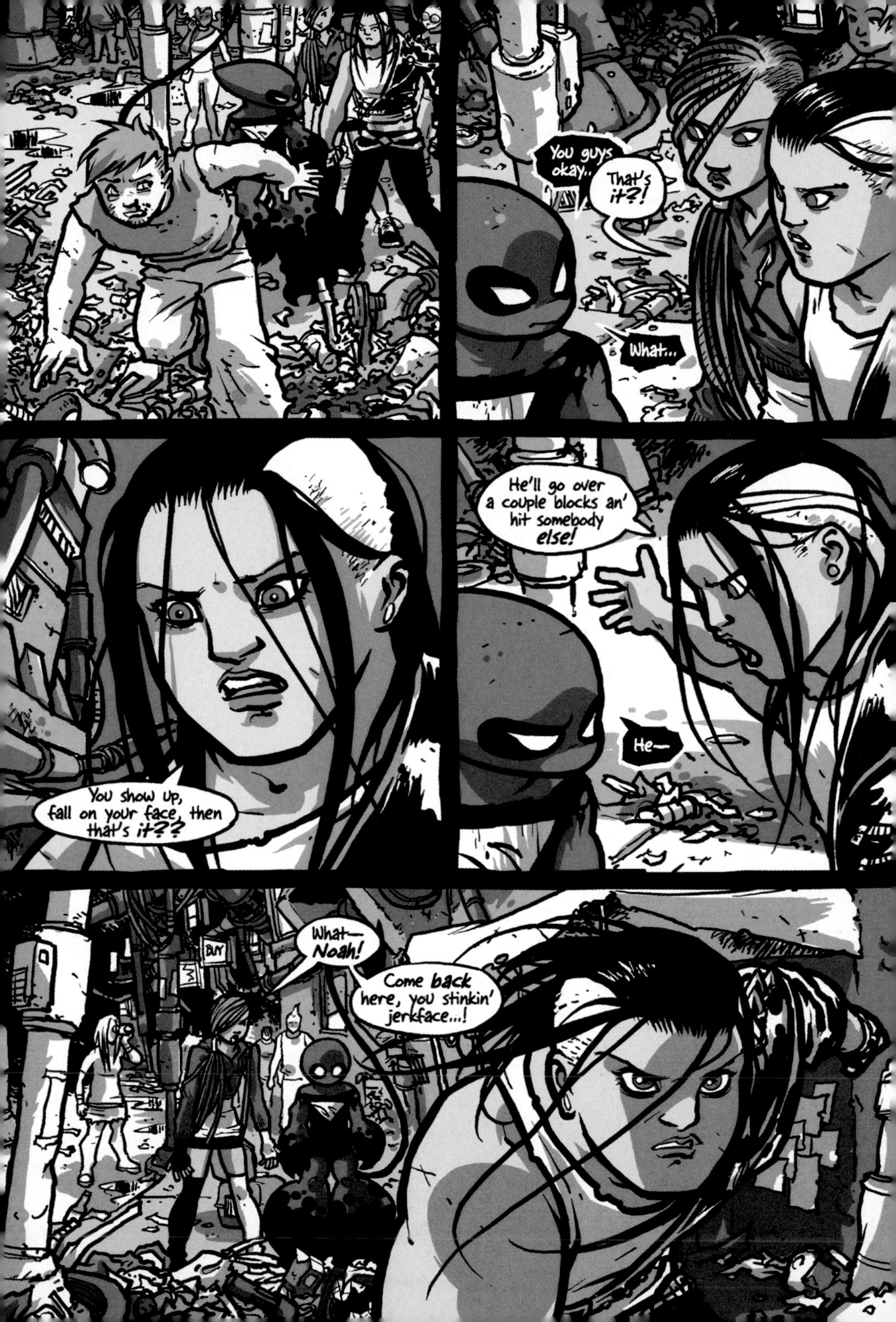
You guys okay..
That's it?!
What...
You show up, fall on your face, then that's it??
He'll go over a couple blocks an' hit somebody else!
He—
BUY
What— Noah!
Come back here, you stinkin' jerkface...!

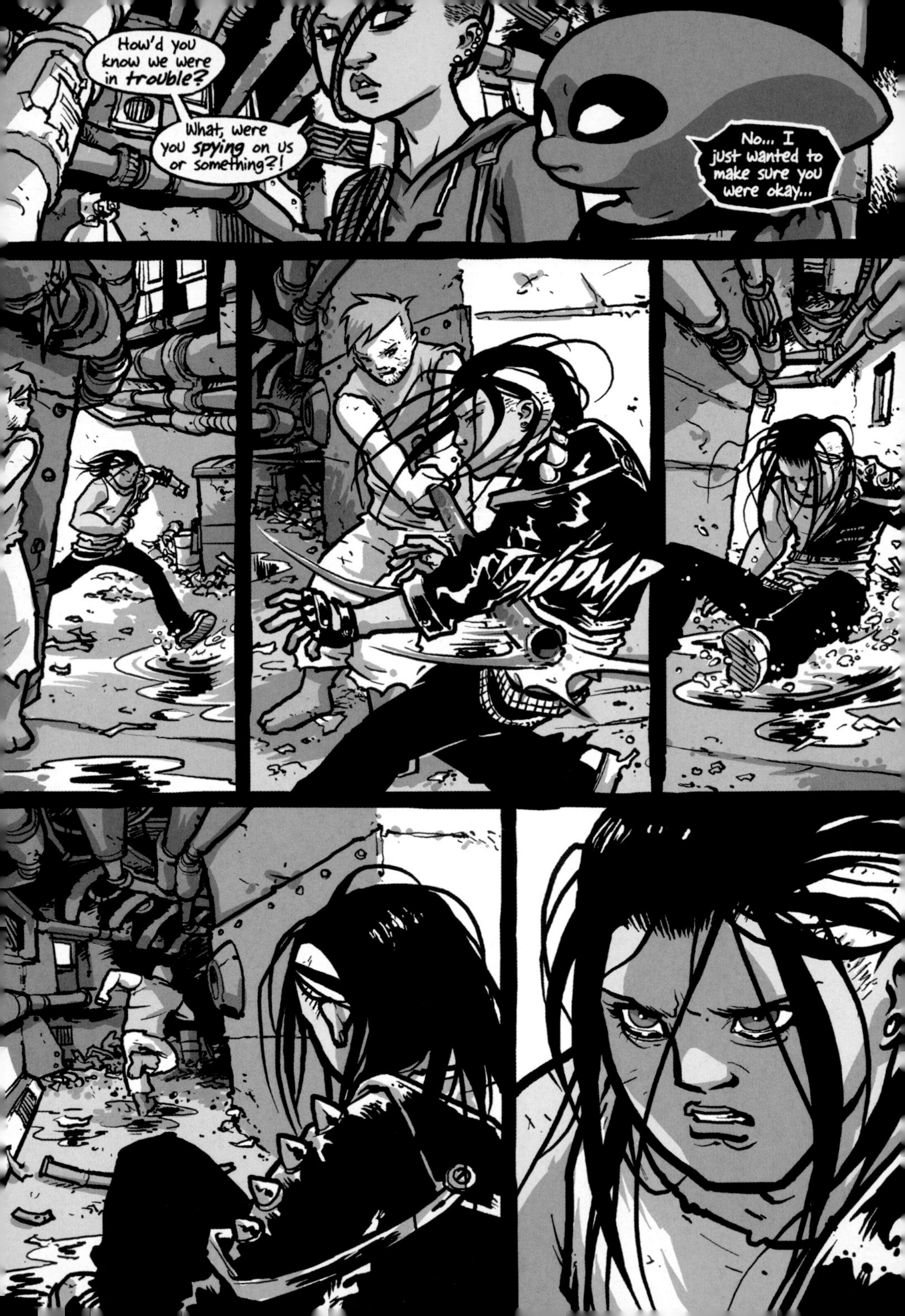
How'd you know we were in trouble?
What, were you spying on us or something?!
No... I just wanted to make sure you were okay...
THOOMP

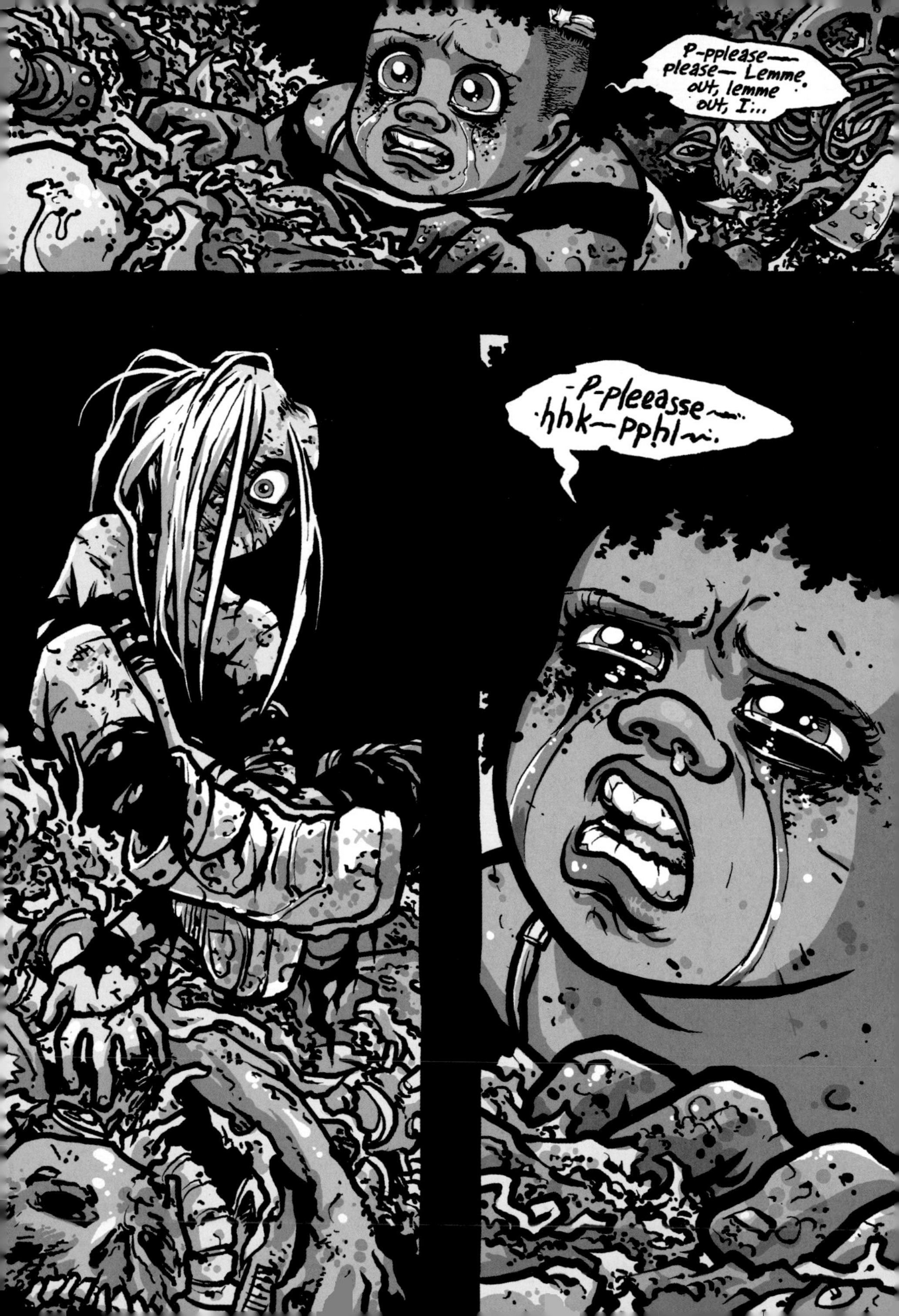
P-pplease— please— Lemme out, lemme out, I...
-P-pleeasse— hhk—pphl—.

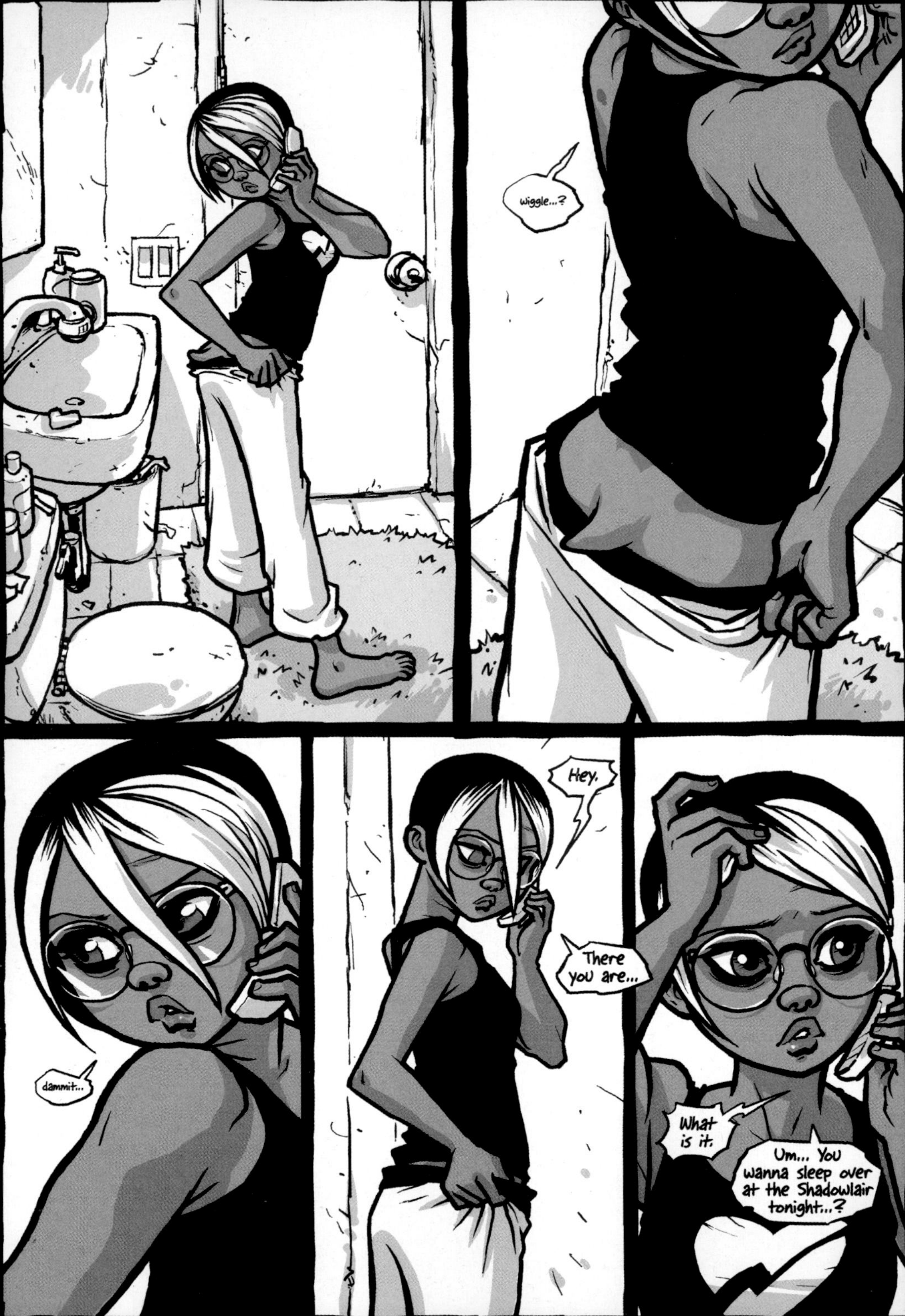
wiggle...?
dammit...
Hey.
There you are...
What is it.
Um... You wanna sleep over at the Shadowlair tonight...?

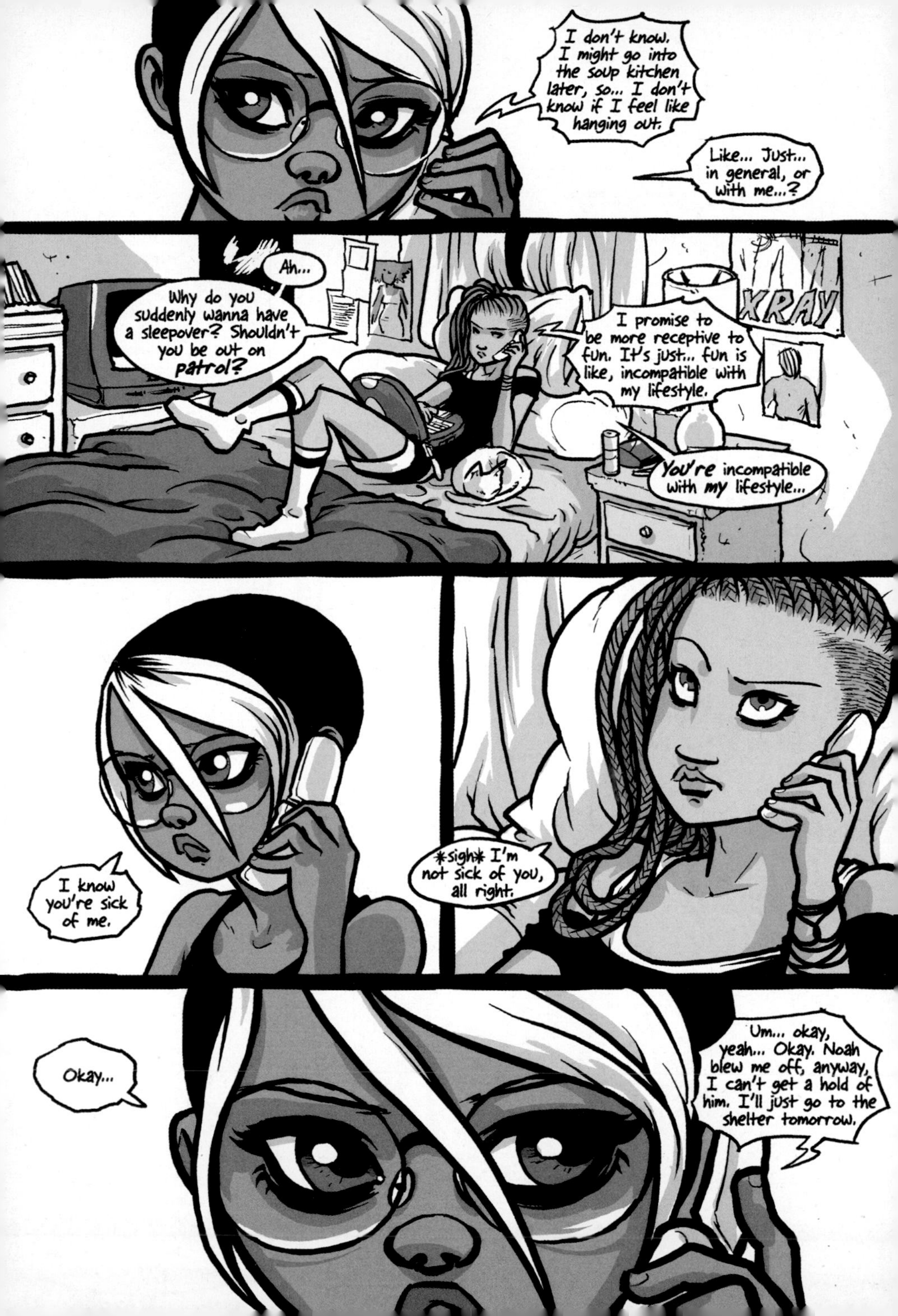
I don't know. I might go into the soup kitchen later, so... I don't know if I feel like hanging out.
Like... Just... in general, or with me...?
Ah...
Why do you suddenly wanna have a sleepover? Shouldn't you be out on patrol?
XRAY
I promise to be more receptive to fun. It's just... fun is like, incompatible with my lifestyle.
You're incompatible with my lifestyle...
I know you're sick of me.
sigh I'm not sick of you, all right.
Okay...
Um... okay, yeah... Okay. Noah blew me off, anyway, I can't get a hold of him. I'll just go to the shelter tomorrow.

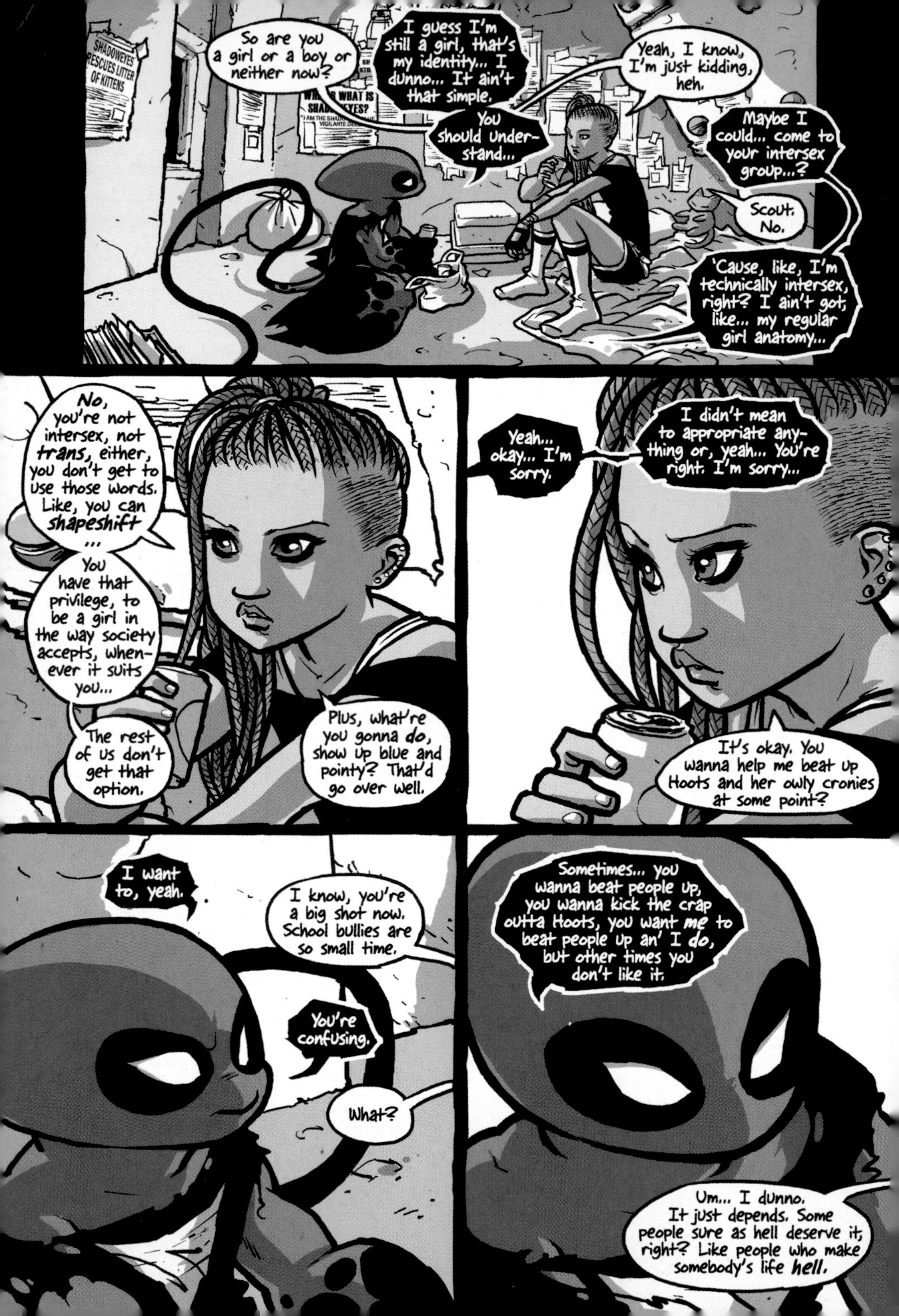
SHADOWEYES RESCUES LITTER OF KITTENS
So are you a girl or a boy or neither now?
I guess I'm still a girl, that's my identity... I dunno... It ain't that simple.
You should understand...
Yeah, I know, I'm just kidding, heh.
Maybe I could... come to your intersex group...?
Scout. No.
'Cause, like, I'm technically intersex, right? I ain't got, like... my regular girl anatomy...
No, you're not intersex, not trans, either, you don't get to use those words. Like, you can shapeshift...
You have that privilege, to be a girl in the way society accepts, whenever it suits you...
The rest of us don't get that option.
Plus, what're you gonna do, show up blue and pointy? That'd go over well.
Yeah... okay... I'm sorry.
I didn't mean to appropriate anything or, yeah... You're right. I'm sorry...
It's okay. You wanna help me beat up Hoots and her owly cronies at some point?
I want to, yeah.
I know, you're a big shot now. School bullies are so small time.
You're confusing.
What?
Sometimes... you wanna beat people up, you wanna kick the crap outta Hoots, you want me to beat people up an' I do, but other times you don't like it.
Um... I dunno. It just depends. Some people sure as hell deserve it, right? Like people who make somebody's life hell.

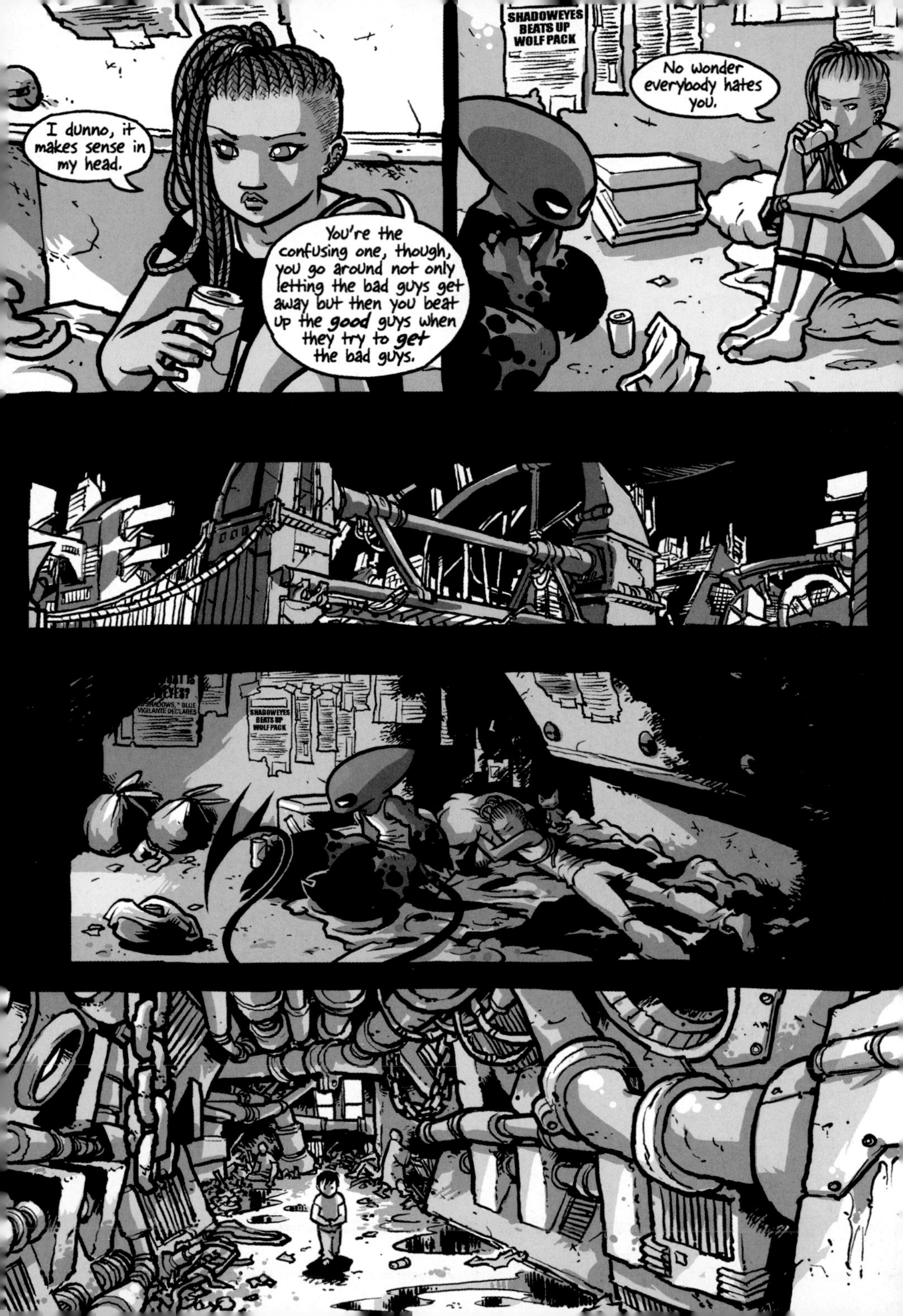
I dunno, it makes sense in my head.
You're the confusing one, though, you go around not only letting the bad guys get away but then you beat up the **good** guys when they try to **get** the bad guys.
SHADOWEYES BEATS UP WOLF PACK
No wonder everybody hates you.
SHADOWEYES BEATS UP WOLF PACK

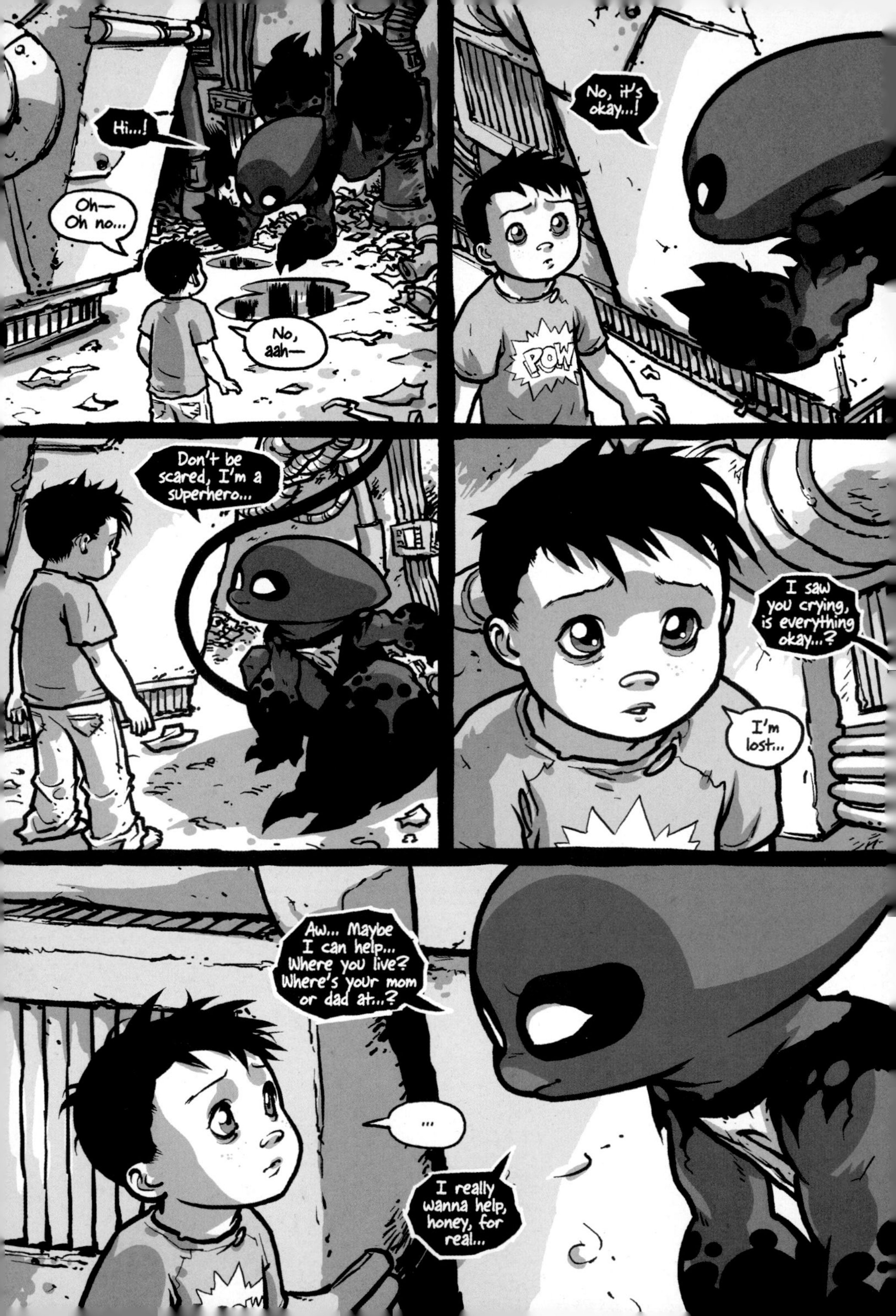
Hi...!
Oh— Oh no...
No, aah—
No, it's okay...!
Don't be scared, I'm a superhero...
I saw you crying, is everything okay...?
I'm lost...
Aw... Maybe I can help... Where you live? Where's your mom or dad at...?
...
I really wanna help, honey, for real...

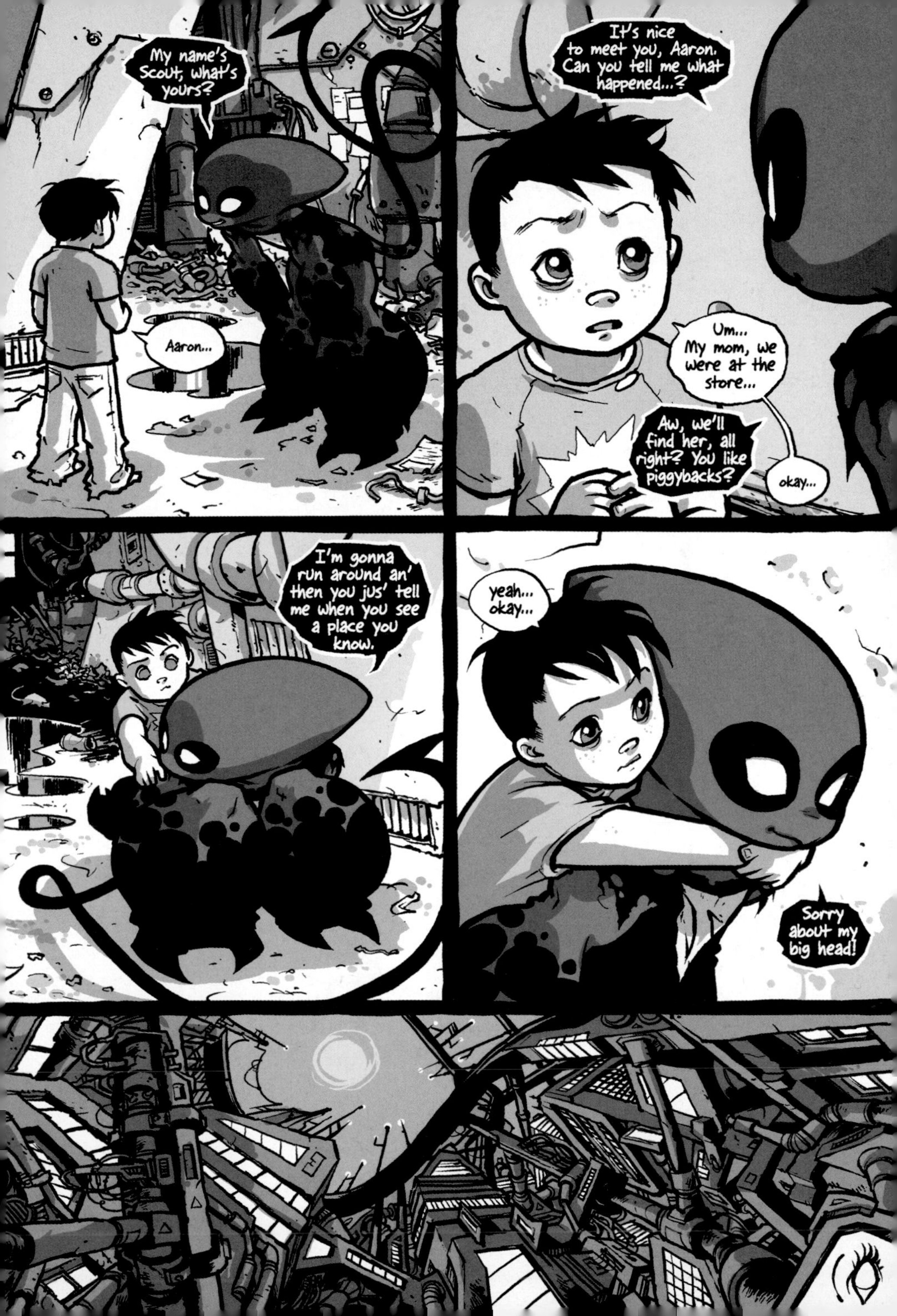
My name's Scout, what's yours?
Aaron...
It's nice to meet you, Aaron. Can you tell me what happened...?
Um... My mom, we were at the store...
Aw, we'll find her, all right? You like piggybacks?
okay...
I'm gonna run around an' then you jus' tell me when you see a place you know.
yeah... okay...
Sorry about my big head!

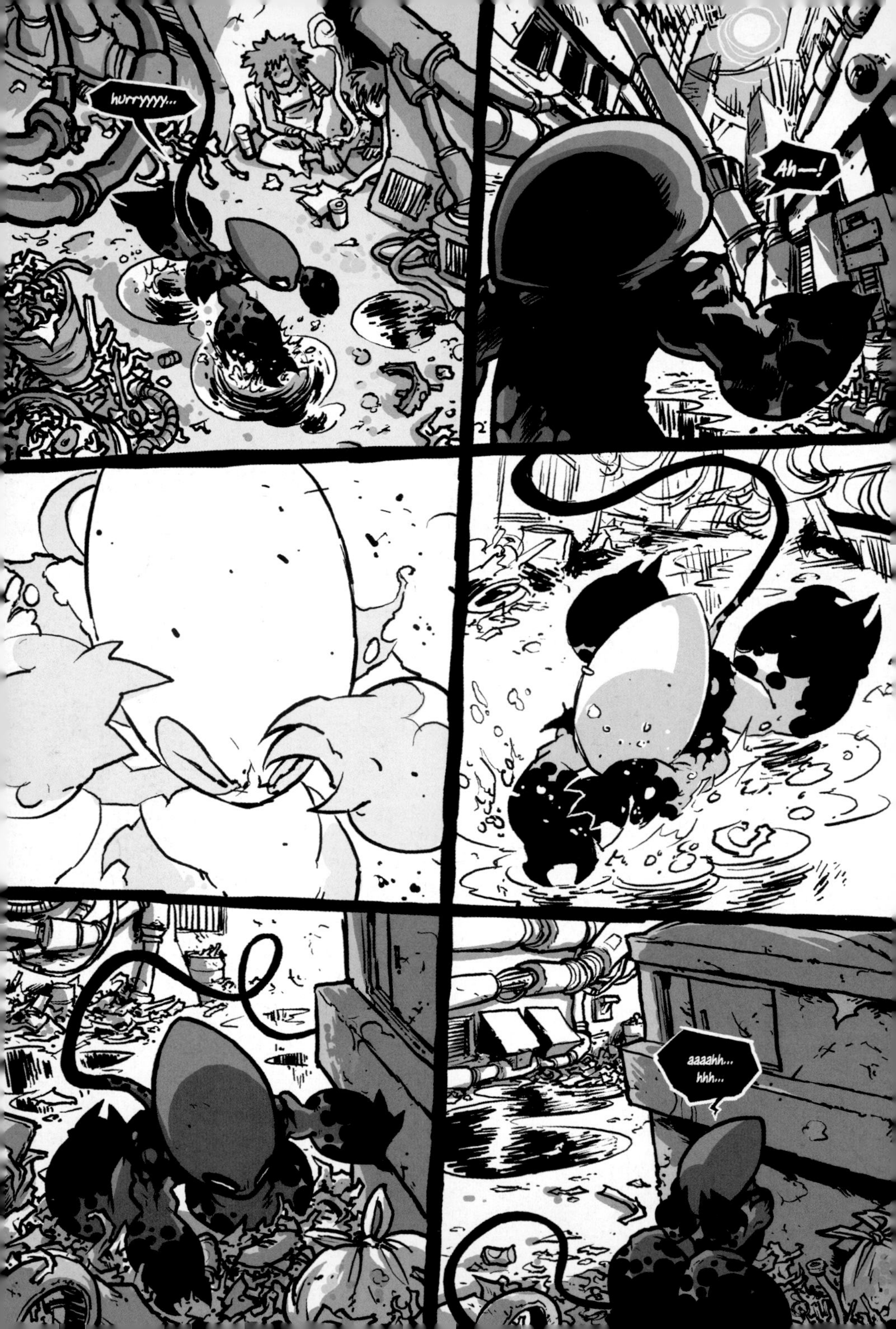
hurryyyy...
Ah—!
aaaahh...
hhh...

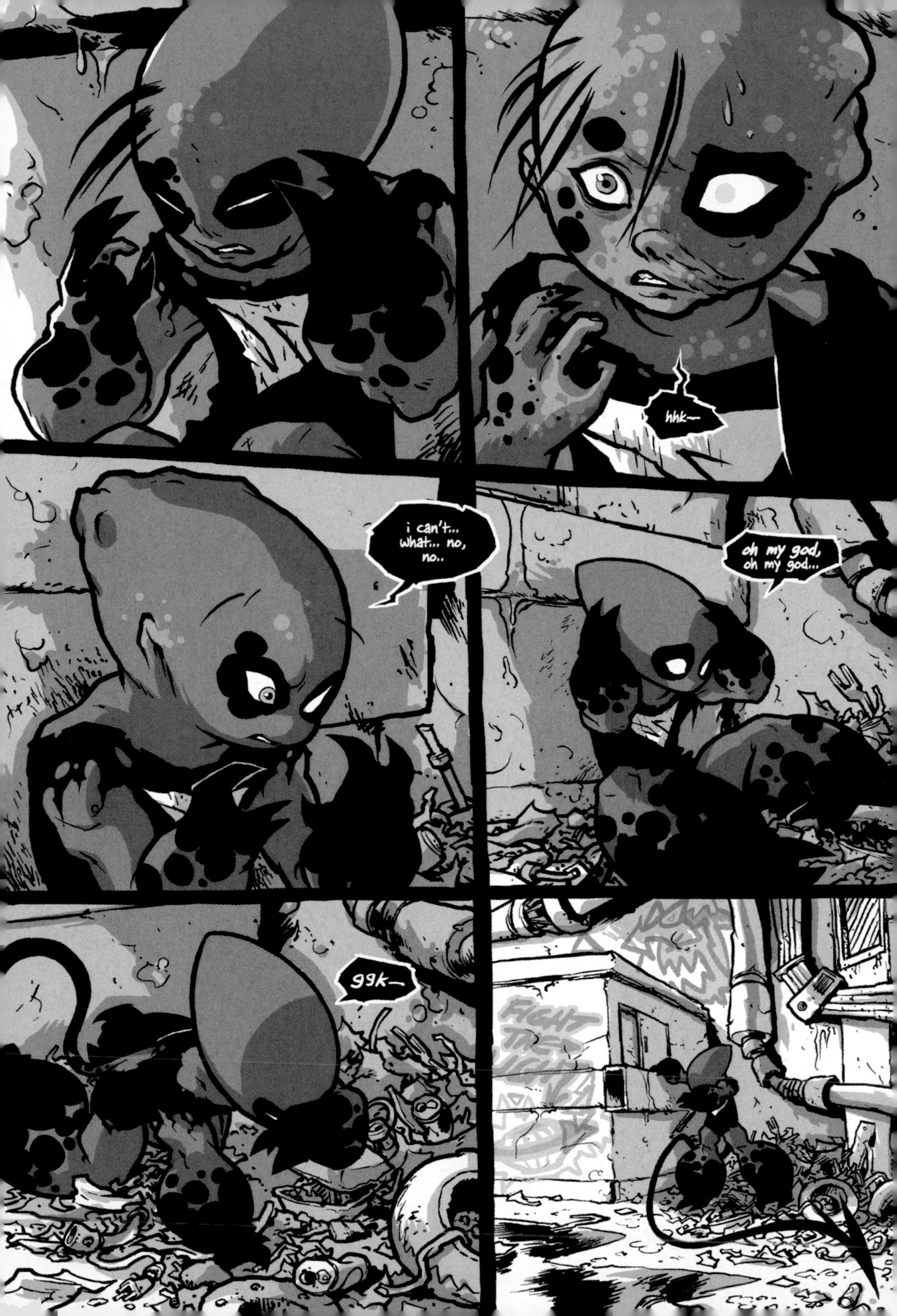
hhk—
i can't... what... no, no..
oh my god, oh my god...
ggk—

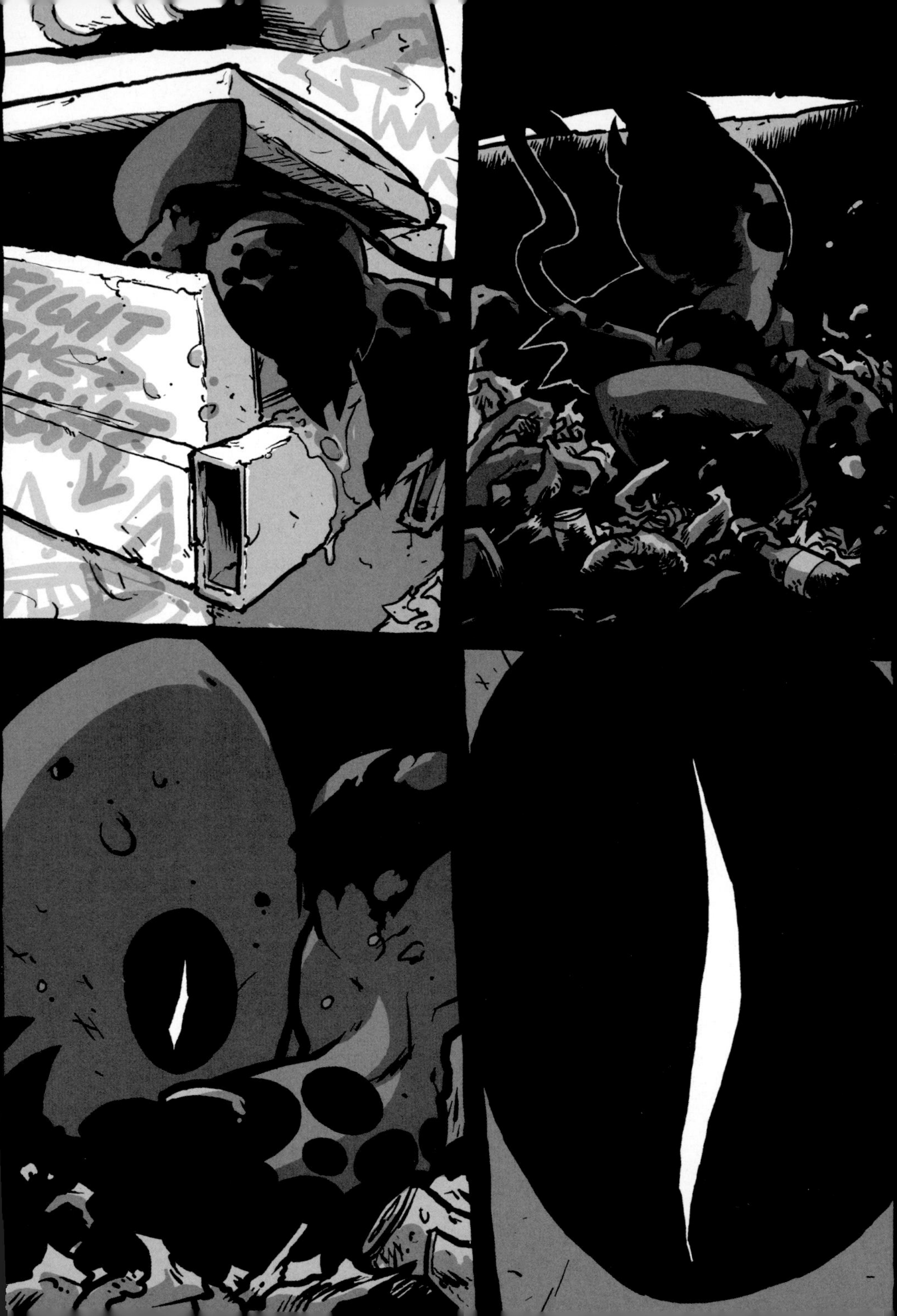

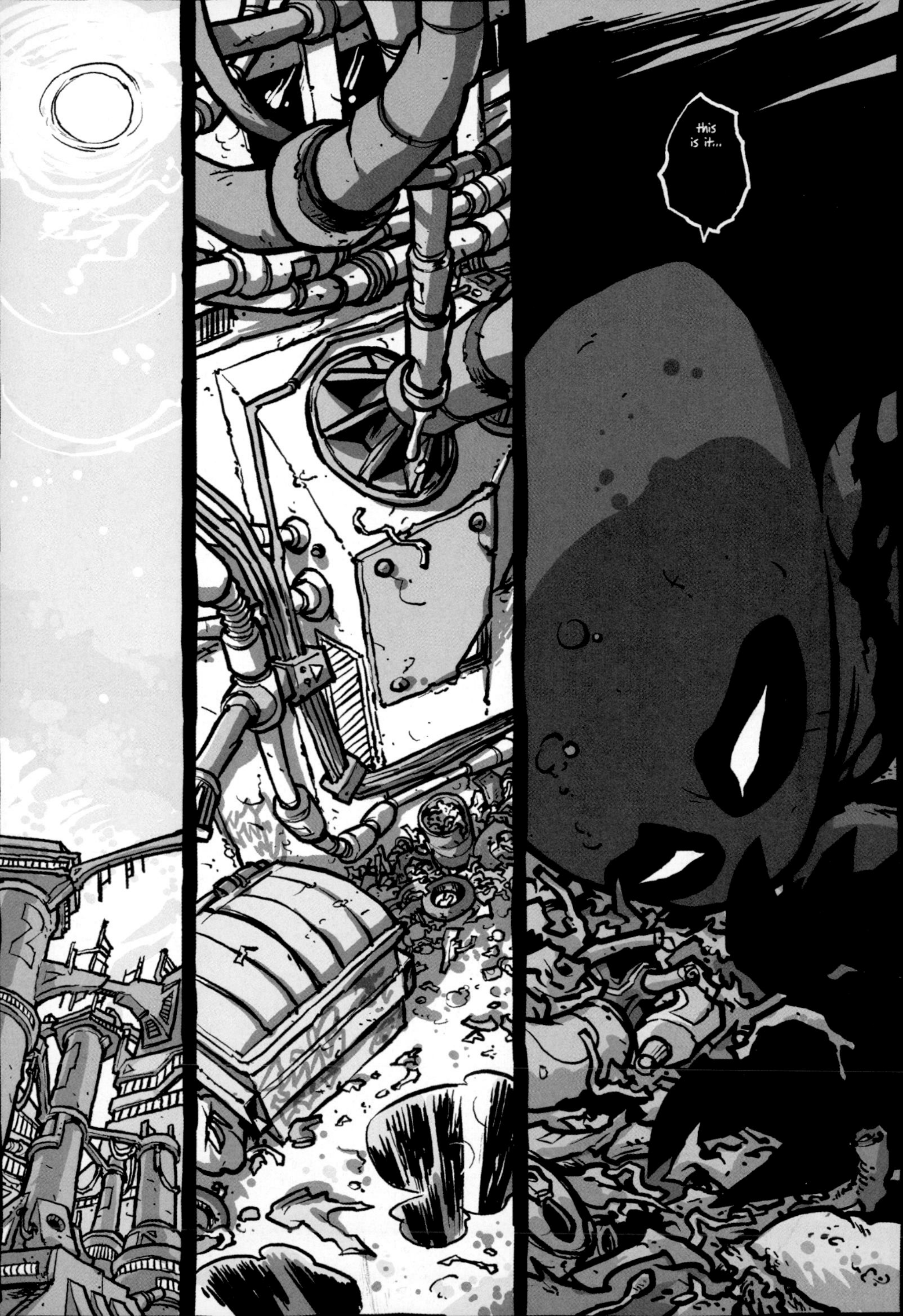
this is it...

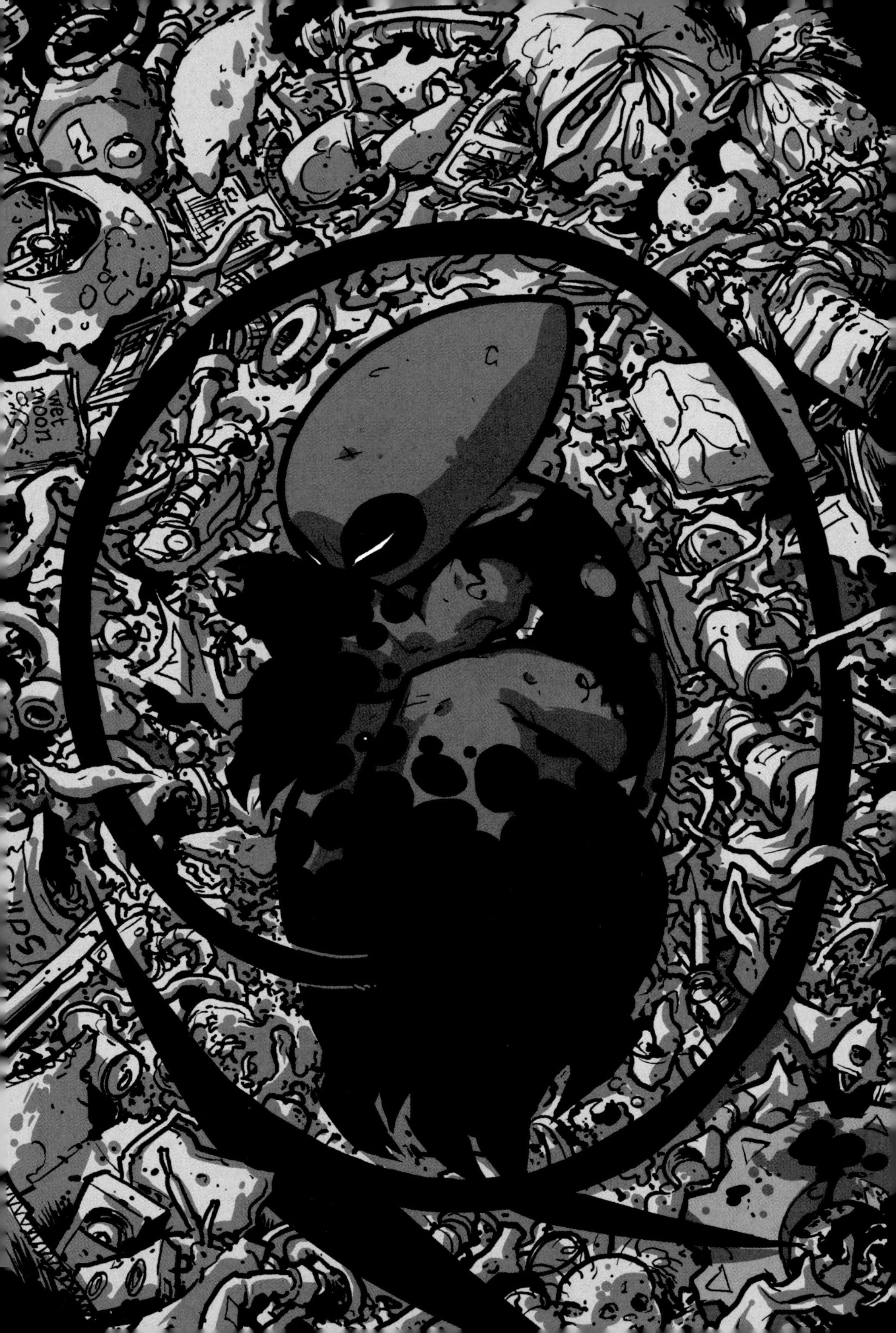
wet moon

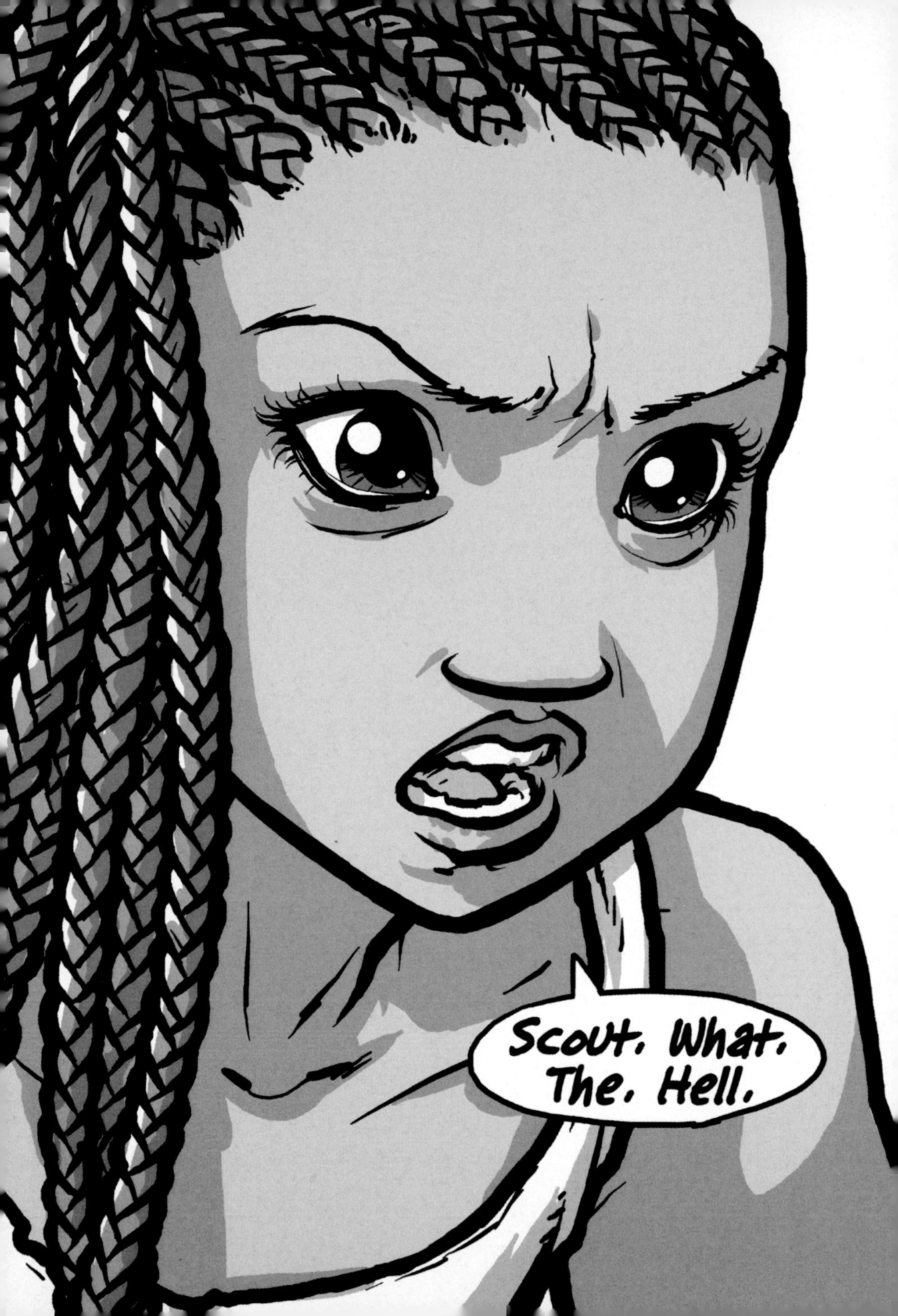
Scout. What. The. Hell.

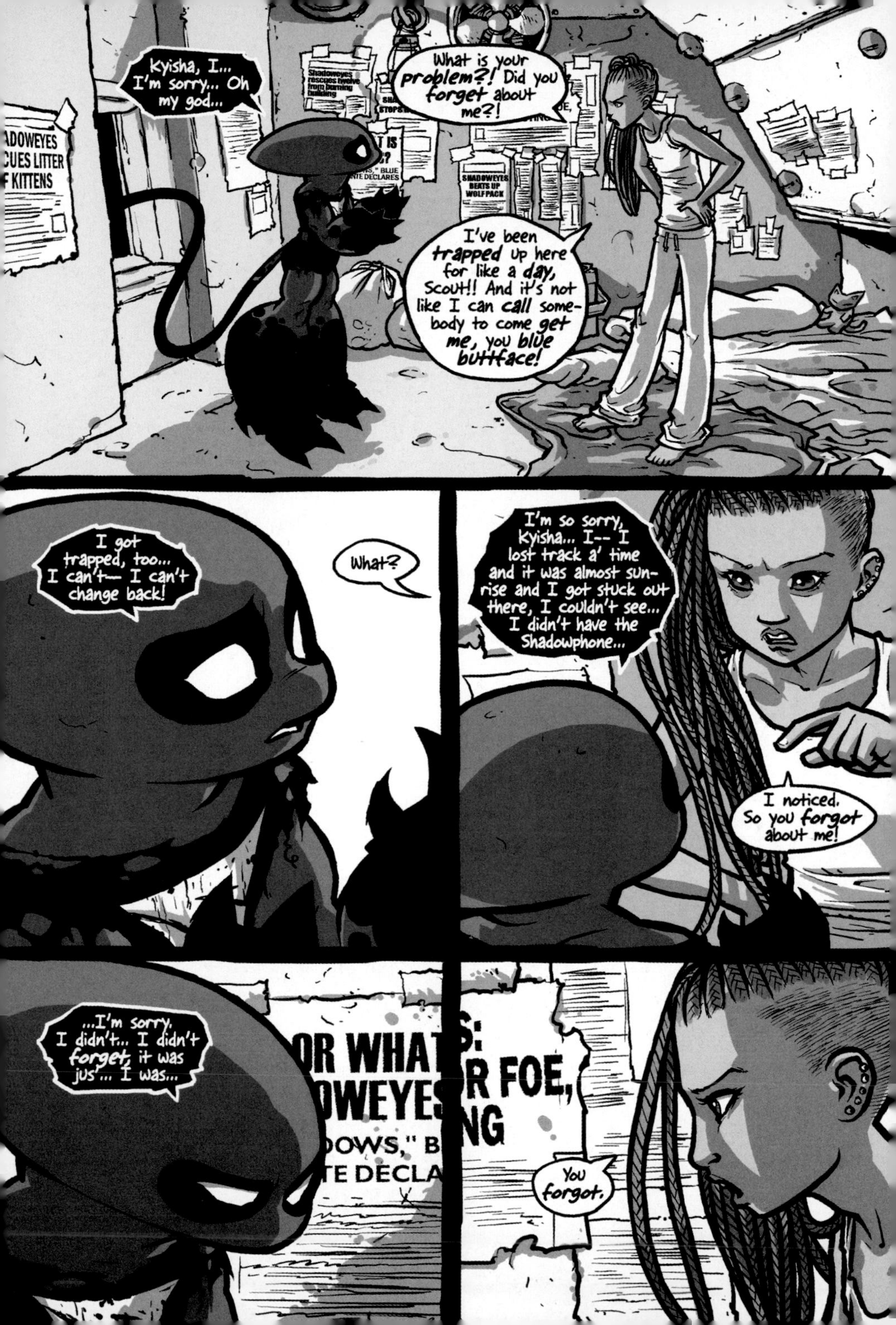
ADOWEYES
CUES LITTER
F KITTENS
Shadoweyes rescues twelve from burning building
SHADOWEYES BEATS UP WOLFPACK
Kyisha, I... I'm sorry... Oh my god...
What is your problem?! Did you forget about me?!
I've been trapped up here for like a day, Scout!! And it's not like I can call somebody to come get me, you blue buttface!
I got trapped, too... I can't— I can't change back!
What?
I'm so sorry, Kyisha... I-- I lost track a' time and it was almost sunrise and I got stuck out there, I couldn't see... I didn't have the Shadowphone...
I noticed. So you forgot about me!
...I'm sorry. I didn't... I didn't forget, it was jus'... I was...
OR WHAT
R FOE,
OWEYES
NG
DOWS," B
TE DECLA
You forgot.

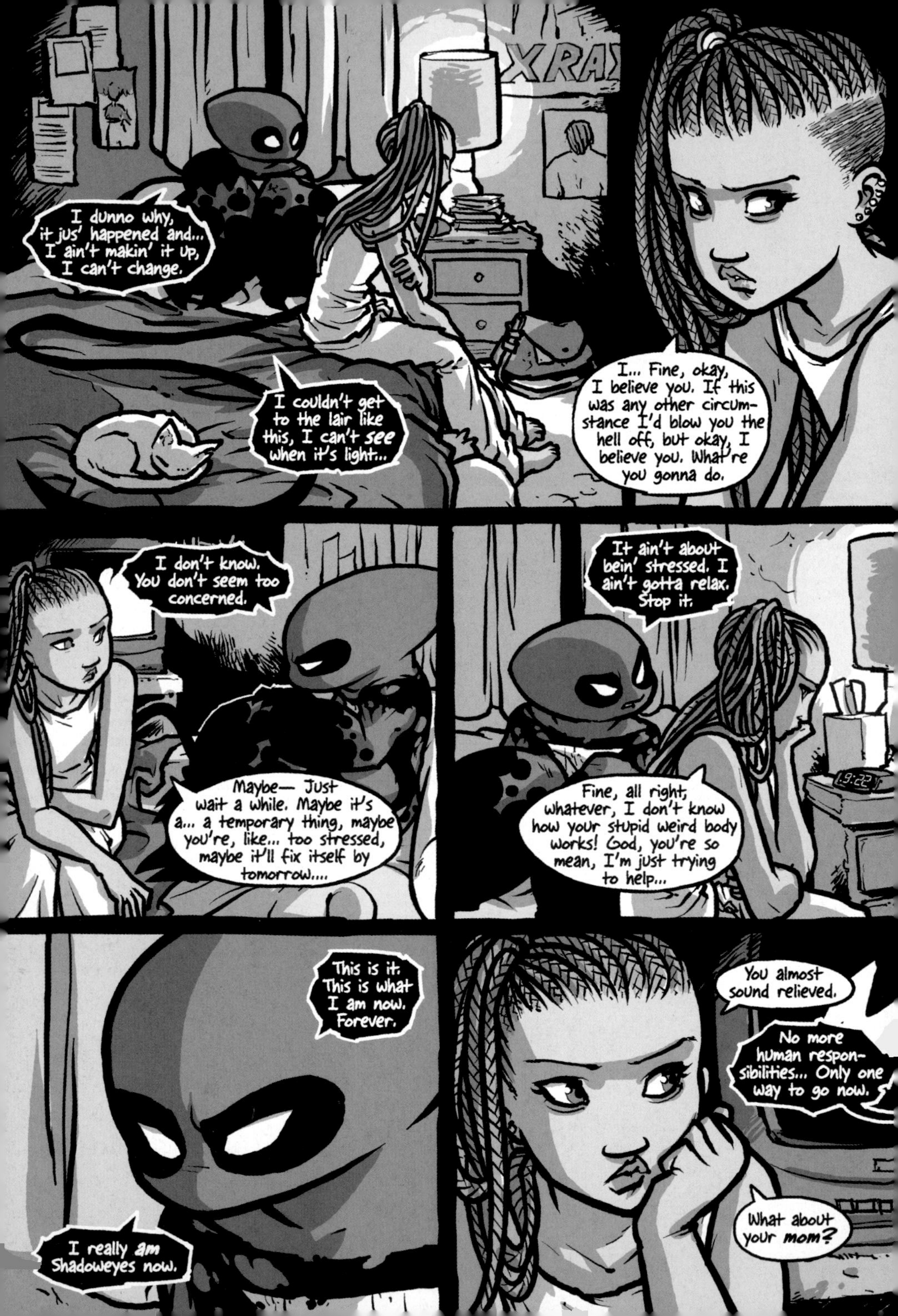
I dunno why, it jus' happened and... I ain't makin' it up, I can't change.
I couldn't get to the lair like this, I can't *see* when it's light...
I... Fine, okay, I believe you. If this was any other circumstance I'd blow you the hell off, but okay, I believe you. What're you gonna do.
I don't know. You don't seem too concerned.
Maybe— Just wait a while. Maybe it's a... a temporary thing, maybe you're, like... too stressed, maybe it'll fix itself by tomorrow....
It ain't about bein' stressed. I ain't gotta relax. Stop it.
Fine, all right, whatever, I don't know how your stupid weird body works! God, you're so mean, I'm just trying to help...
9:22
This is it. This is what I am now. Forever.
I really *am* Shadoweyes now.
You almost sound relieved.
No more human responsibilities... Only one way to go now.
What about your *mom?*

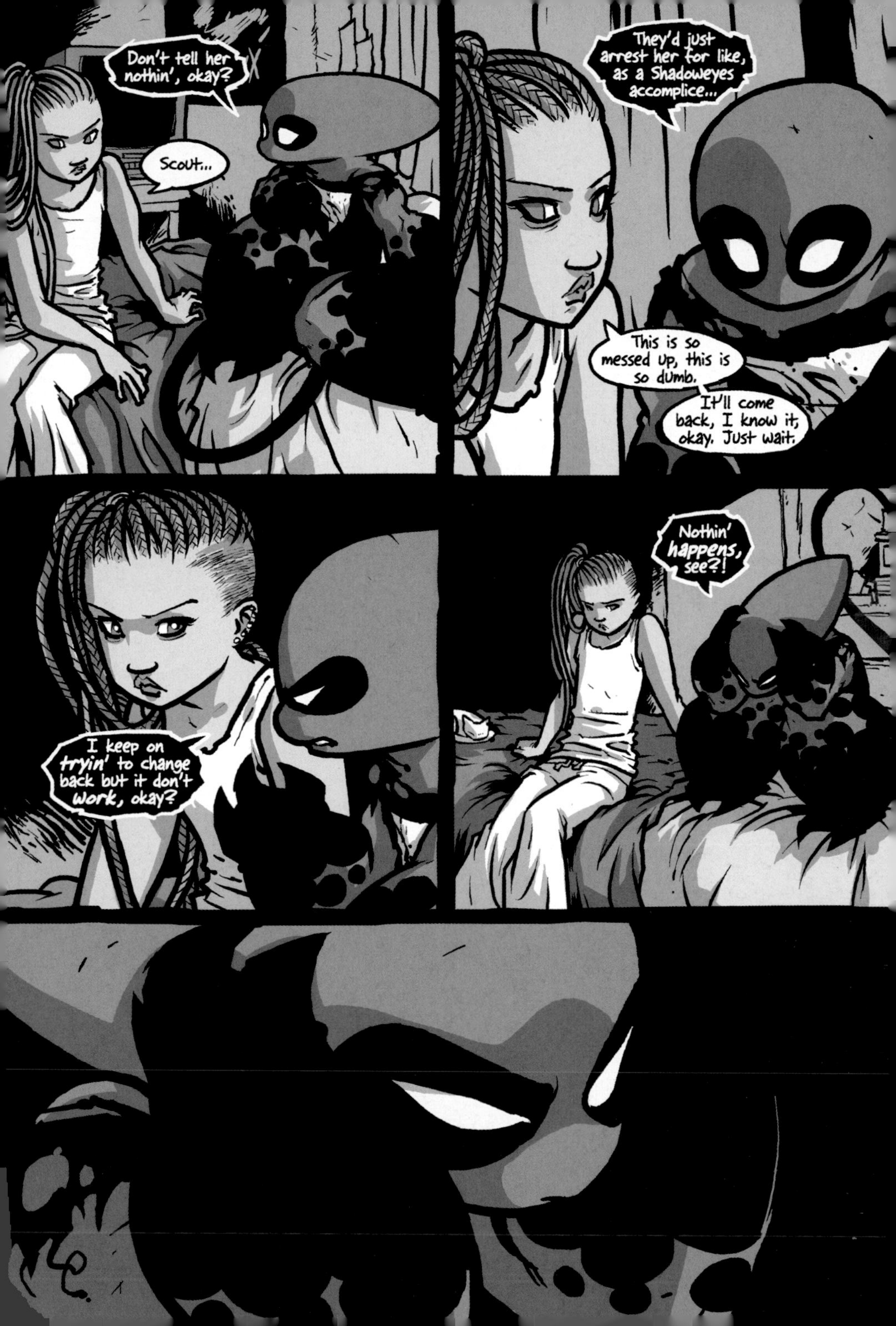
Don't tell her nothin', okay?
Scout...
They'd just arrest her for like, as a Shadoweyes accomplice...
This is so messed up, this is so dumb.
It'll come back, I know it, okay. Just wait.
I keep on *tryin'* to change back but it don't *work*, okay?
Nothin' *happens*, see?!

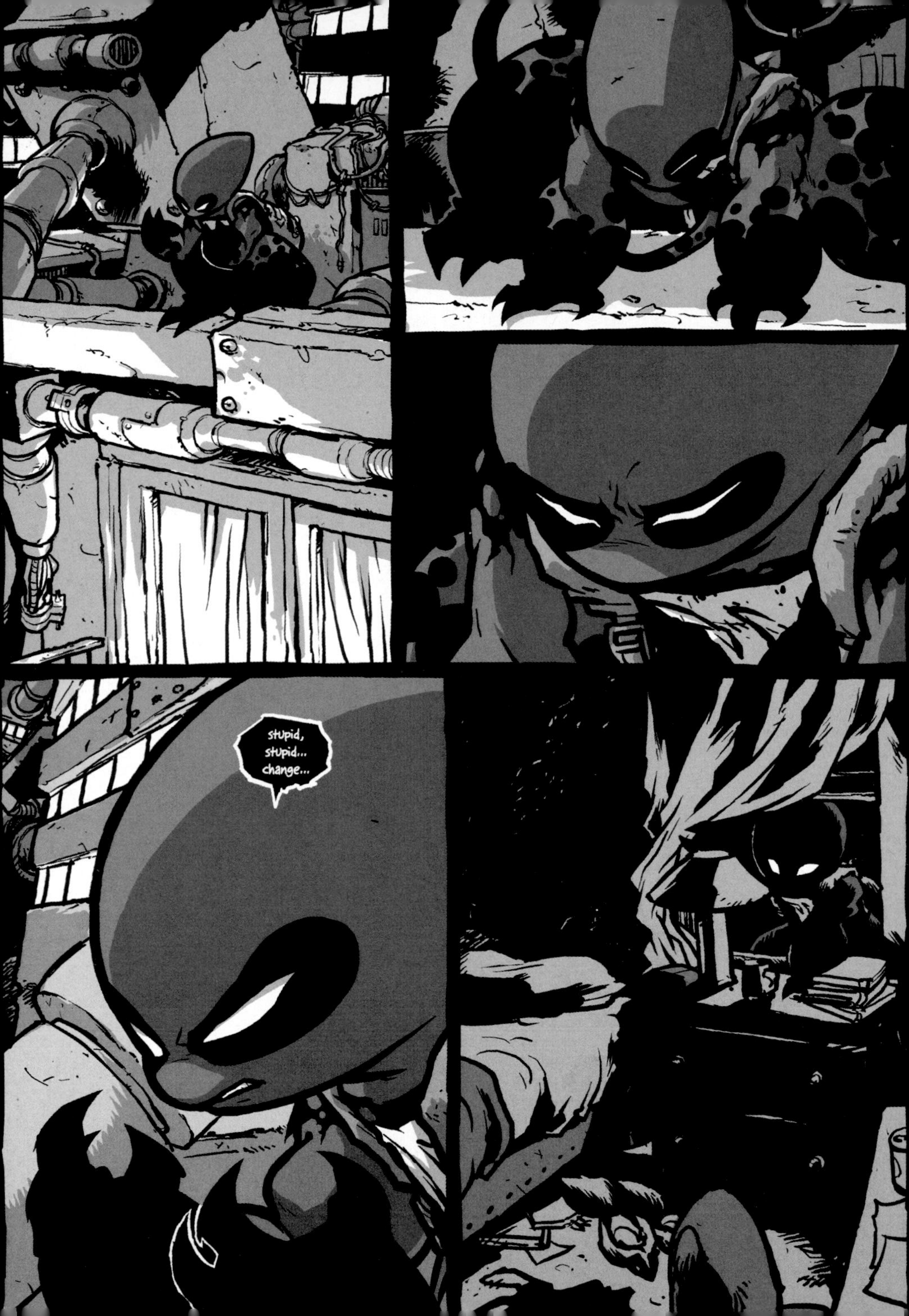
stupid,
stupid...
change...

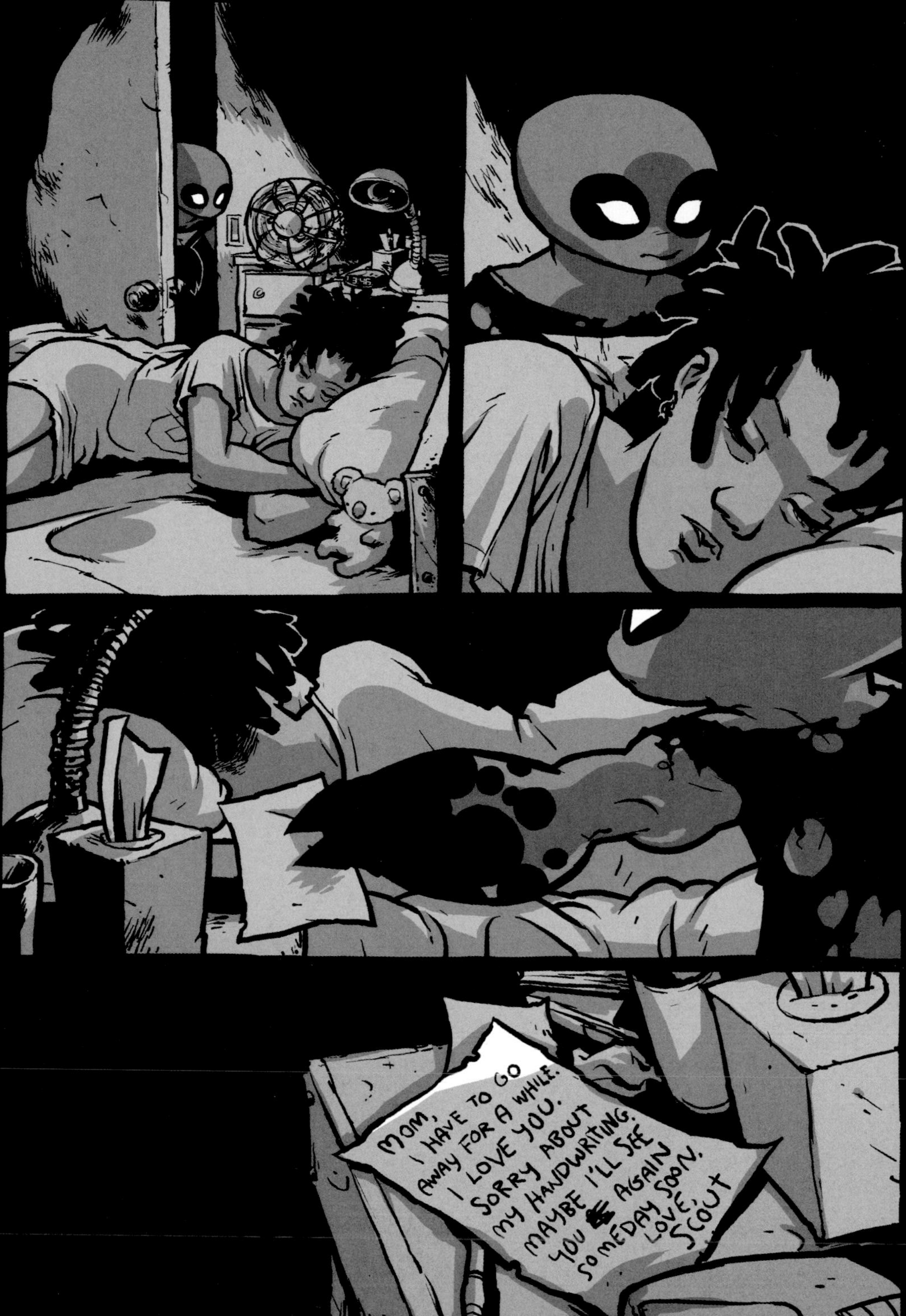
MOM,
I HAVE TO GO
AWAY FOR A WHILE.
I LOVE YOU.
SORRY ABOUT
MY HANDWRITING.
MAYBE I'LL SEE
YOU AGAIN
SOMEDAY SOON.
LOVE,
SCOUT

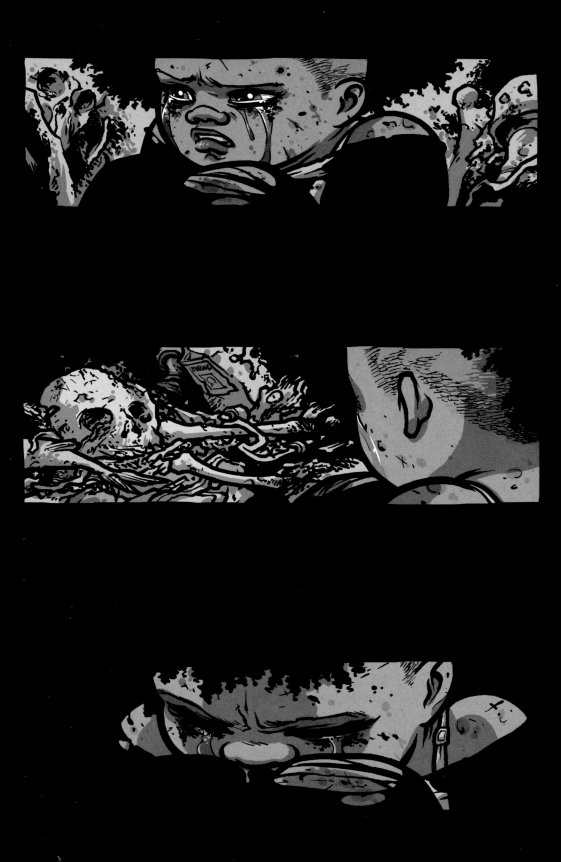

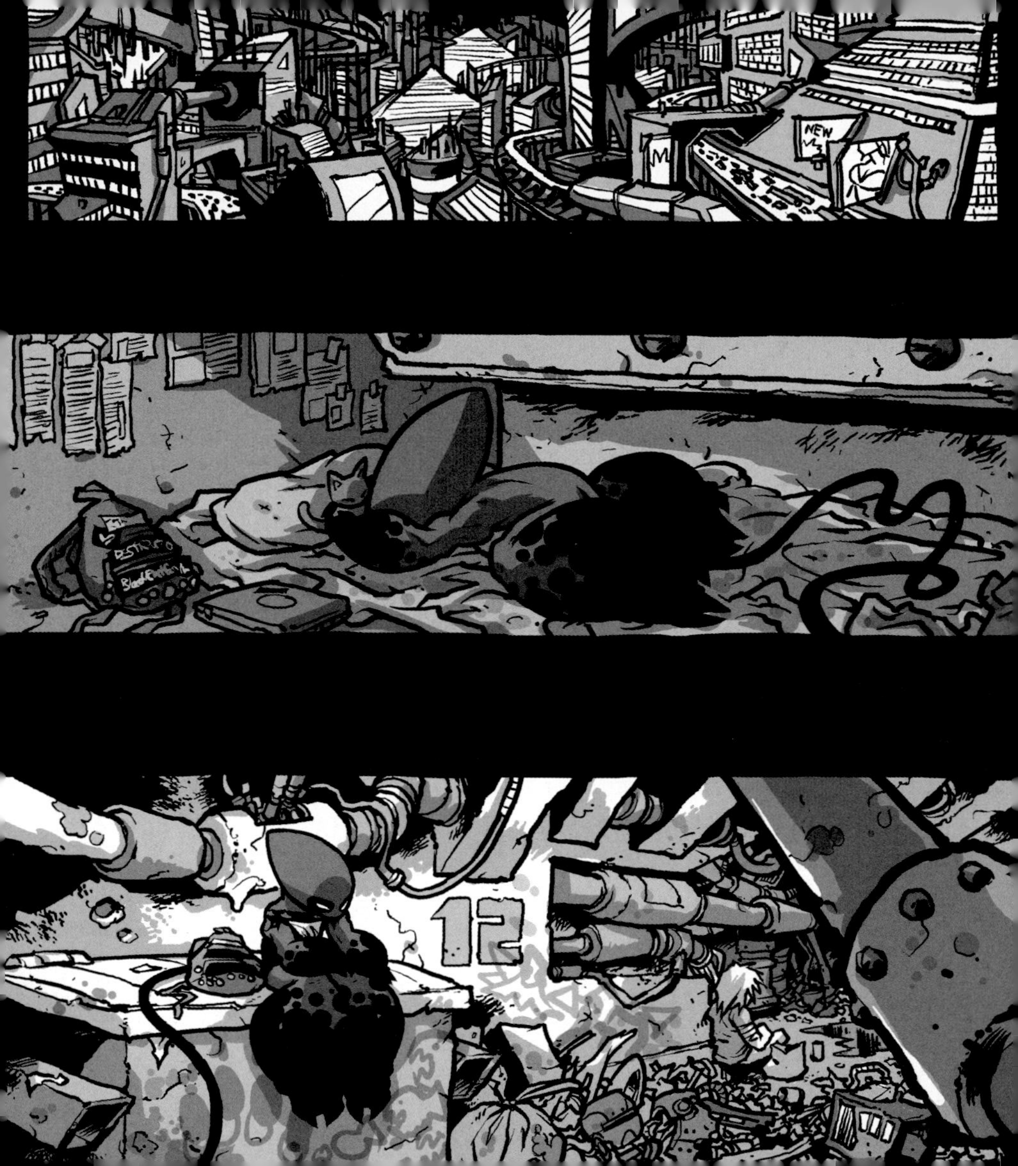
NEW
12

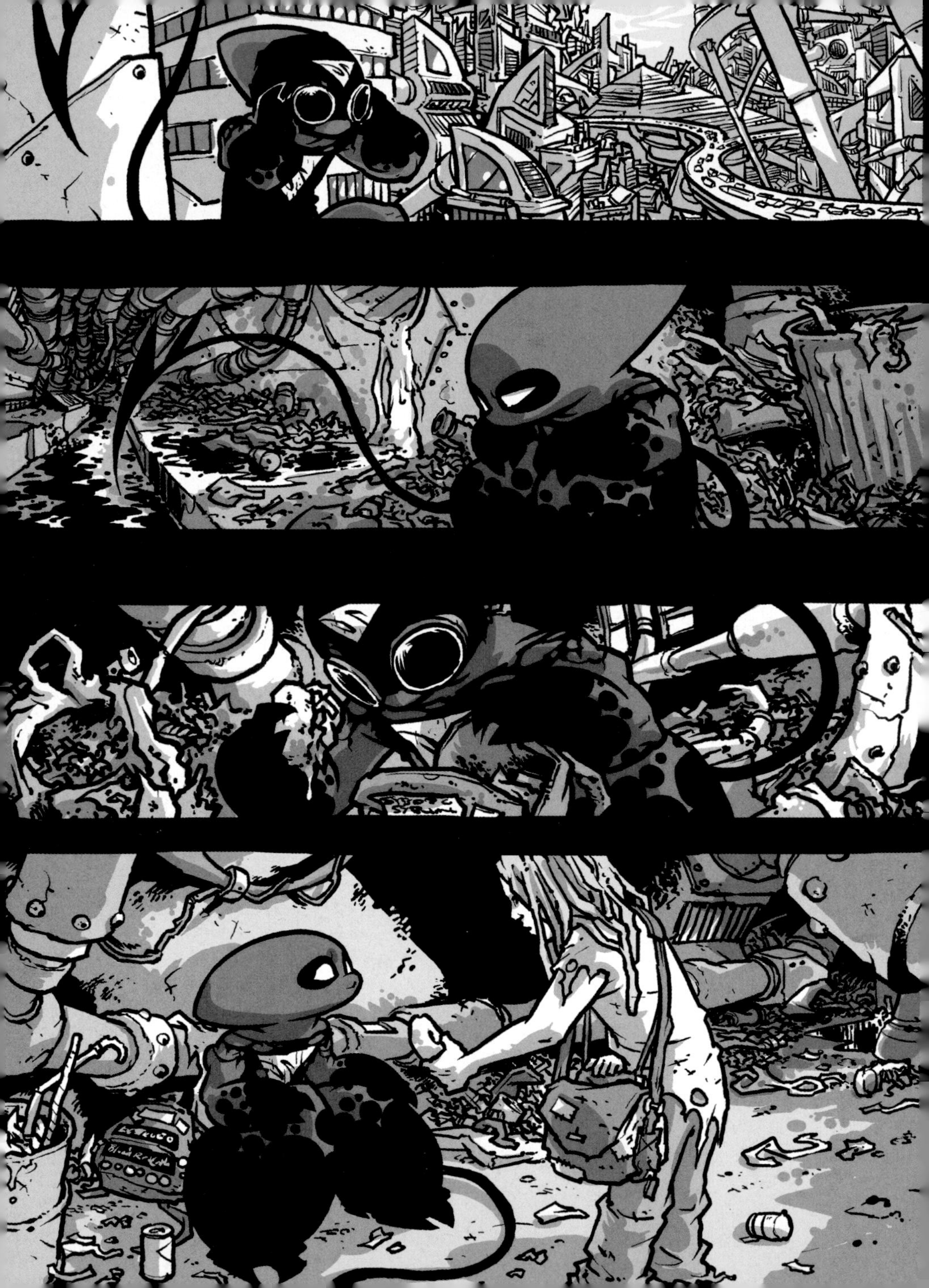

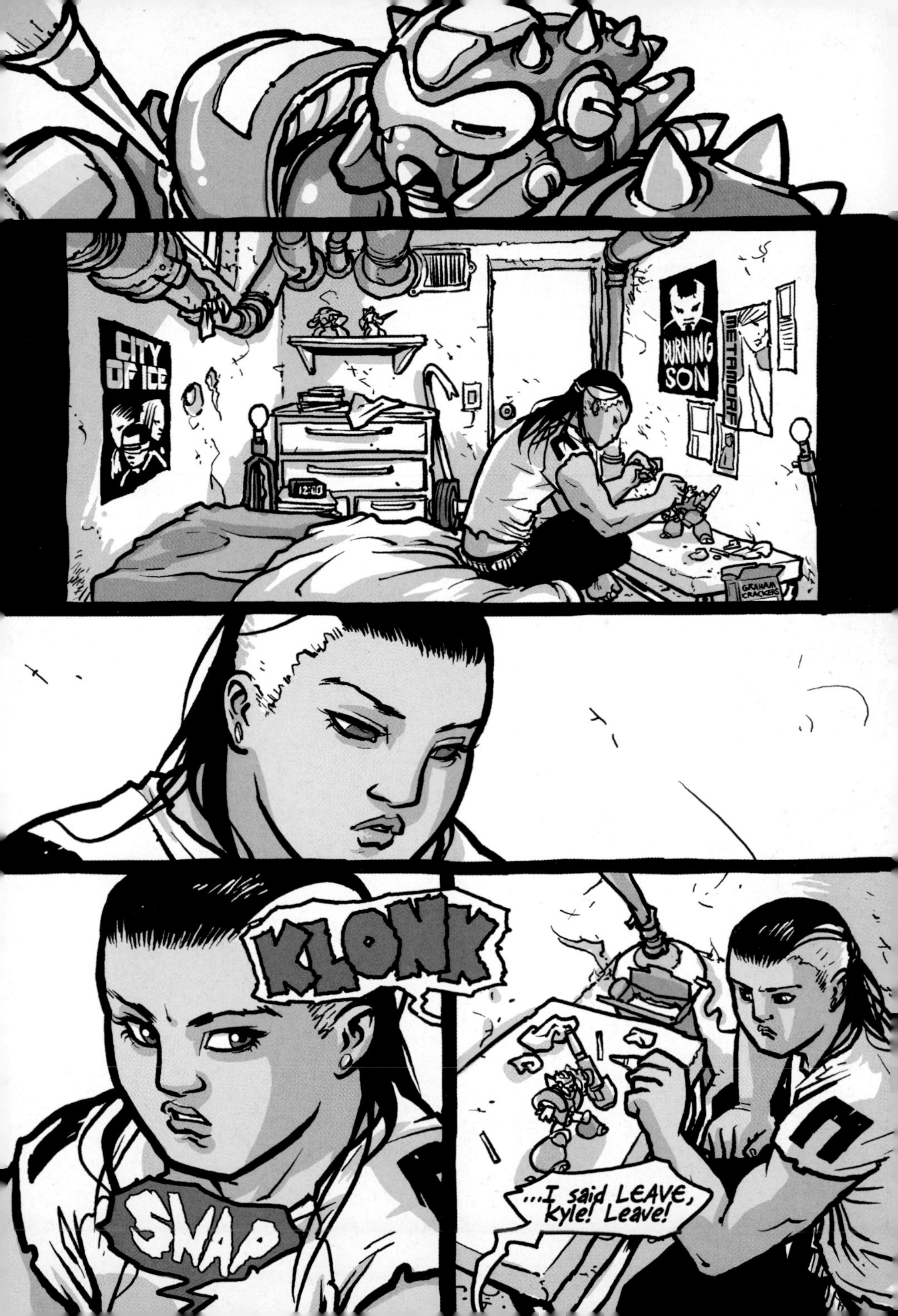
CITY OF ICE
BURNING SON
METAMORF
GRAHAM CRACKERS
KLONK
SNAP
...I said LEAVE, kyle! Leave!

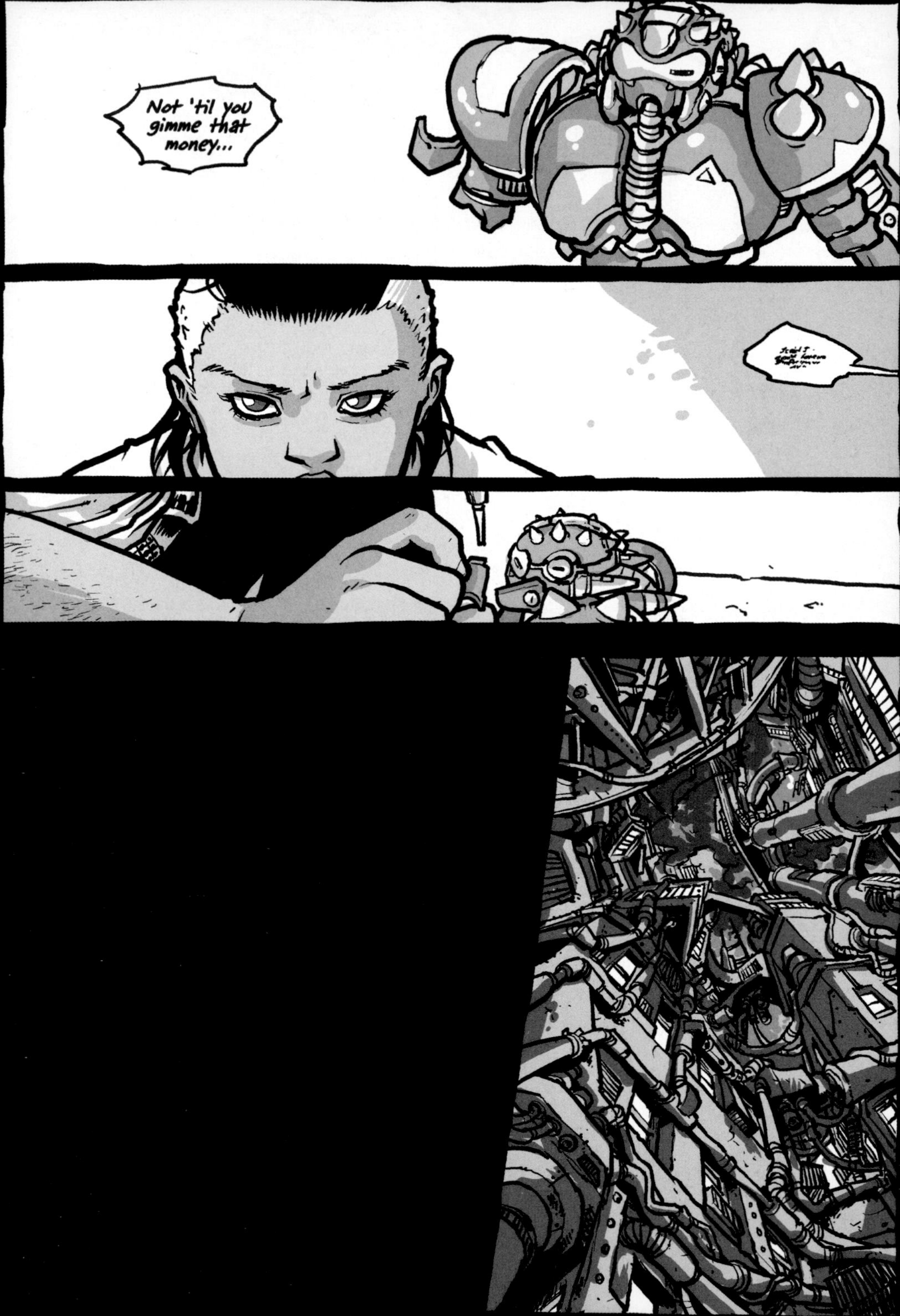
Not 'til you gimme that money...

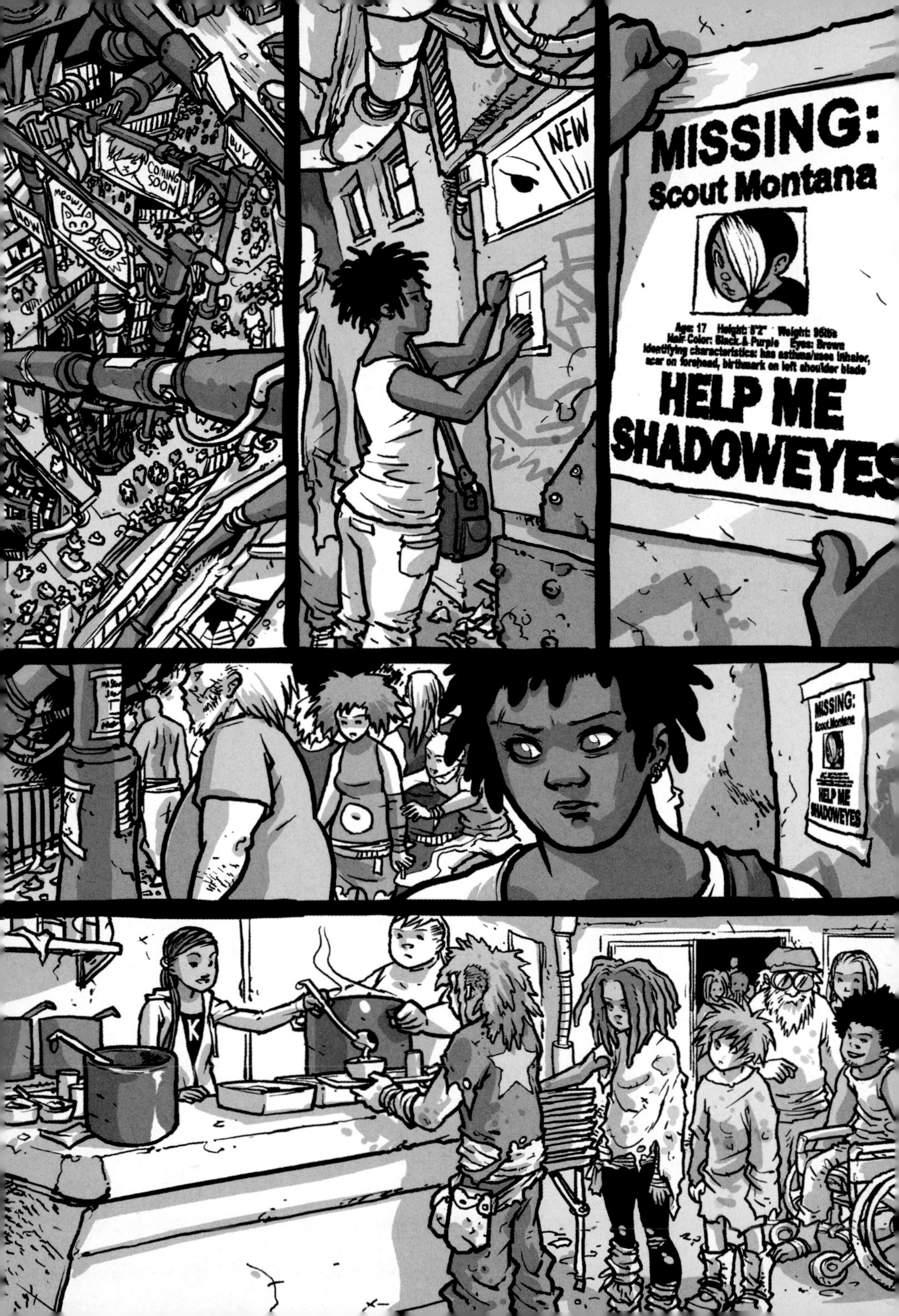
BUY
COMING SOON
NOW
MEOW!
NEW
MISSING:
Scout Montana
Age: 17 Height: 5'2" Weight: 95lbs
Hair-Color: Black & Purple Eyes: Brown
Identifying characteristics: has asthma/uses inhaler, scar on forehead, birthmark on left shoulder blade
HELP ME
SHADOWEYES
MISSING:
Scout Montana
HELP ME
SHADOWEYES

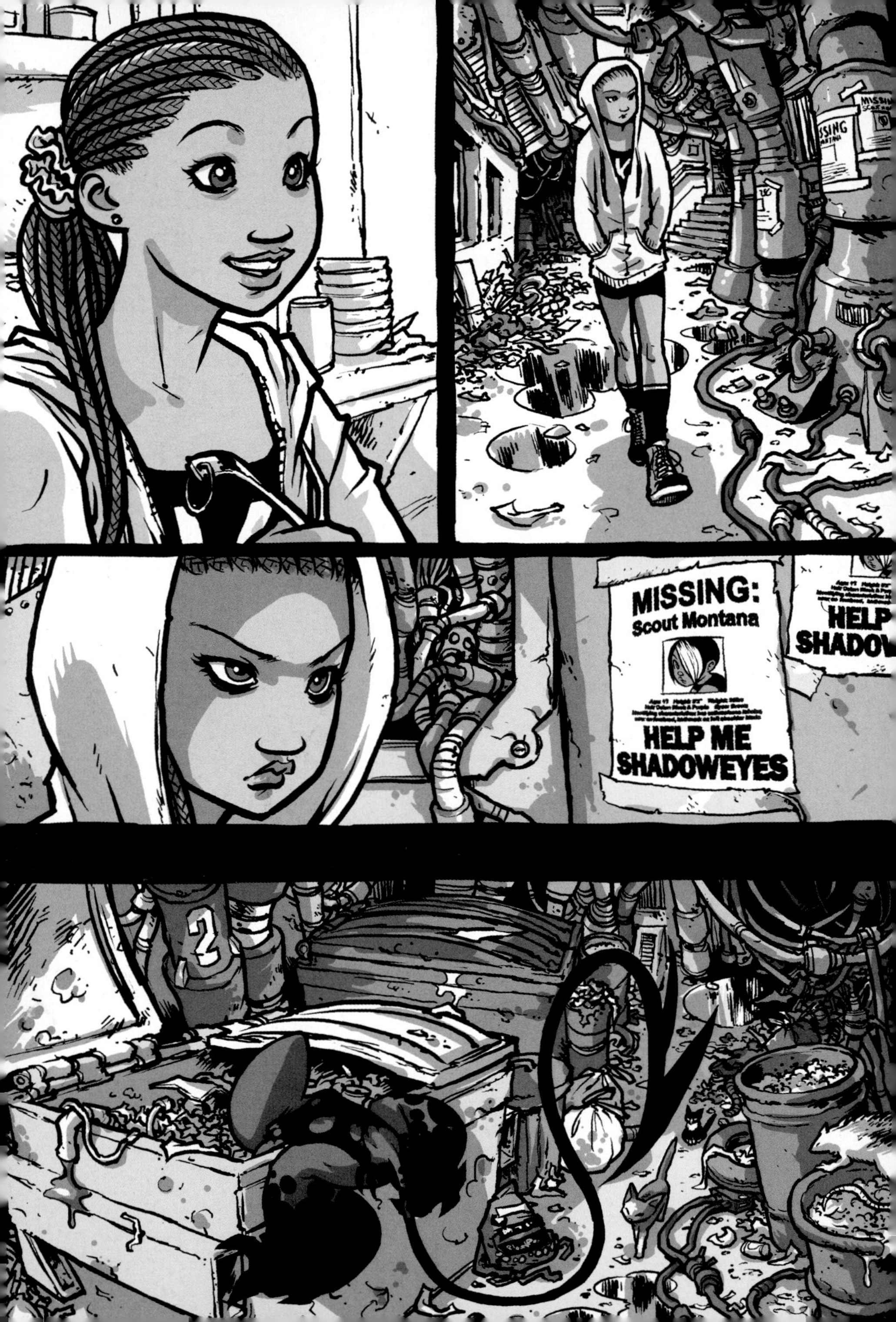
MISSING
MISSING:
Scout Montana
HELP ME
SHADOWEYES
HELP

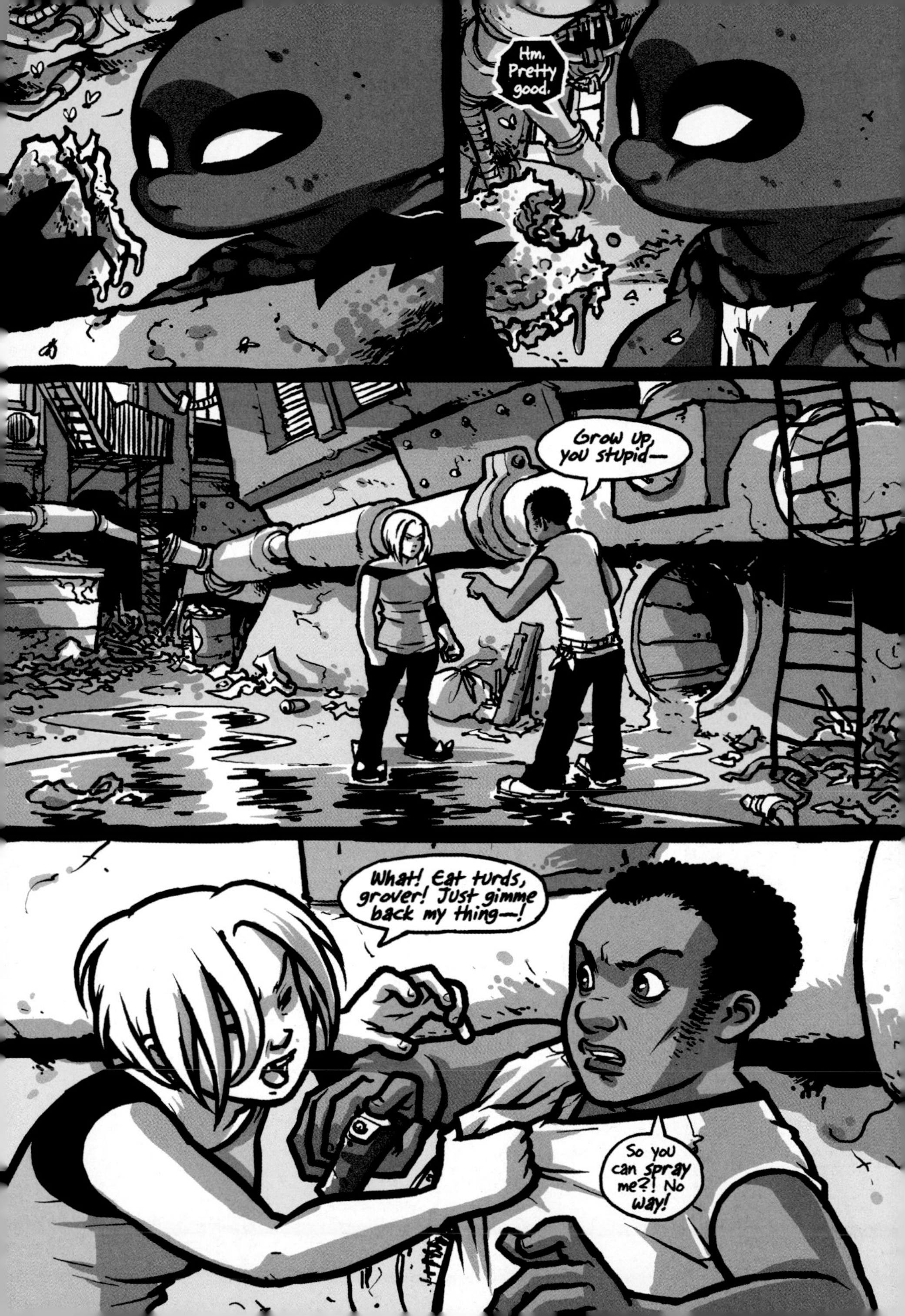
Hm. Pretty good.
Grow up, you stupid—
What! Eat turds, grover! Just gimme back my thing—!
So you can spray me?! No way!

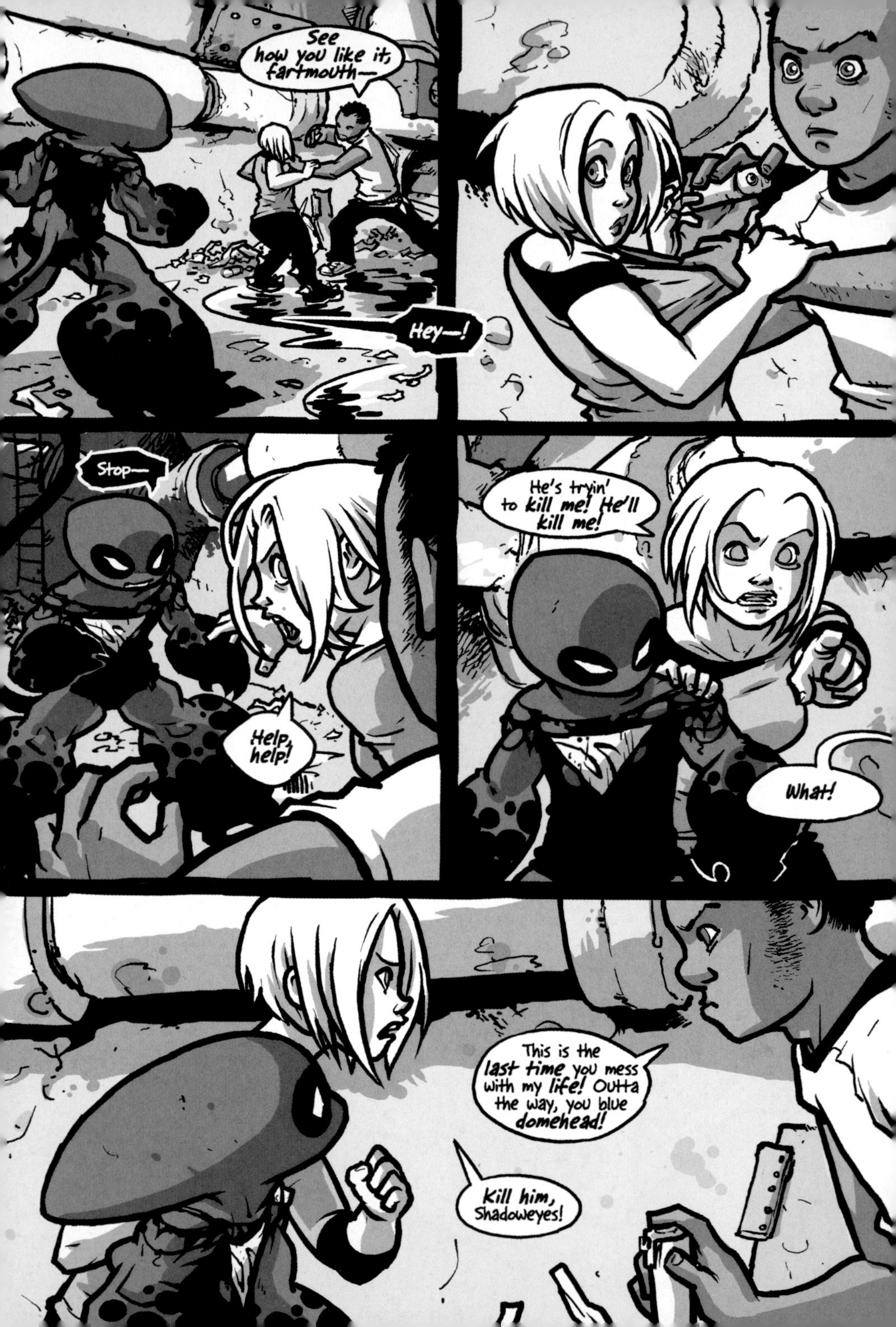
See how you like it, fartmouth—
Hey—!
Stop—
Help, help!
He's tryin' to kill me! He'll kill me!
What!
This is the last time you mess with my life! Outta the way, you blue domehead!
Kill him, Shadoweyes!

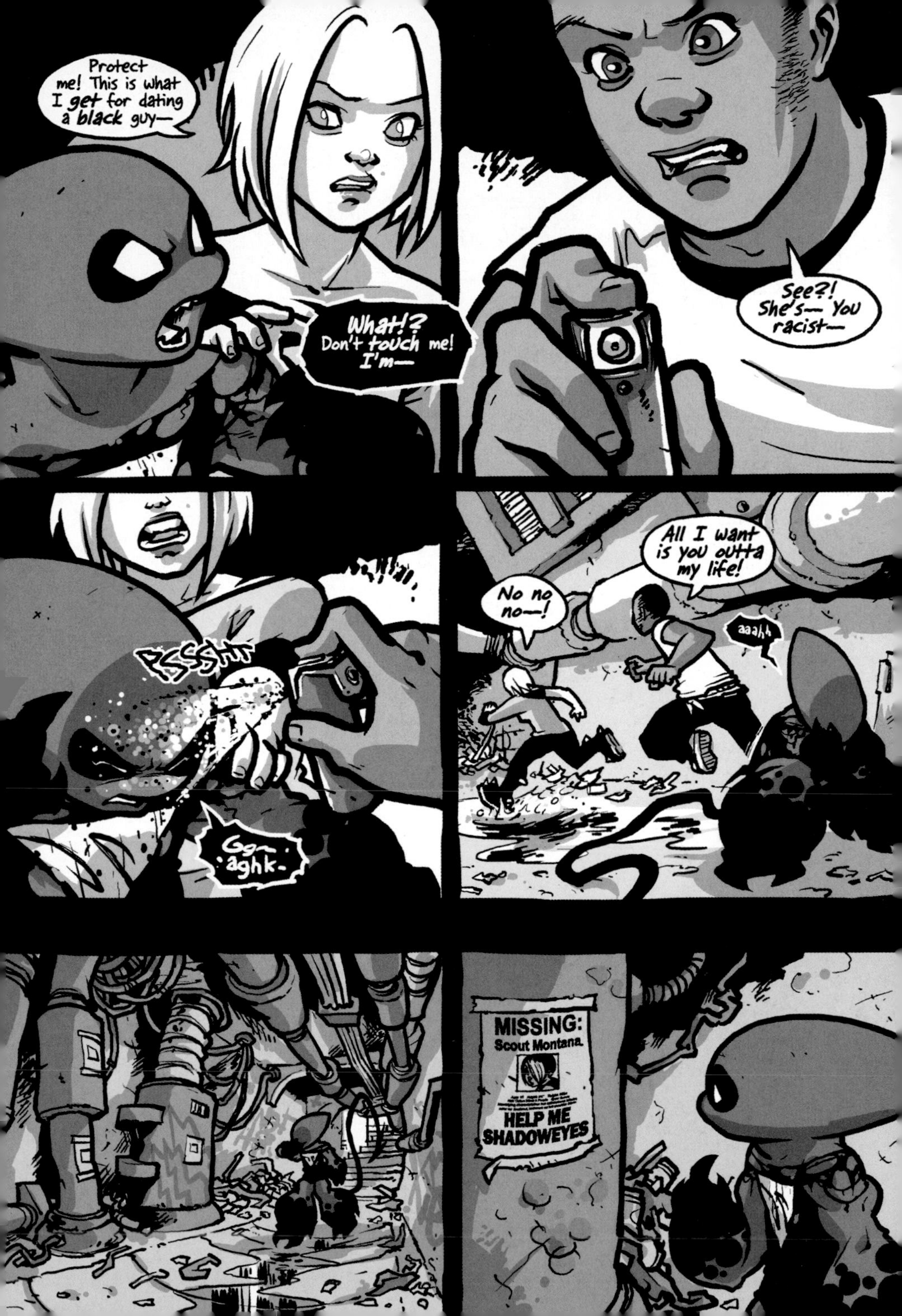
Protect me! This is what I *get* for dating a ***black*** guy—
What!? Don't *touch* me! I'm—
See?! She's— You racist—
PSSHT
Gg- aghk-
All I want is you outta my life!
No no no—!
aaahh
MISSING:
Scout Montana
HELP ME SHADOWEYES

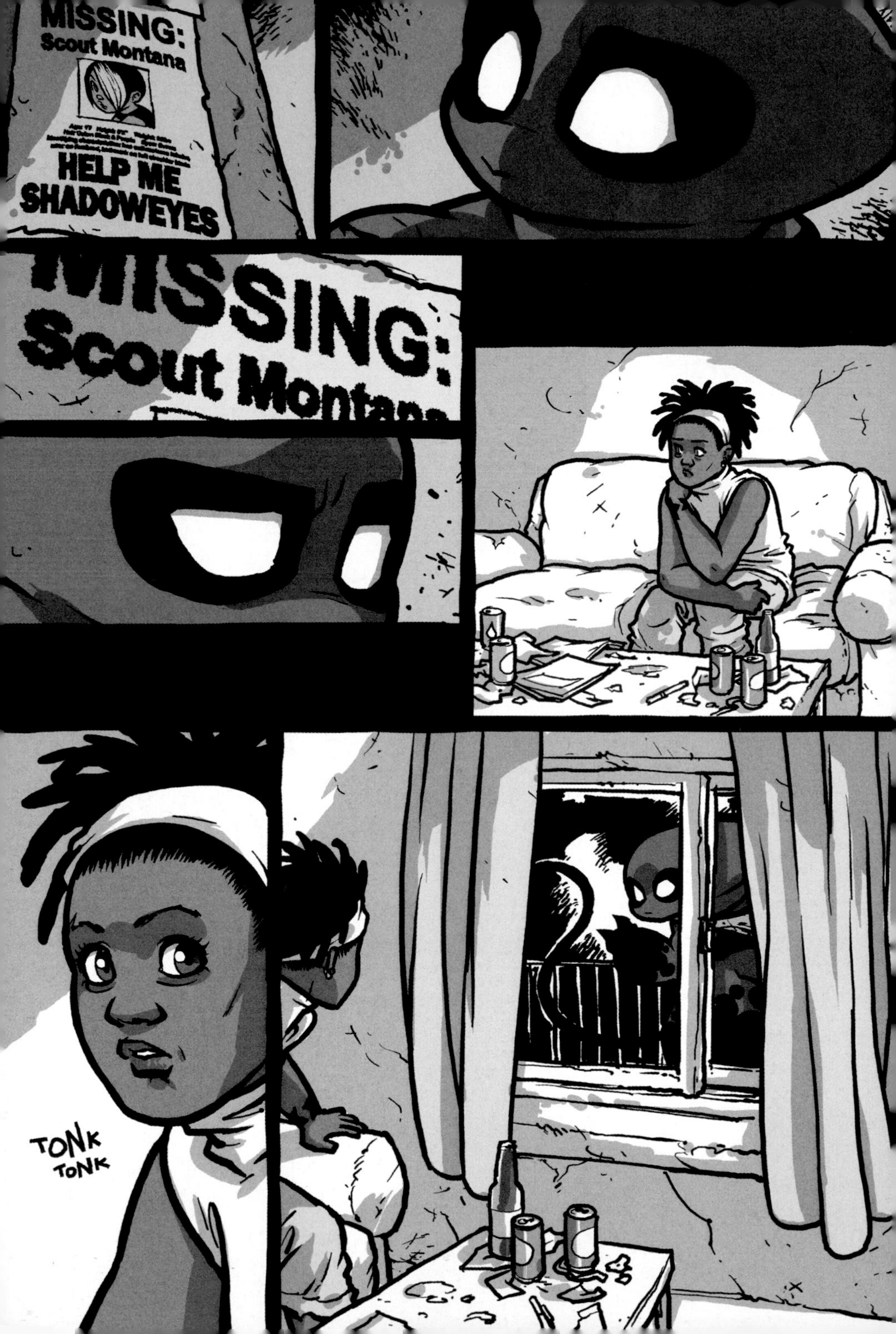
MISSING:
Scout Montana
HELP ME
SHADOWEYES
MISSING:
Scout Monta
TONK
TONK

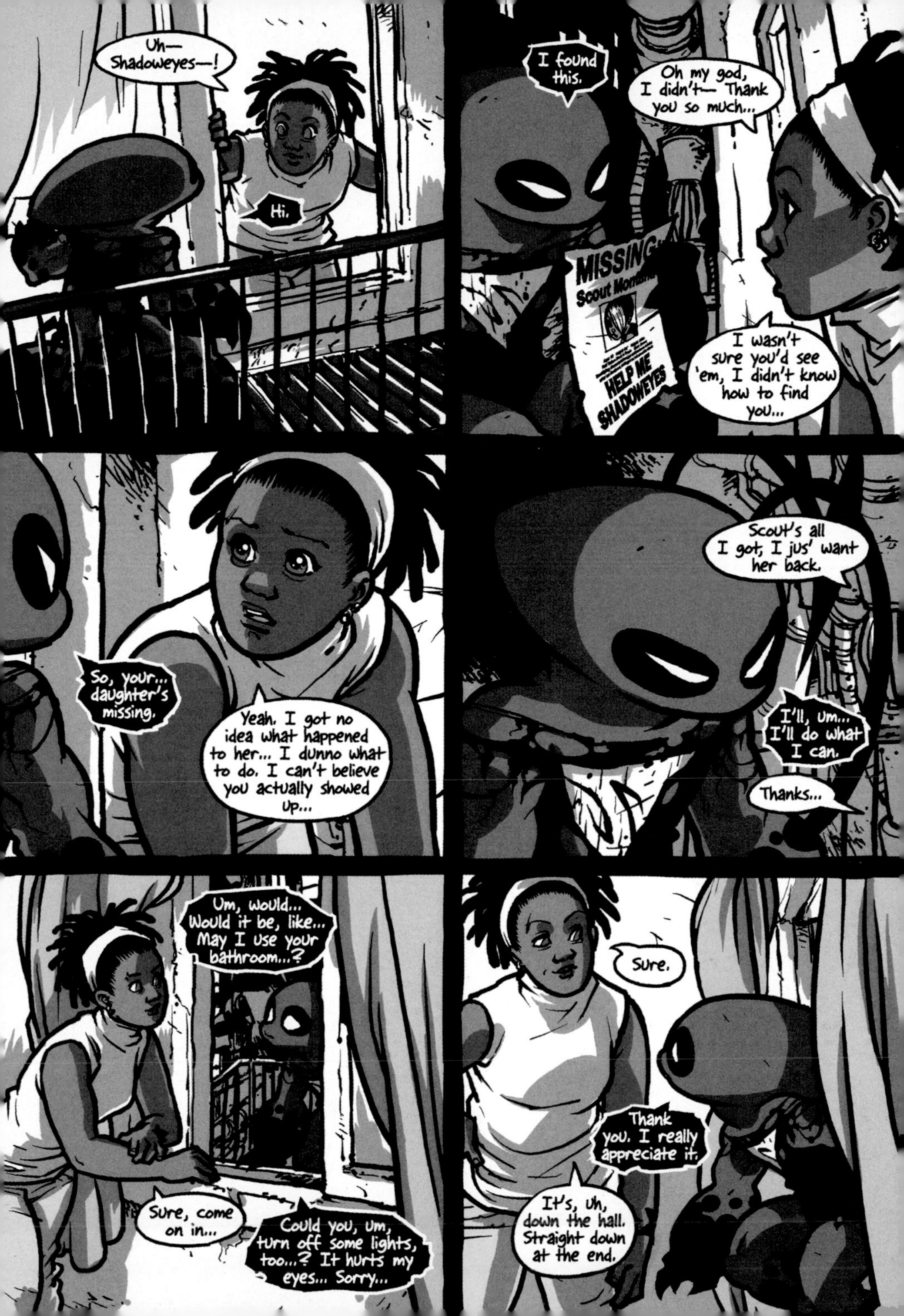
Uh— Shadoweyes—!
Hi.
I found this.
Oh my god, I didn't— Thank you so much...
MISSING
Scout Mont
HELP ME SHADOWEYES
I wasn't sure you'd see 'em, I didn't know how to find you...
So, your... daughter's missing.
Yeah. I got no idea what happened to her... I dunno what to do. I can't believe you actually showed up...
Scout's all I got, I jus' want her back.
I'll, um... I'll do what I can.
Thanks...
Um, would... Would it be, like... May I use your bathroom...?
Sure, come on in...
Could you, um, turn off some lights, too...? It hurts my eyes... Sorry...
Sure.
Thank you. I really appreciate it.
It's, uh, down the hall. Straight down at the end.

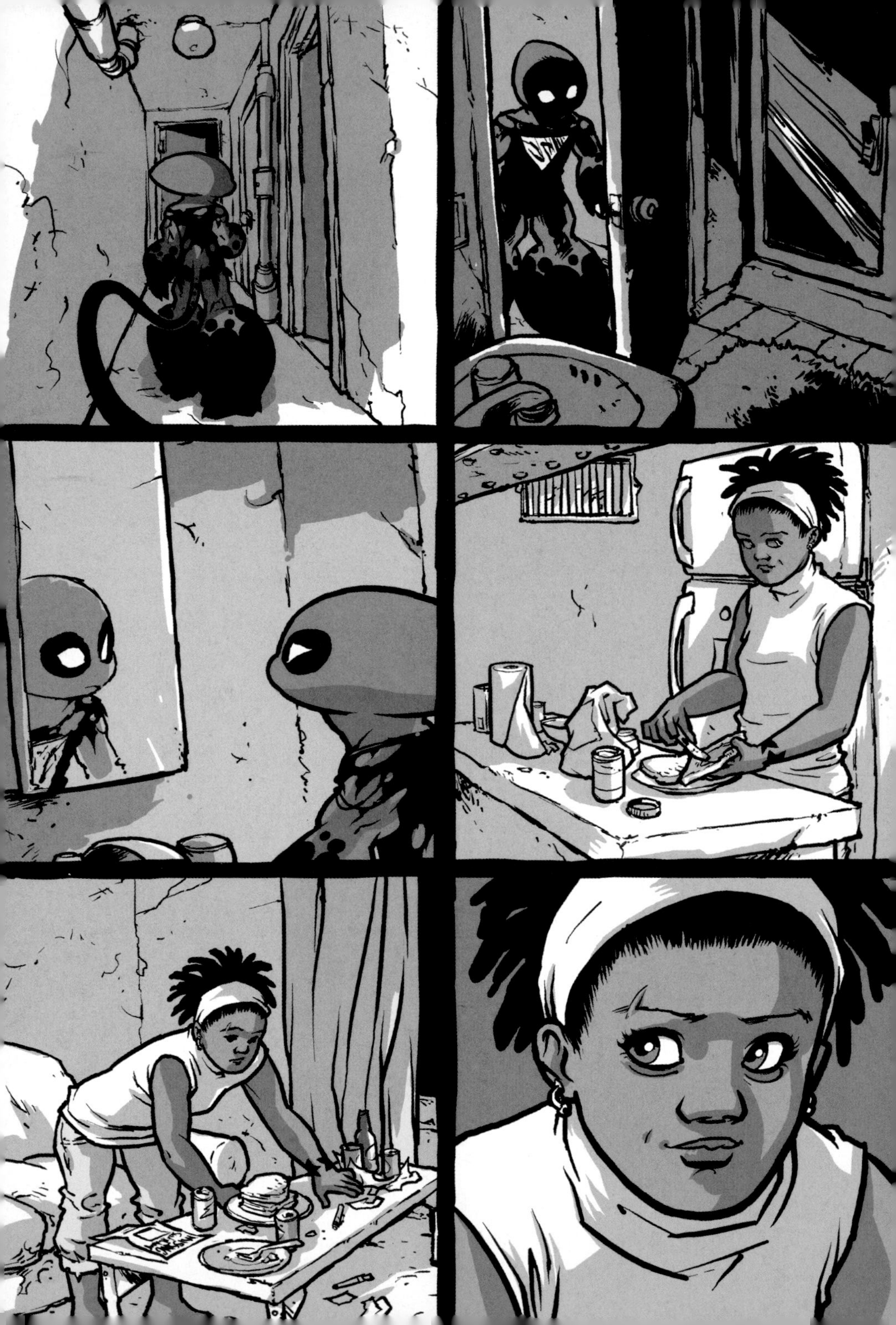

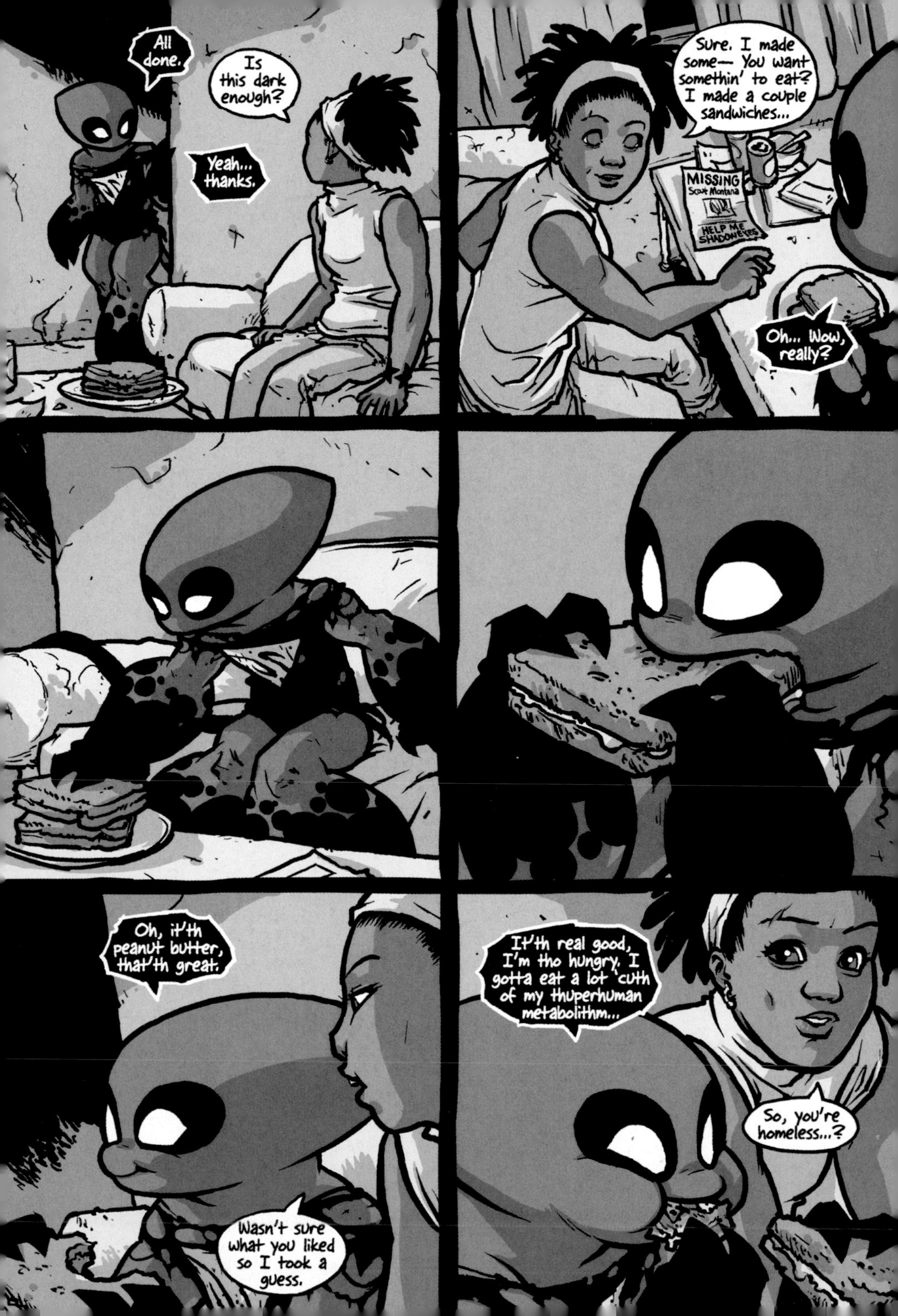
All done.
Is this dark enough?
Yeah... thanks.
Sure. I made some— You want somethin' to eat? I made a couple sandwiches...
MISSING
Scout Montana
HELP ME SHADOWEYES
Oh... Wow, really?
Oh, it'th peanut butter, that'th great.
Wasn't sure what you liked so I took a guess.
It'th real good, I'm tho hungry. I gotta eat a lot 'cuth of my thuperhuman metabolithm...
So, you're homeless...?

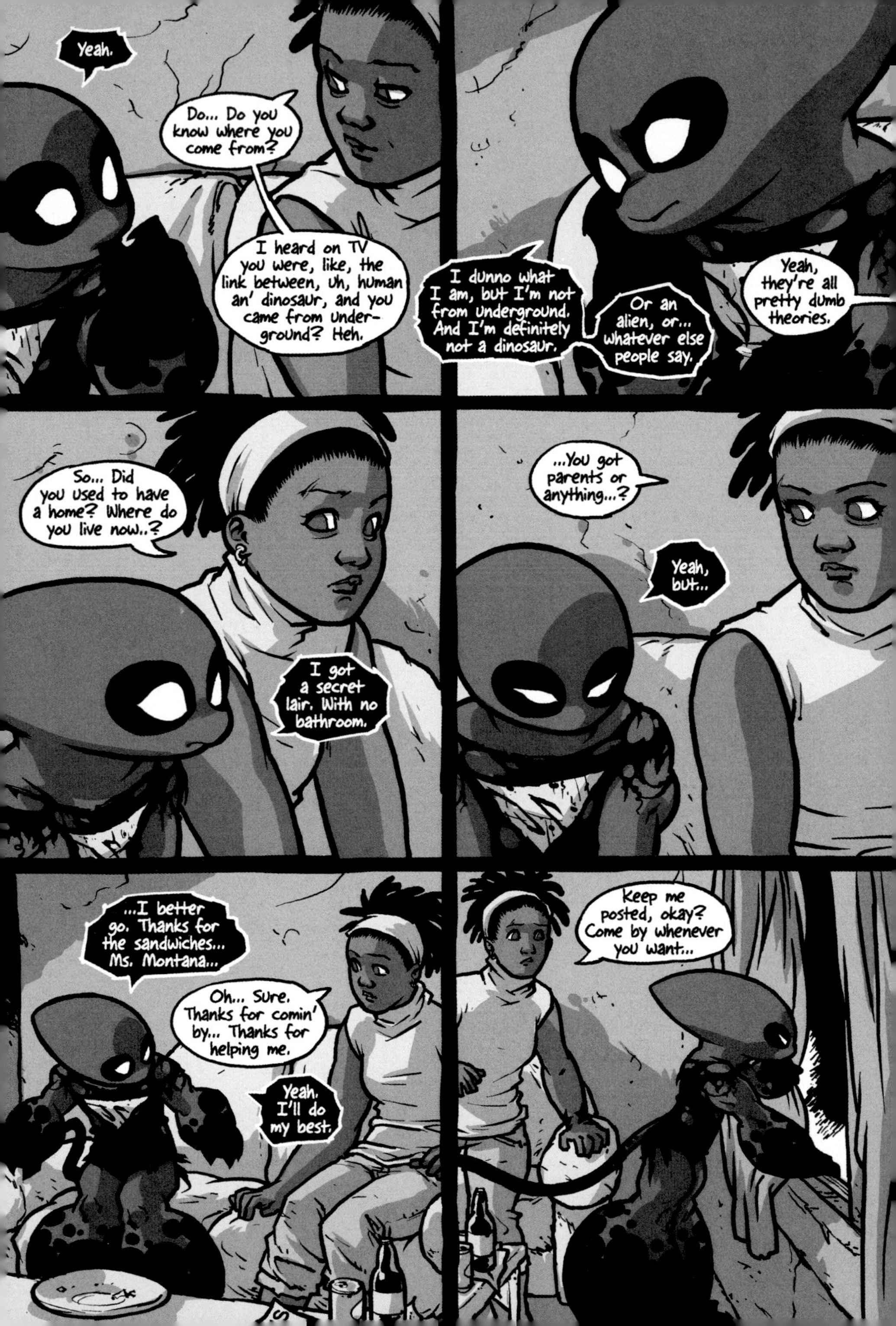

Yeah.
Do... Do you know where you come from?
I heard on TV you were, like, the link between, uh, human an' dinosaur, and you came from under-ground? Heh.
I dunno what I am, but I'm not from underground. And I'm definitely not a dinosaur.
Or an alien, or... whatever else people say.
Yeah, they're all pretty dumb theories.
So... Did you used to have a home? Where do you live now..?
I got a secret lair. With no bathroom.
...You got parents or anything...?
Yeah, but...
...I better go. Thanks for the sandwiches... Ms. Montana...
Oh... Sure. Thanks for comin' by... Thanks for helping me.
Yeah. I'll do my best.
Keep me posted, okay? Come by whenever you want...

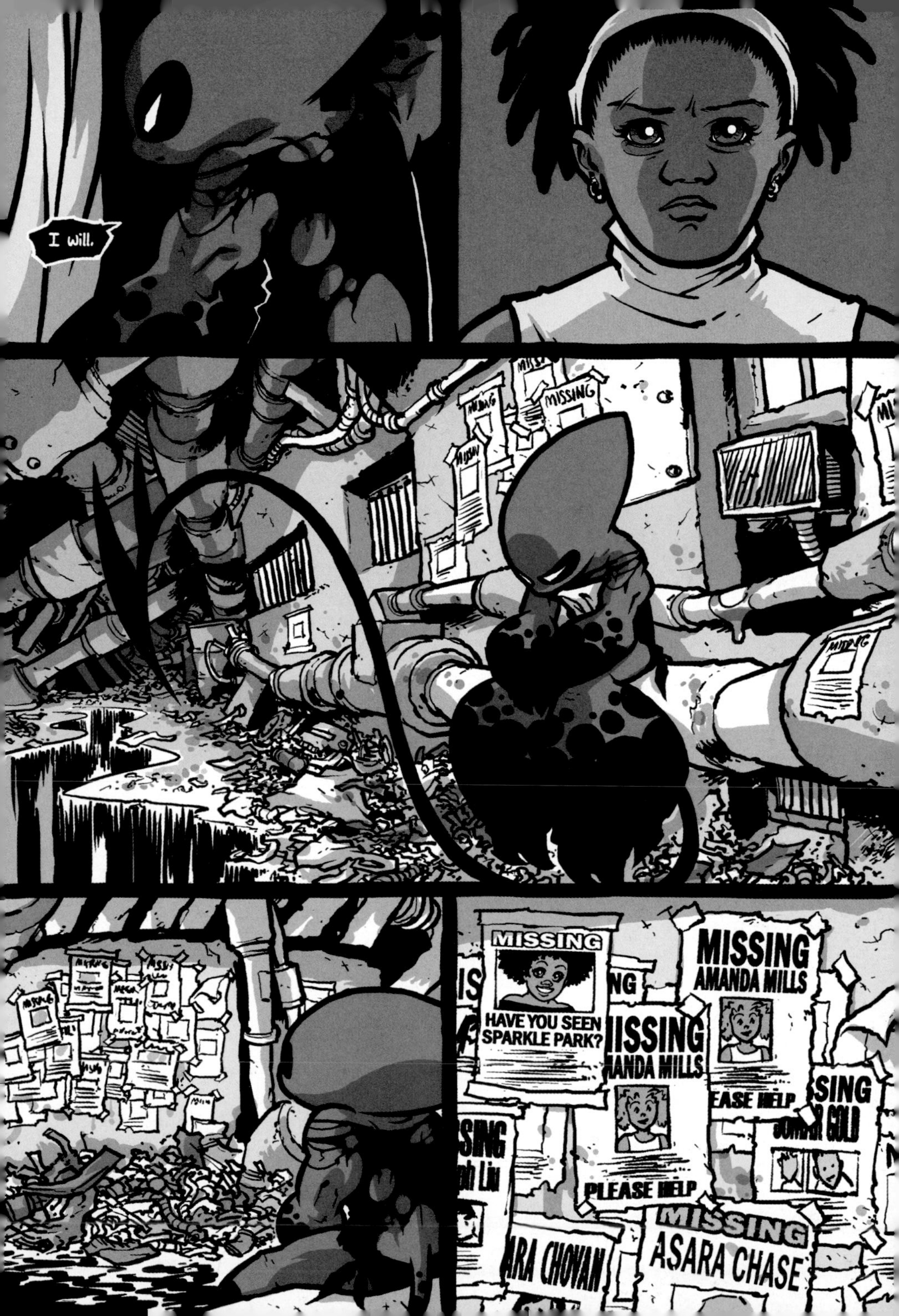

I will.
MISSING
HAVE YOU SEEN SPARKLE PARK?
MISSING
AMANDA MILLS
PLEASE HELP
MISSING
ASARA CHASE

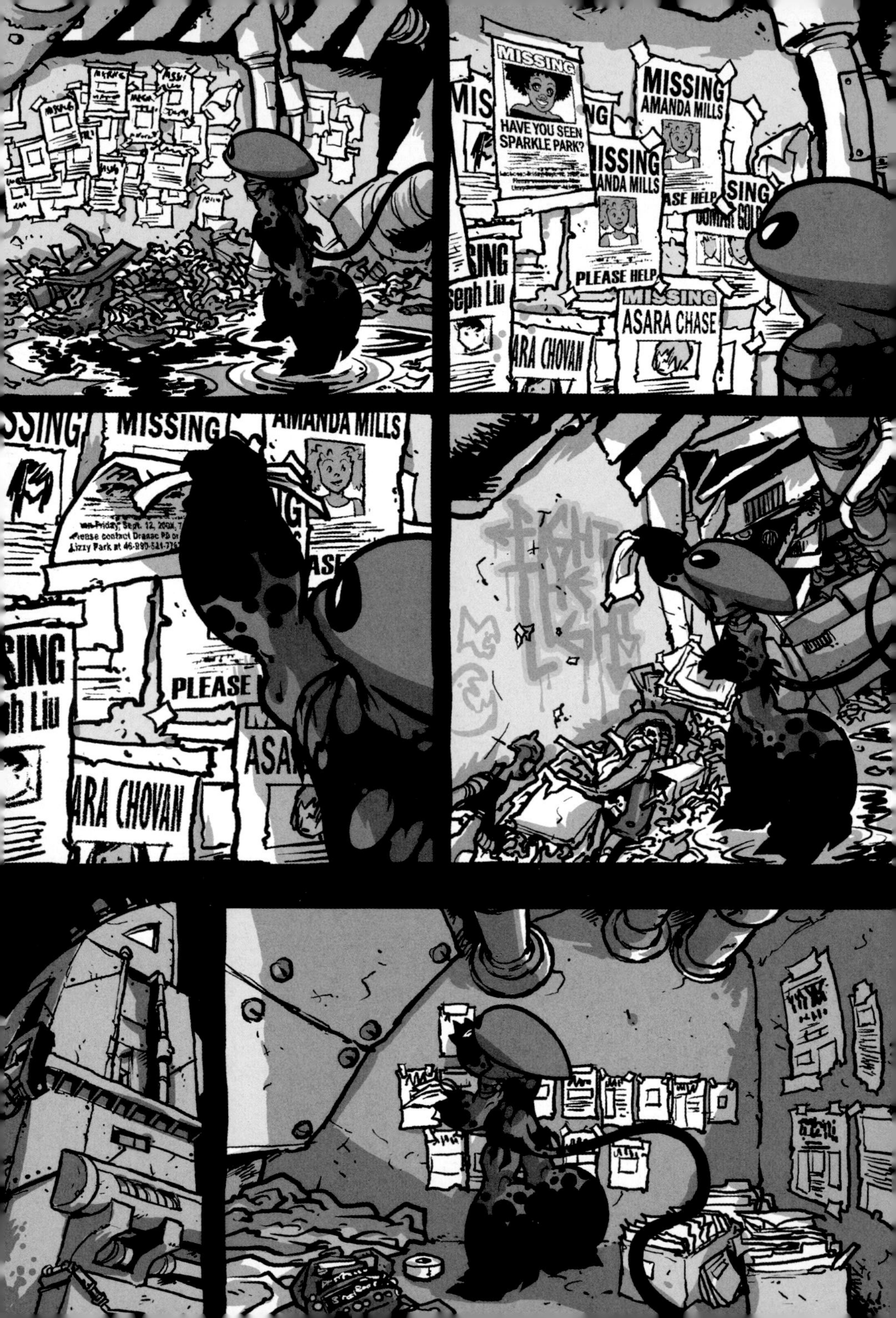
MISSING
HAVE YOU SEEN SPARKLE PARK?
MISSING
AMANDA MILLS
ISSING
ANDA MILLS
PLEASE HELP
ASE HELP
SING
seph Liu
MISSING
ASARA CHASE
ARA CHOVAN
SSING
MISSING
AMANDA MILLS
SING
h Liu
PLEASE
ASA
ARA CHOVAN

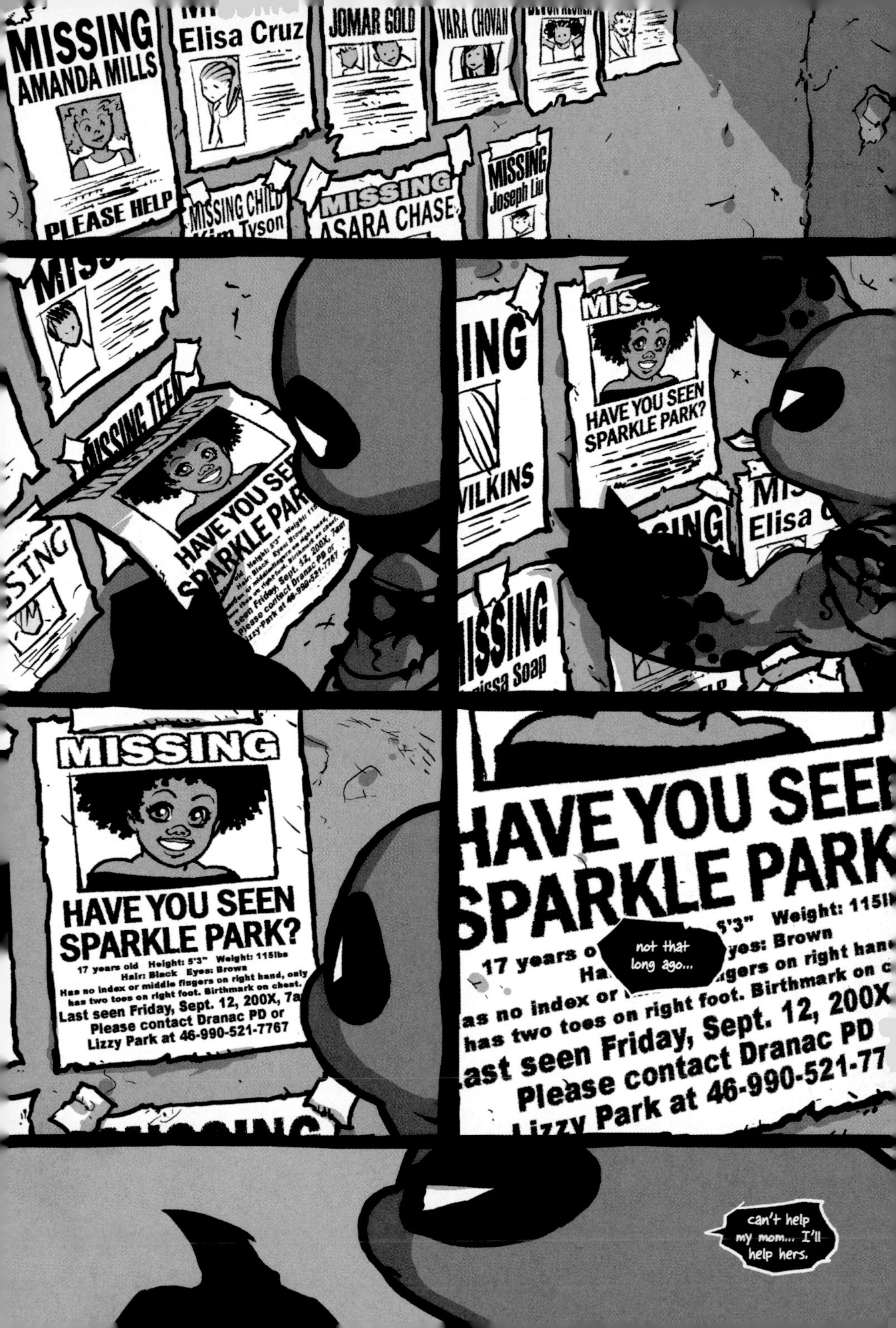
MISSING AMANDA MILLS
PLEASE HELP
Elisa Cruz
JOMAR GOLD
VARA CHOVAN
MISSING CHILD
Kim Tyson
MISSING
ASARA CHASE
MISSING
Joseph Liu
MISSING TEEN
HAVE YOU SEEN SPARKLE PARK?
HAVE YOU SEEN SPARKLE PARK?
WILKINS
Elisa
MISSING
Soap
MISSING
HAVE YOU SEEN SPARKLE PARK?
17 years old Height: 5'3" Weight: 115lbs
Hair: Black Eyes: Brown
Has no index or middle fingers on right hand, only has two toes on right foot. Birthmark on chest.
Last seen Friday, Sept. 12, 200X, 7a
Please contact Dranac PD or
Lizzy Park at 46-990-521-7767
not that long ago...
can't help my mom... I'll help hers.

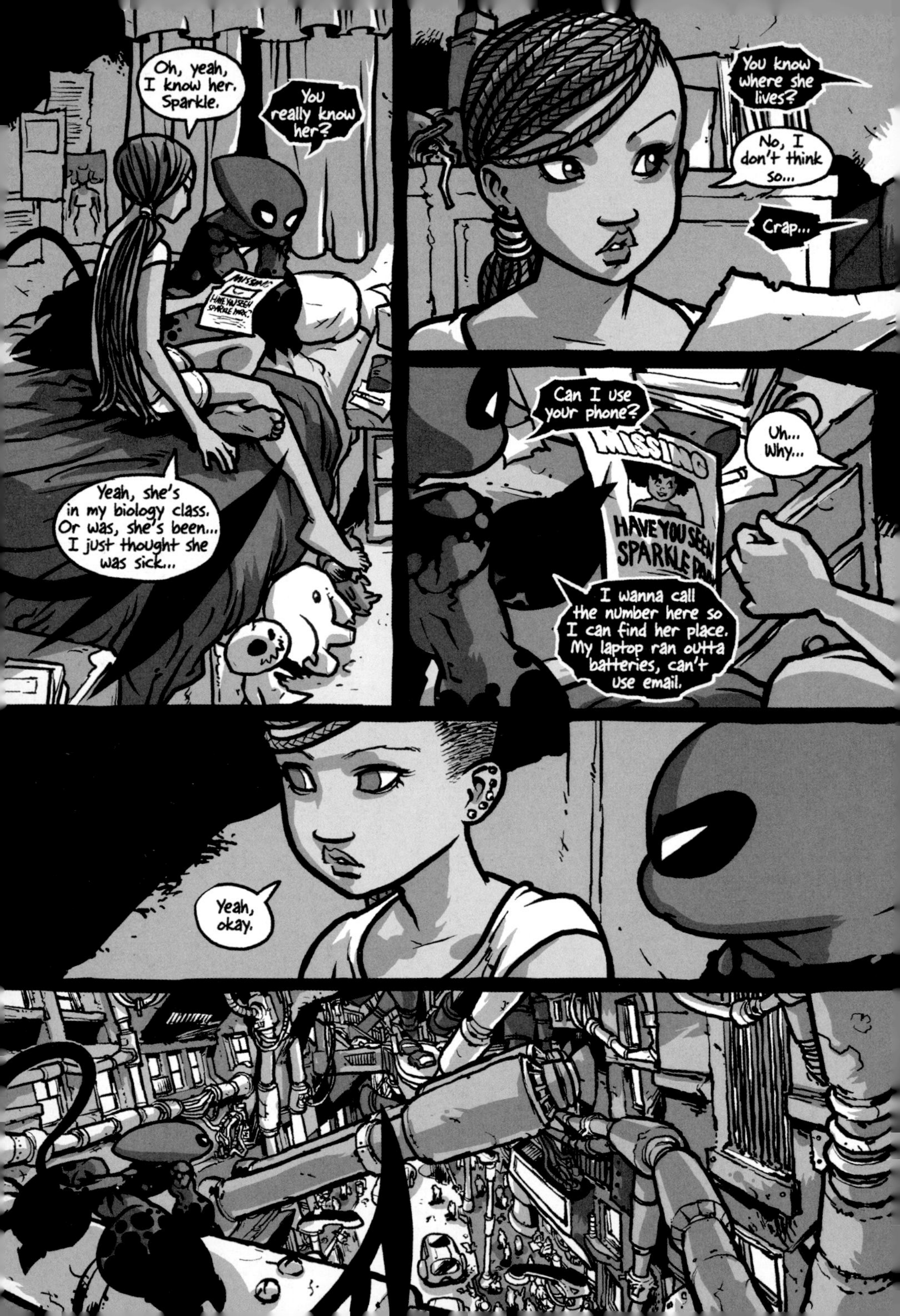

Oh, yeah, I know her. Sparkle.
You really know her?
MISSING
HAVE YOU SEEN SPARKLE PARK?
Yeah, she's in my biology class. Or was, she's been... I just thought she was sick...
You know where she lives?
No, I don't think so...
Crap...
Can I use your phone?
MISSING
HAVE YOU SEEN SPARKLE PA
Uh... Why...
I wanna call the number here so I can find her place. My laptop ran outta batteries, can't use email.
Yeah, okay.

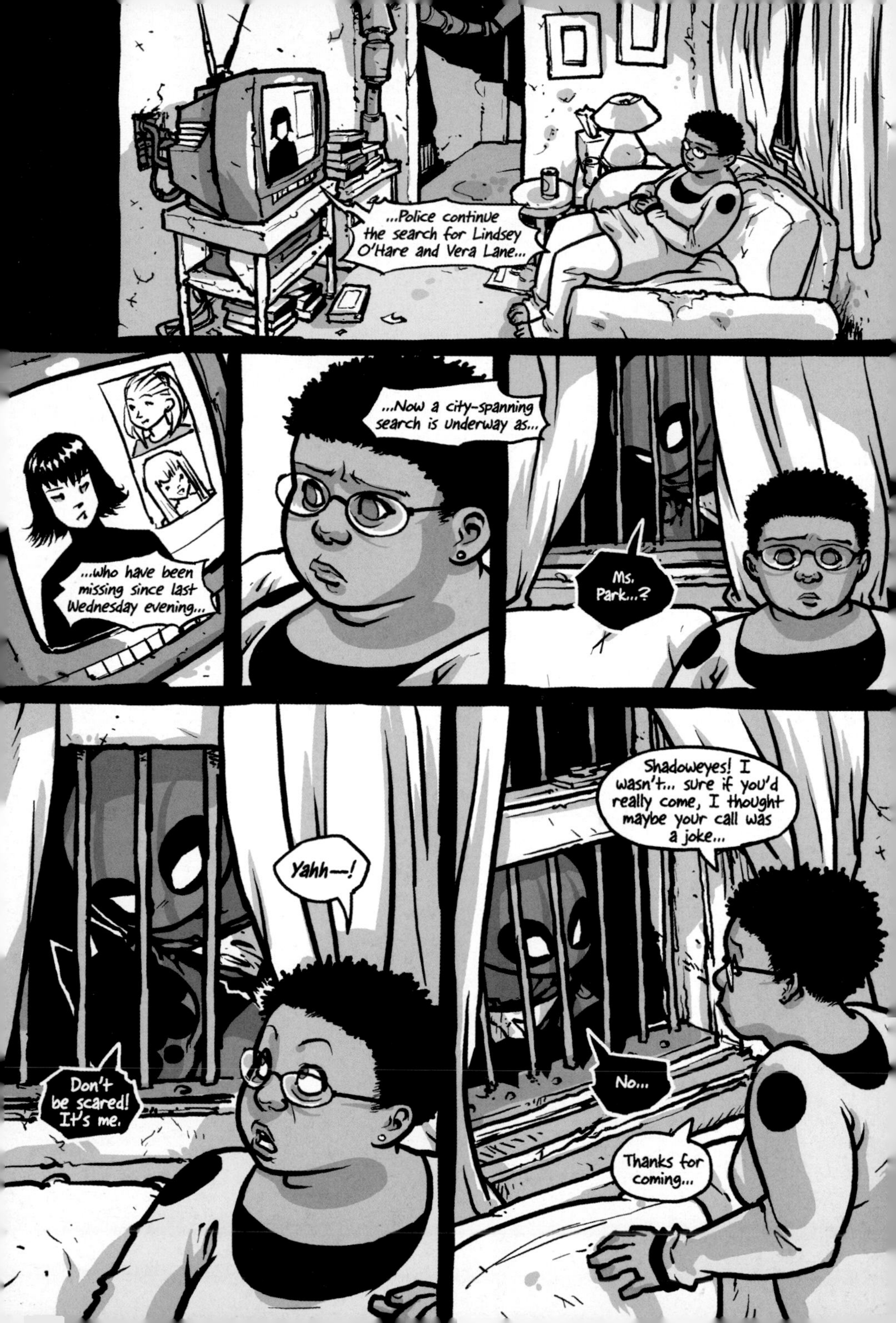
...Police continue the search for Lindsey O'Hare and Vera Lane...
...who have been missing since last Wednesday evening...
...Now a city-spanning search is underway as...
Ms. Park...?
Don't be scared! It's me.
Yahh—!
Shadoweyes! I wasn't... sure if you'd really come, I thought maybe your call was a joke...
No...
Thanks for coming...

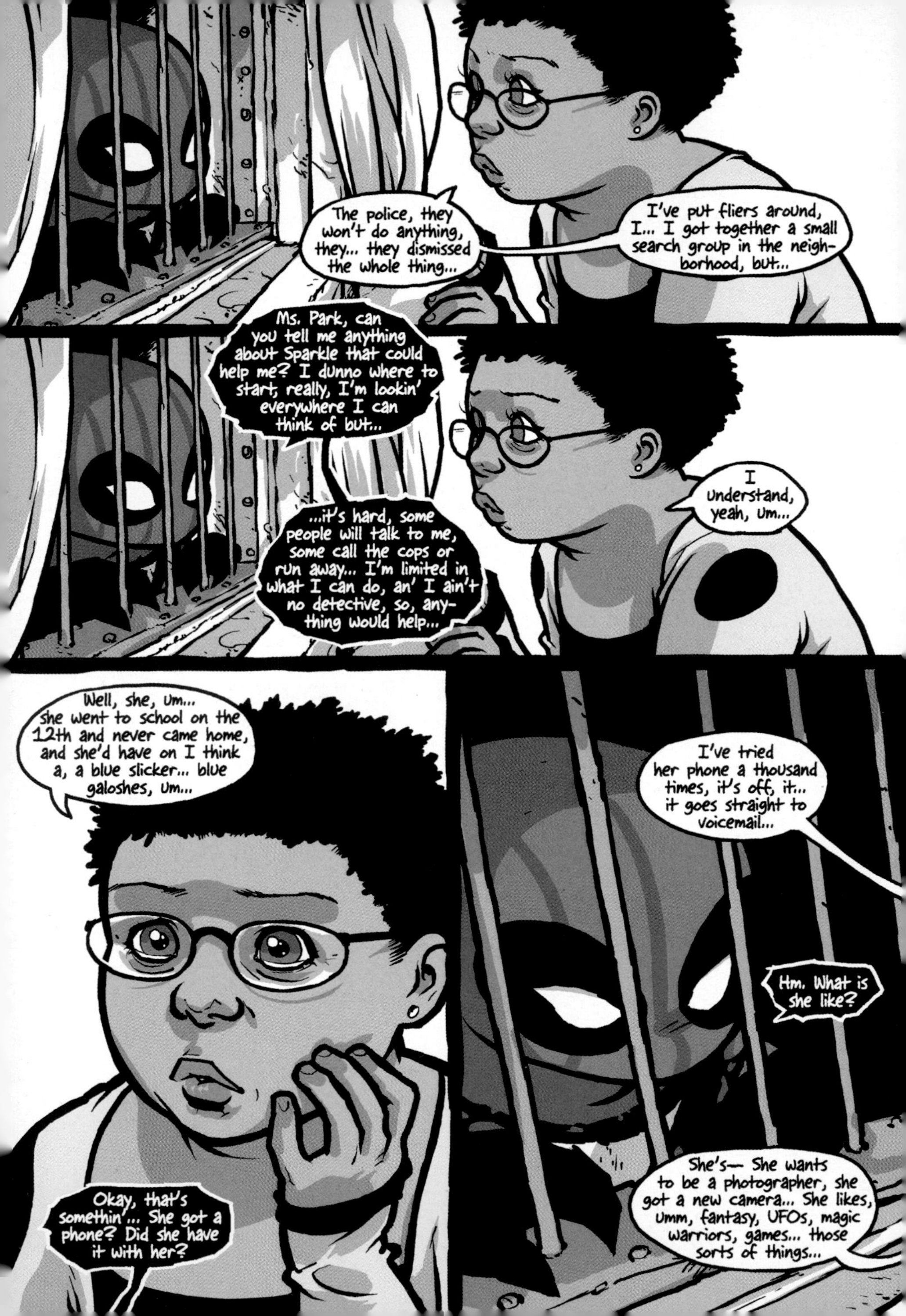
The police, they won't do anything, they... they dismissed the whole thing...
I've put fliers around, I... I got together a small search group in the neighborhood, but...
Ms. Park, can you tell me anything about Sparkle that could help me? I dunno where to start, really, I'm lookin' everywhere I can think of but...
...it's hard, some people will talk to me, some call the cops or run away... I'm limited in what I can do, an' I ain't no detective, so, anything would help...
I understand, yeah, um...
Well, she, um... she went to school on the 12th and never came home, and she'd have on I think a, a blue slicker... blue galoshes, um...
Okay, that's somethin'... She got a phone? Did she have it with her?
I've tried her phone a thousand times, it's off, it... it goes straight to voicemail...
Hm. What is she like?
She's— She wants to be a photographer, she got a new camera... She likes, umm, fantasy, UFOs, magic warriors, games... those sorts of things...

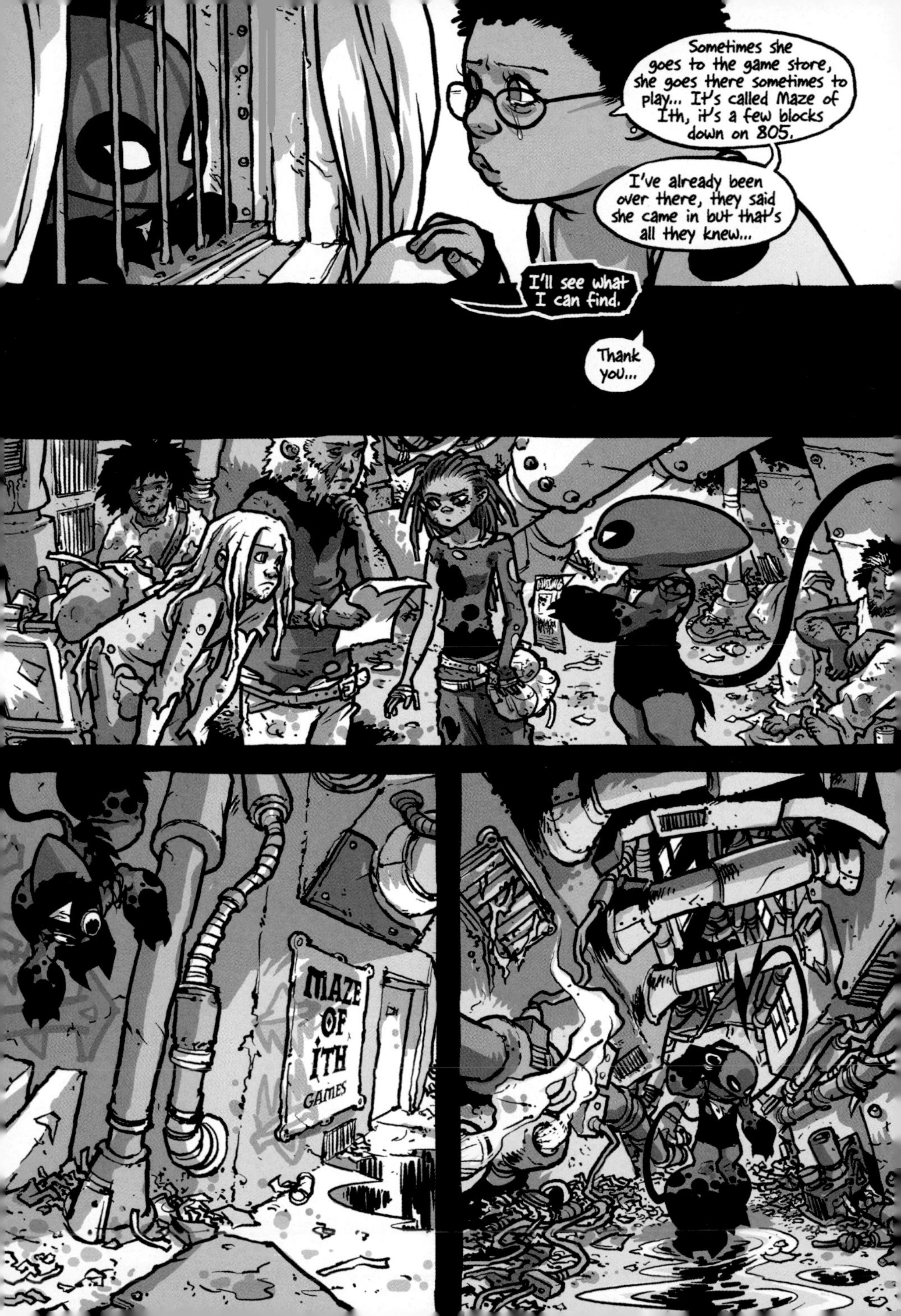
Sometimes she goes to the game store, she goes there sometimes to play... It's called Maze of Ith, it's a few blocks down on 805.
I've already been over there, they said she came in but that's all they knew...
I'll see what I can find.
Thank you...
MAZE OF ITH GAMES

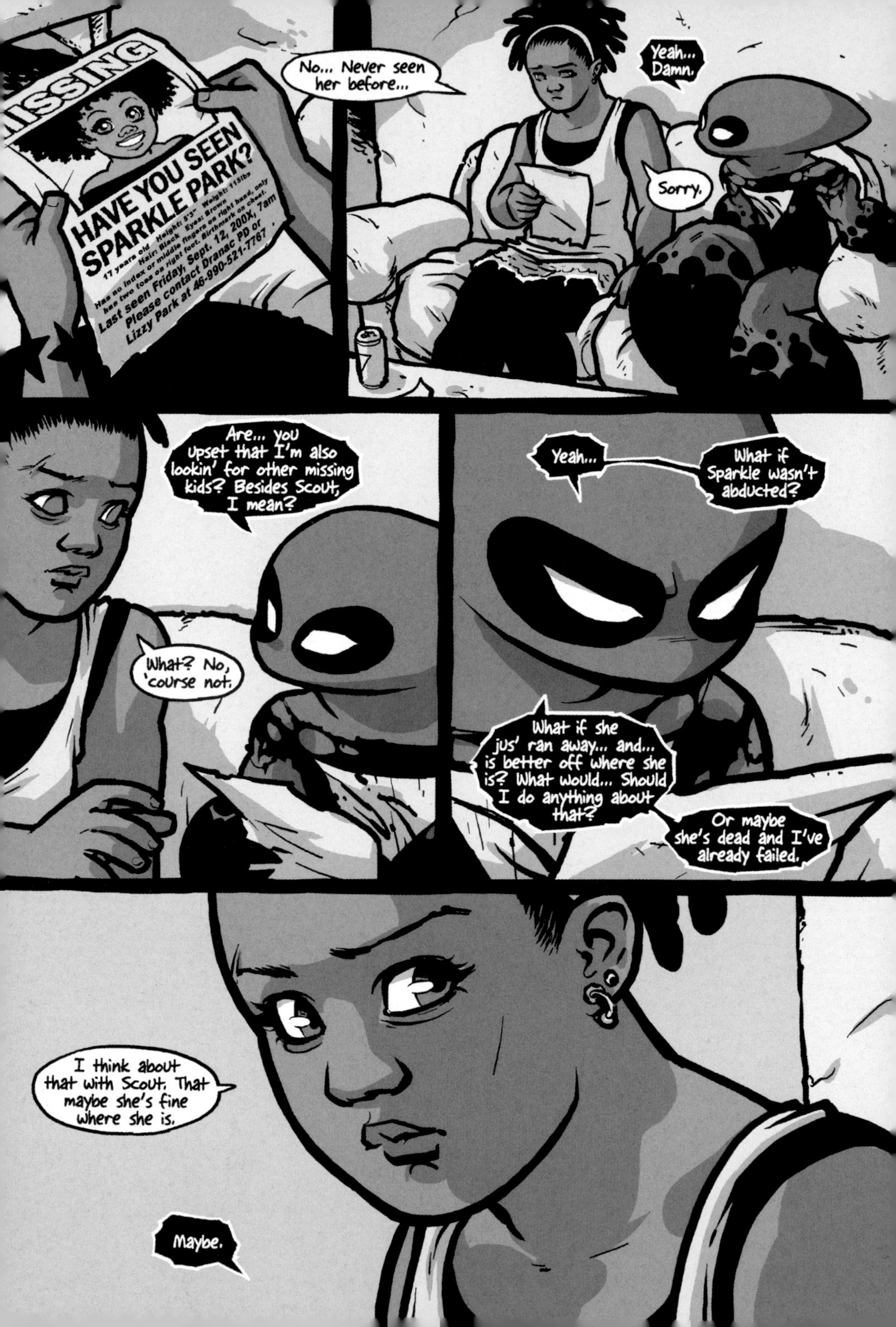
MISSING
HAVE YOU SEEN SPARKLE PARK?
17 years old Height: 5'3" Weight: 115lbs
Hair: Black Eyes: Brown
Has no index or middle fingers on right hand, only has two toes on right foot. Birthmark on chest.
Last seen Friday, Sept. 12, 200X, 7am
Please contact Dranac PD or Lizzy Park at 46-990-521-7767
No... Never seen her before...
Yeah... Damn.
Sorry.
Are... you upset that I'm also lookin' for other missing kids? Besides Scout, I mean?
What? No, 'course not.
Yeah...
What if Sparkle wasn't abducted?
What if she jus' ran away... and... is better off where she is? What would... Should I do anything about that?
Or maybe she's dead and I've already failed.
I think about that with Scout. That maybe she's fine where she is.
Maybe.

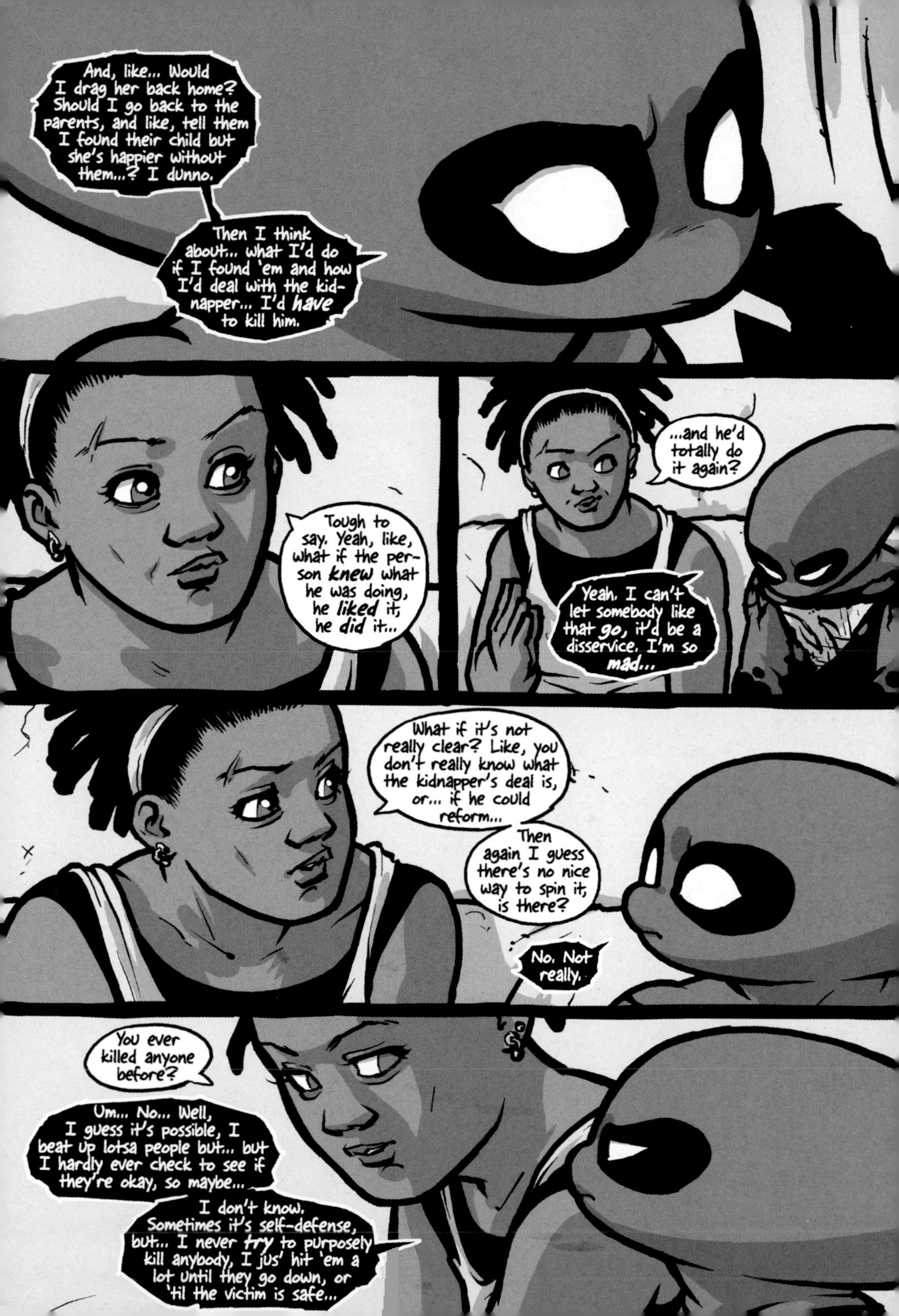
And, like... Would I drag her back home? Should I go back to the parents, and like, tell them I found their child but she's happier without them...? I dunno.
Then I think about... what I'd do if I found 'em and how I'd deal with the kid-napper... I'd *have* to kill him.
Tough to say. Yeah, like, what if the per-son *knew* what he was doing, he *liked* it, he *did* it...
...and he'd totally do it again?
Yeah. I can't let somebody like that *go*, it'd be a disservice. I'm so *mad*...
What if it's not really clear? Like, you don't really know what the kidnapper's deal is, or... if he could reform...
Then again I guess there's no nice way to spin it, is there?
No. Not really.
You ever killed anyone before?
Um... No... Well, I guess it's possible, I beat up lotsa people but... but I hardly ever check to see if they're okay, so maybe...
I don't know. Sometimes it's self-defense, but... I never *try* to purposely kill anybody, I jus' hit 'em a lot until they go down, or 'til the victim is safe...

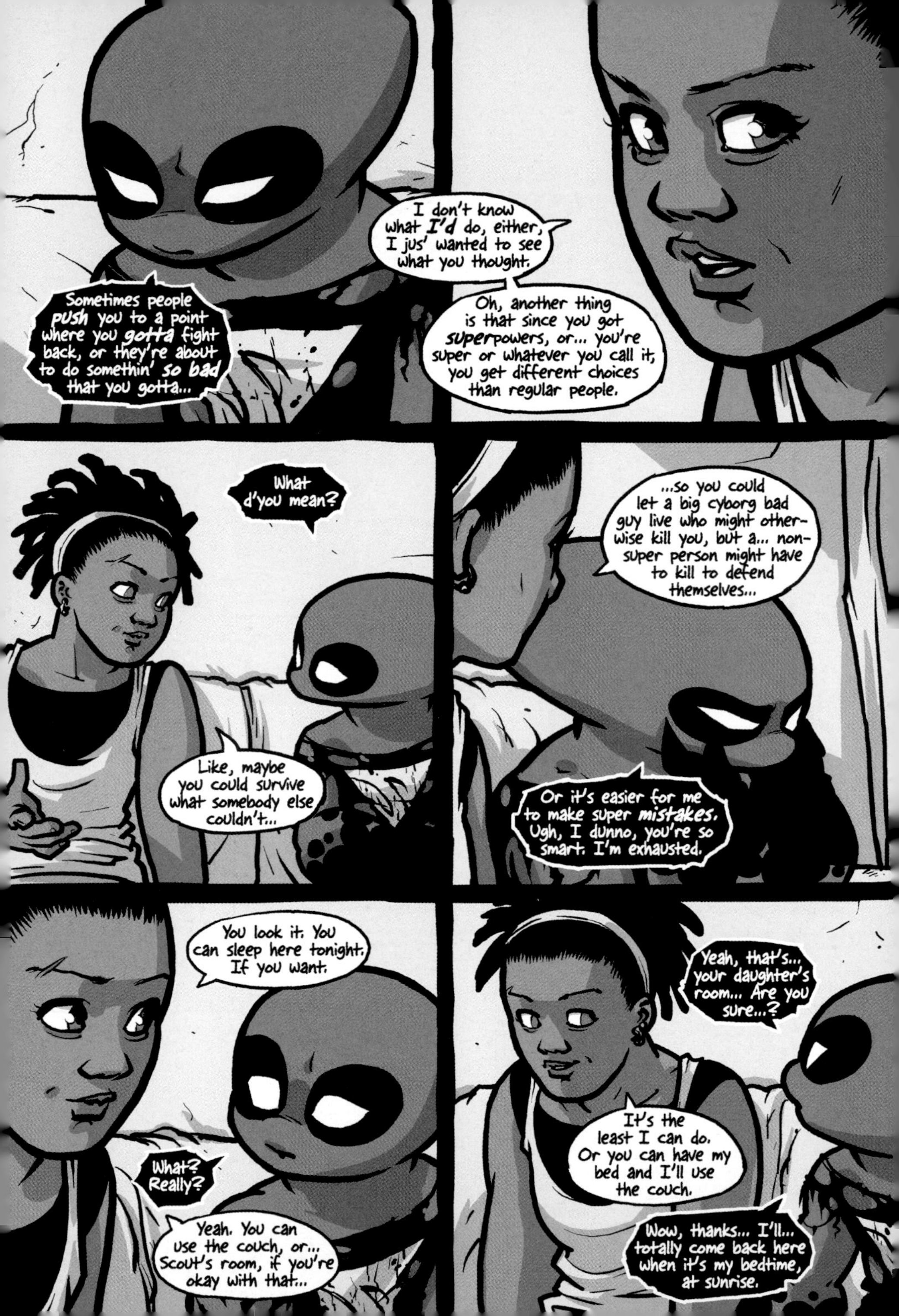
Sometimes people push you to a point where you gotta fight back, or they're about to do somethin' so bad that you gotta...
I don't know what I'd do, either, I jus' wanted to see what you thought.
Oh, another thing is that since you got superpowers, or... you're super or whatever you call it, you get different choices than regular people.
What d'you mean?
Like, maybe you could survive what somebody else couldn't...
...so you could let a big cyborg bad guy live who might other-wise kill you, but a... non-super person might have to kill to defend themselves...
Or it's easier for me to make super mistakes. Ugh, I dunno, you're so smart. I'm exhausted.
You look it. You can sleep here tonight. If you want.
What? Really?
Yeah. You can use the couch, or... Scout's room, if you're okay with that...
Yeah, that's... your daughter's room... Are you sure...?
It's the least I can do. Or you can have my bed and I'll use the couch.
Wow, thanks... I'll... totally come back here when it's my bedtime, at sunrise.

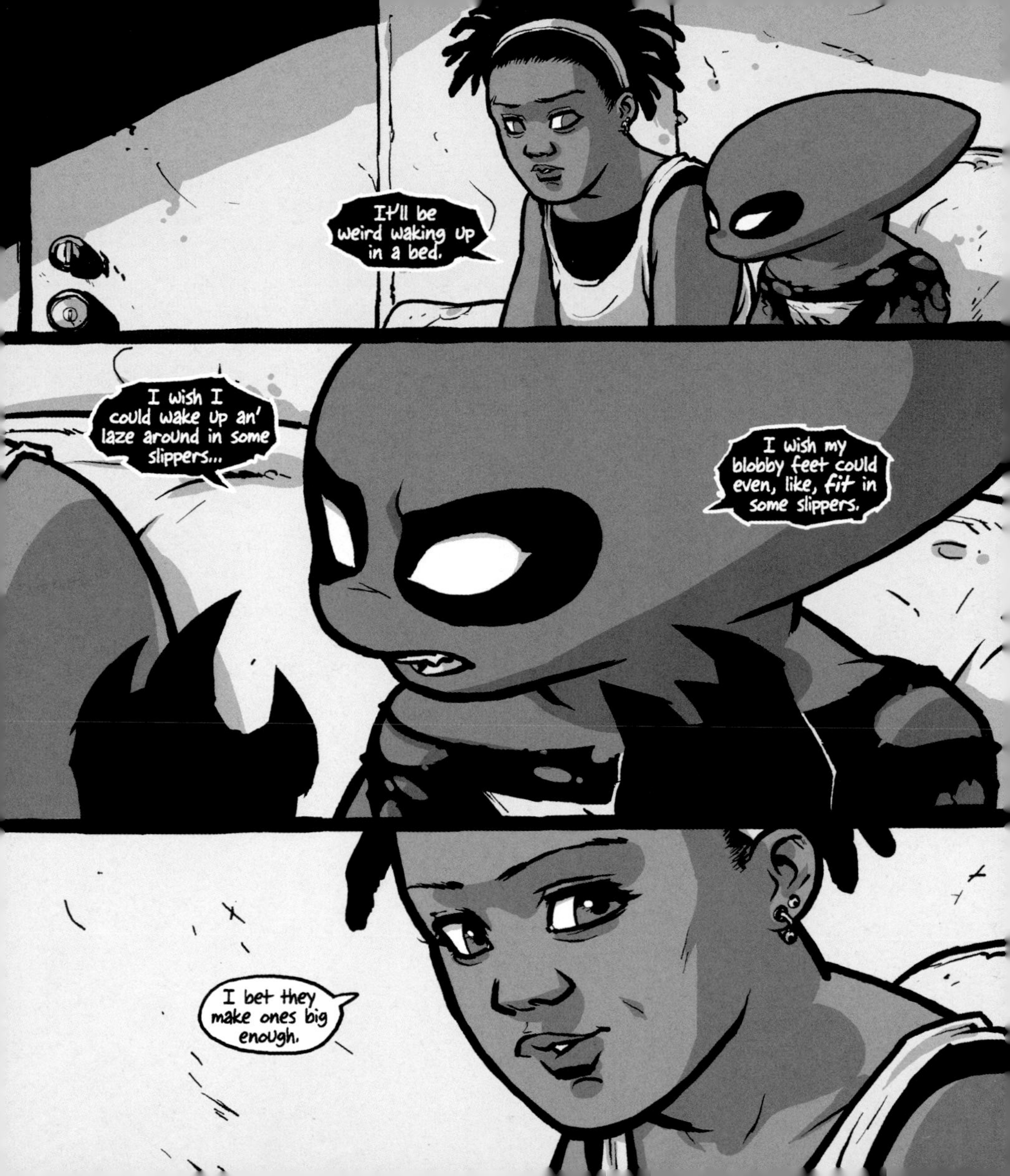
It'll be weird waking up in a bed.
I wish I could wake up an' laze around in some slippers...
I wish my blobby feet could even, like, fit in some slippers.
I bet they make ones big enough.

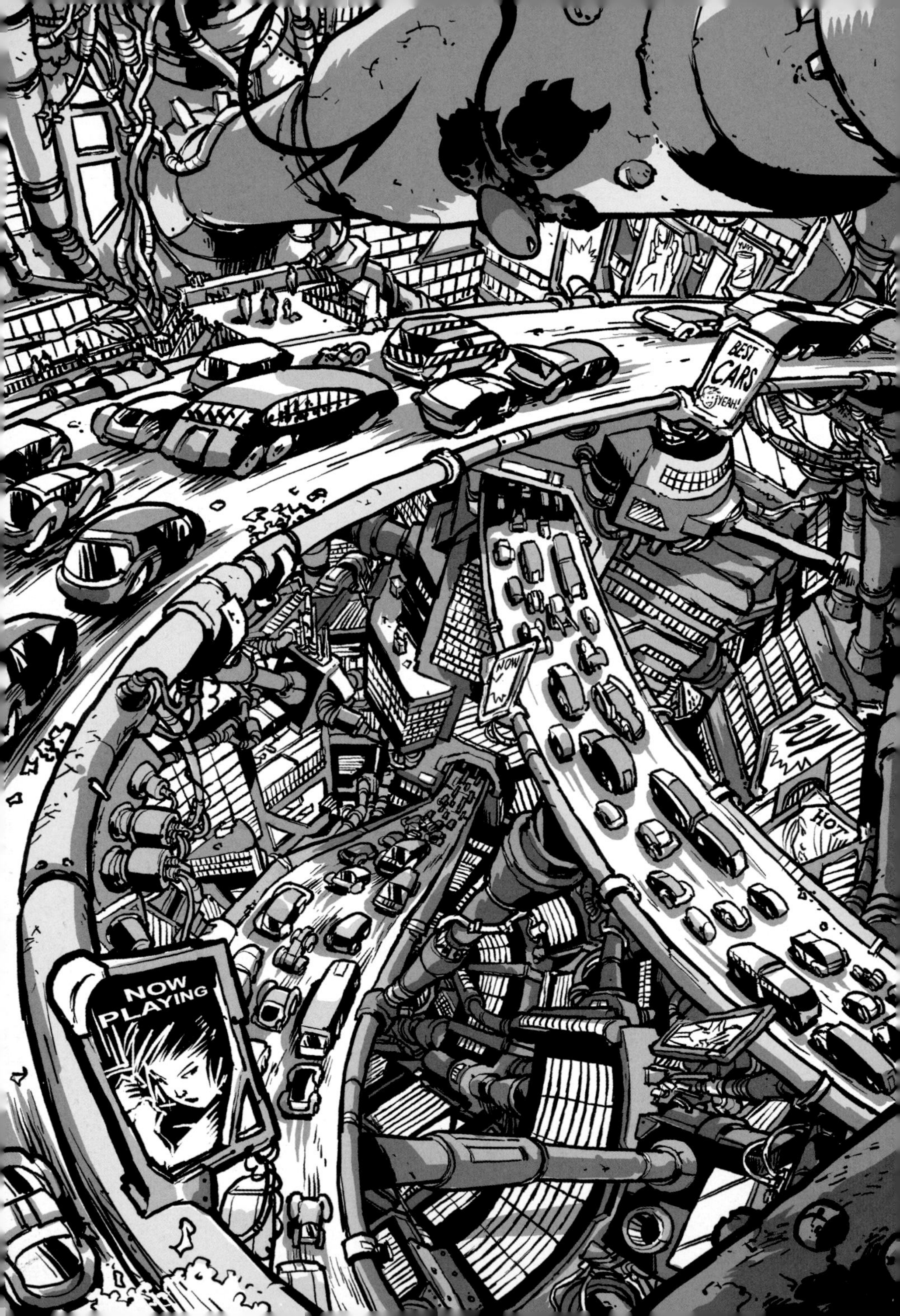
BEST
CARS
YEAH!
NOW
HOT
NOW
PLAYING

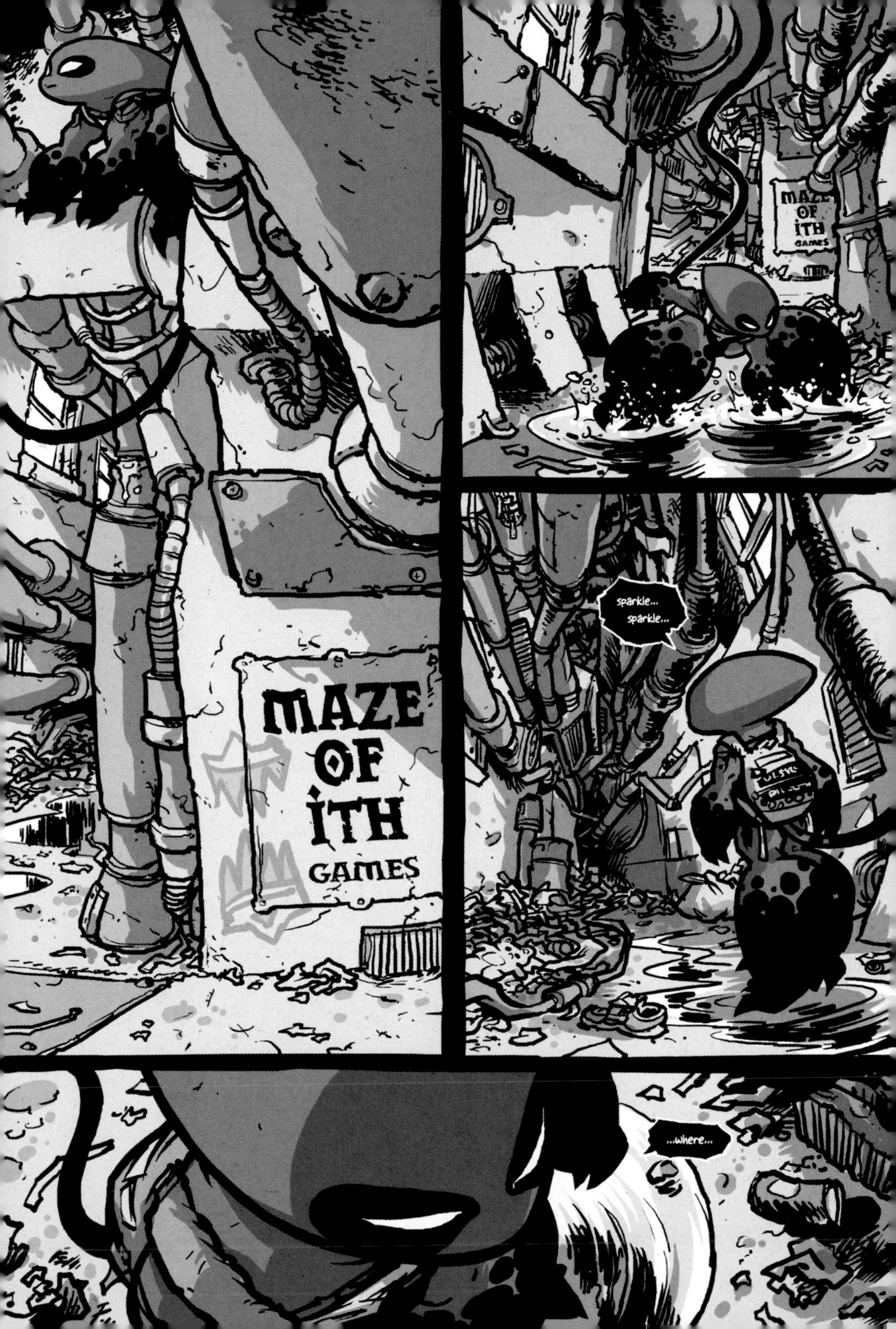
MAZE OF ITH GAMES
MAZE OF ITH GAMES
sparkle... sparkle...
...where...

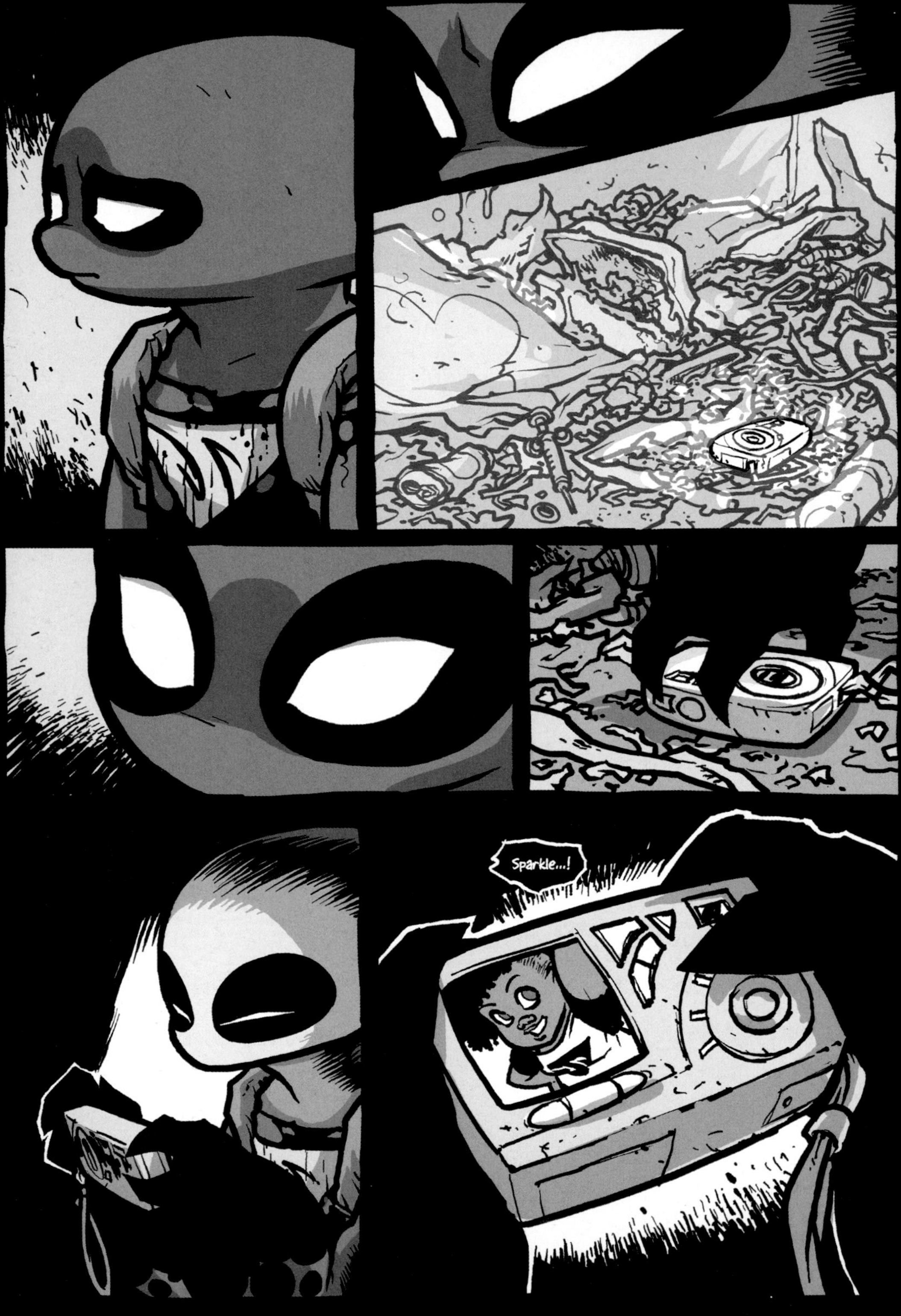
Sparkle...!

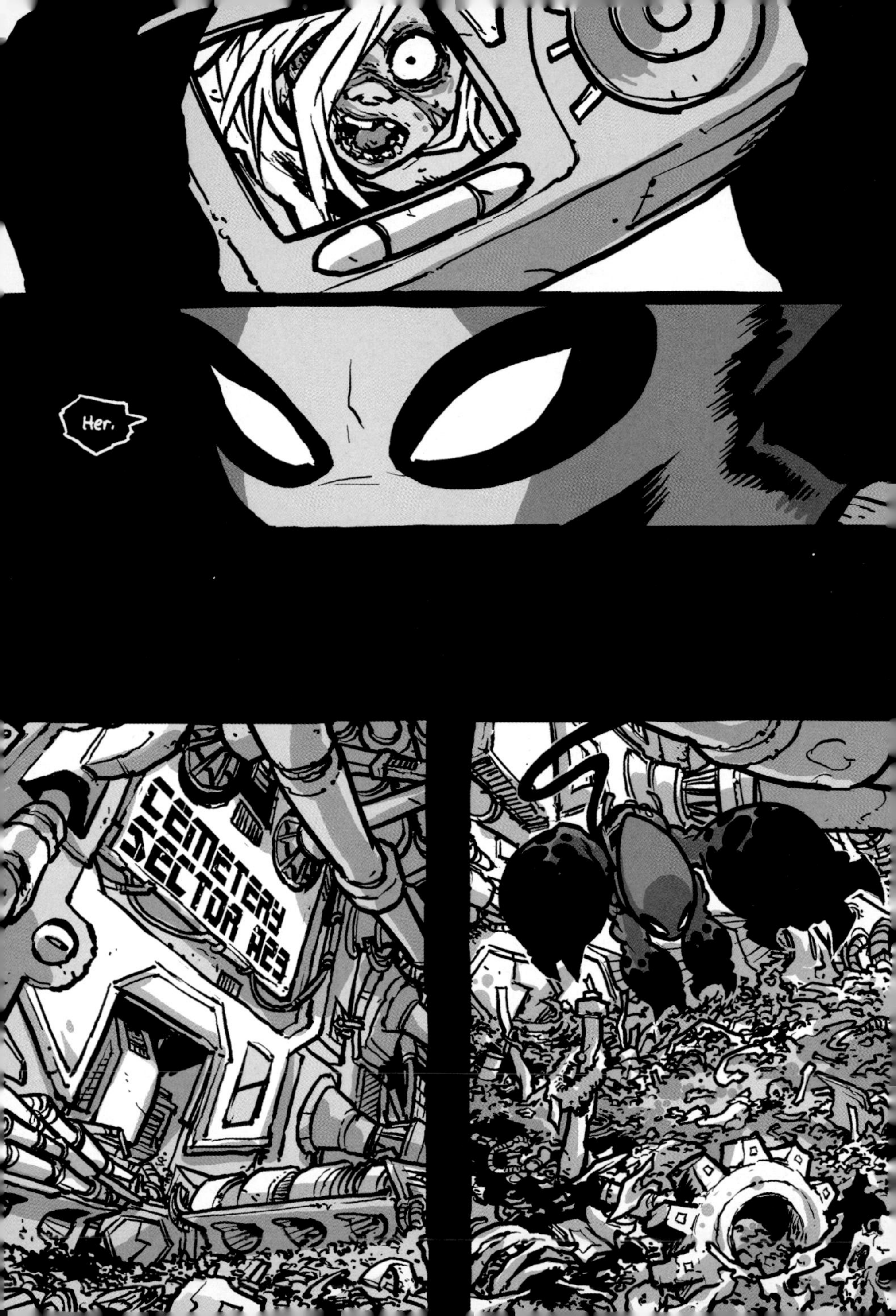
Her.
CEMETERY SECTOR A23

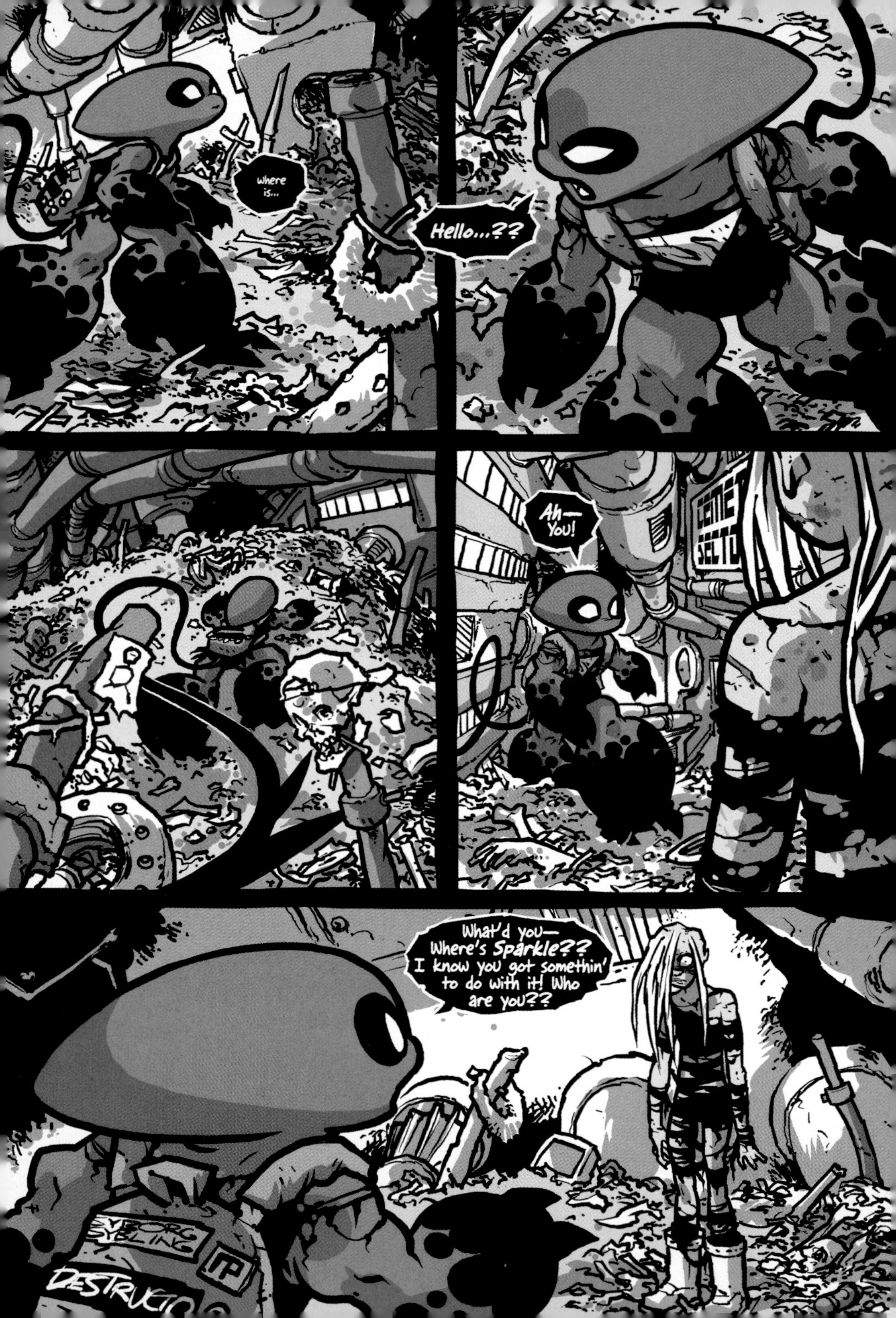
where is...
Hello...??
Ah— You!
What'd you— Where's Sparkle?? I know you got somethin' to do with it! Who are you??
CYBORG SYBLING

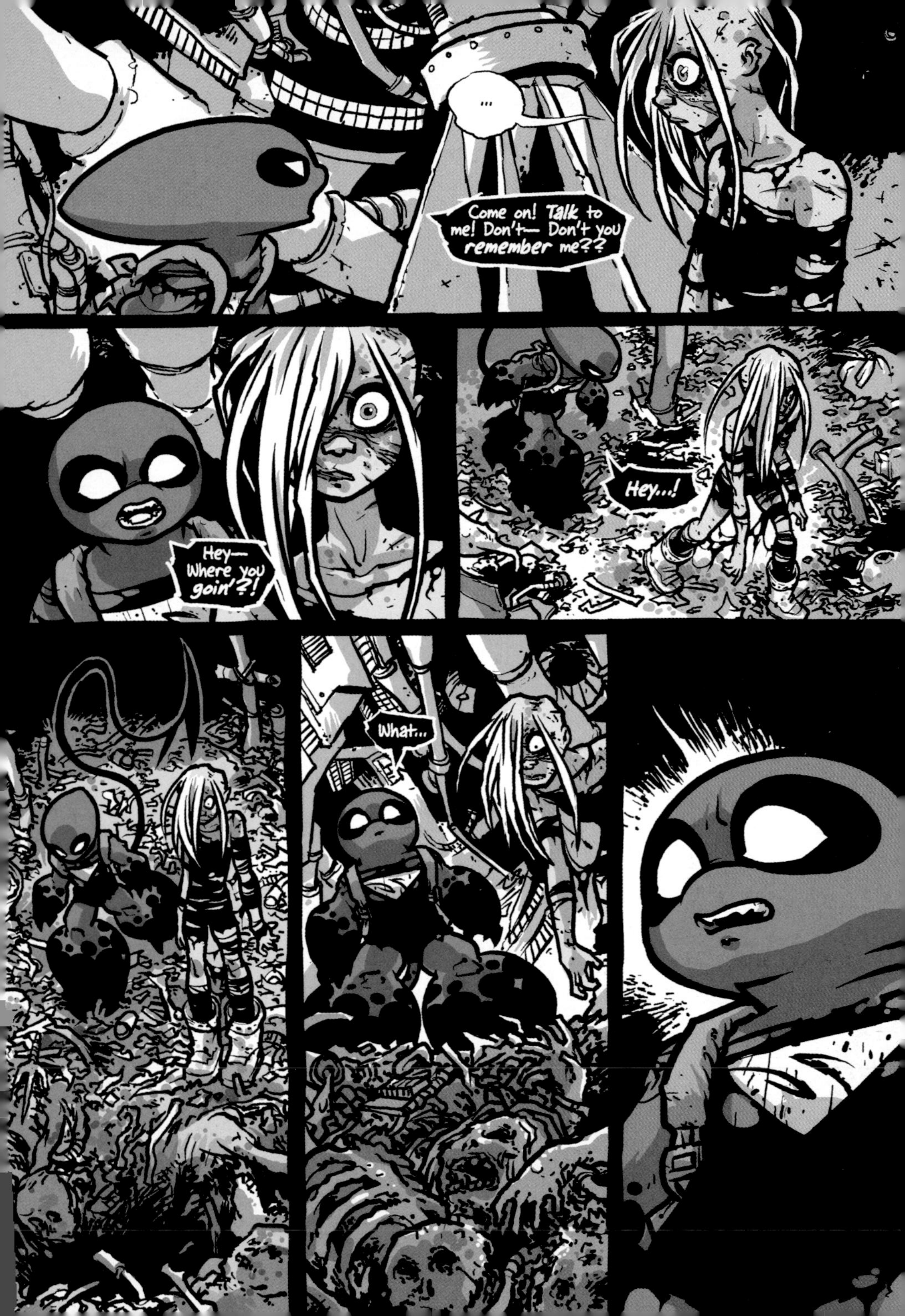
...
Come on! Talk to me! Don't— Don't you remember me??
Hey— Where you goin'?!
Hey...!
What...

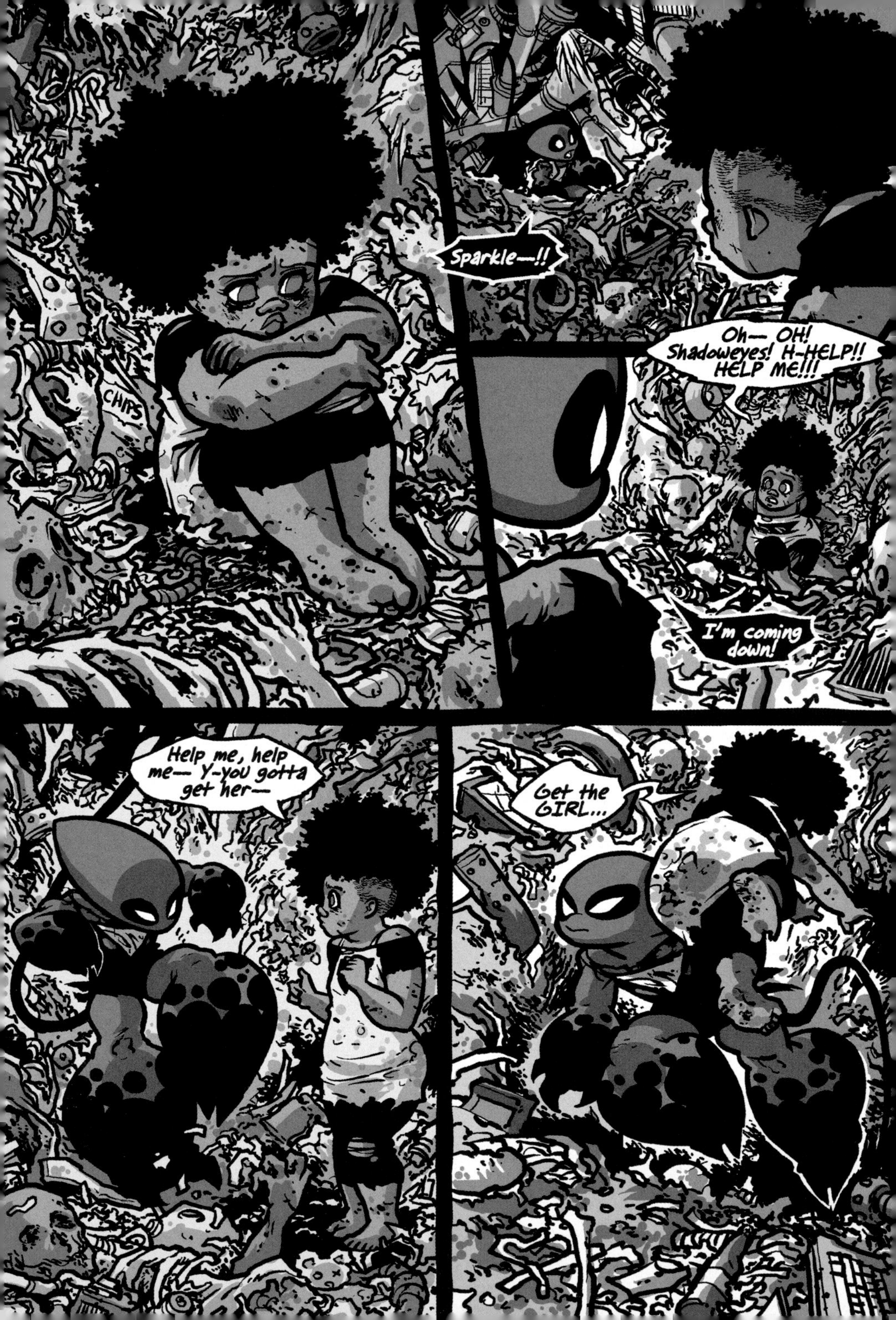
CHIPS
Sparkle—!!
Oh— OH! Shadoweyes! H-HELP!! HELP ME!!!
I'm coming down!
Help me, help me— Y-you gotta get her—
Get the GIRL...

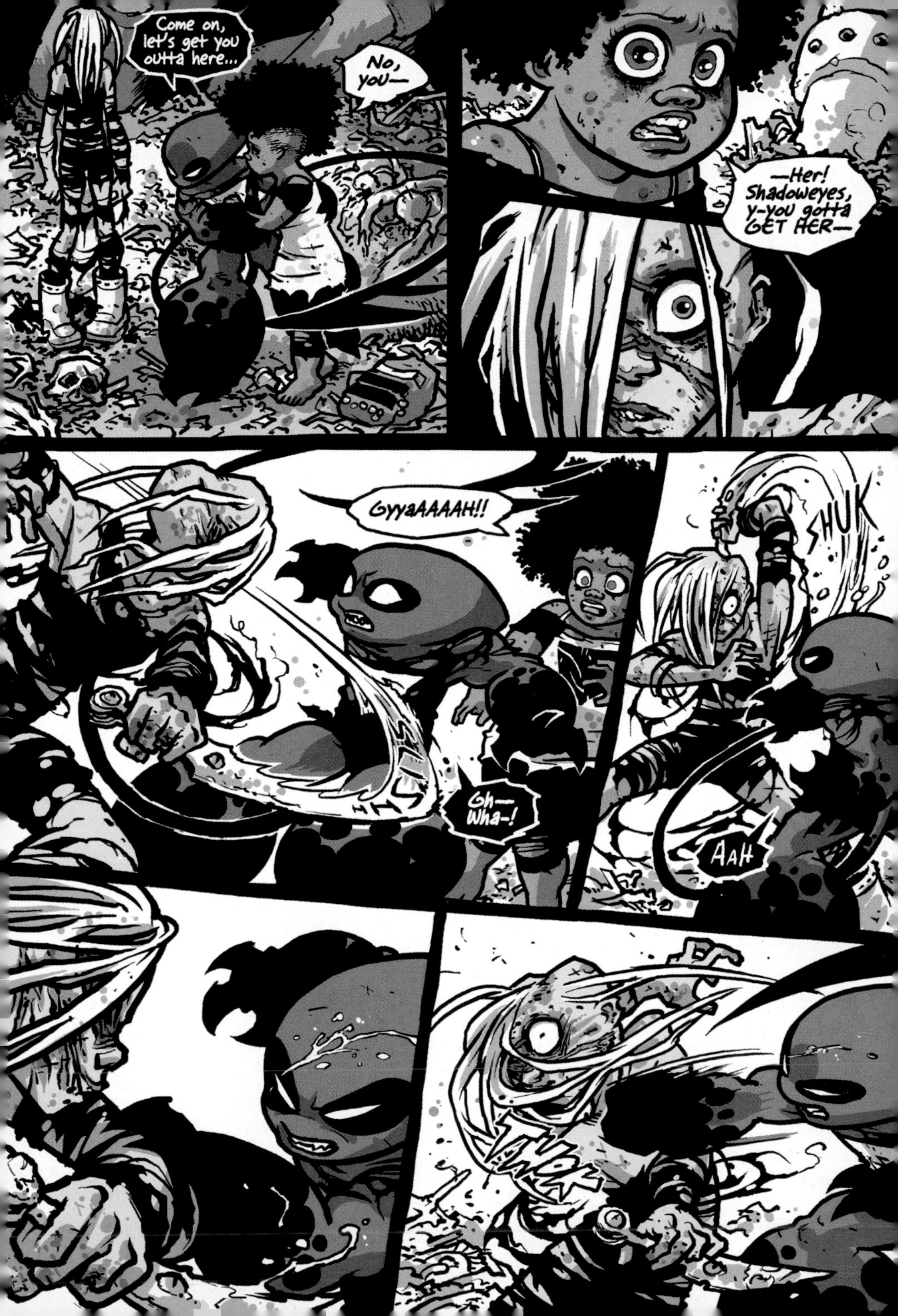

Come on, let's get you outta here...
No, you—
—Her! Shadoweyes, y-you gotta GET HER—
GyyaAAAAH!!
Gh— Wha-!
SHUK
AAH

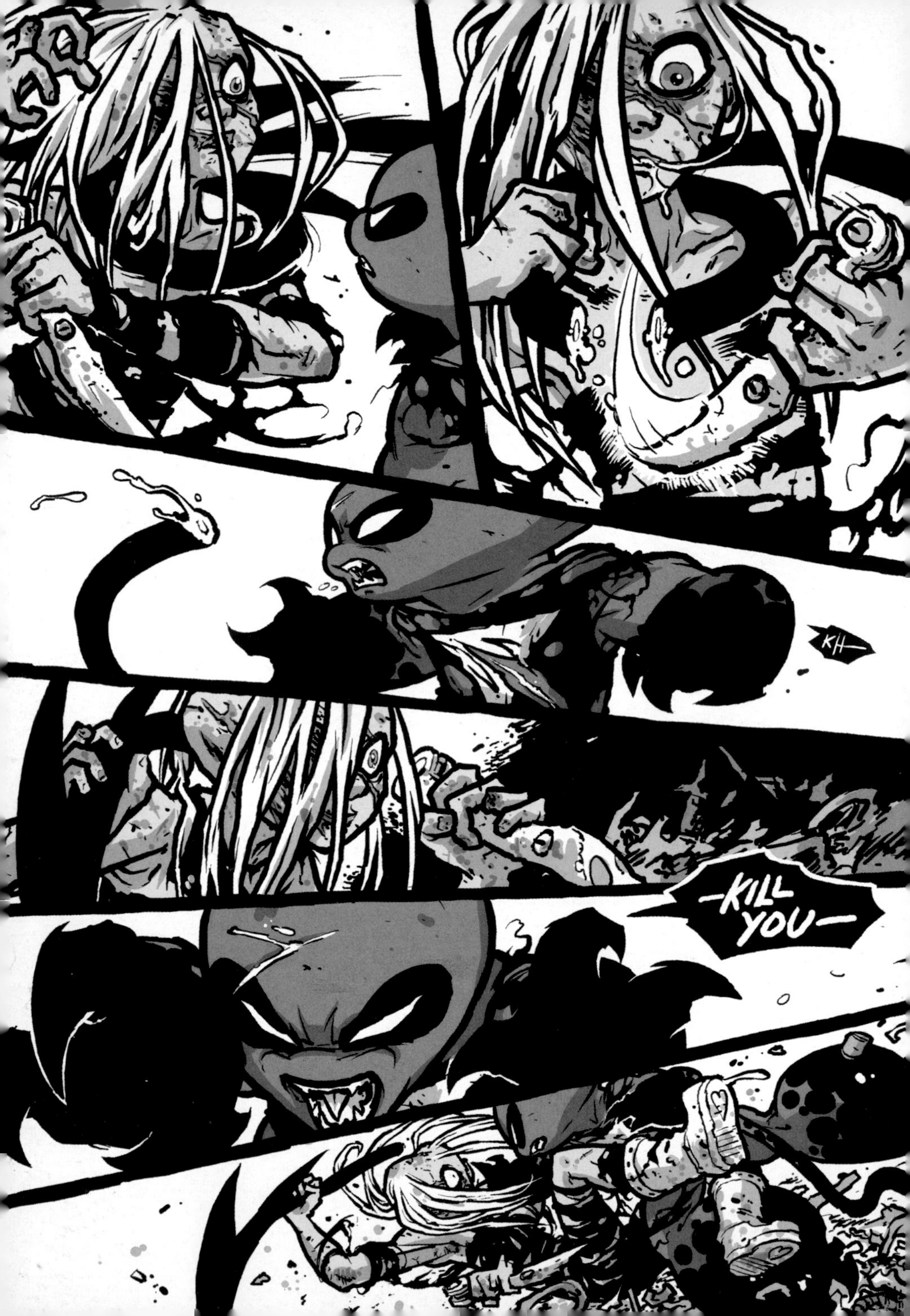
-KILL YOU-

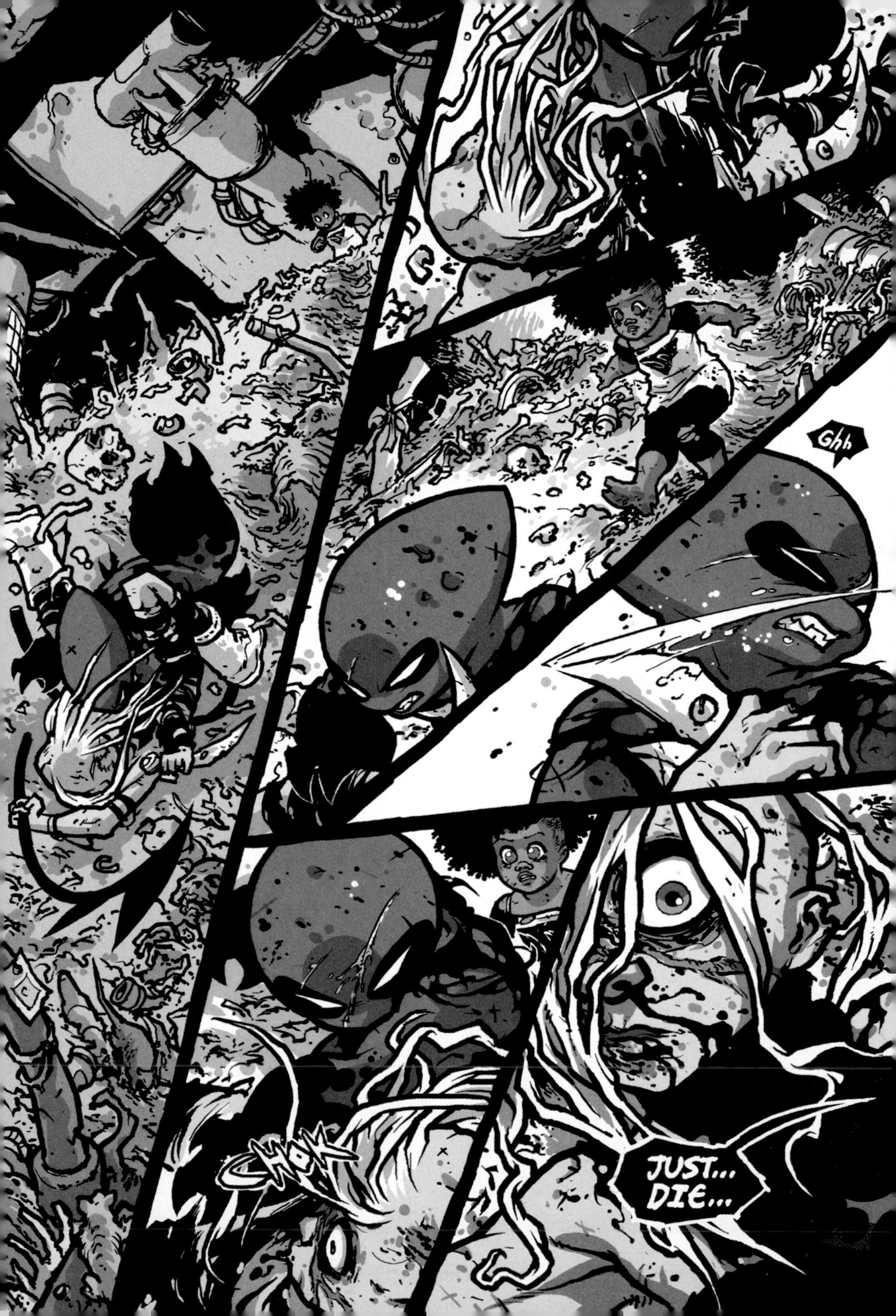
Ghh
CHOK
JUST... DIE...

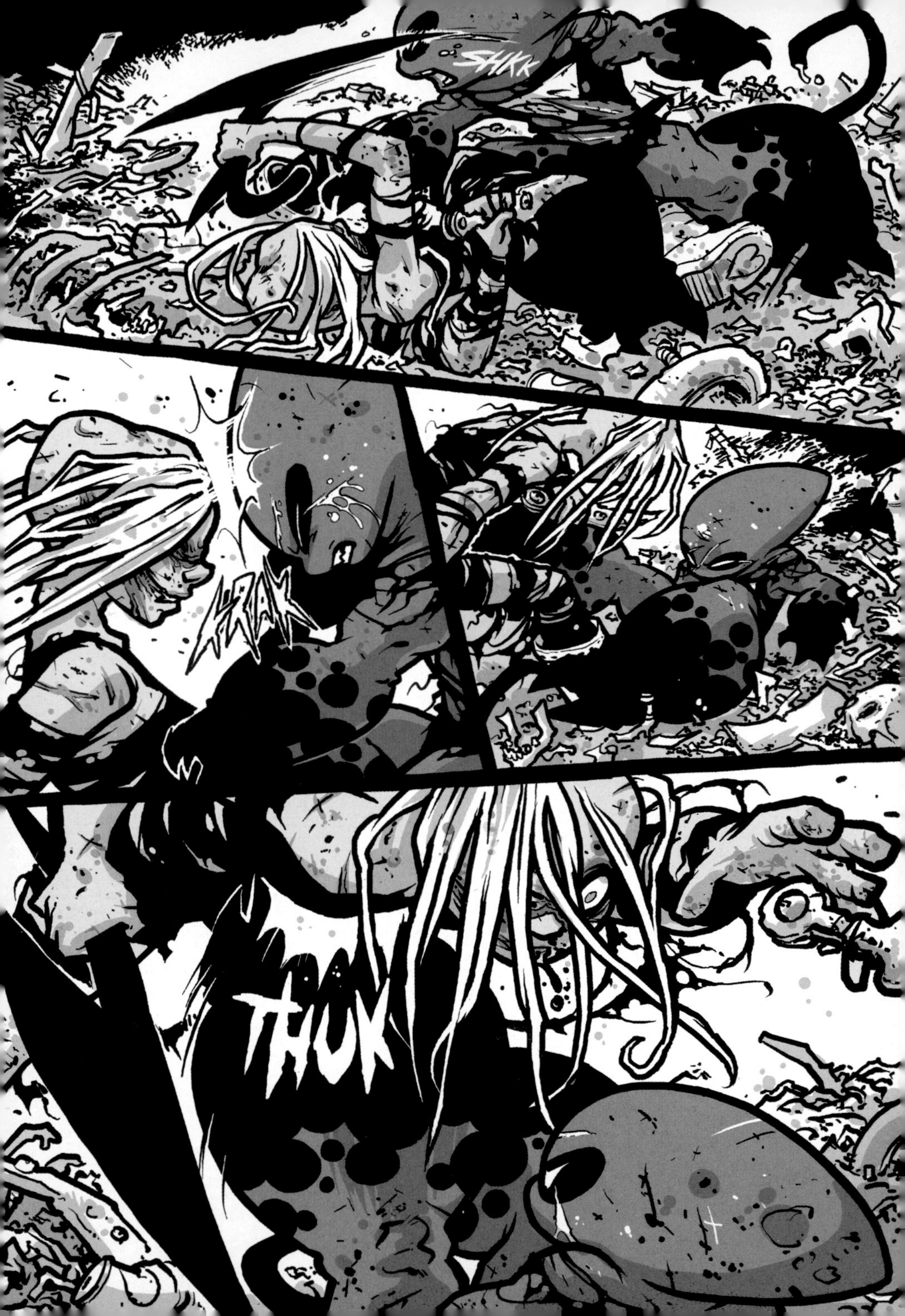
SHKK
THUK

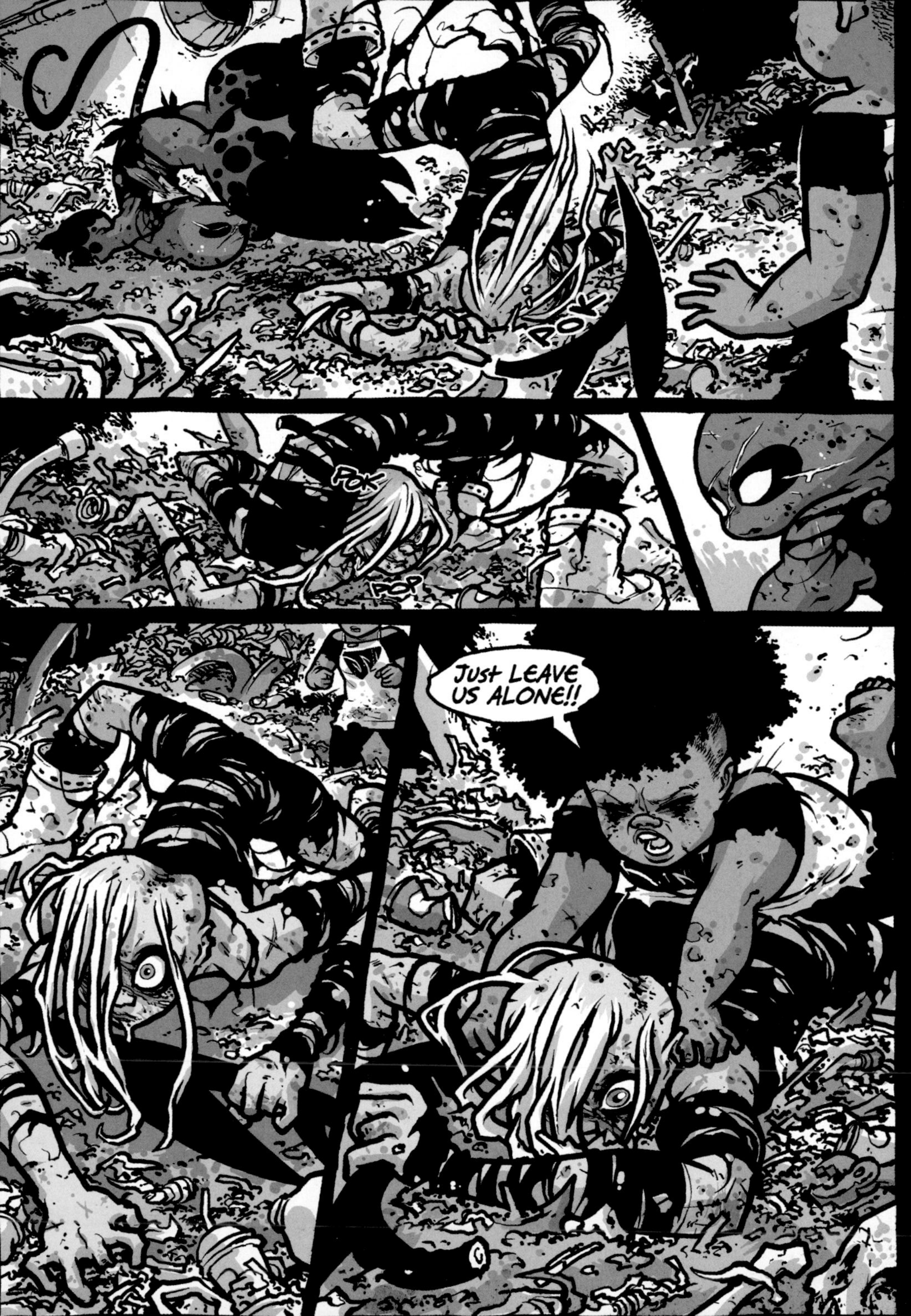
POK
POK
POP
JUST LEAVE US ALONE!!

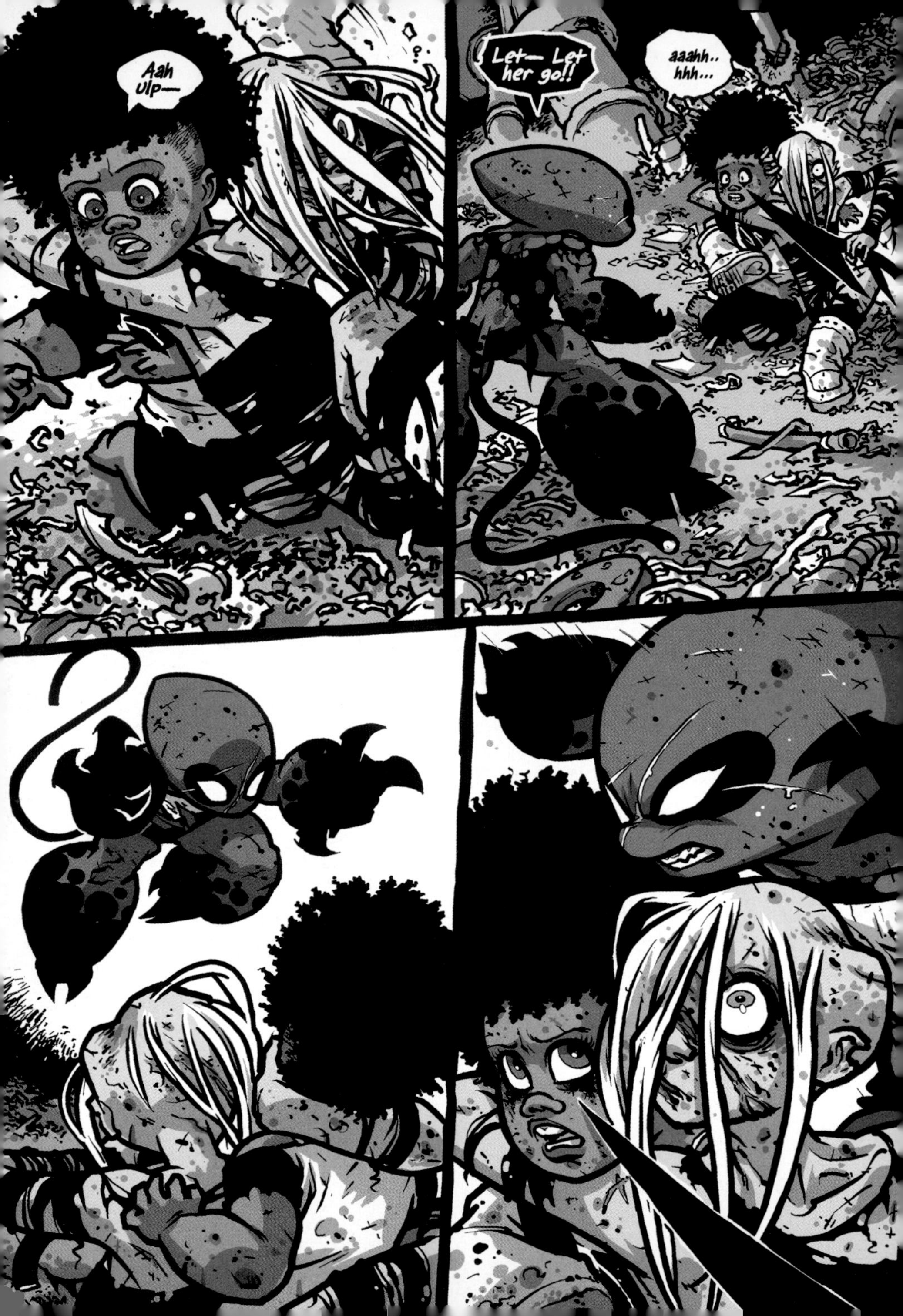
Aah Ulp—
Let— Let her go!!
aaahh.. hhh...

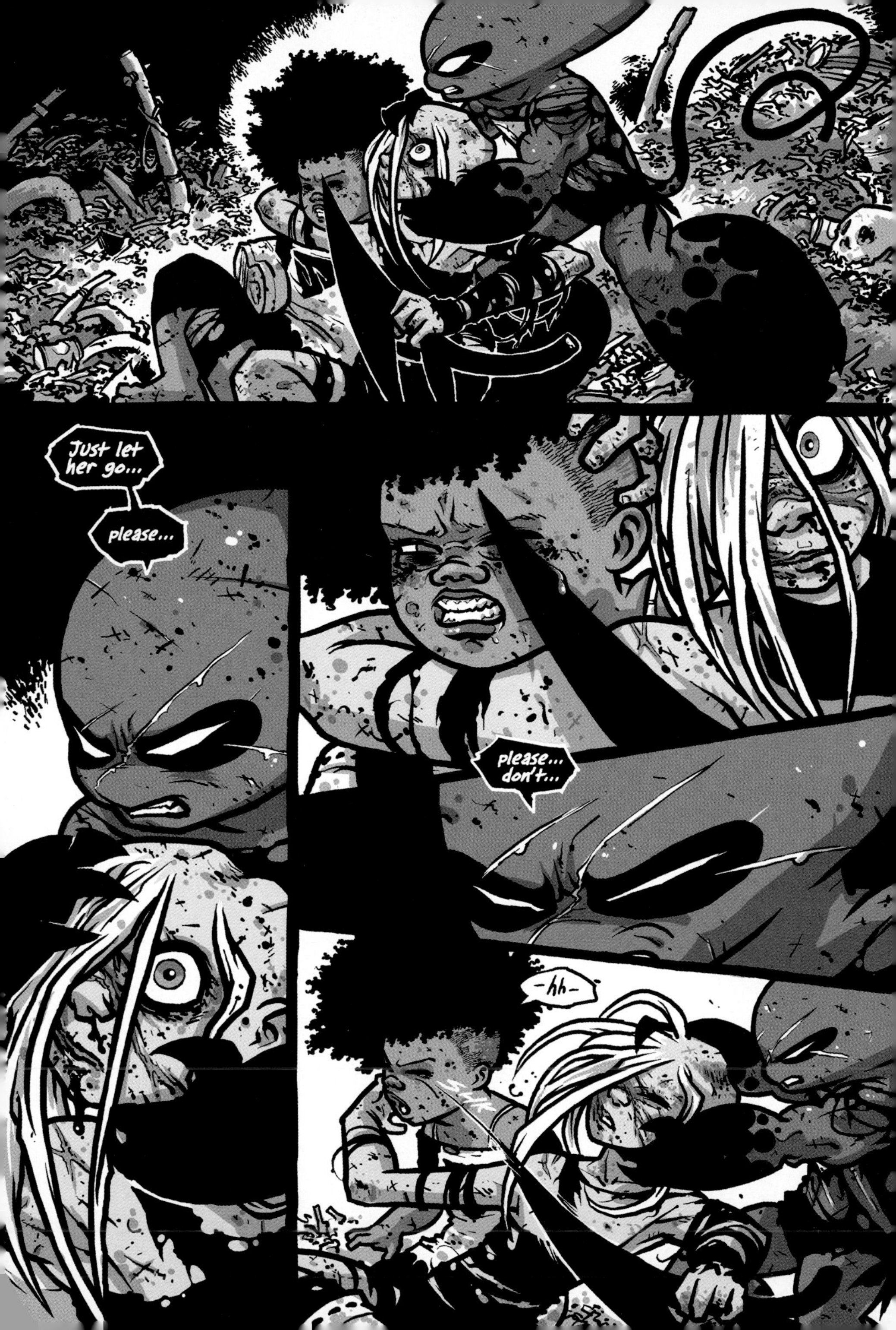
Just let her go...
please...
please... don't...
-hh-
SLIK

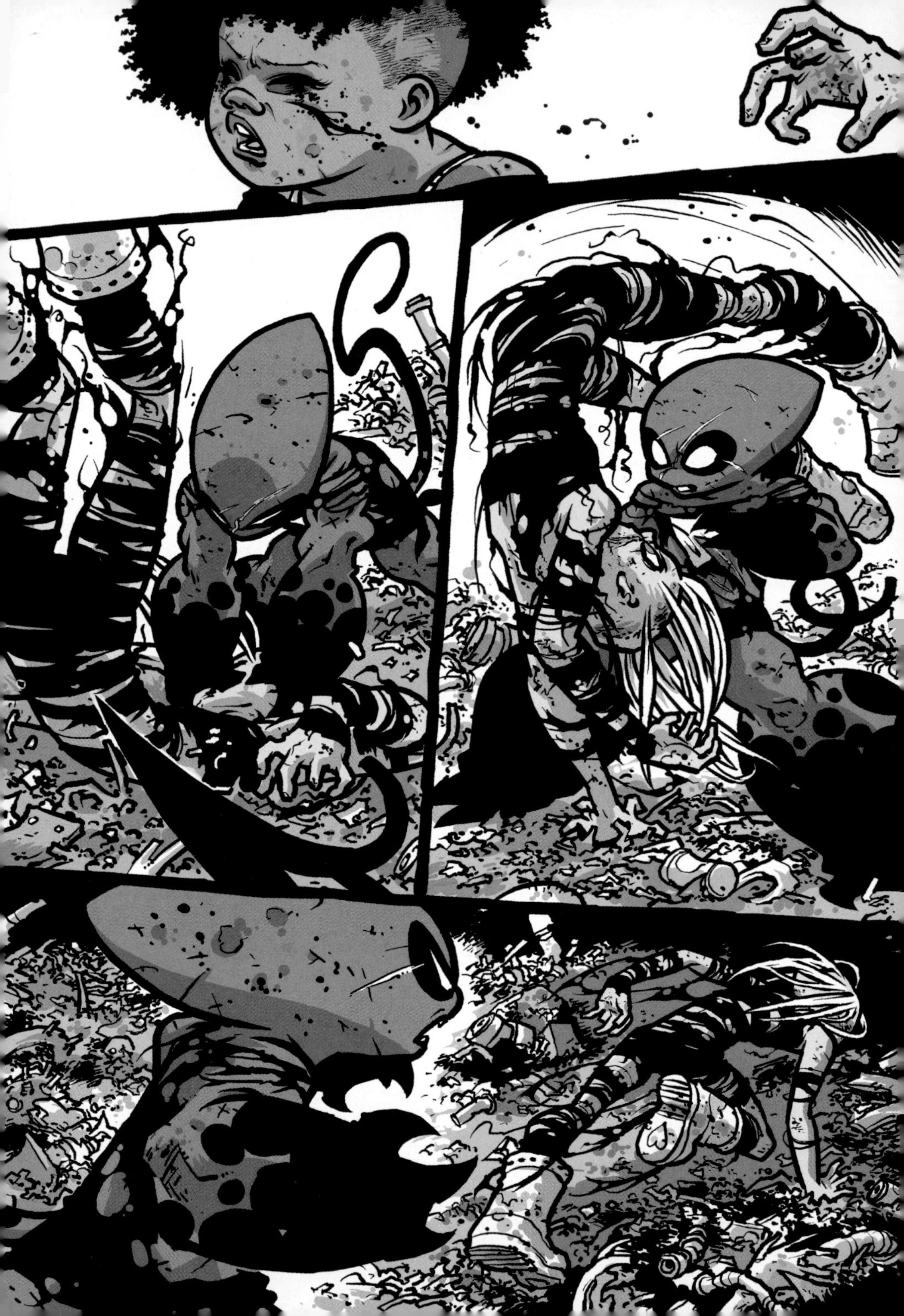

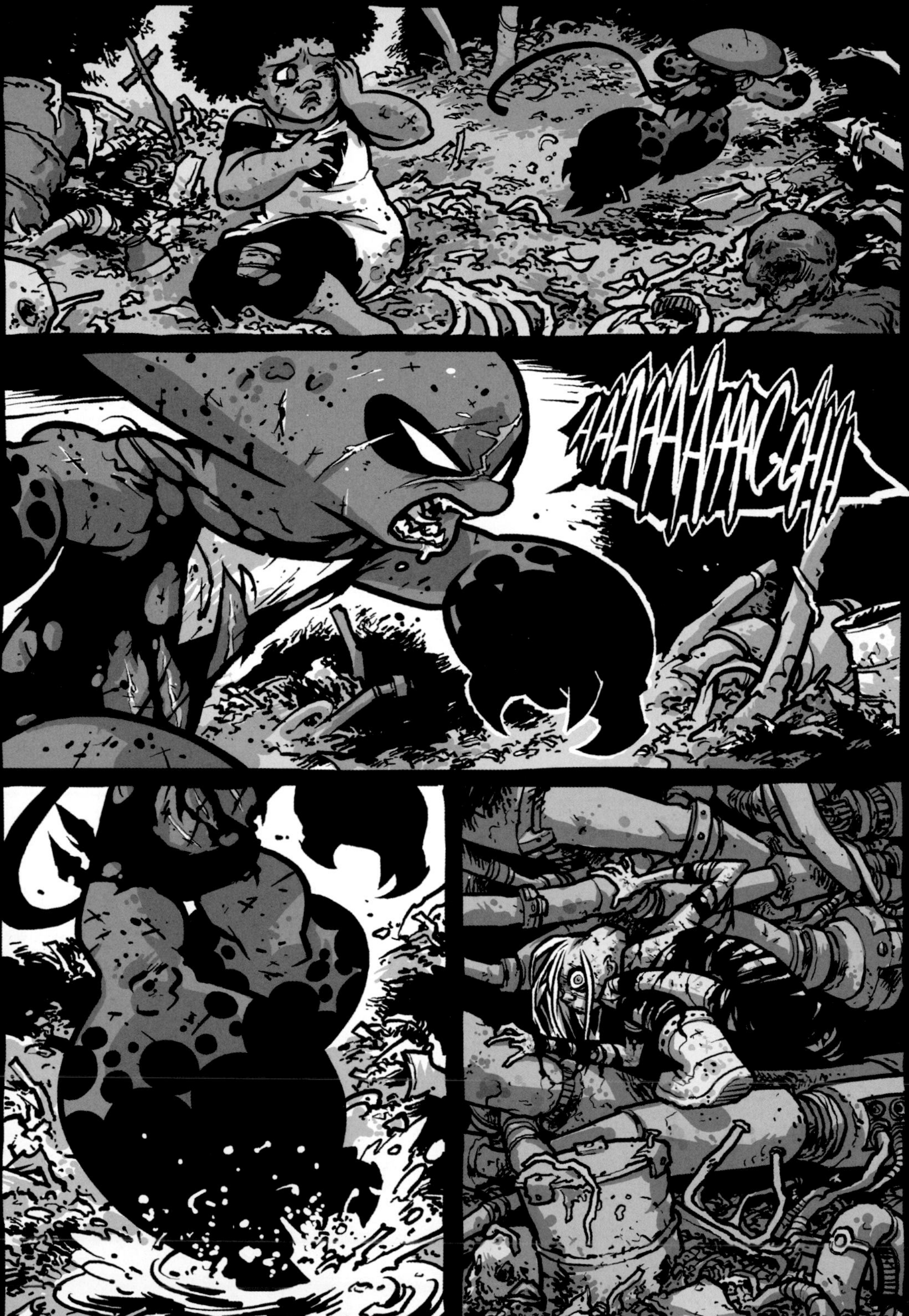
AAAAAAAAAGHH

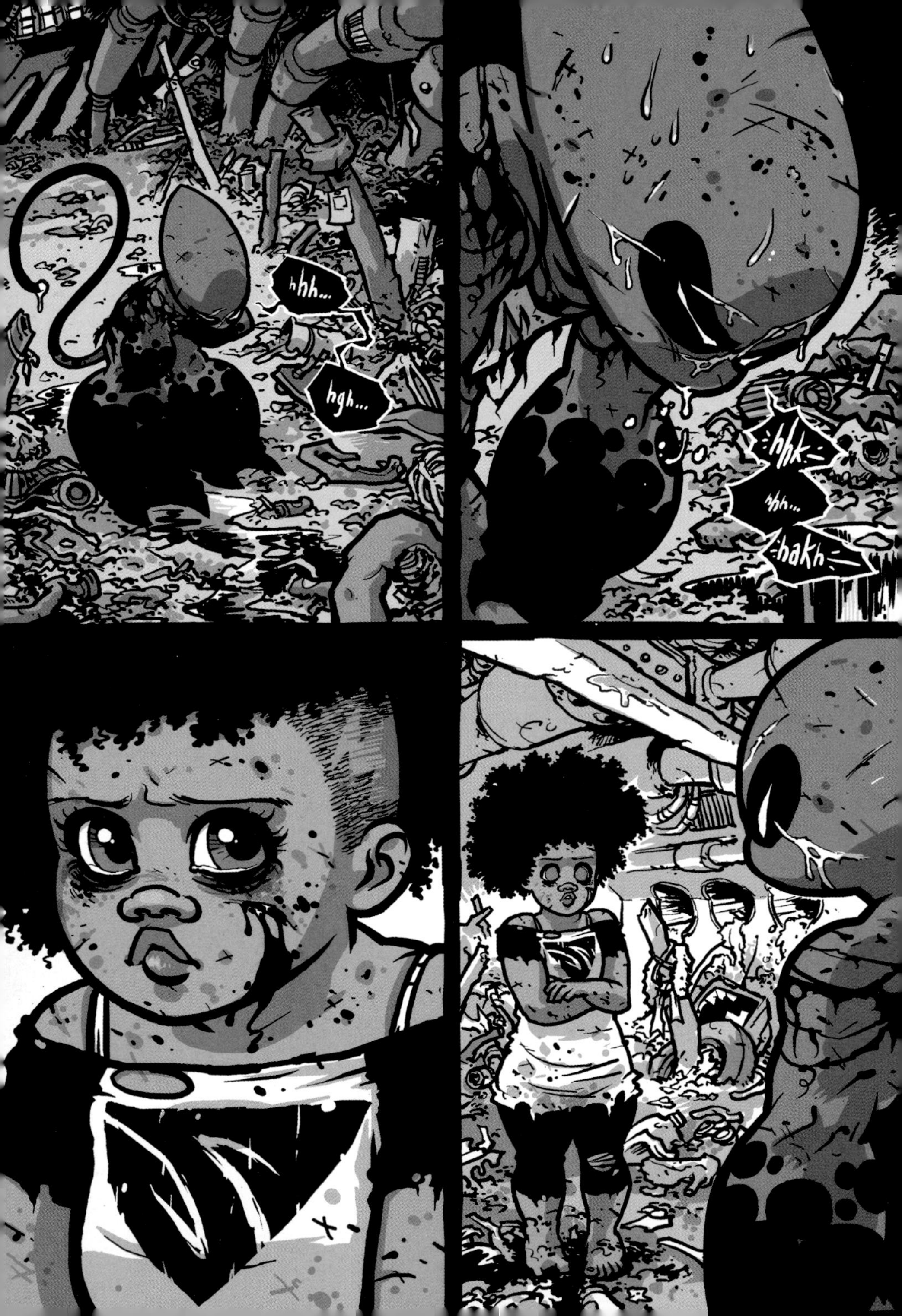
hhh...
hgh...
hhk
hhh...
hakh

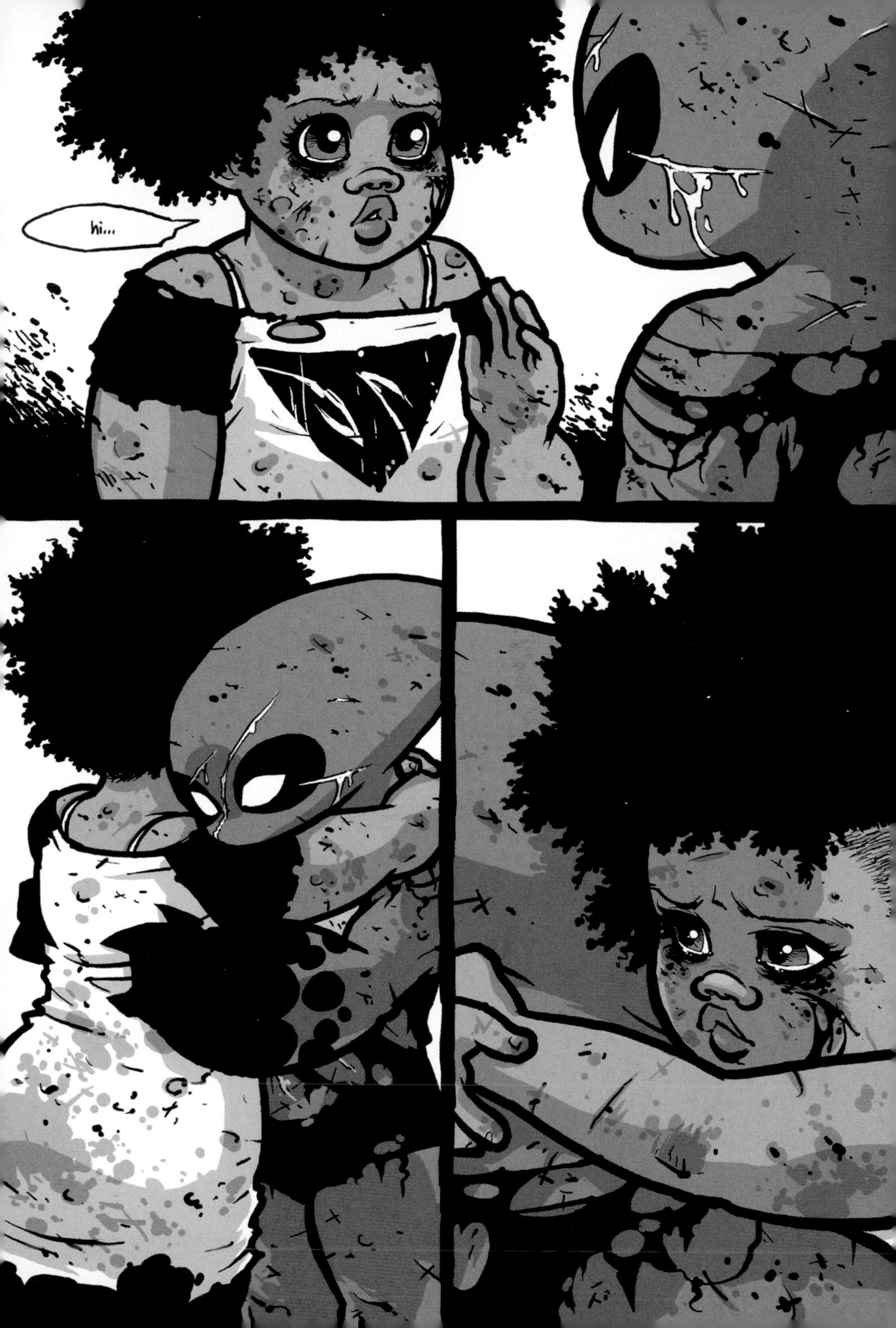
hi...

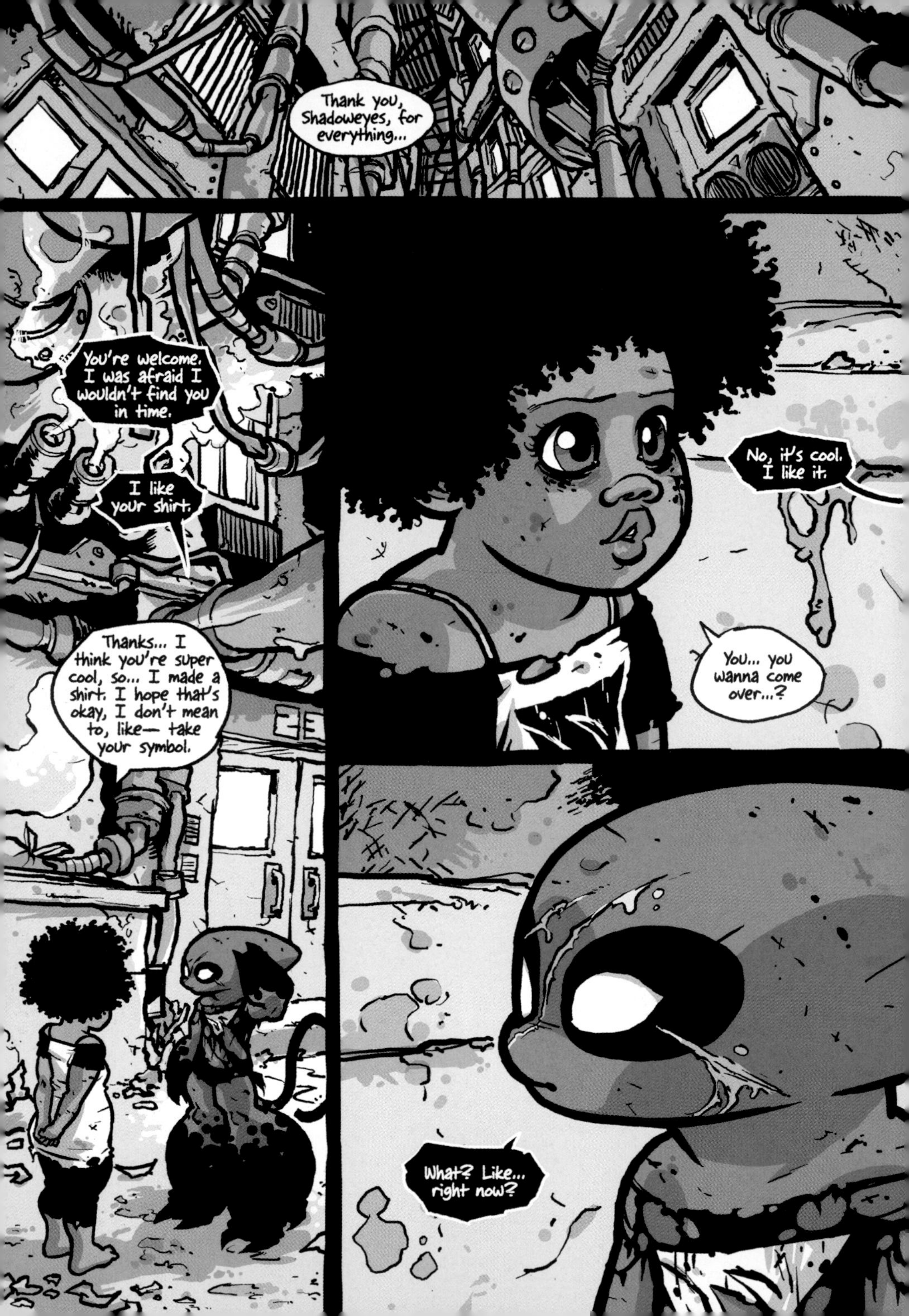
Thank you, Shadoweyes, for everything...
You're welcome. I was afraid I wouldn't find you in time.
I like your shirt.
Thanks... I think you're super cool, so... I made a shirt. I hope that's okay, I don't mean to, like— take your symbol.
No, it's cool. I like it.
You... you wanna come over...?
What? Like... right now?

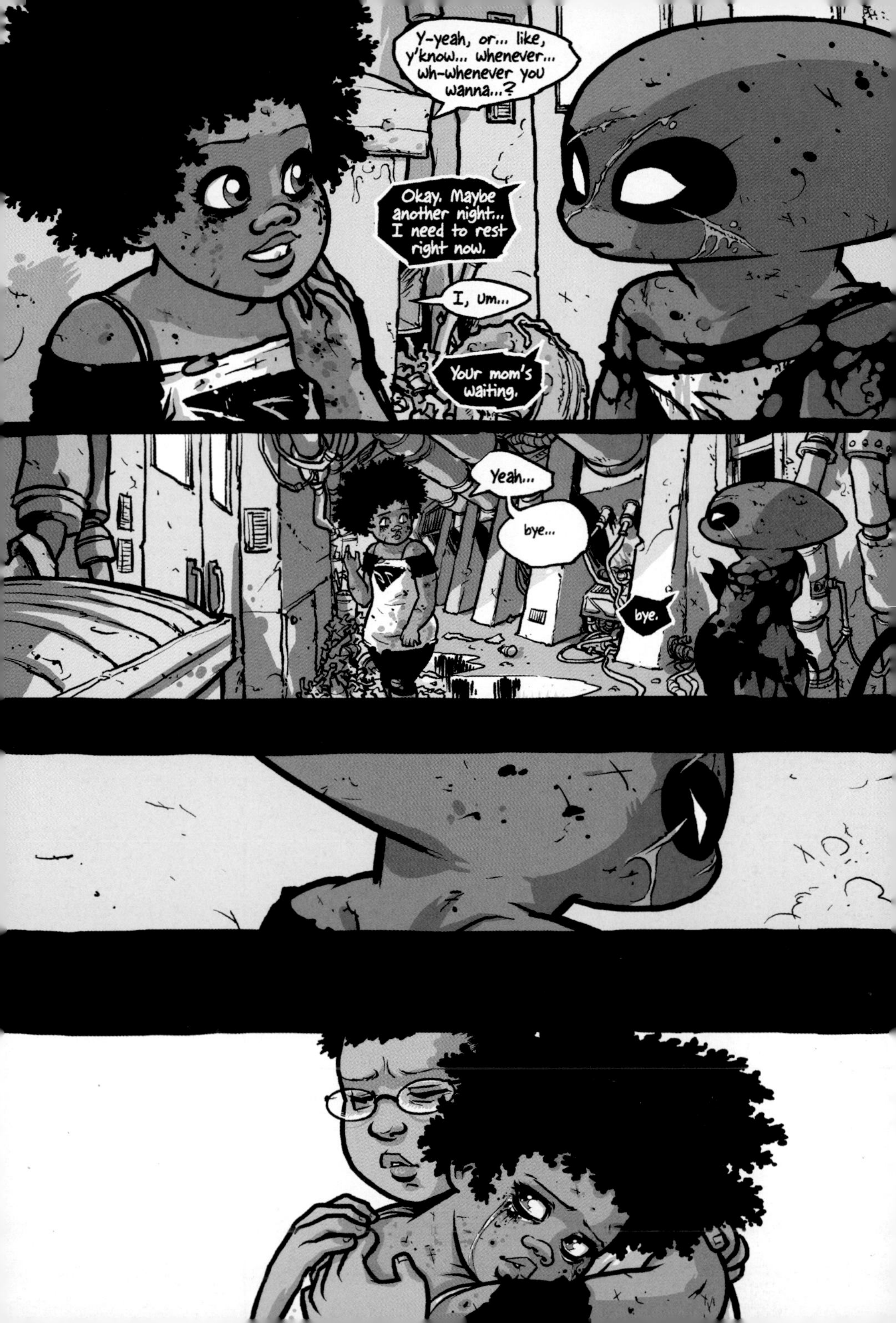

Y-yeah, or... like, y'know... whenever... wh-whenever you wanna...?
Okay. Maybe another night... I need to rest right now.
I, um...
Your mom's waiting.
Yeah...
bye...
bye.

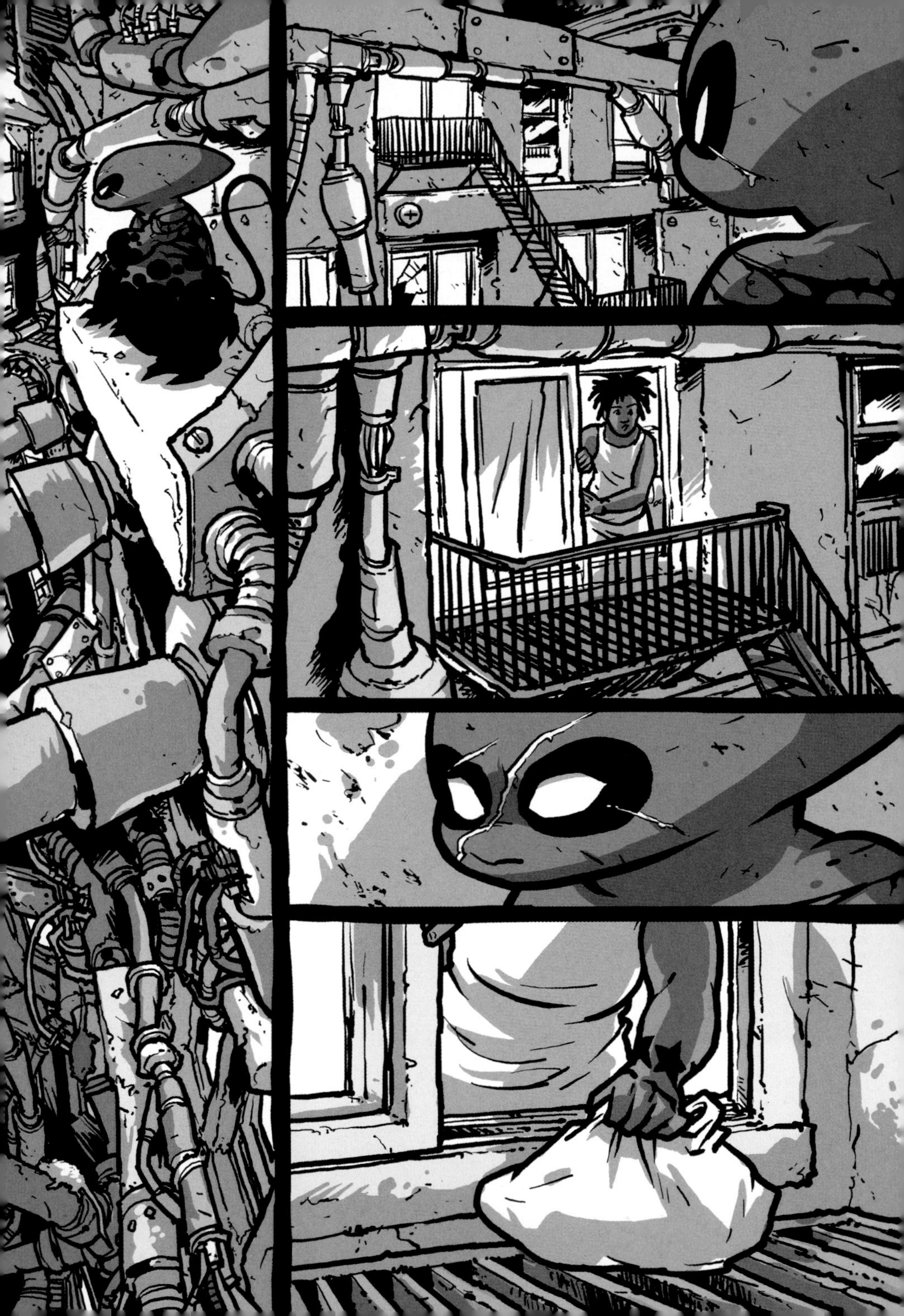

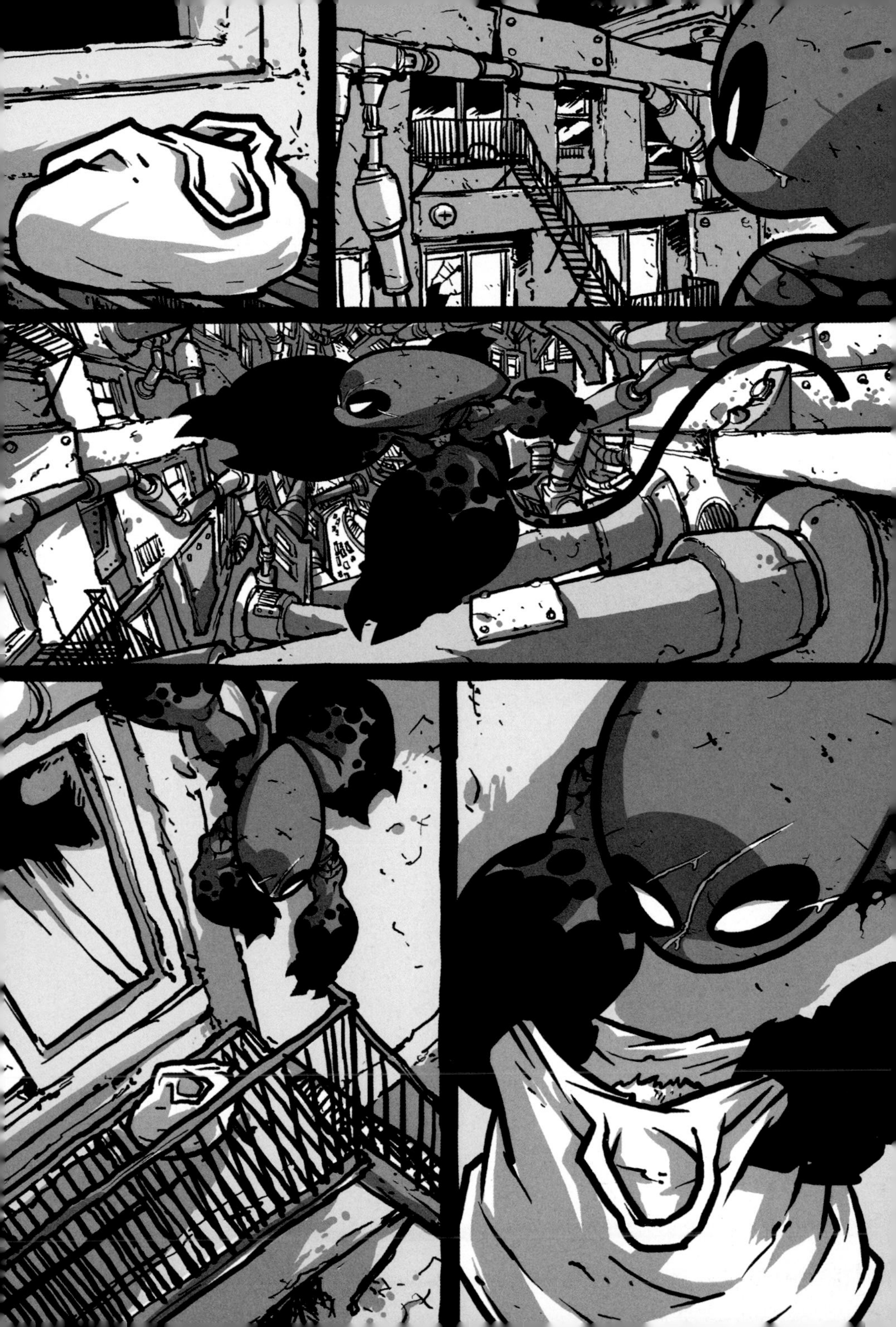

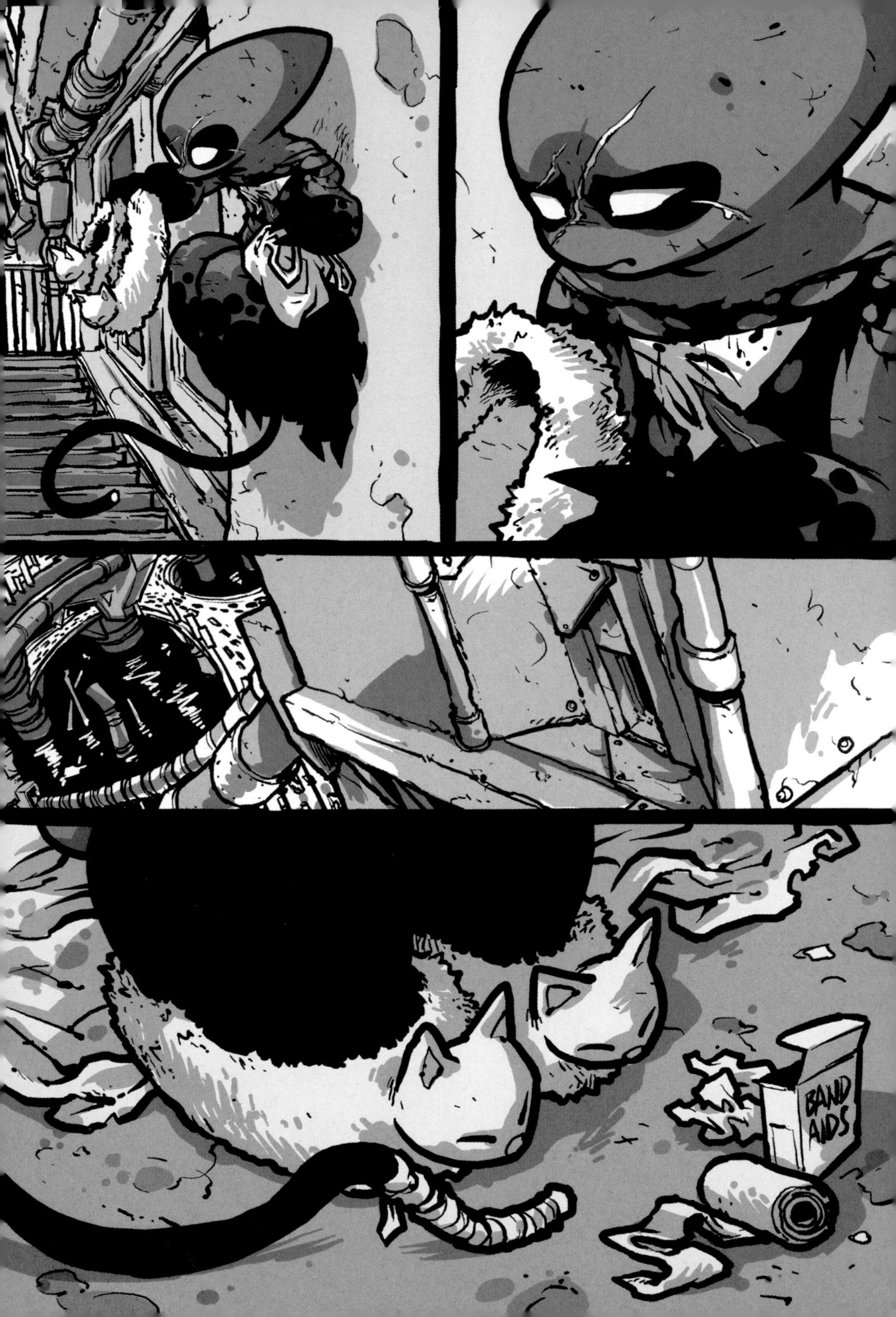
BAND AIDS

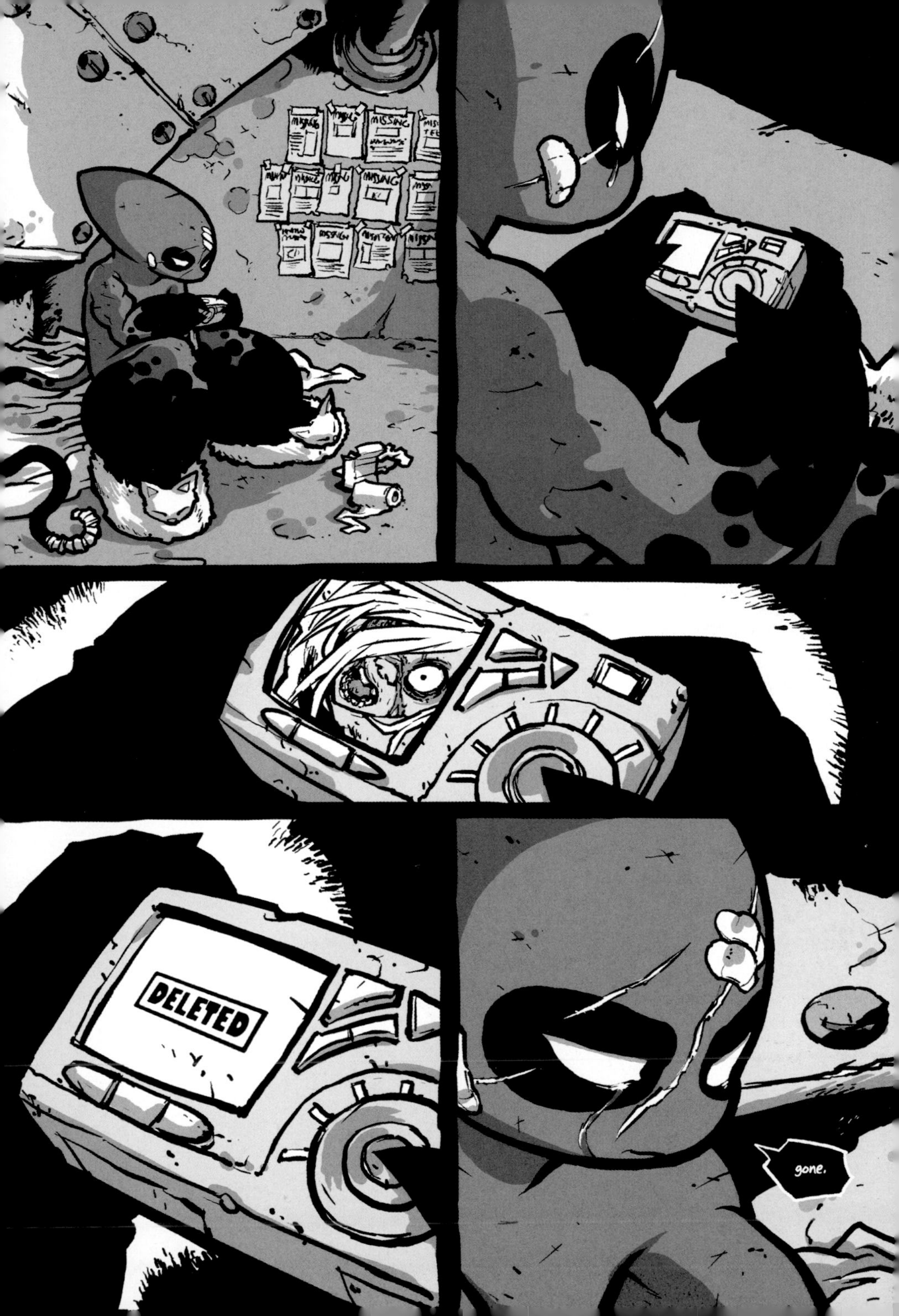
MISSING
MISSING
DELETED
gone.

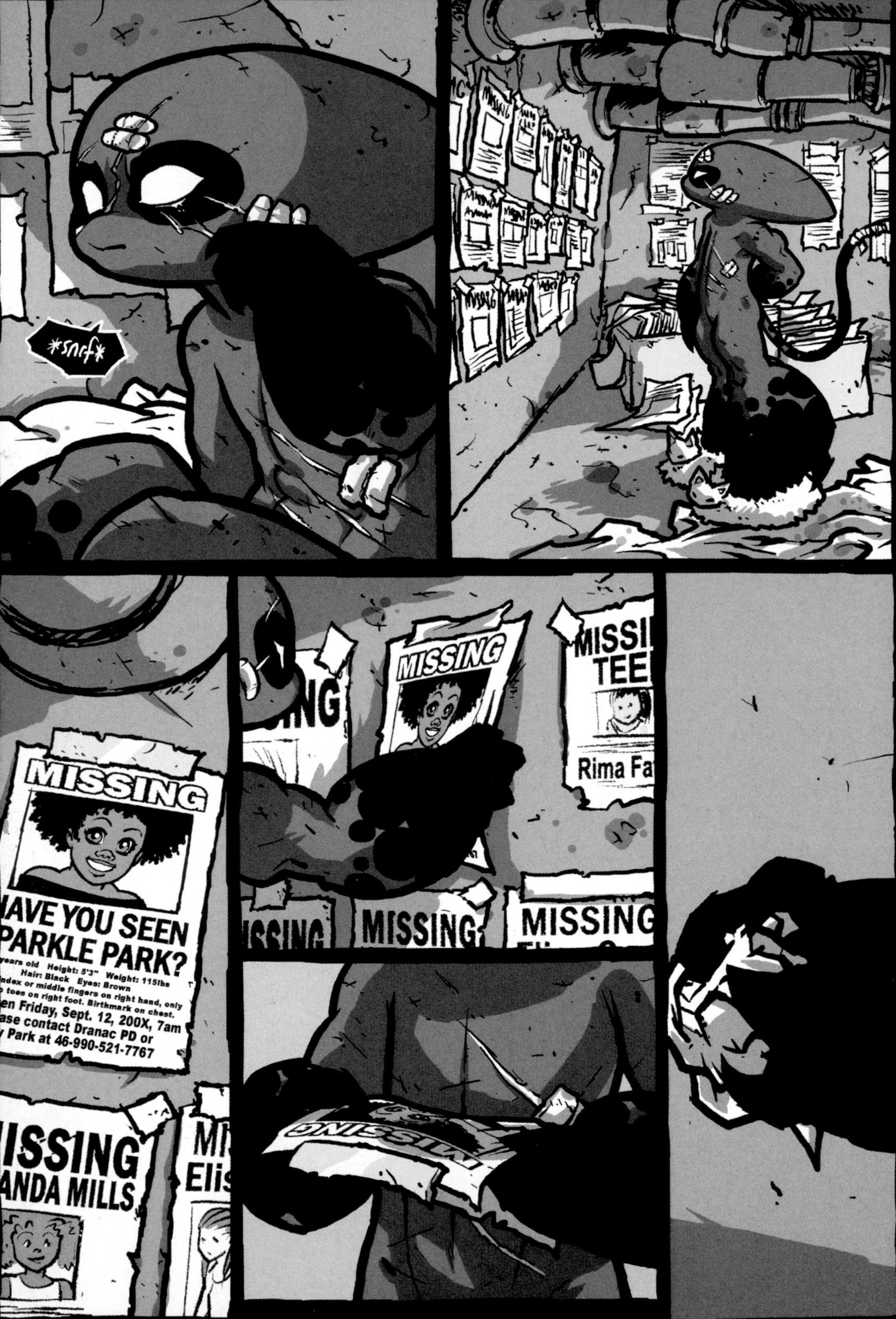
snrf
MISSING
AVE YOU SEEN
PARKLE PARK?
years old Height: 5'3" Weight: 115lbs
Hair: Black Eyes: Brown
ndex or middle fingers on right hand, only
toes on right foot. Birthmark on chest.
en Friday, Sept. 12, 200X, 7am
ase contact Dranac PD or
y Park at 46-990-521-7767
ISSING
ANDA MILLS
MI
Elis
ING
MISSING
MISSI
TEE
Rima Fa
ISSING
MISSING
MISSING
MISSING

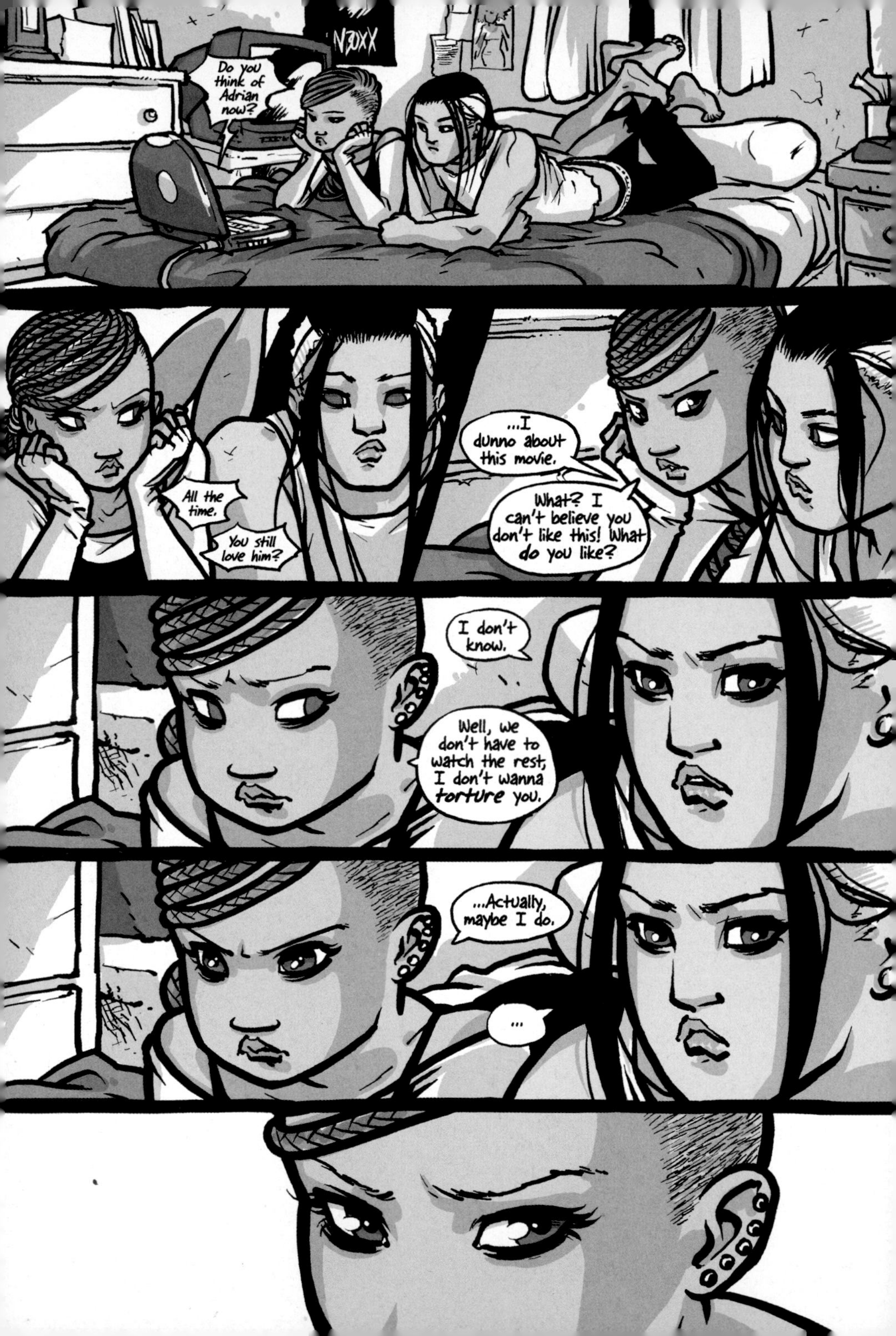
N3OXX
Do you think of Adrian now?
All the time.
You still love him?
...I dunno about this movie.
What? I can't believe you don't like this! What do you like?
I don't know.
Well, we don't have to watch the rest, I don't wanna torture you.
...Actually, maybe I do.
...

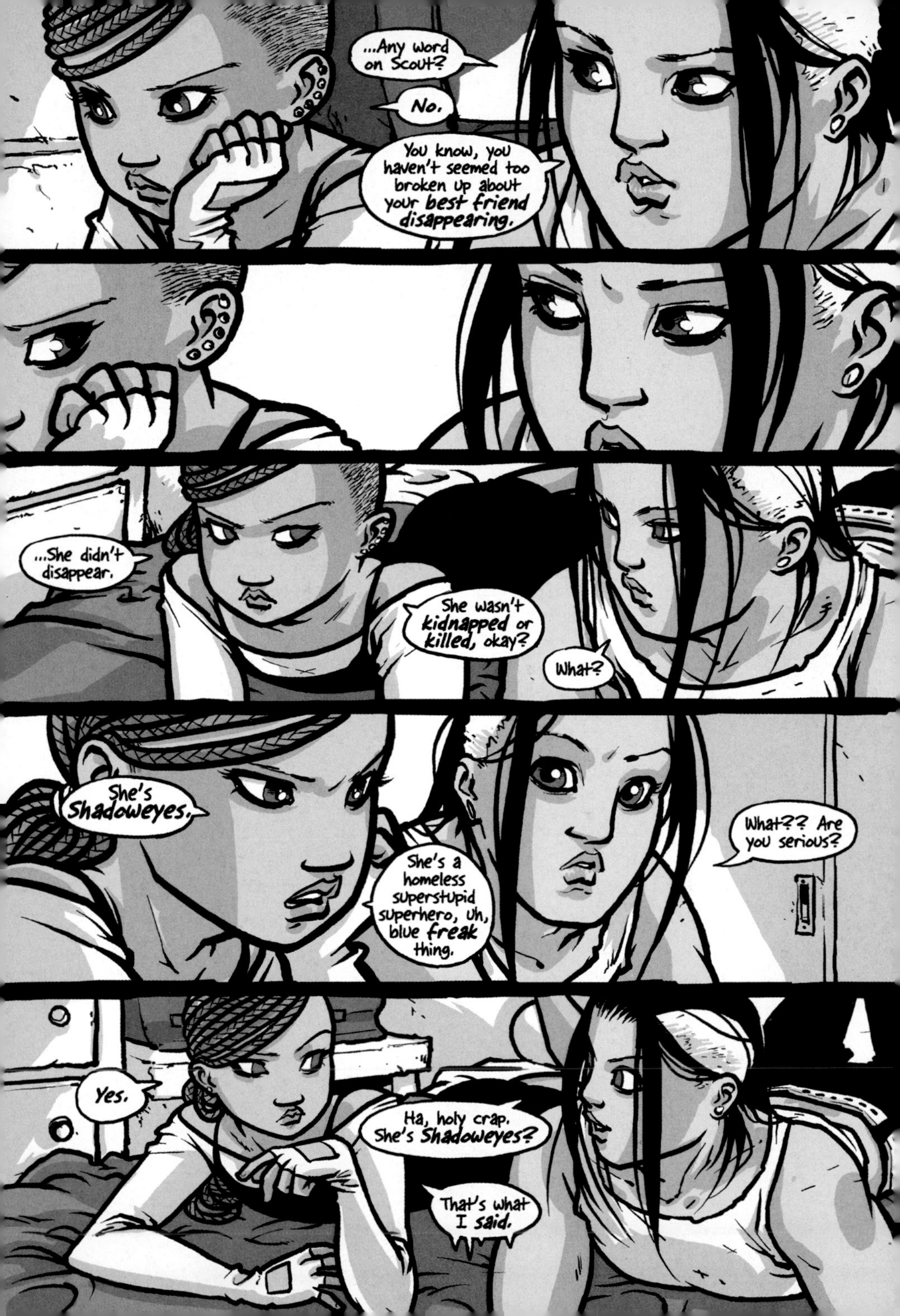
...Any word on Scout?
No.
You know, you haven't seemed too broken up about your best friend disappearing.
...She didn't disappear.
She wasn't kidnapped or killed, okay?
What?
She's Shadoweyes.
She's a homeless superstupid superhero, uh, blue freak thing.
What?? Are you serious?
Yes.
Ha, holy crap. She's Shadoweyes?
That's what I said.

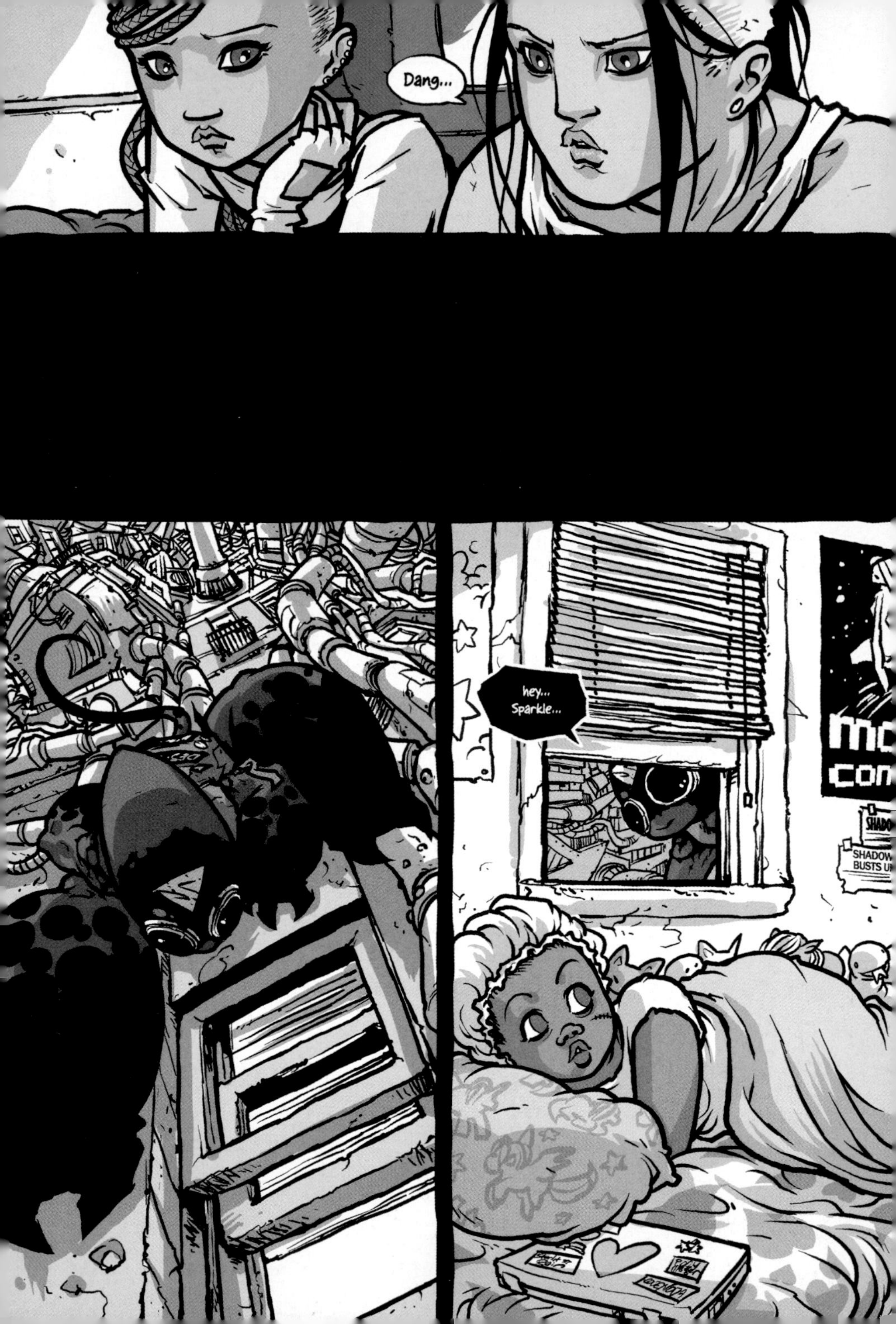
Dang...
hey... Sparkle...

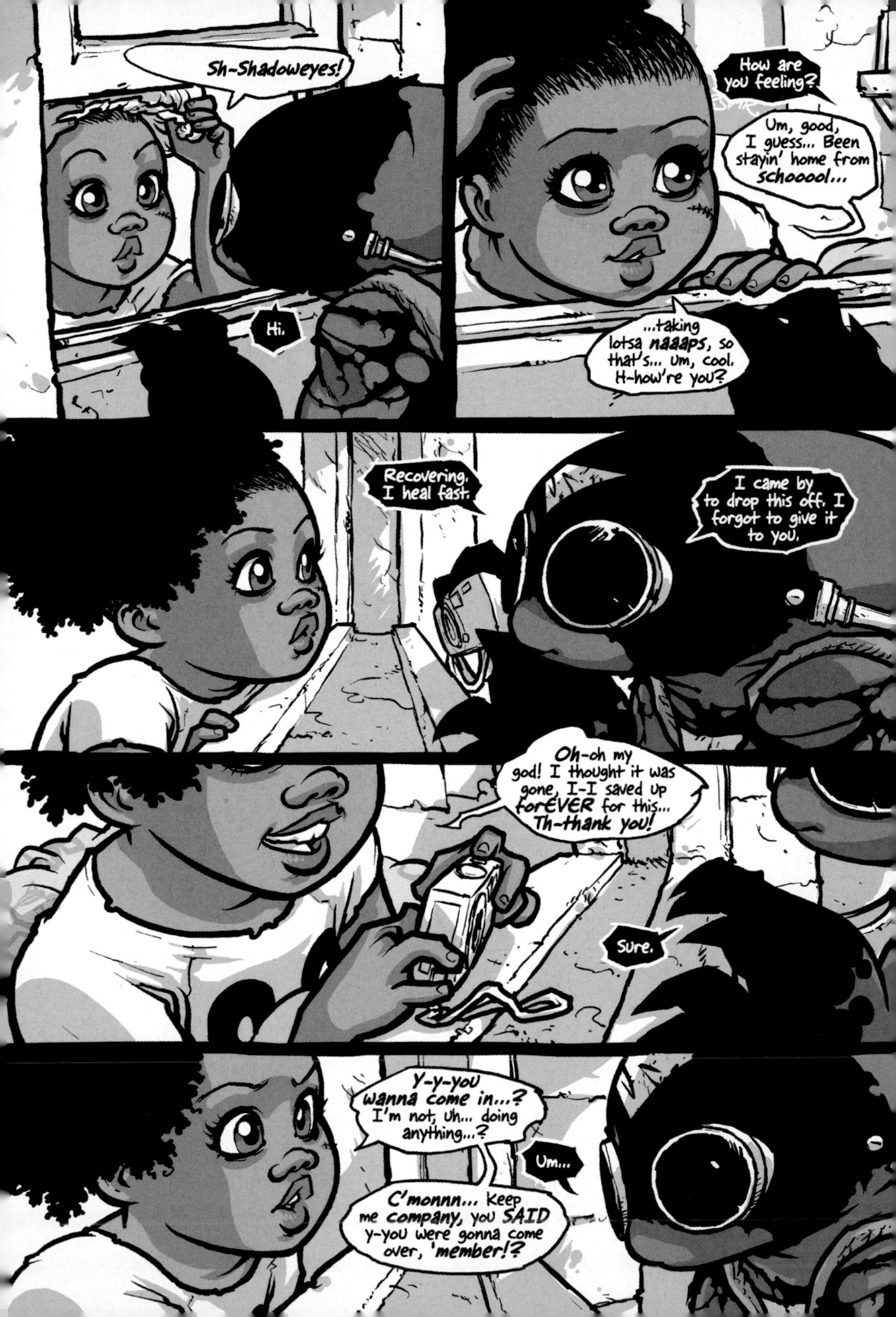
Sh-Shadoweyes!
Hi.
How are you feeling?
Um, good, I guess... Been stayin' home from schooool...
...taking lotsa naaaps, so that's... um, cool. H-how're you?
Recovering. I heal fast.
I came by to drop this off. I forgot to give it to you.
Oh-oh my god! I thought it was gone, I-I saved up forEVER for this... Th-thank you!
Sure.
Y-y-you wanna come in...? I'm not, uh... doing anything...?
Um...
C'monnn... keep me company, you SAID y-you were gonna come over, 'member!?

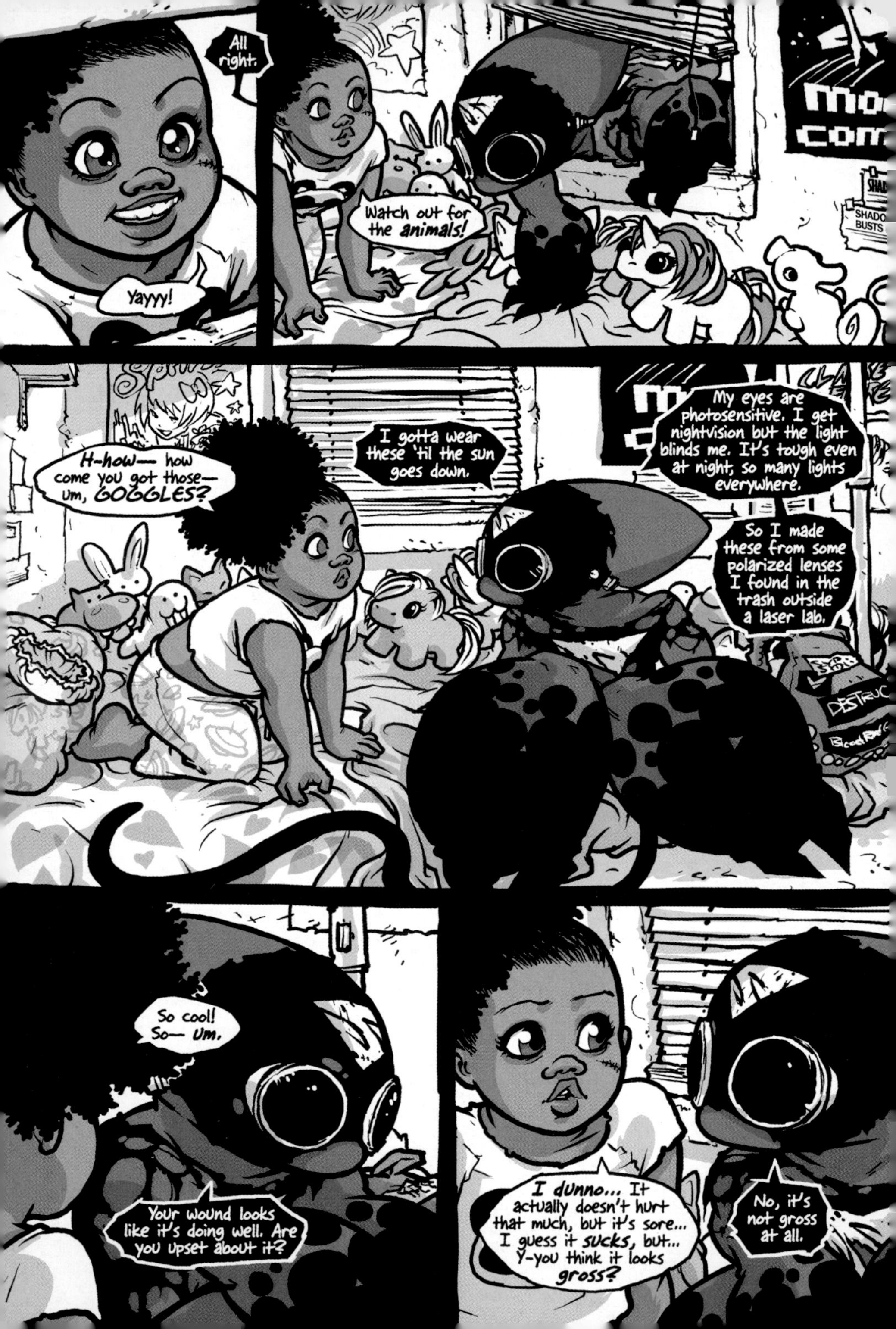
All right.
Yayyy!
Watch out for the animals!
moo
com
SHAD
SHADO BUSTS
H-how— how come you got those— um, GOGGLES?
I gotta wear these 'til the sun goes down.
My eyes are photosensitive. I get nightvision but the light blinds me. It's tough even at night, so many lights everywhere.
So I made these from some polarized lenses I found in the trash outside a laser lab.
DESTRUC
So cool! So— um.
Your wound looks like it's doing well. Are you upset about it?
I dunno... It actually doesn't hurt that much, but it's sore... I guess it sucks, but... Y-you think it looks gross?
No, it's not gross at all.

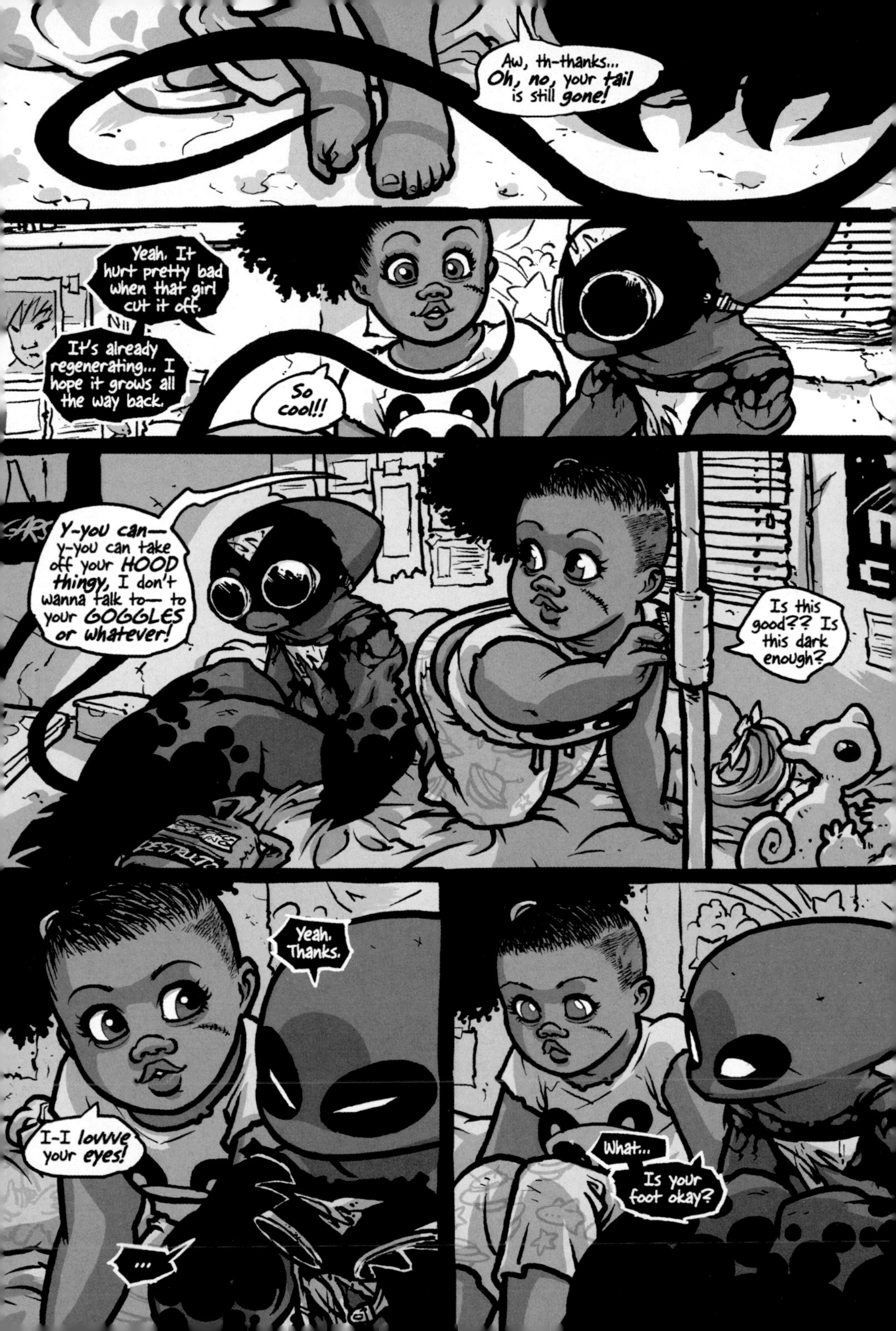

Aw, th-thanks... Oh, no, your tail is still gone!
Yeah. It hurt pretty bad when that girl cut it off.
It's already regenerating... I hope it grows all the way back.
So cool!!
Y-you can— y-you can take off your HOOD thingy, I don't wanna talk to— to your GOGGLES or whatever!
Is this good?? Is this dark enough?
Yeah. Thanks.
I-I lovvve your eyes!
...
What...
Is your foot okay?

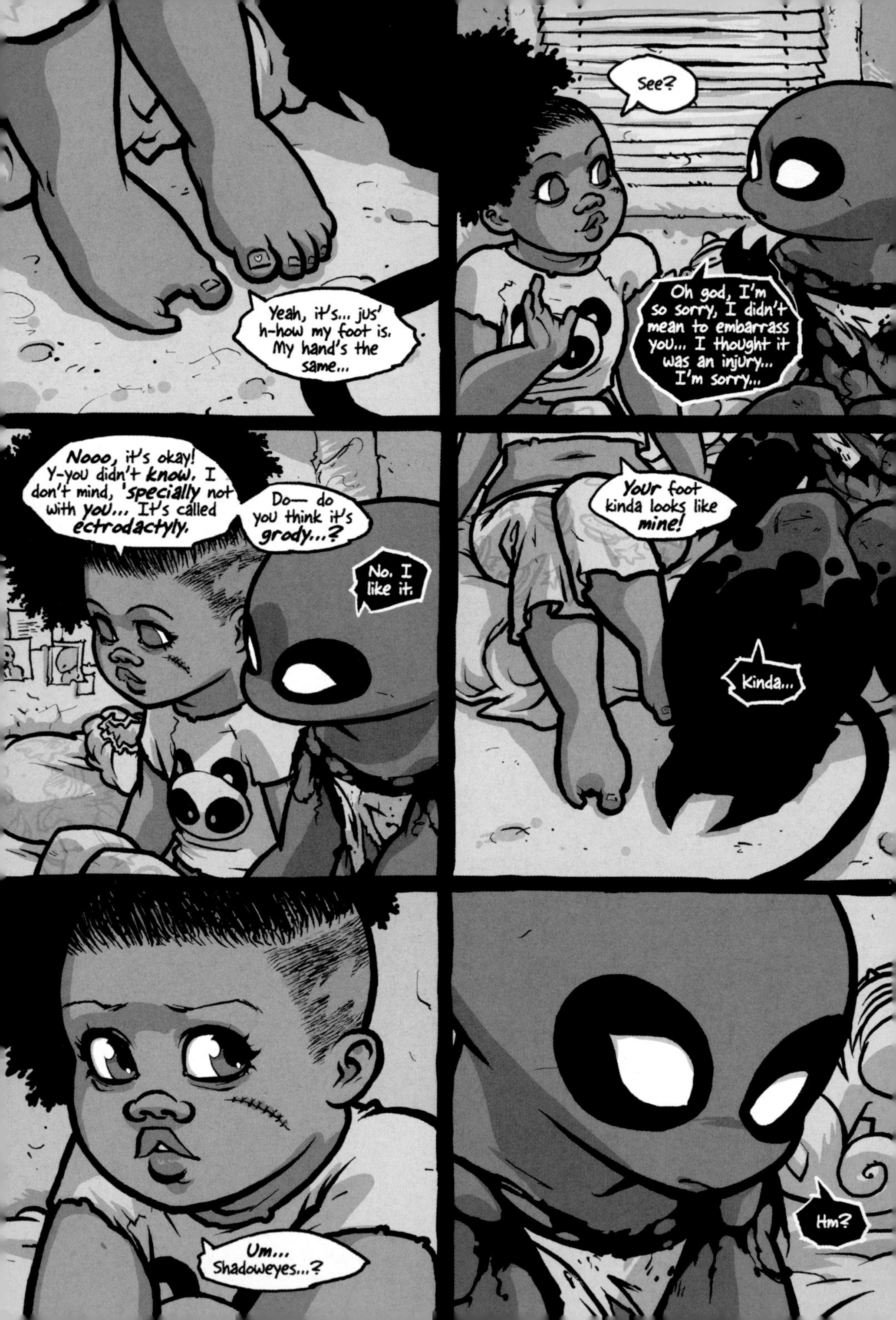
Yeah, it's... jus' h-how my foot is. My hand's the same...
See?
Oh god, I'm so sorry, I didn't mean to embarrass you... I thought it was an injury... I'm sorry...
Nooo, it's okay! Y-you didn't know. I don't mind, 'specially not with you... It's called ectrodactyly.
Do— do you think it's grody...?
No. I like it.
Your foot kinda looks like mine!
Kinda...
Um... Shadoweyes...?
Hm?

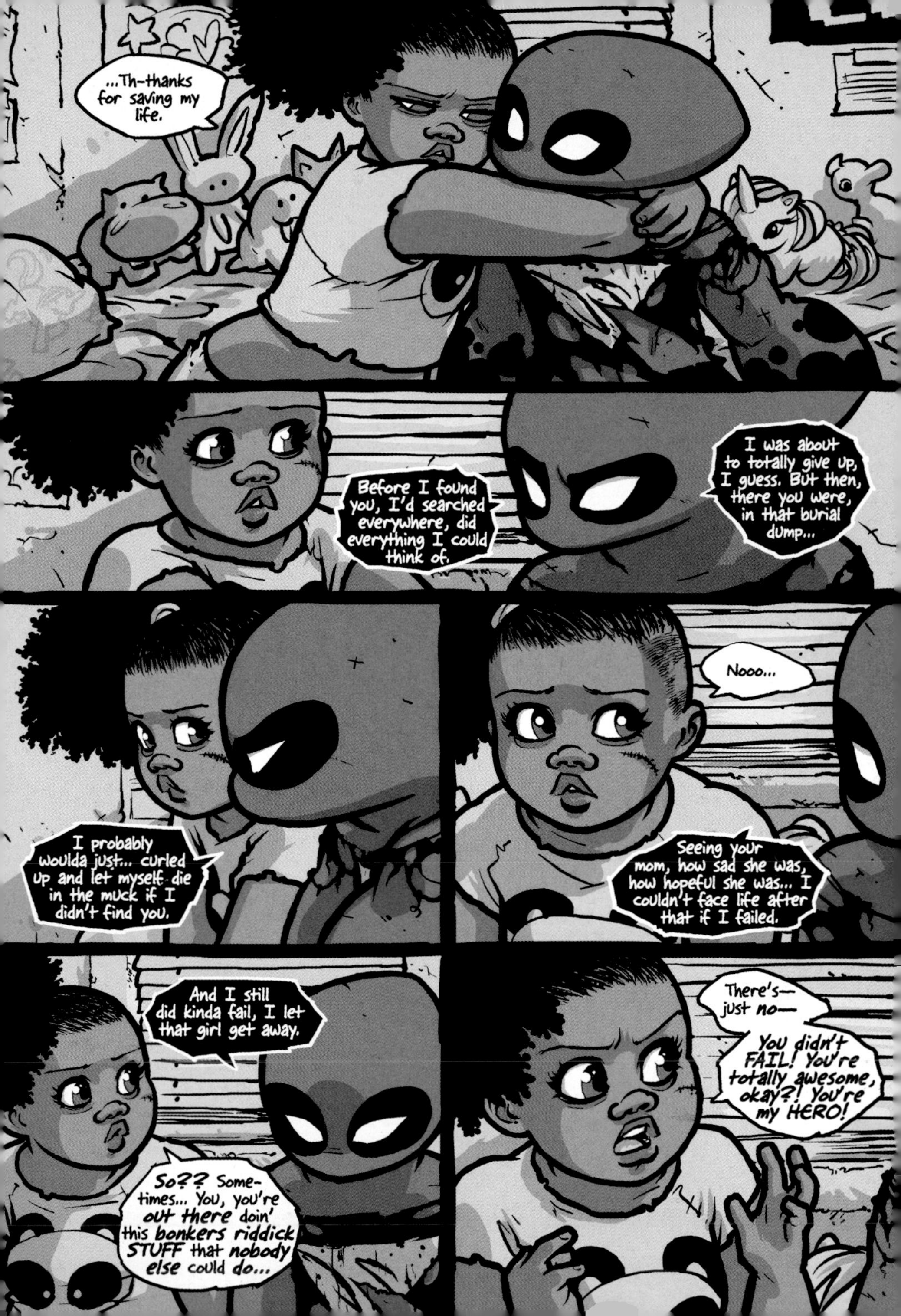
...Th-thanks for saving my life.
Before I found you, I'd searched everywhere, did everything I could think of.
I was about to totally give up, I guess. But then, there you were, in that burial dump...
I probably woulda just... curled up and let myself die in the muck if I didn't find you.
Nooo...
Seeing your mom, how sad she was, how hopeful she was... I couldn't face life after that if I failed.
And I still did kinda fail, I let that girl get away.
So?? Sometimes... You, you're out there doin' this bonkers riddick STUFF that nobody else could do...
There's— just no—
You didn't FAIL! You're totally awesome, okay?! You're my HERO!

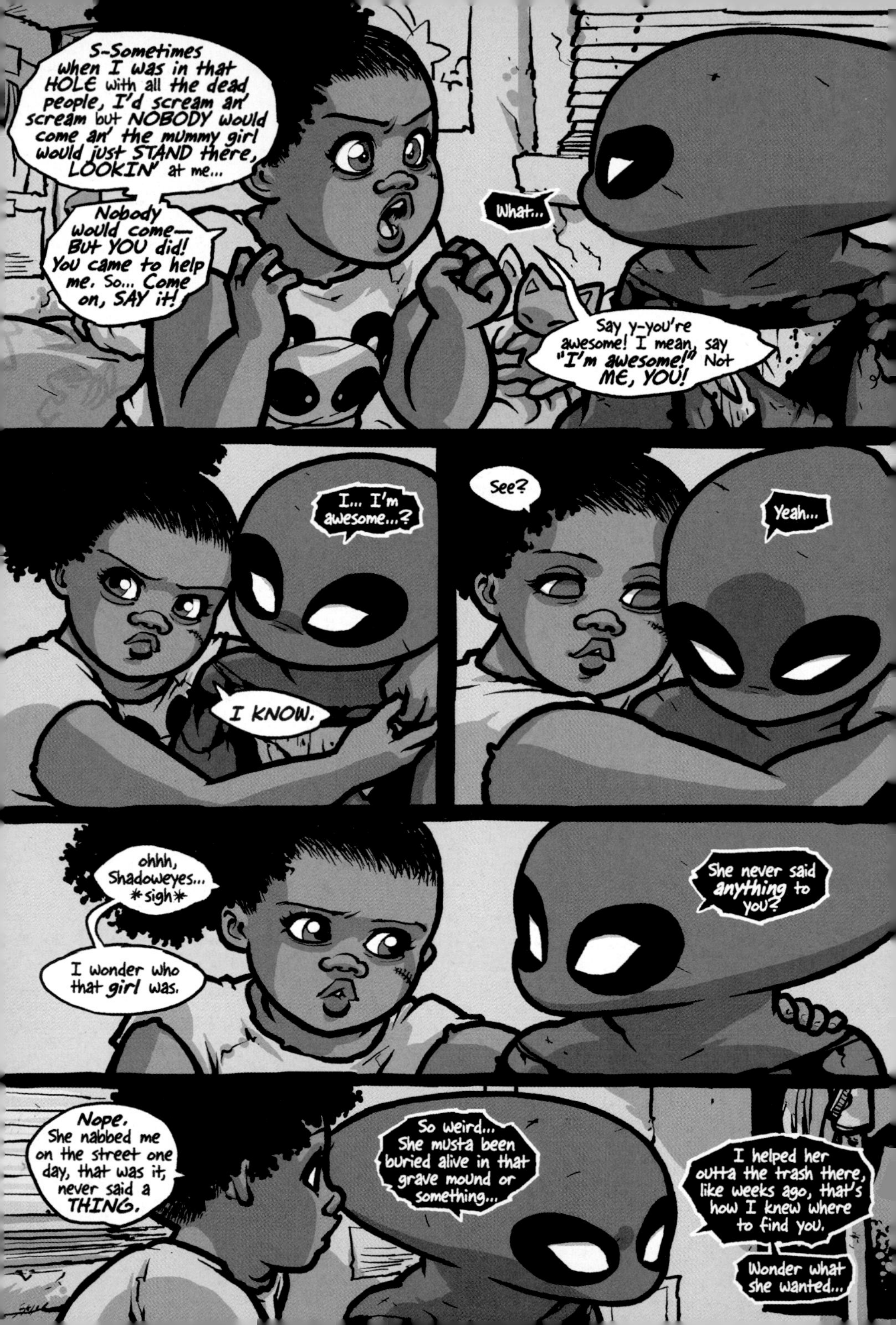
S-Sometimes when I was in that HOLE with all the dead people, I'd scream an' scream but NOBODY would come an' the mummy girl would just STAND there, LOOKIN' at me...
Nobody would come— But YOU did! You came to help me. So... Come on, SAY it!
What...
Say y-you're awesome! I mean, say "I'm awesome!" Not ME, YOU!
I... I'm awesome...?
I KNOW.
See?
Yeah...
ohhh, Shadoweyes... *sigh*
I wonder who that girl was.
She never said anything to you?
Nope. She nabbed me on the street one day, that was it, never said a THING.
So weird... She musta been buried alive in that grave mound or something...
I helped her outta the trash there, like weeks ago, that's how I knew where to find you.
Wonder what she wanted...

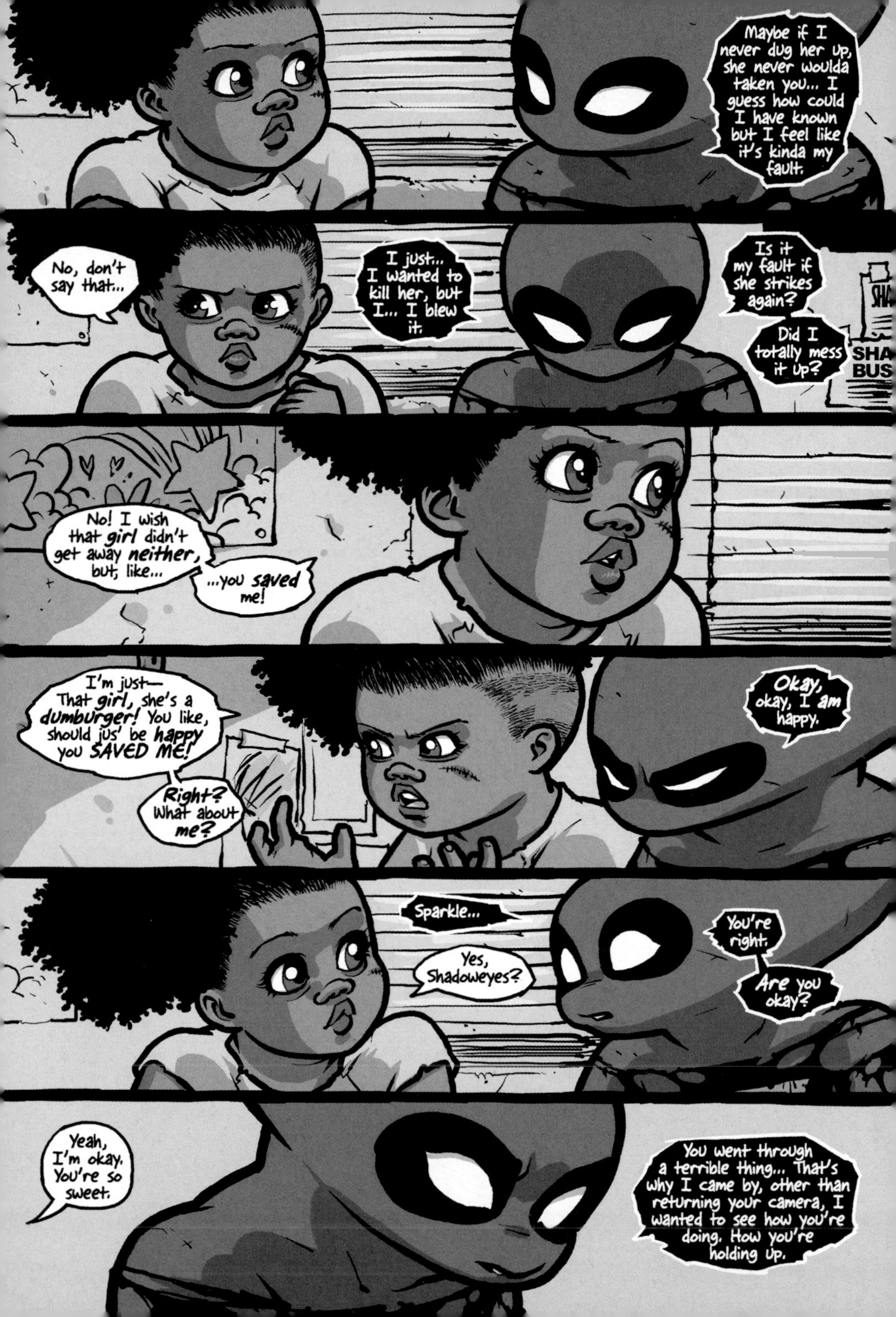
Maybe if I never dug her up, she never woulda taken you... I guess how could I have known but I feel like it's kinda my fault.
No, don't say that...
I just... I wanted to kill her, but I... I blew it.
Is it my fault if she strikes again?
Did I totally mess it up?
No! I wish that *girl* didn't get away *neither*, but, like...
...you *saved* me!
I'm just— That *girl*, she's a *dumburger!* You like, should jus' be *happy* you *SAVED ME!*
Right? What about *me?*
Okay, okay, I *am* happy.
Sparkle...
Yes, Shadoweyes?
You're right.
Are you okay?
Yeah, I'm okay. You're so sweet.
You went through a terrible thing... That's why I came by, other than returning your camera, I wanted to see how you're doing. How you're holding up.

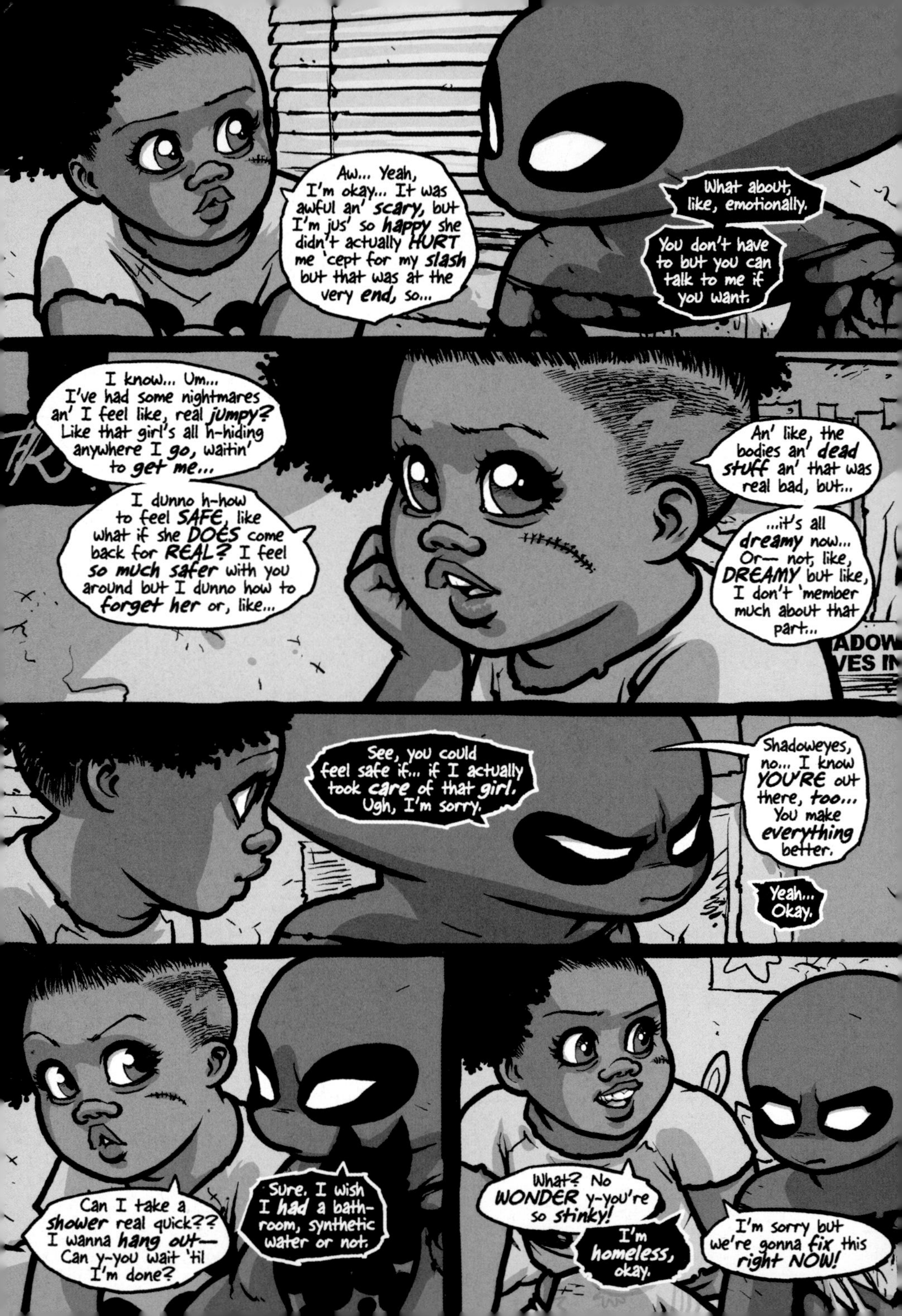
Aw... Yeah, I'm okay... It was awful an' scary, but I'm jus' so happy she didn't actually HURT me 'cept for my slash but that was at the very end, so...
What about, like, emotionally.
You don't have to but you can talk to me if you want.
I know... Um... I've had some nightmares an' I feel like, real jumpy? Like that girl's all h-hiding anywhere I go, waitin' to get me...
I dunno h-how to feel SAFE, like what if she DOES come back for REAL? I feel so much safer with you around but I dunno how to forget her or, like...
An' like, the bodies an' dead stuff an' that was real bad, but...
...it's all dreamy now... Or— not, like, DREAMY but like, I don't 'member much about that part...
ADOW
VES IN
See, you could feel safe if... if I actually took care of that girl. Ugh, I'm sorry.
Shadoweyes, no... I know YOU'RE out there, too... You make everything better.
Yeah... Okay.
Can I take a shower real quick?? I wanna hang out— Can y-you wait 'til I'm done?
Sure. I wish I had a bath-room, synthetic water or not.
What? No WONDER y-you're so stinky!
I'm homeless, okay.
I'm sorry but we're gonna fix this right NOW!

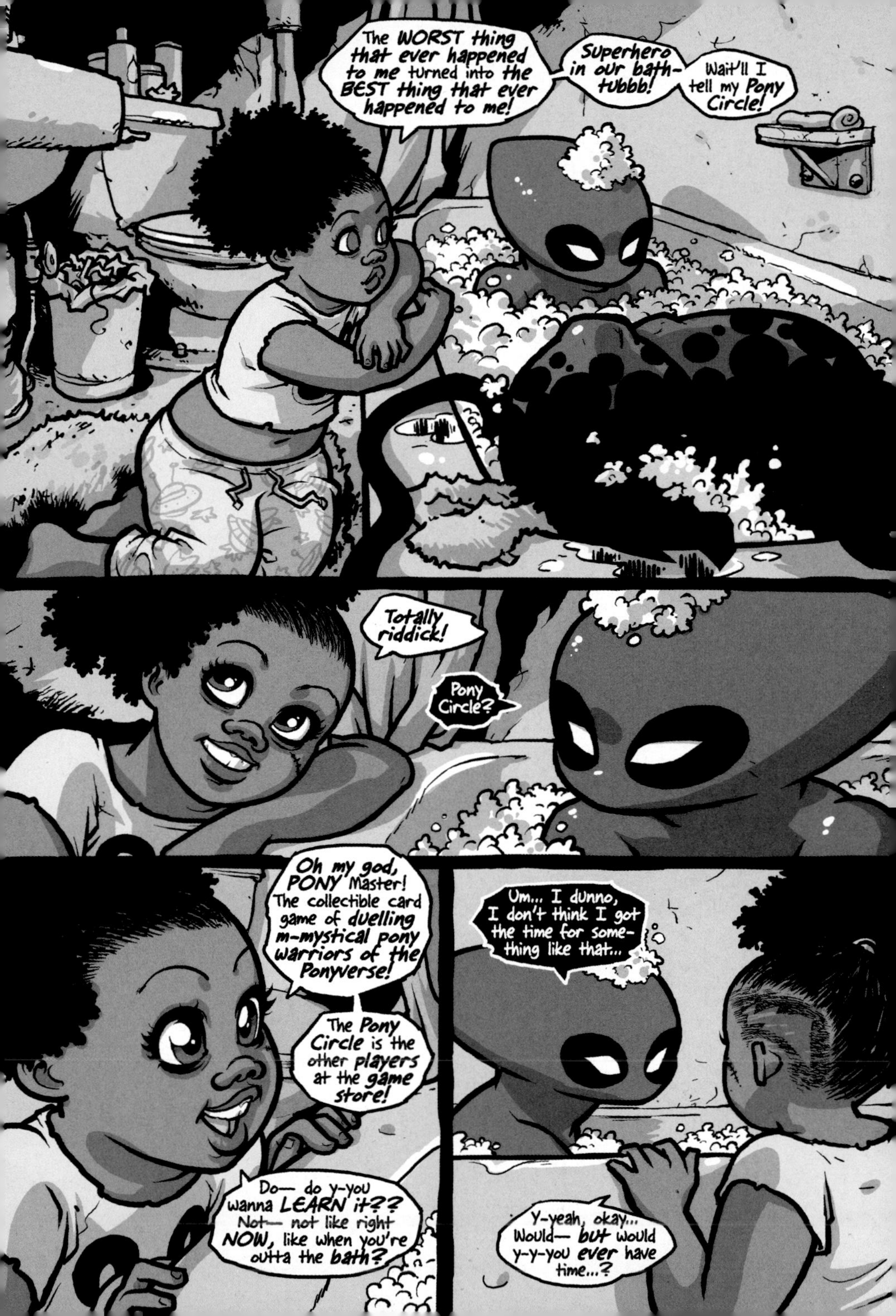
The WORST thing that ever happened to me turned into the BEST thing that ever happened to me!
Superhero in our bath-tubbb!
Wait'll I tell my Pony Circle!
Totally riddick!
Pony Circle?
Oh my god, PONY Master! The collectible card game of duelling m-mystical pony warriors of the Ponyverse!
The Pony Circle is the other players at the game store!
Do— do y-you wanna LEARN it?? Not— not like right NOW, like when you're outta the bath?
Um... I dunno, I don't think I got the time for some-thing like that...
Y-yeah, okay... Would— but would y-y-you ever have time...?

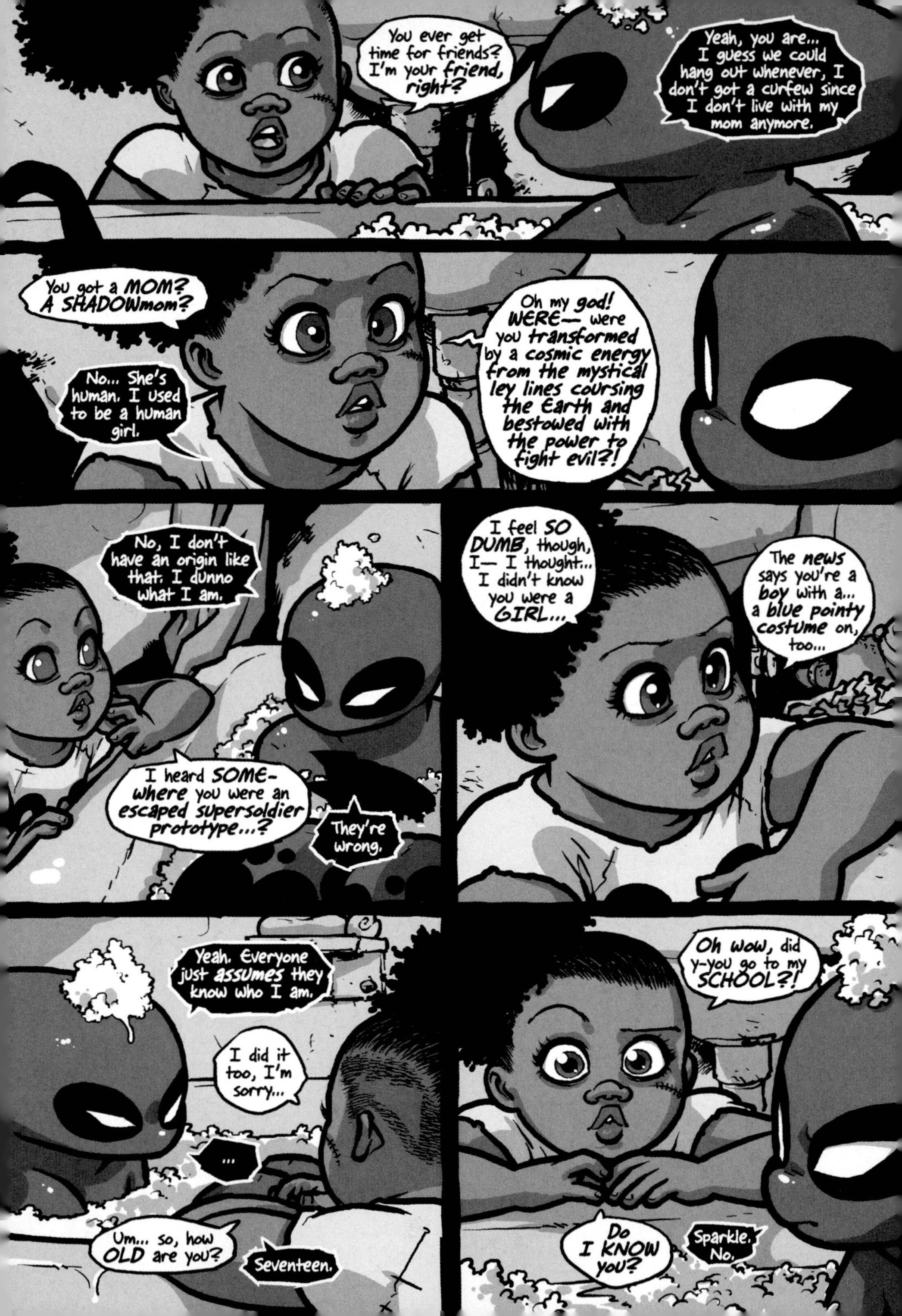
You ever get time for friends? I'm your friend, right?
Yeah, you are... I guess we could hang out whenever, I don't got a curfew since I don't live with my mom anymore.
You got a MOM? A SHADOWmom?
No... She's human. I used to be a human girl.
Oh my god! WERE— were you transformed by a cosmic energy from the mystical ley lines coursing the Earth and bestowed with the power to fight evil?!
No, I don't have an origin like that. I dunno what I am.
I heard SOME-where you were an escaped supersoldier prototype...?
They're wrong.
I feel SO DUMB, though, I— I thought... I didn't know you were a GIRL...
The news says you're a boy with a... a blue pointy costume on, too...
Yeah. Everyone just assumes they know who I am.
I did it too, I'm sorry...
...
Um... so, how OLD are you?
Seventeen.
Oh wow, did y-you go to my SCHOOL?!
Do I KNOW you?
Sparkle. No.

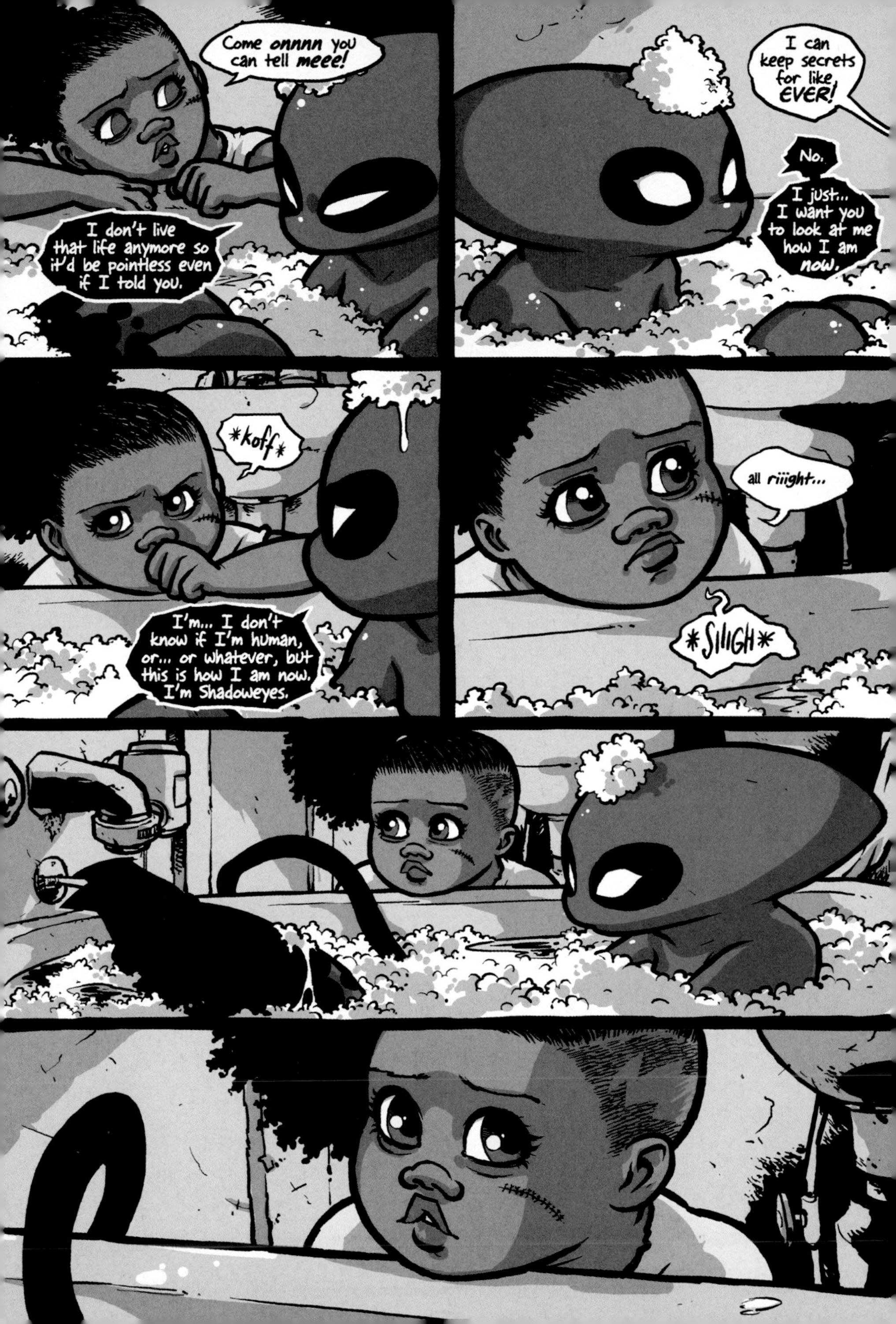
Come onnnn you can tell meee!
I don't live that life anymore so it'd be pointless even if I told you.
I can keep secrets for like, EVER!
No.
I just... I want you to look at me how I am now.
koff
I'm... I don't know if I'm human, or... or whatever, but this is how I am now. I'm Shadoweyes.
all riiight...
SIIIGH

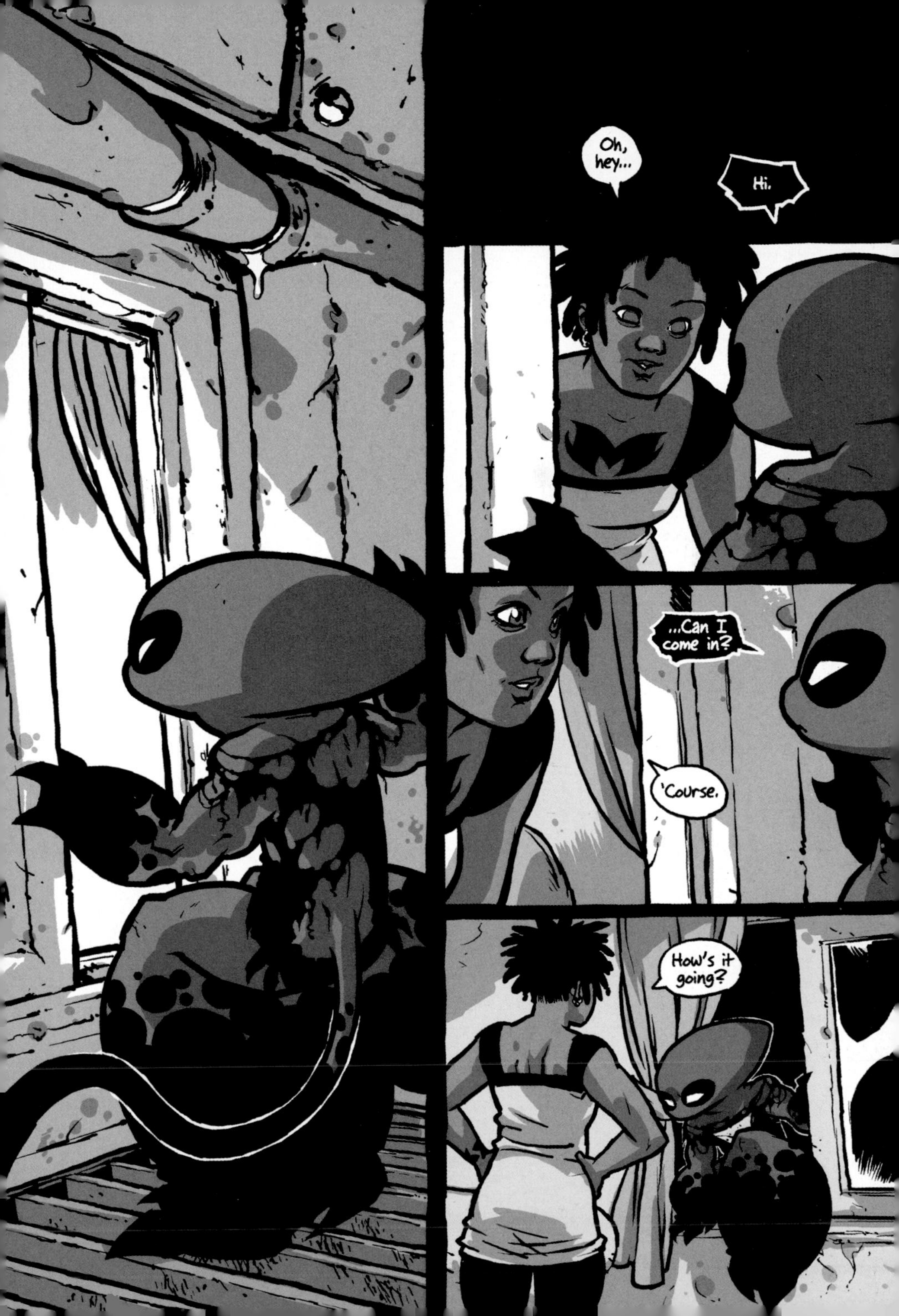
Oh, hey...
Hi.
...Can I come in?
'Course.
How's it going?

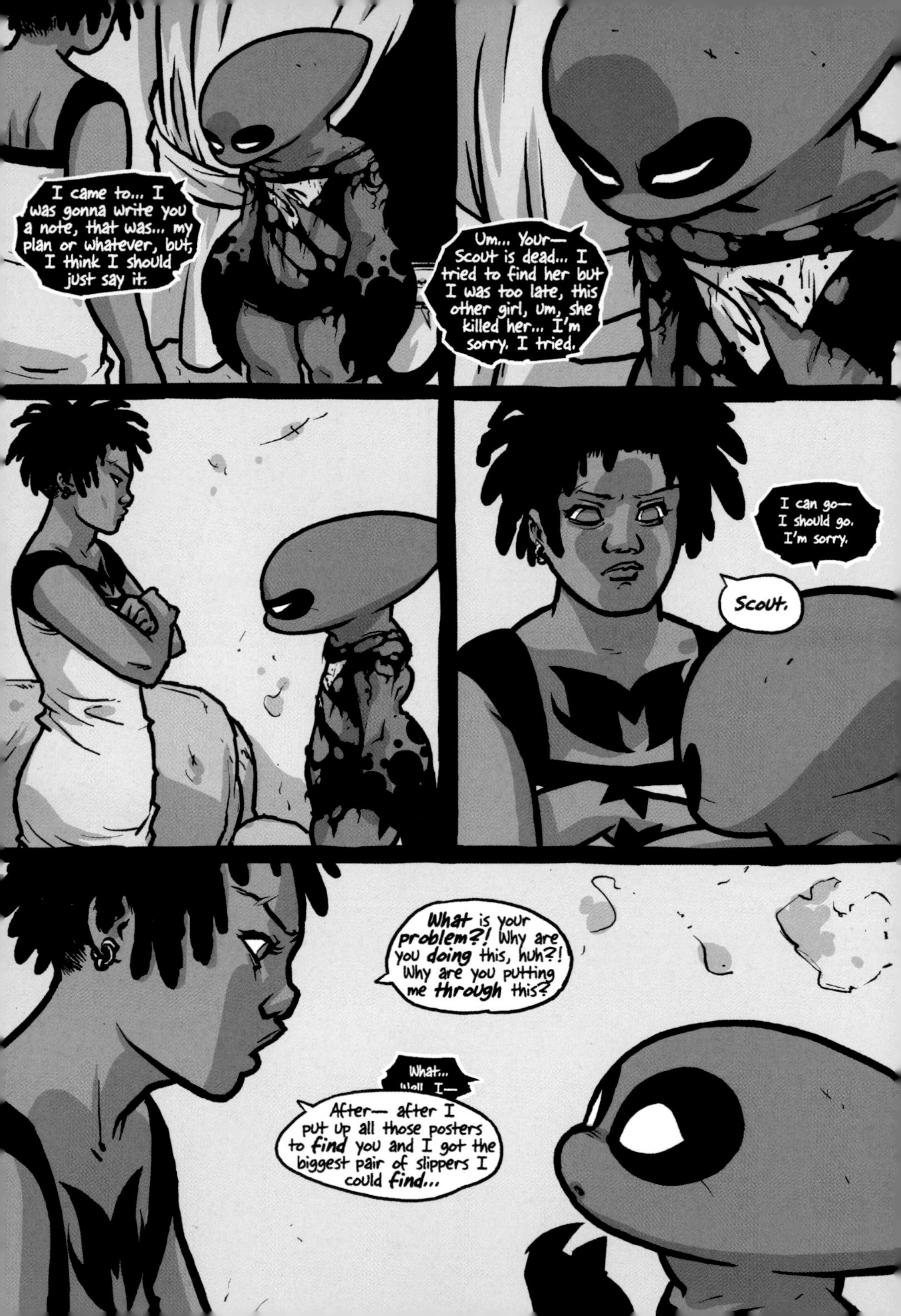
I came to... I was gonna write you a note, that was... my plan or whatever, but, I think I should just say it.
Um... Your— Scout is dead... I tried to find her but I was too late, this other girl, um, she killed her... I'm sorry. I tried.
I can go— I should go. I'm sorry.
Scout.
What is your problem?! Why are you doing this, huh?! Why are you putting me through this?
What... Well I—
After— after I put up all those posters to find you and I got the biggest pair of slippers I could find...

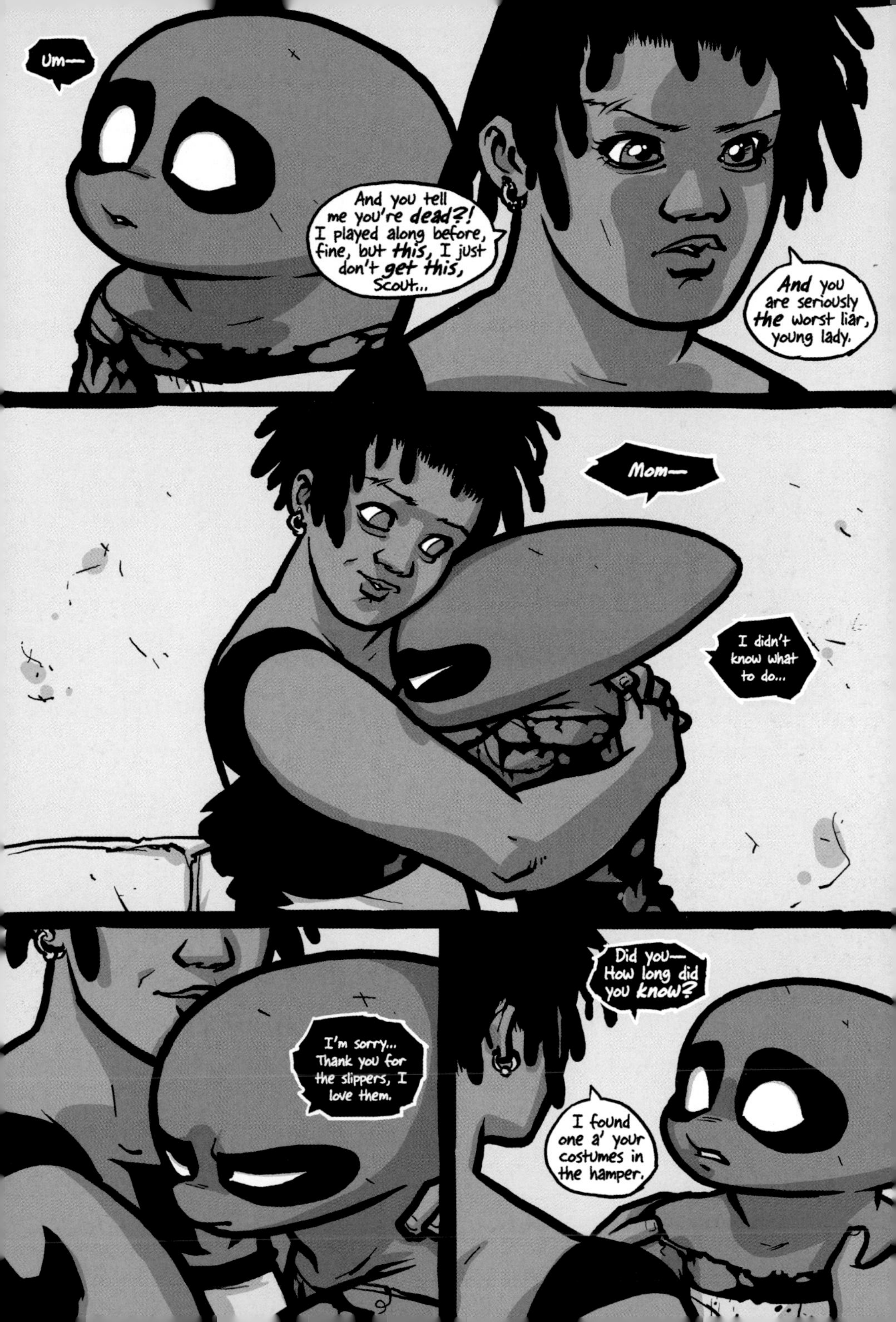
Um—
And you tell me you're dead?! I played along before, fine, but this, I just don't get this, Scout...
And you are seriously the worst liar, young lady.
Mom—
I didn't know what to do...
I'm sorry... Thank you for the slippers, I love them.
Did you— How long did you know?
I found one a' your costumes in the hamper.

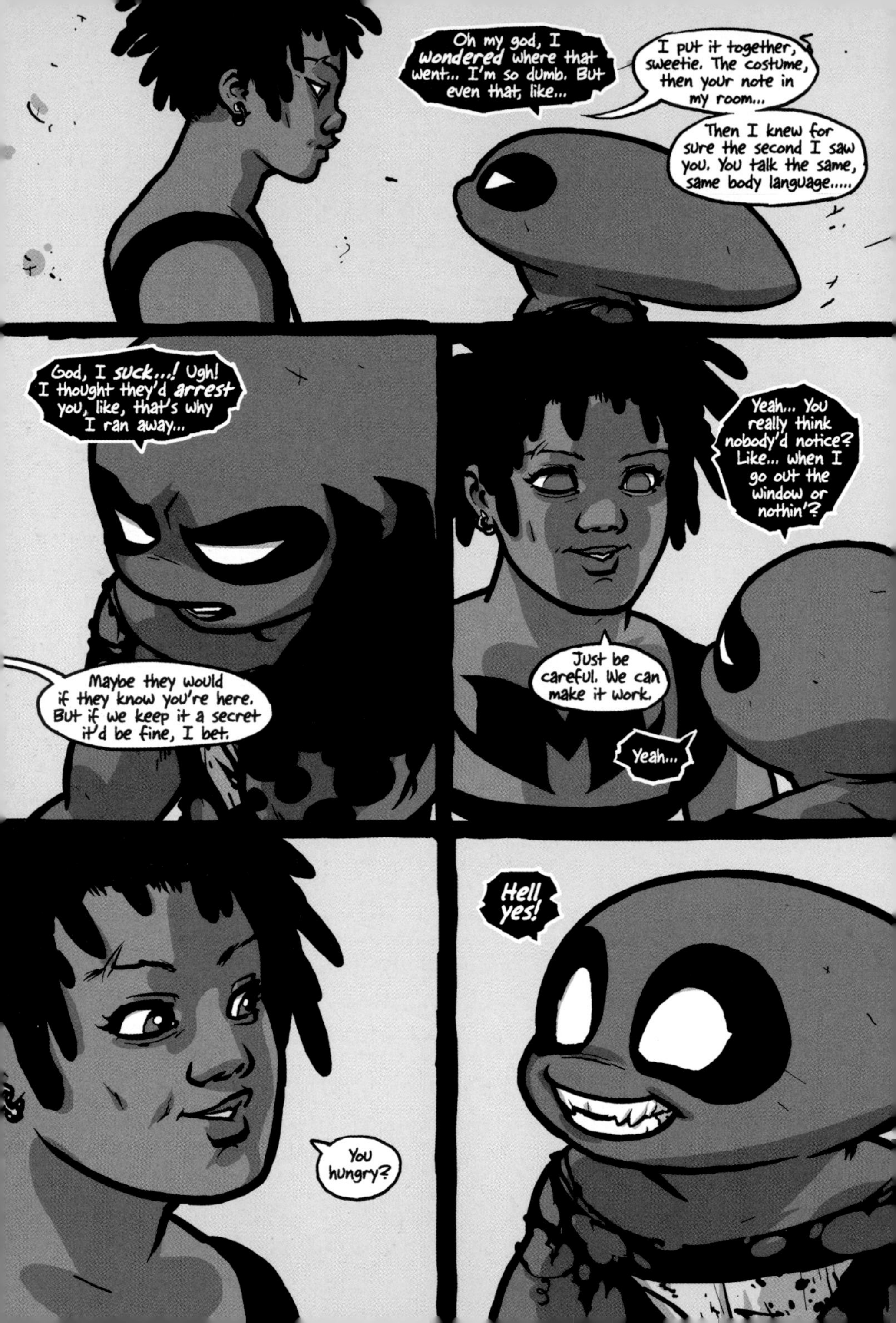
Oh my god, I wondered where that went... I'm so dumb. But even that, like...
I put it together, sweetie. The costume, then your note in my room...
Then I knew for sure the second I saw you. You talk the same, same body language.....
God, I suck...! Ugh! I thought they'd arrest you, like, that's why I ran away...
Maybe they would if they know you're here. But if we keep it a secret it'd be fine, I bet.
Yeah... You really think nobody'd notice? Like... when I go out the window or nothin'?
Just be careful. We can make it work.
Yeah...
You hungry?
Hell yes!

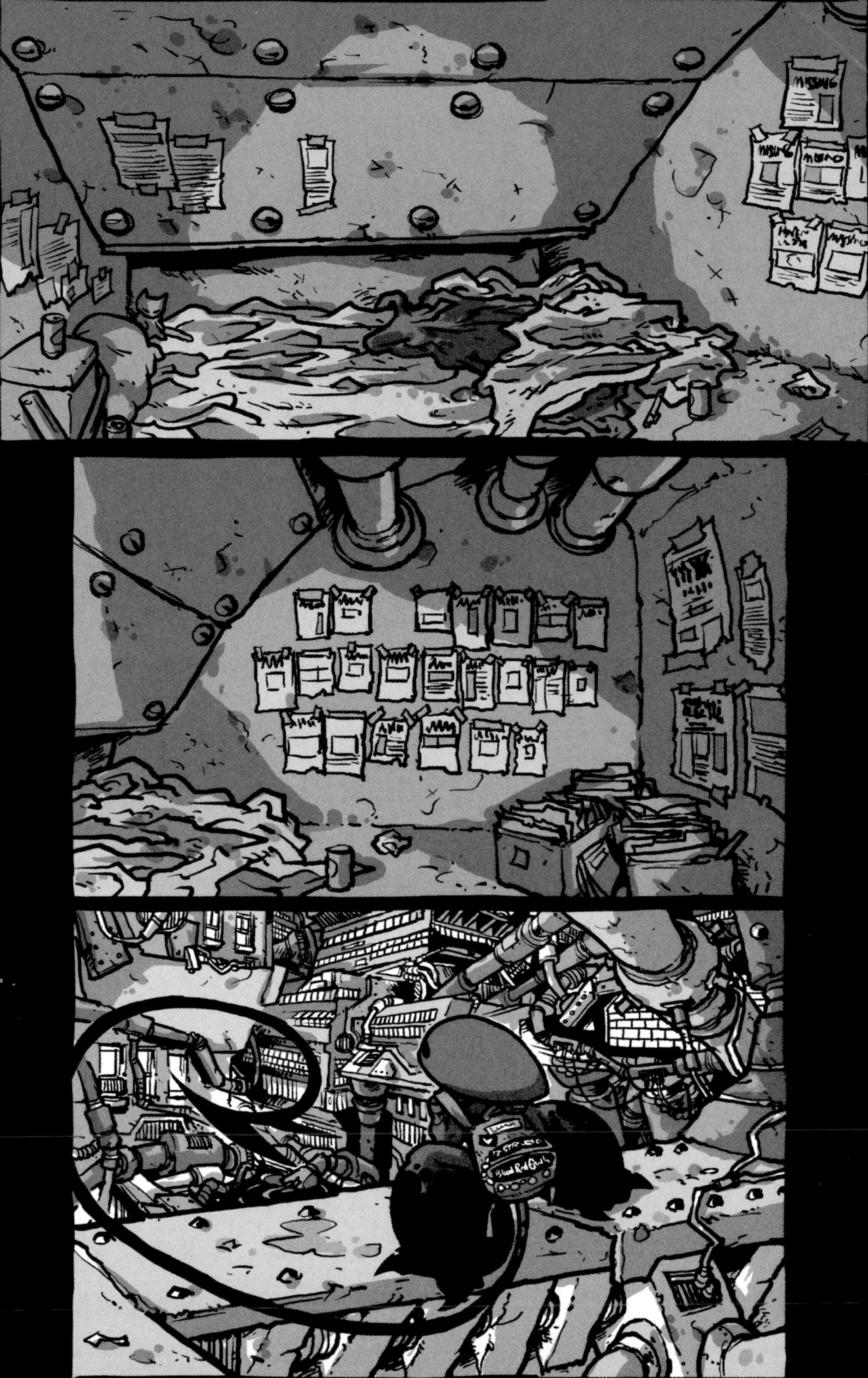
MISSING

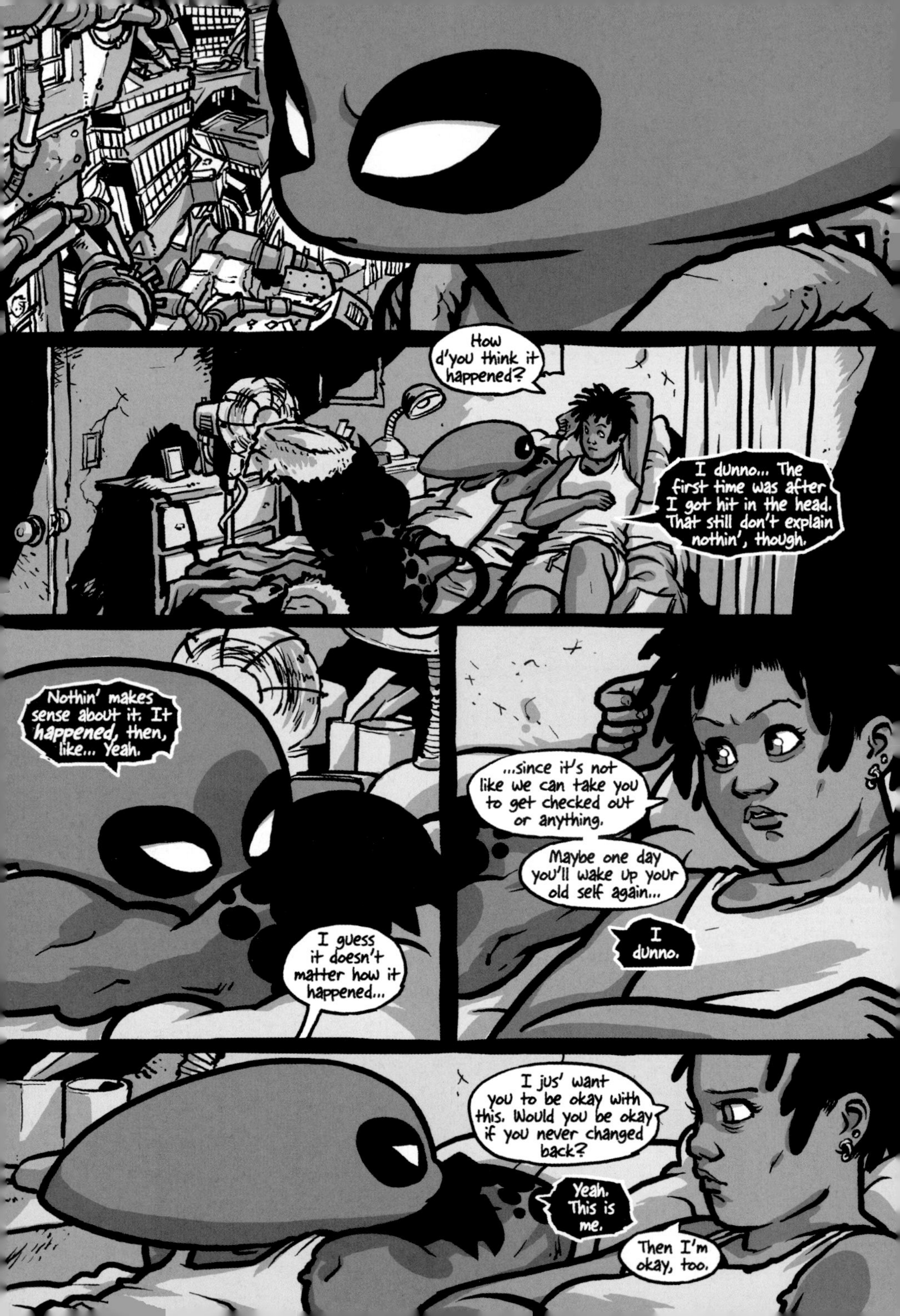
How d'you think it happened?
I dunno... The first time was after I got hit in the head. That still don't explain nothin', though.
Nothin' makes sense about it. It *happened*, then, like... Yeah.
I guess it doesn't matter how it happened...
...since it's not like we can take you to get checked out or anything.
Maybe one day you'll wake up your old self again...
I dunno.
I jus' want you to be okay with this. Would you be okay if you never changed back?
Yeah. This is me.
Then I'm okay, too.

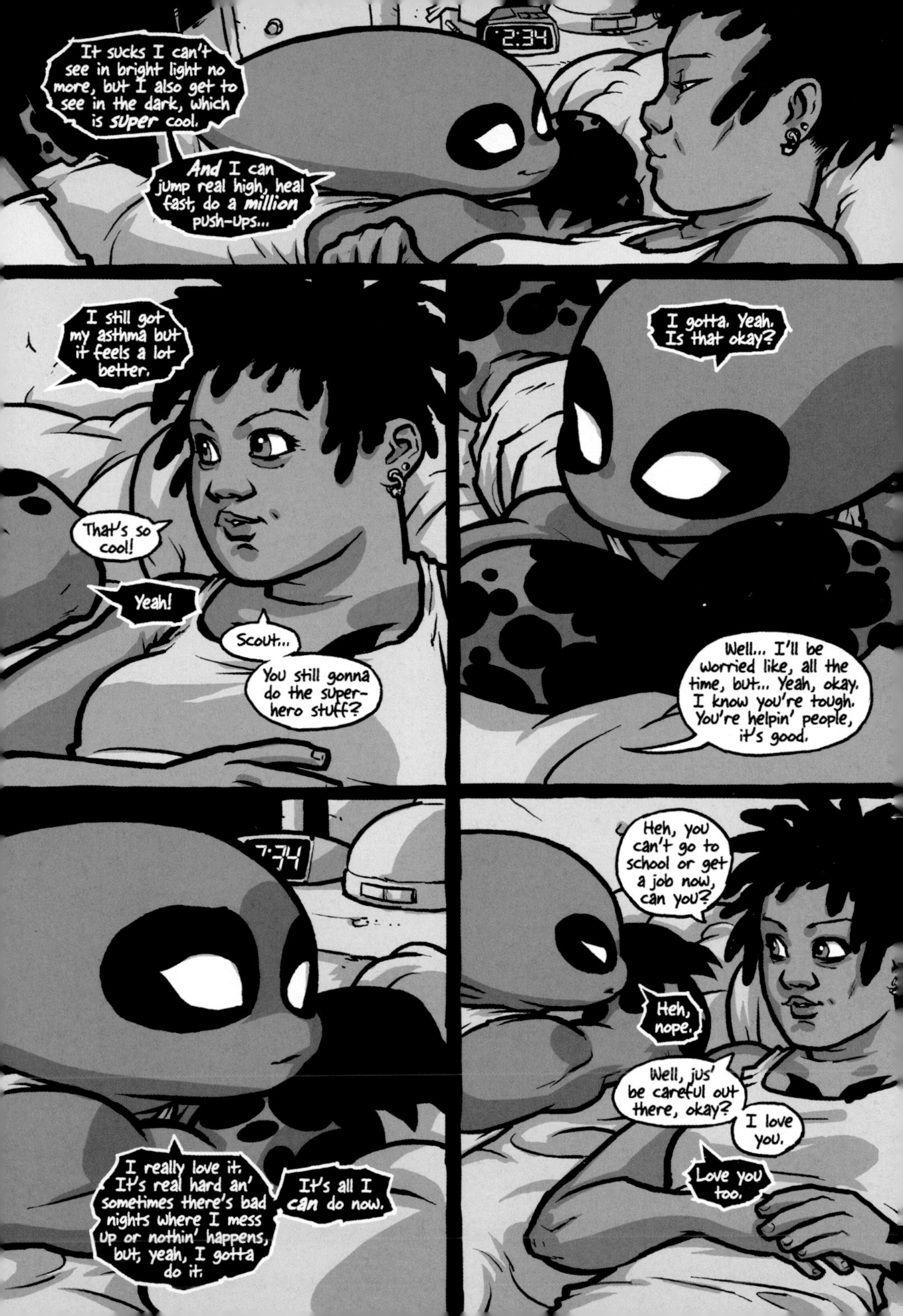
2:34
It sucks I can't see in bright light no more, but I also get to see in the dark, which is super cool.
And I can jump real high, heal fast, do a million push-ups...
I still got my asthma but it feels a lot better.
That's so cool!
Yeah!
Scout...
You still gonna do the super-hero stuff?
I gotta. Yeah. Is that okay?
Well... I'll be worried like, all the time, but... Yeah, okay. I know you're tough. You're helpin' people, it's good.
7:34
I really love it. It's real hard an' sometimes there's bad nights where I mess up or nothin' happens, but, yeah, I gotta do it.
It's all I can do now.
Heh, you can't go to school or get a job now, can you?
Heh, nope.
Well, jus' be careful out there, okay?
I love you.
Love you too.

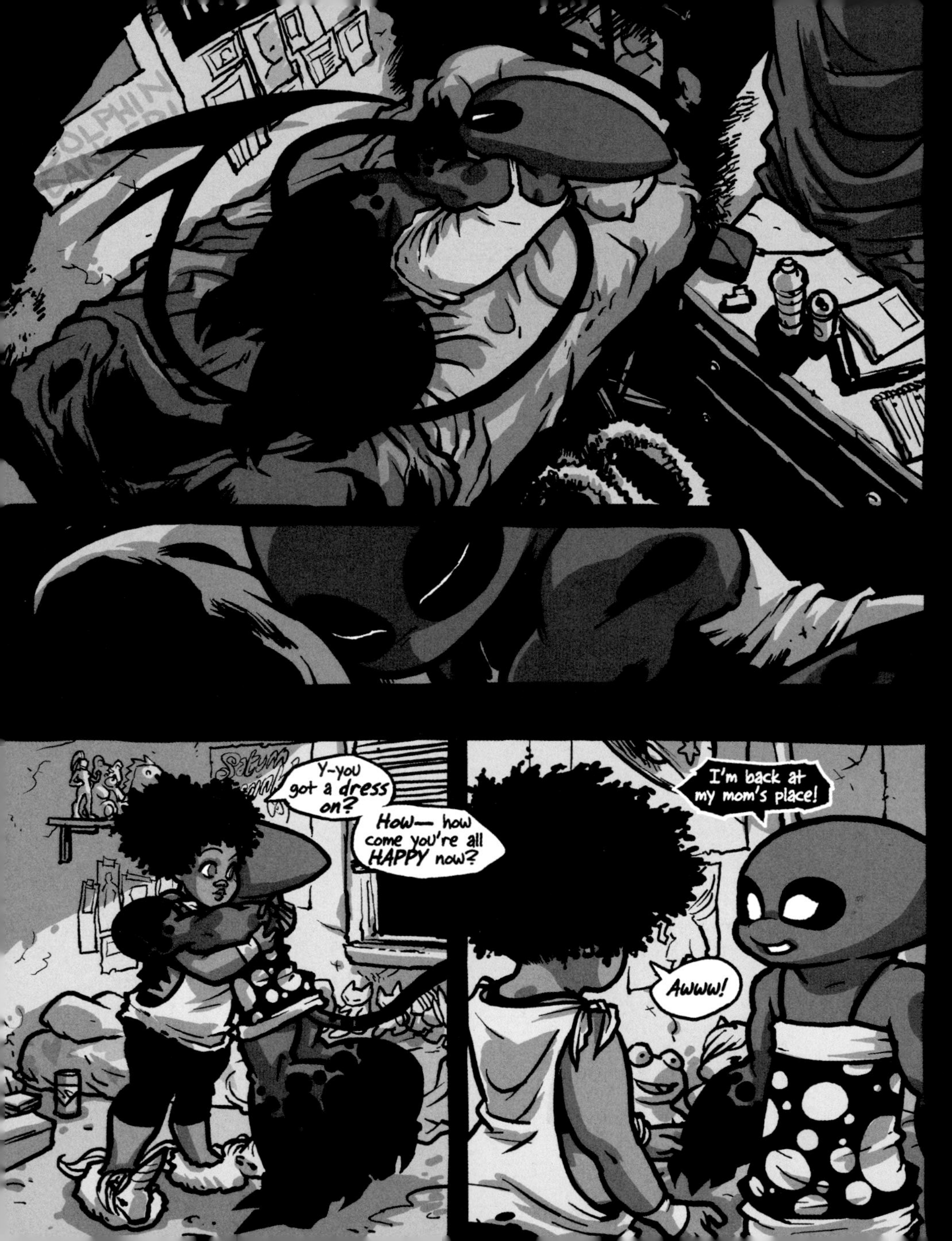
Y-you got a dress on?
How— how come you're all HAPPY now?
I'm back at my mom's place!
AWWW!

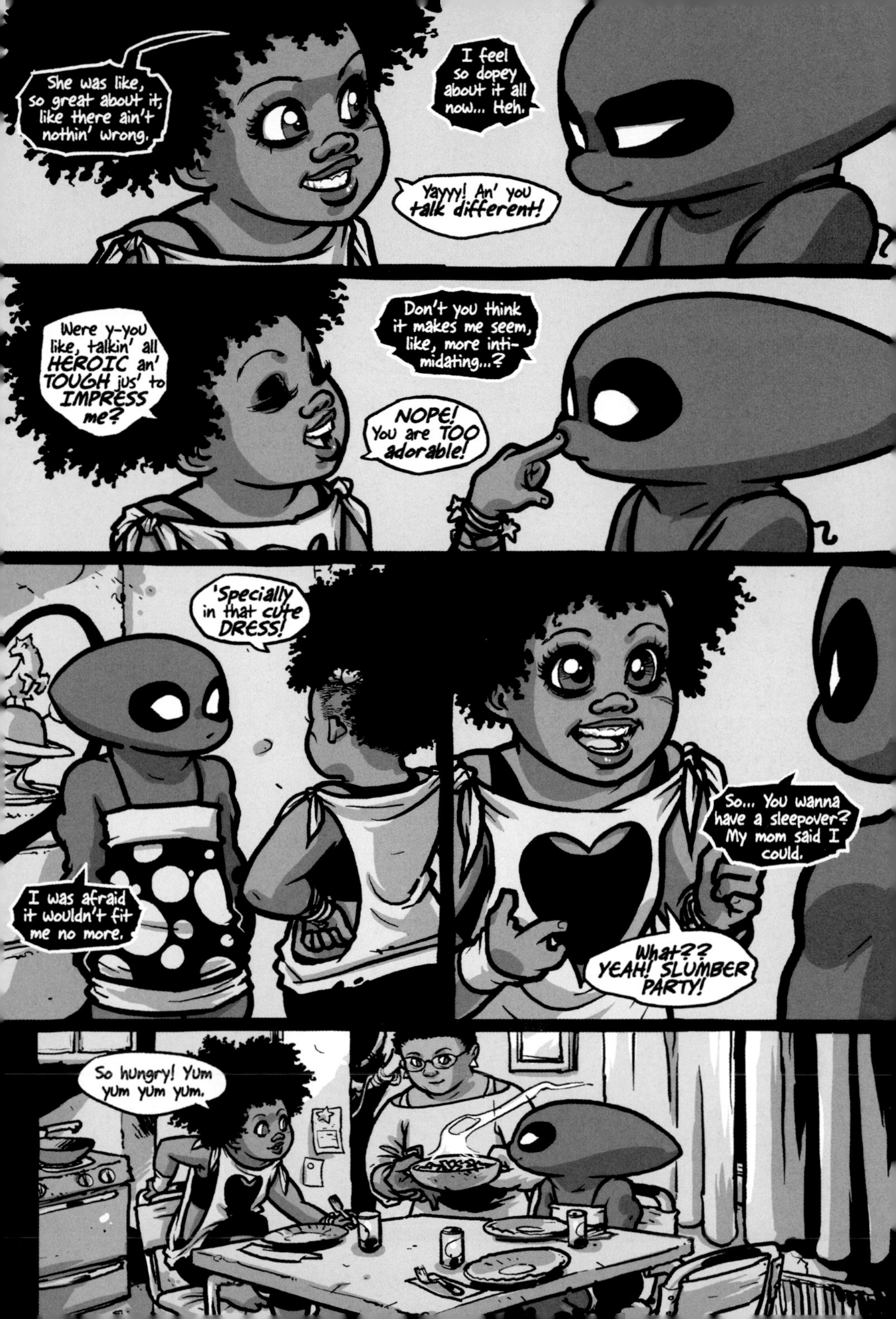
She was like, so great about it, like there ain't nothin' wrong.
I feel so dopey about it all now... Heh.
Yayyy! An' you talk different!
Were y-you like, talkin' all HEROIC an' TOUGH jus' to IMPRESS me?
Don't you think it makes me seem, like, more intimidating...?
NOPE! You are TOO adorable!
'Specially in that cute DRESS!
I was afraid it wouldn't fit me no more.
So... You wanna have a sleepover? My mom said I could.
What?? YEAH! SLUMBER PARTY!
So hungry! Yum yum yum yum.

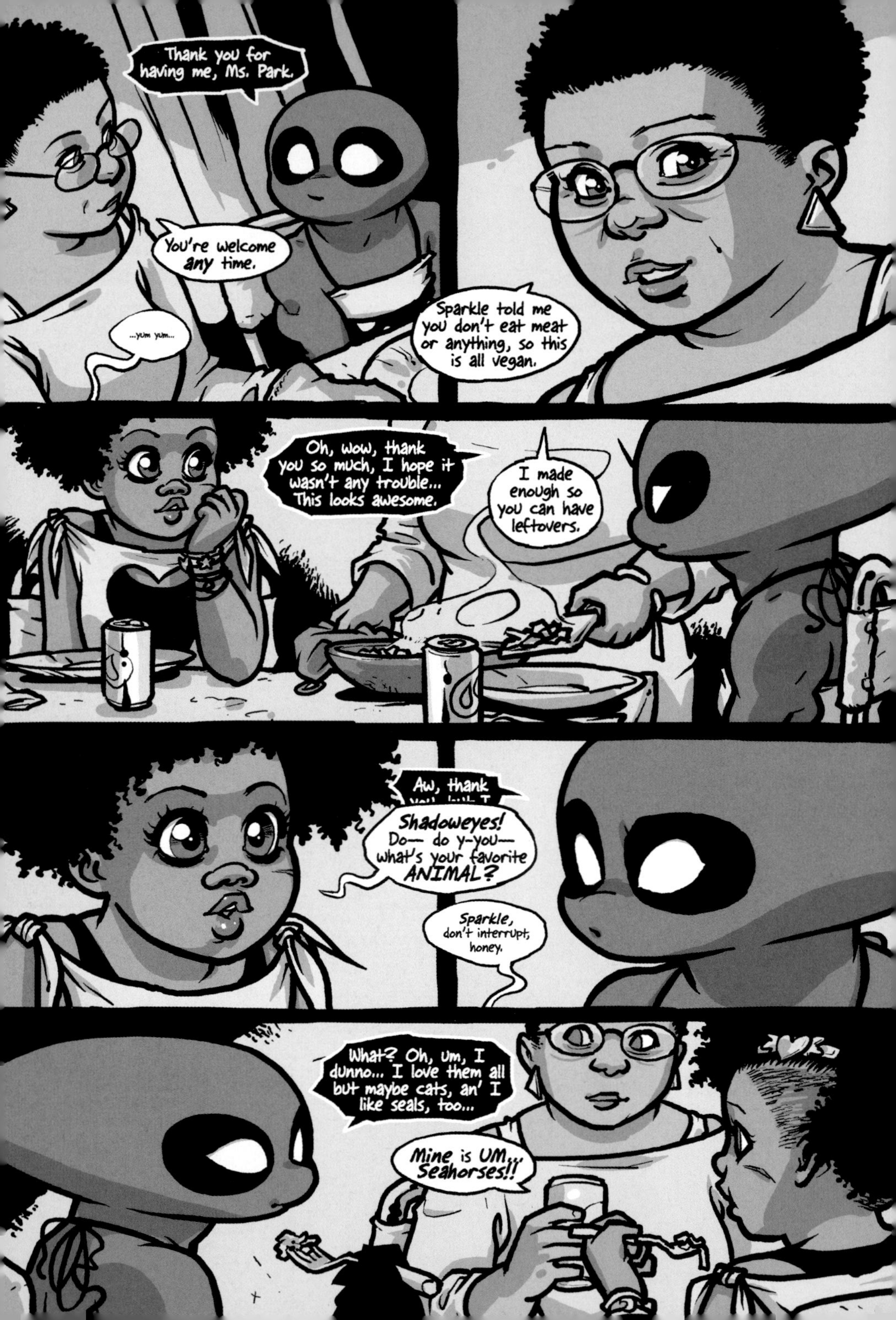

Thank you for having me, Ms. Park.
You're welcome any time.
...yum yum...
Sparkle told me you don't eat meat or anything, so this is all vegan.
Oh, wow, thank you so much, I hope it wasn't any trouble... This looks awesome.
I made enough so you can have leftovers.
Aw, thank
Shadoweyes! Do— do y-you— what's your favorite ANIMAL?
Sparkle, don't interrupt, honey.
What? Oh, um, I dunno... I love them all but maybe cats, an' I like seals, too...
Mine is UM... Seahorses!!

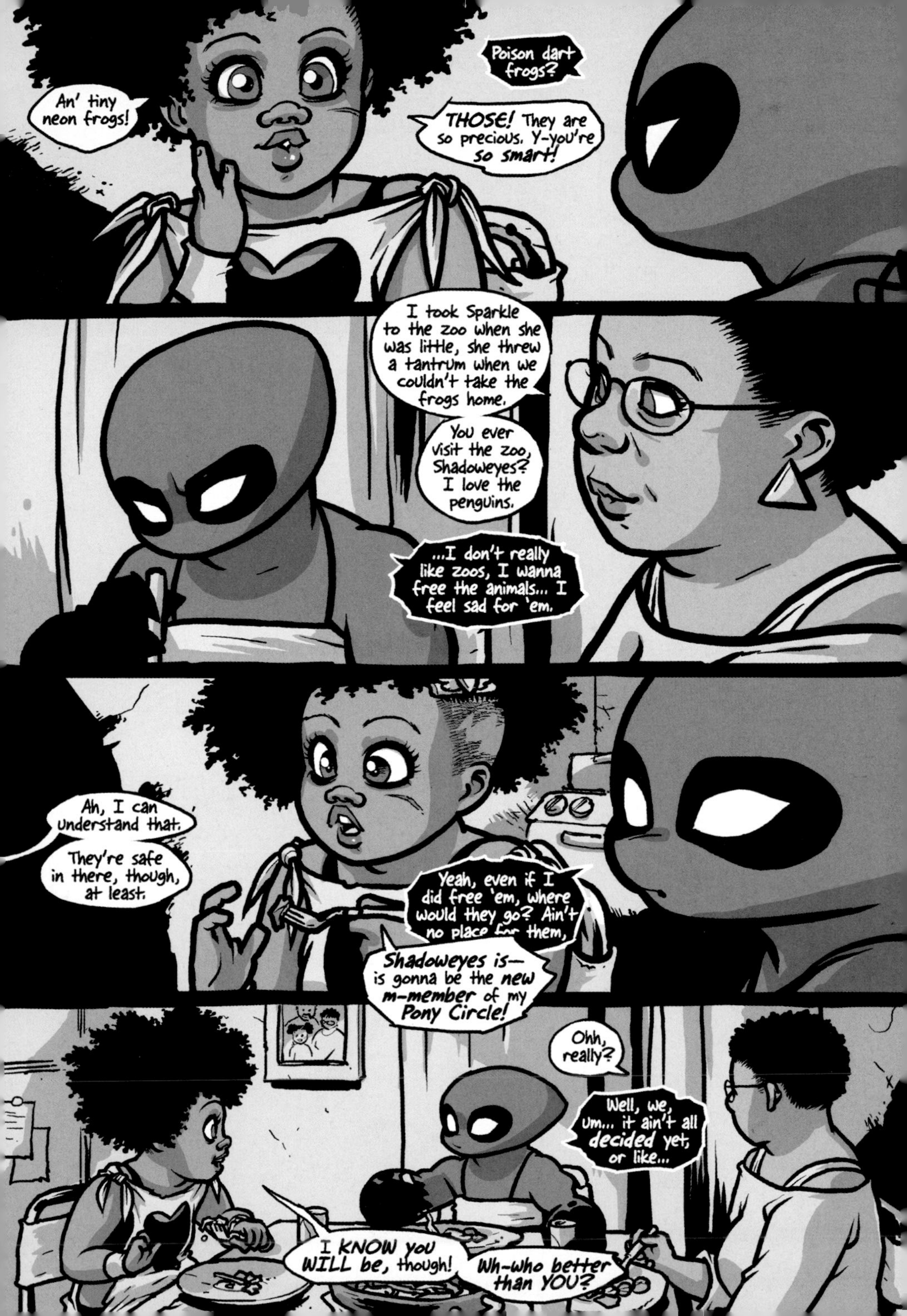
An' tiny neon frogs!
Poison dart frogs?
THOSE! They are so precious. Y-you're so smart!
I took Sparkle to the zoo when she was little, she threw a tantrum when we couldn't take the frogs home.
You ever visit the zoo, Shadoweyes? I love the penguins.
...I don't really like zoos, I wanna free the animals... I feel sad for 'em.
Ah, I can understand that.
They're safe in there, though, at least.
Yeah, even if I did free 'em, where would they go? Ain't no place for them,
Shadoweyes is—is gonna be the new m-member of my Pony Circle!
Ohh, really?
Well, we, um... it ain't all decided yet, or like...
I KNOW you WILL be, though!
Wh-who better than YOU?

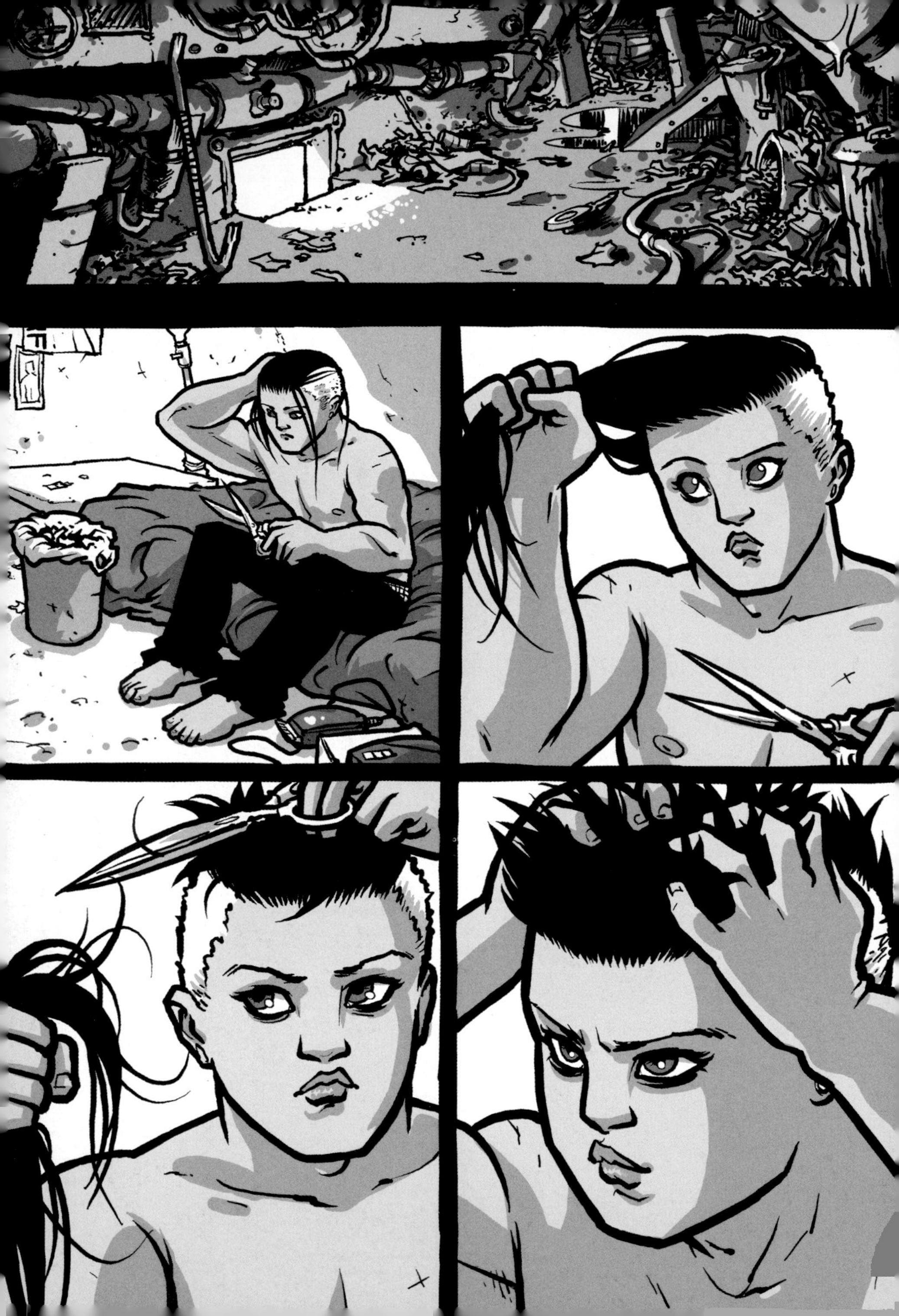

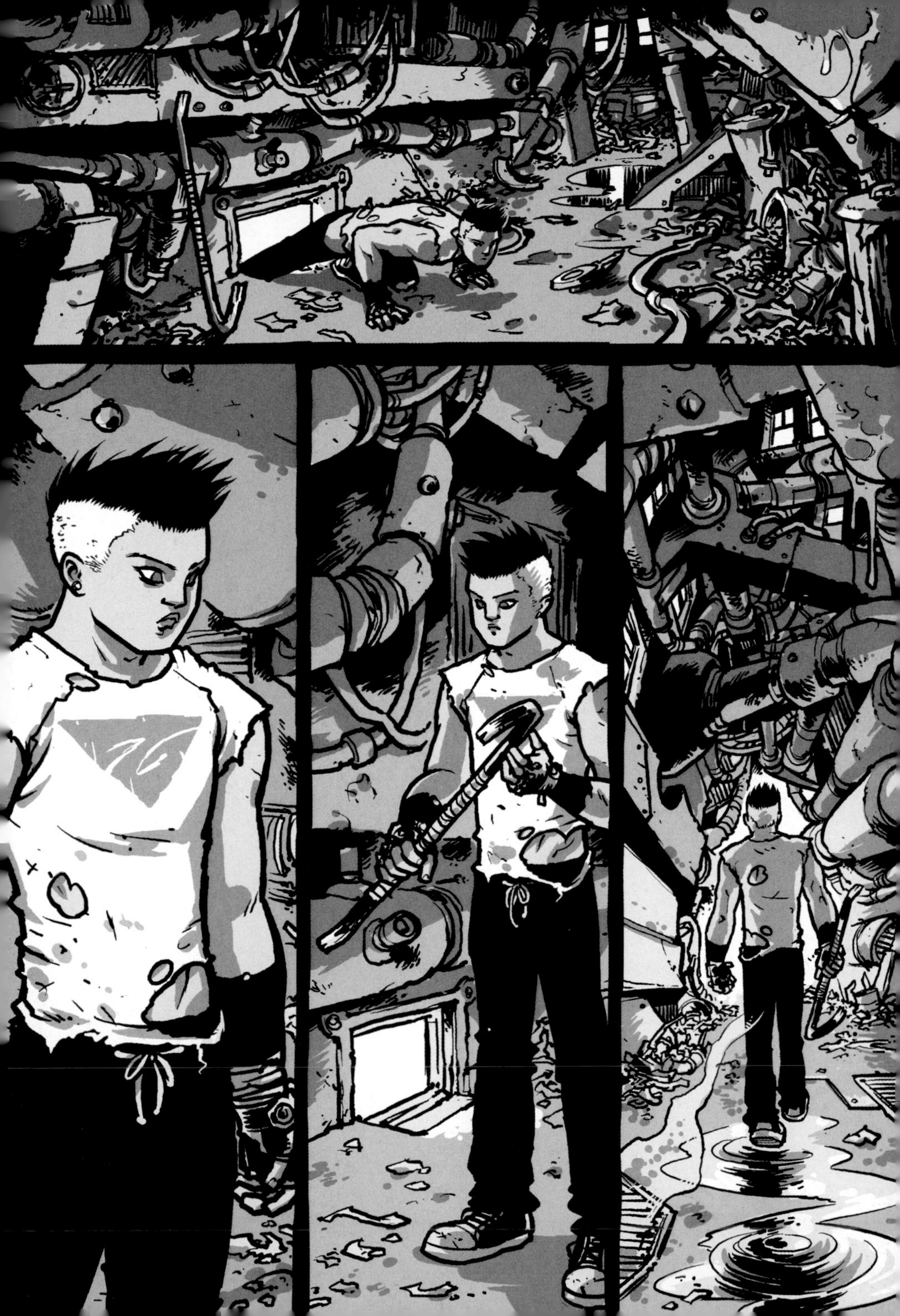

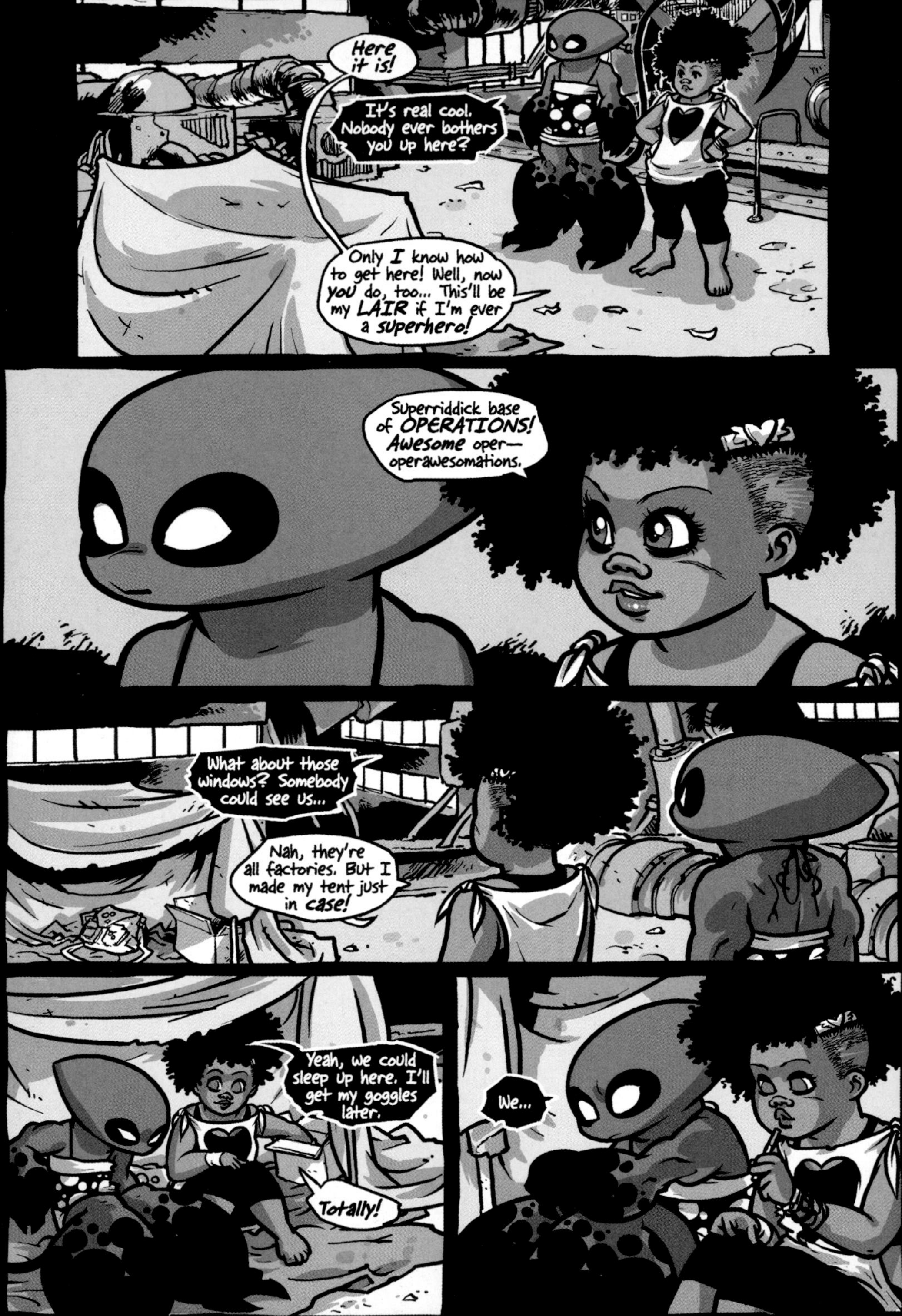
Here it is!
It's real cool. Nobody ever bothers you up here?
Only I know how to get here! Well, now you do, too... This'll be my LAIR if I'm ever a superhero!
Superriddick base of OPERATIONS! Awesome oper— operawesomations.
What about those windows? Somebody could see us...
Nah, they're all factories. But I made my tent just in case!
Yeah, we could sleep up here. I'll get my goggles later.
Totally!
We...

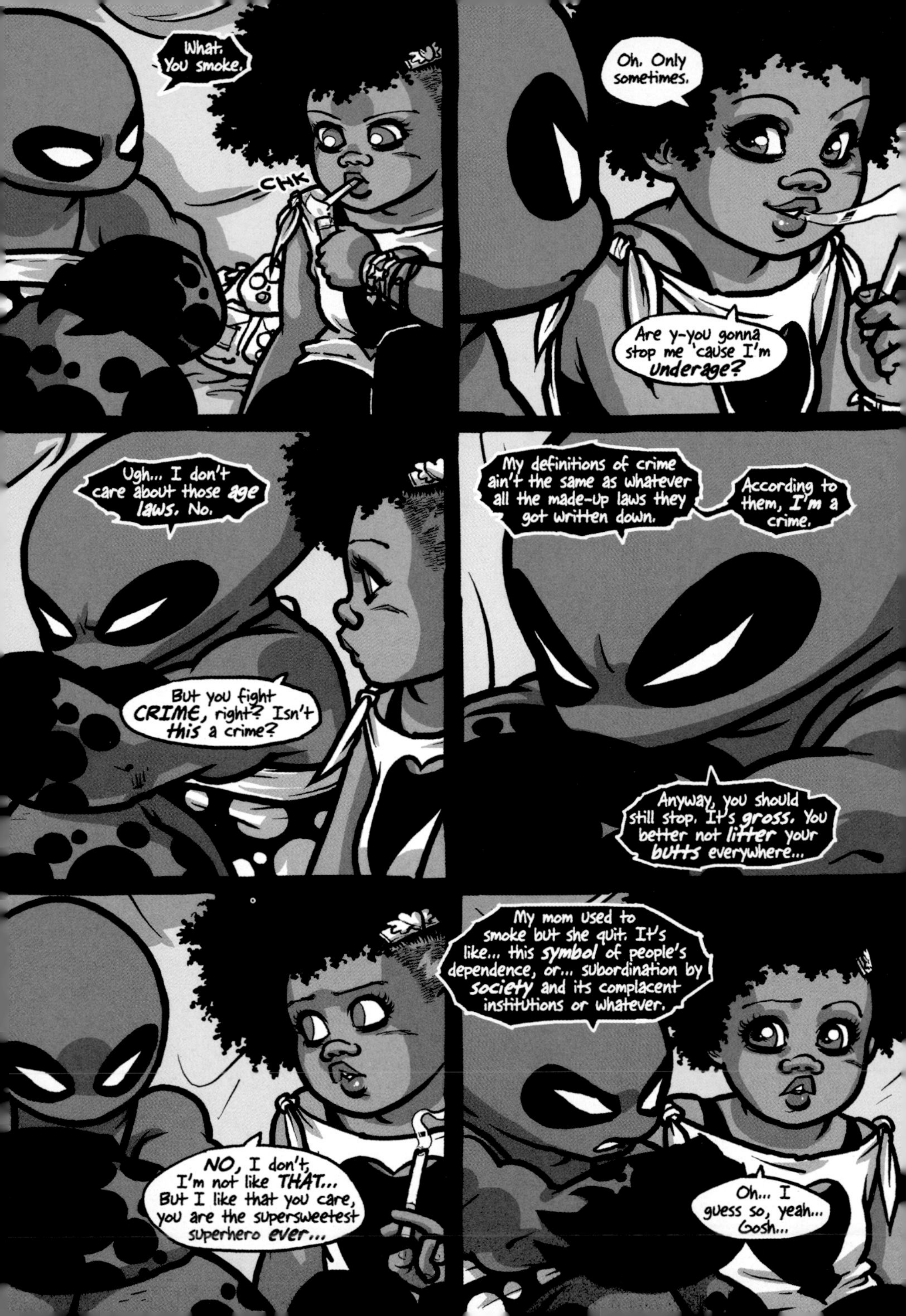
What. You smoke.
CHK
Oh. Only sometimes.
Are y-you gonna stop me 'cause I'm underage?
Ugh... I don't care about those age laws. No.
But you fight CRIME, right? Isn't this a crime?
My definitions of crime ain't the same as whatever all the made-up laws they got written down.
According to them, I'm a crime.
Anyway, you should still stop. It's gross. You better not litter your butts everywhere...
NO, I don't, I'm not like THAT... But I like that you care, you are the supersweetest superhero ever...
My mom used to smoke but she quit. It's like... this symbol of people's dependence, or... subordination by society and its complacent institutions or whatever.
Oh... I guess so, yeah... Gosh...

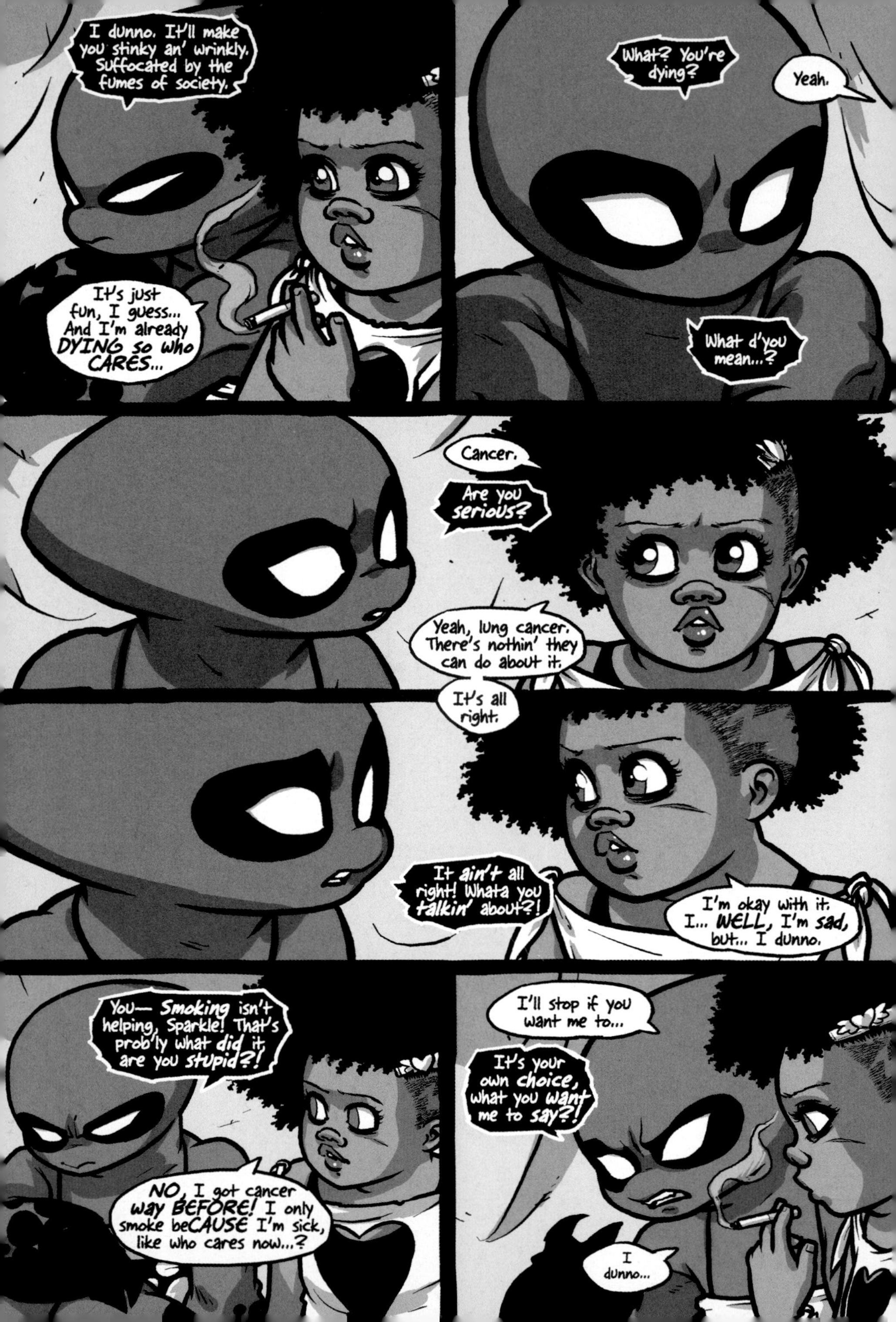
I dunno. It'll make you stinky an' wrinkly. Suffocated by the fumes of society.
It's just fun, I guess... And I'm already DYING so who CARES...
What? You're dying?
Yeah.
What d'you mean...?
Cancer.
Are you serious?
Yeah, lung cancer. There's nothin' they can do about it.
It's all right.
It ain't all right! Whata you talkin' about?!
I'm okay with it. I... WELL, I'm sad, but... I dunno.
You— Smoking isn't helping, Sparkle! That's prob'ly what did it, are you stupid?!
NO, I got cancer way BEFORE! I only smoke beCAUSE I'm sick, like who cares now...?
I'll stop if you want me to...
It's your own choice, what you want me to say?!
I dunno...

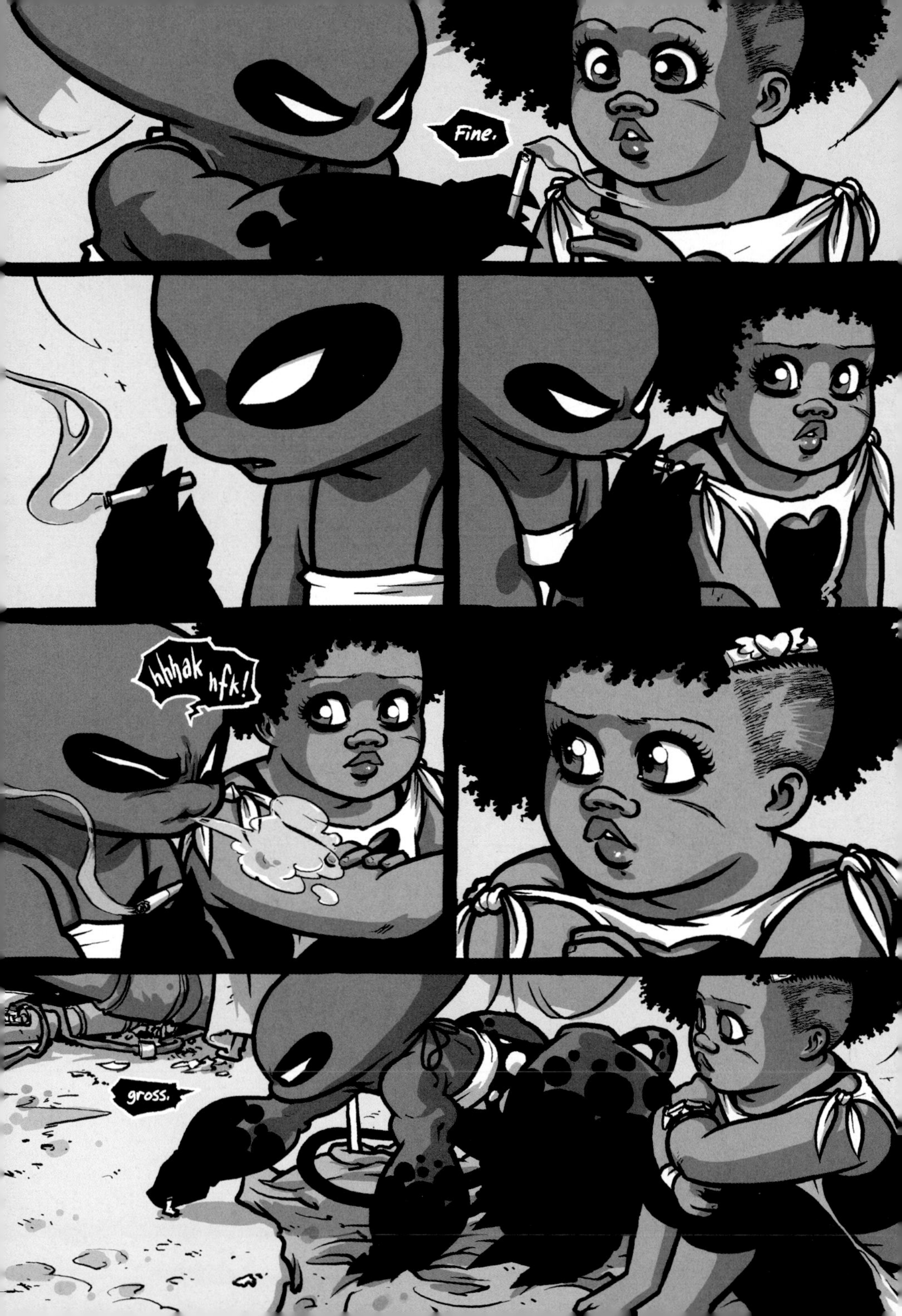
Fine.
hhhak hfk!
gross.

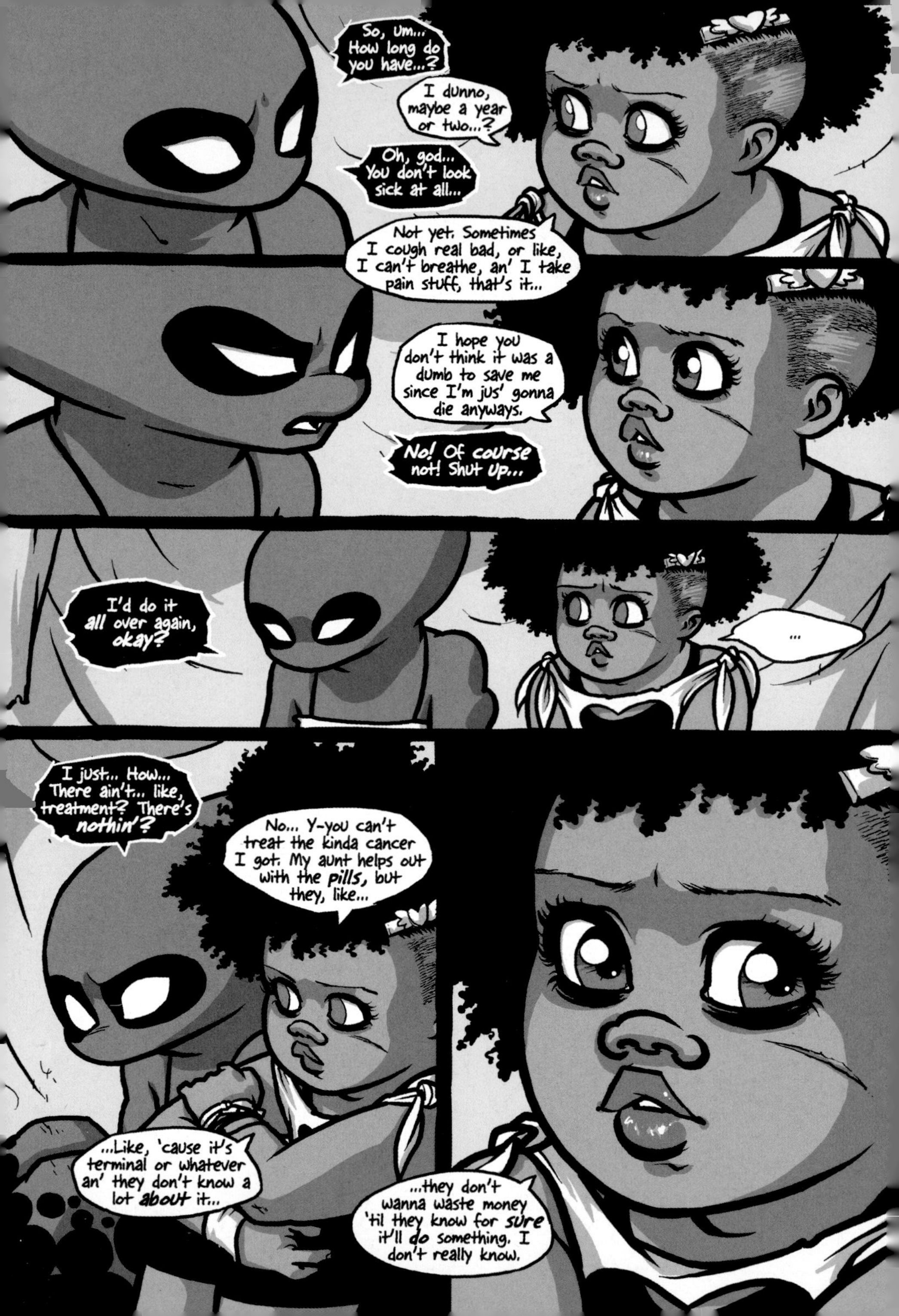
So, um... How long do you have...?
I dunno, maybe a year or two...?
Oh, god... You don't look sick at all...
Not yet. Sometimes I cough real bad, or like, I can't breathe, an' I take pain stuff, that's it...
I hope you don't think it was a dumb to save me since I'm jus' gonna die anyways.
No! Of course not! Shut up...
I'd do it all over again, okay?
...
I just... How... There ain't... like, treatment? There's nothin'?
No... Y-you can't treat the kinda cancer I got. My aunt helps out with the pills, but they, like...
...Like, 'cause it's terminal or whatever an' they don't know a lot about it...
...they don't wanna waste money 'til they know for sure it'll do something. I don't really know.

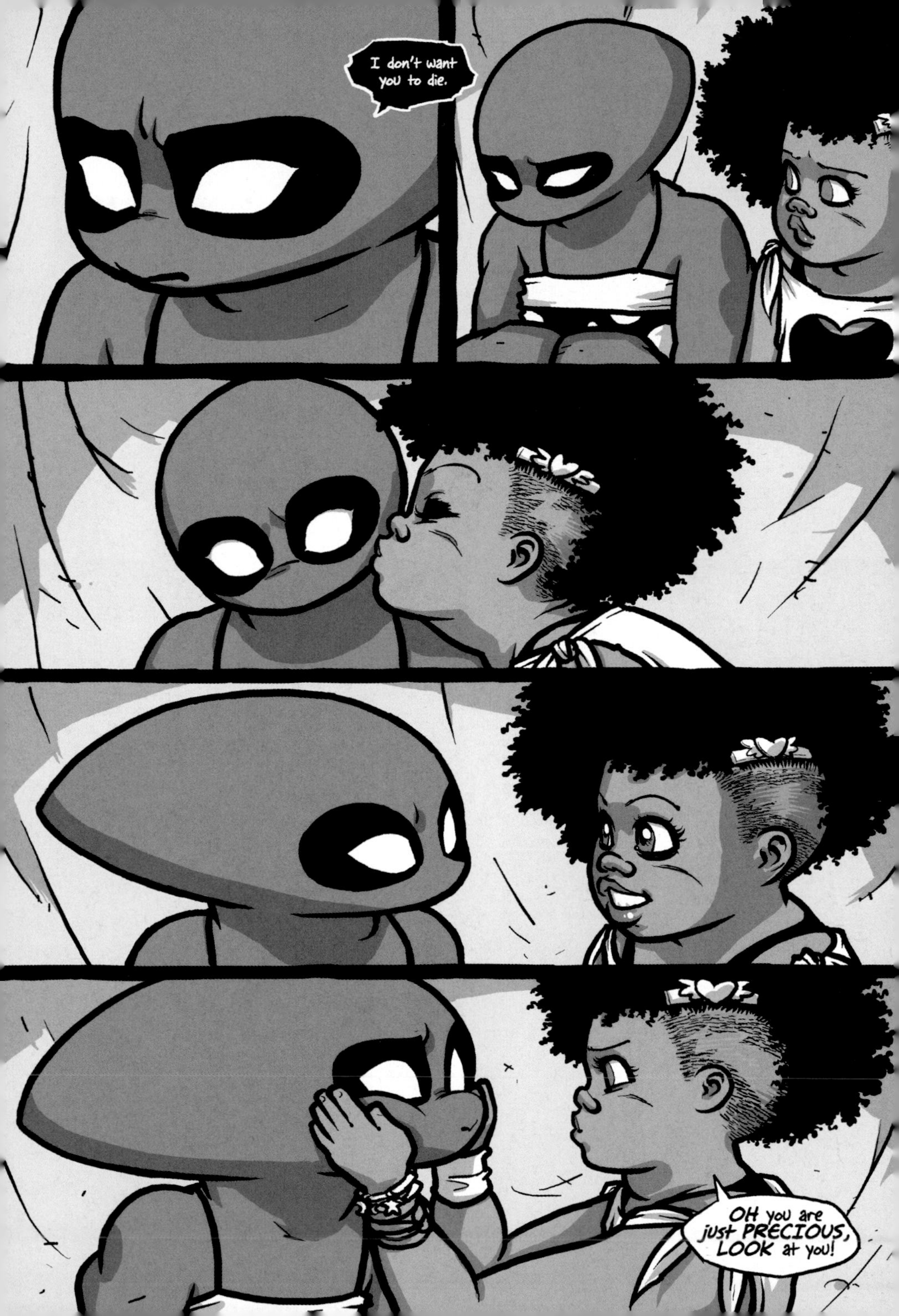
I don't want you to die.
OH you are just PRECIOUS, LOOK at you!

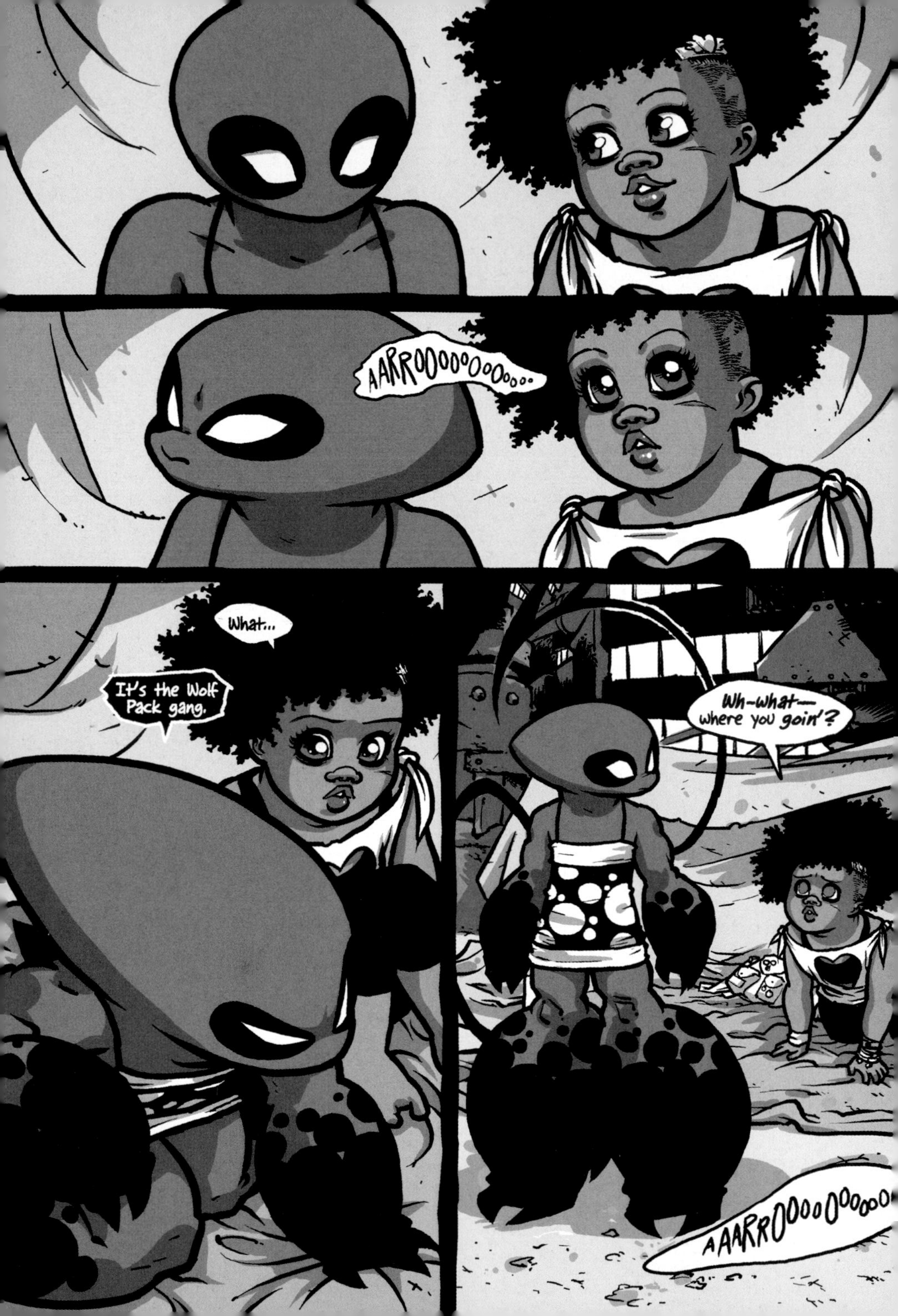
AARROOOOOOOOooo
What...
It's the Wolf Pack gang.
Wh-what— where you goin'?
AAARROOOOOOOOOOOO

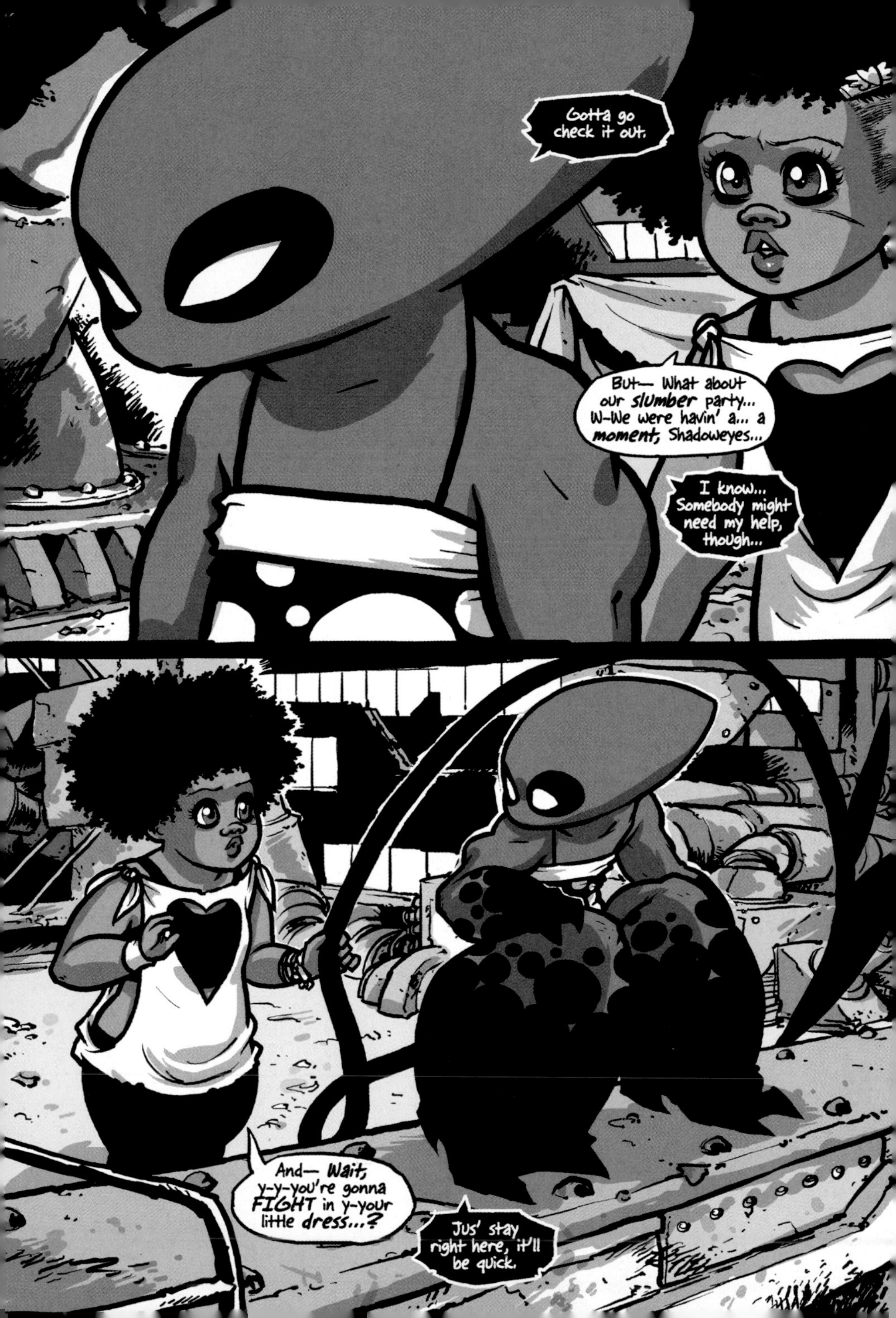
Gotta go check it out.
But— What about our slumber party... W-We were havin' a... a moment, Shadoweyes...
I know... Somebody might need my help, though...
And— Wait, y-y-you're gonna FIGHT in y-your little dress...?
Jus' stay right here, it'll be quick.

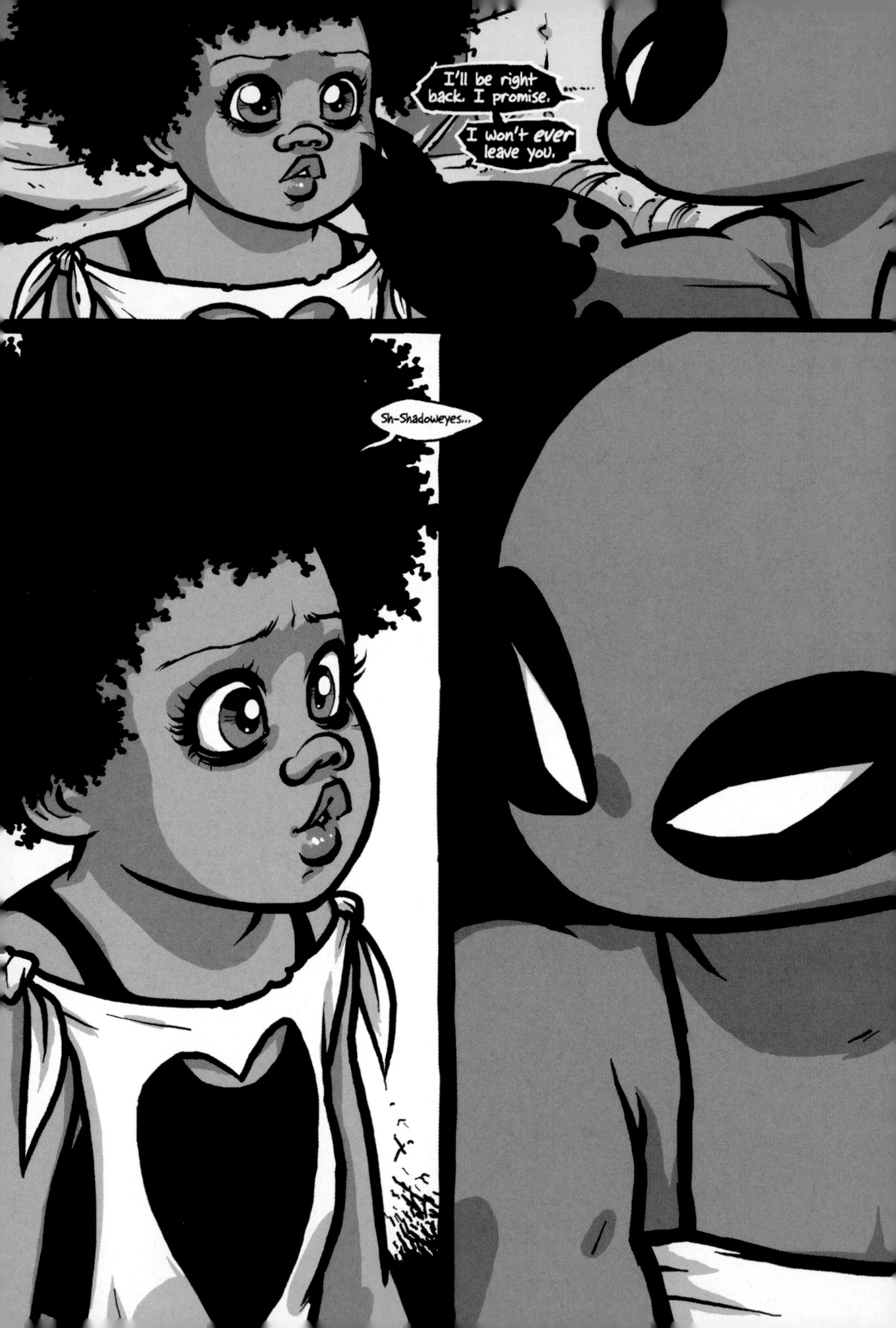
I'll be right back. I promise.
I won't ever leave you.
Sh-Shadoweyes...

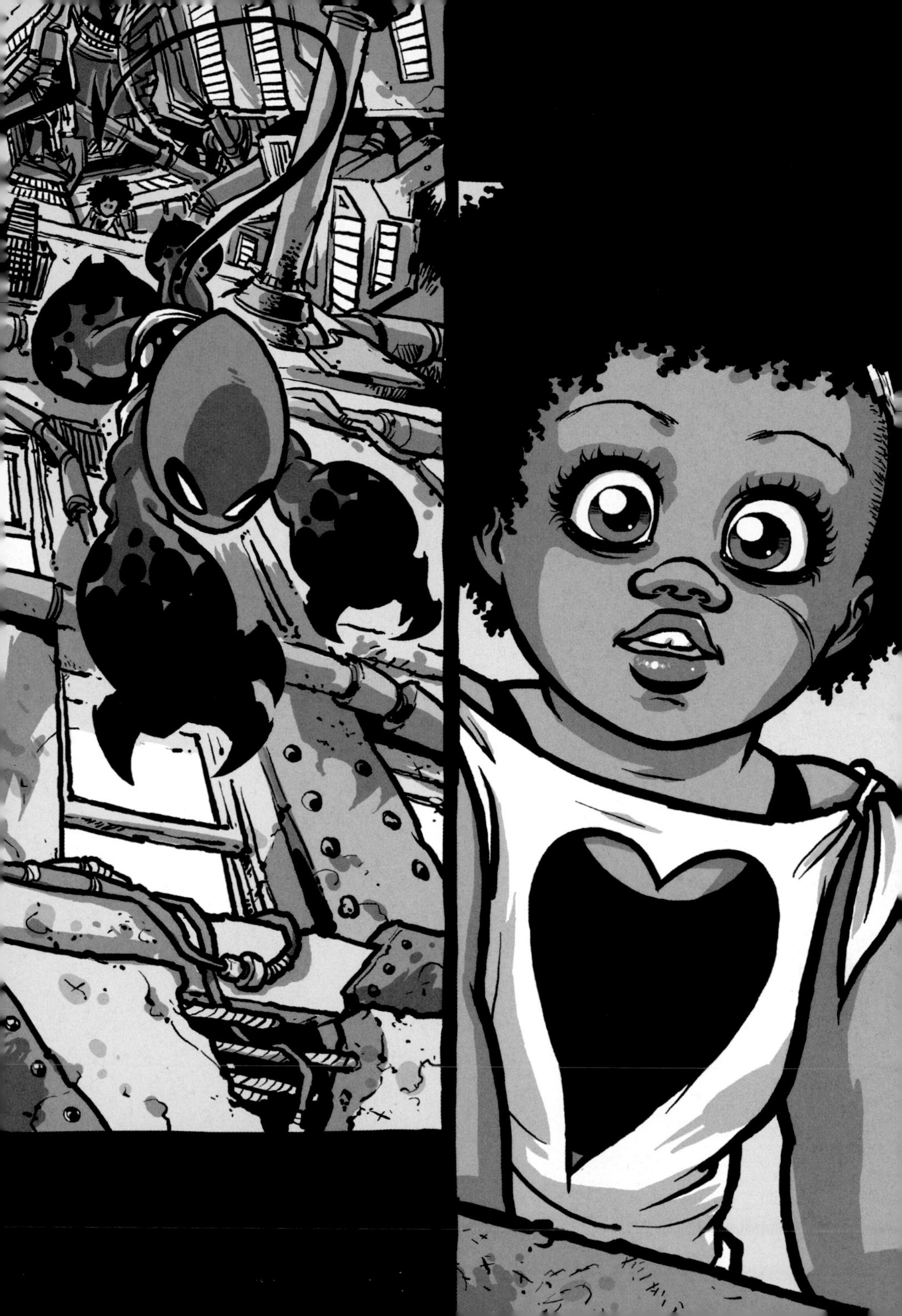

to be continued in
SHADOWEYES IN LOVE

Ross Campbell lives in Rochester, New York and is a full-time freelance artist (for now). His work includes the series *Wet Moon*, *The Abandoned*, *Water Baby*, *Spooked*, some short stories for DC/Vertigo's *House of Mystery*, Oni Press's *Resurrection*, and Tim Seeley's *Hack/Slash*, and his self-published comic *Mountain Girl* (which is currently on hiatus but will return with fury). He was nominated for an Eisner Award in 2006. He likes alien terror, Vin Diesel, Carl Weathers, monsters, tea, brussels sprouts, and cats. He hates frogs, summer, traveling, and ketchup.

thanks to: Kelly Thompson, Nnedi Okorafor, Zach Smith, Dan Rozman, Nick Marino, Candace McAfee, Kaylie McDougal, Jessica Rider, Tim Seeley, John Parkin, Chris Arrant, everyone who reads my comics, everyone at Oni, and last but not least Jennifer de Guzman and Dan Vado for taking a chance on a blue, pointy superhero.

visit Ross at
www.greenoblivion.com
mooncalfe.deviantart.com
mooncalfe.livejournal.com
www.shadoweyes.net

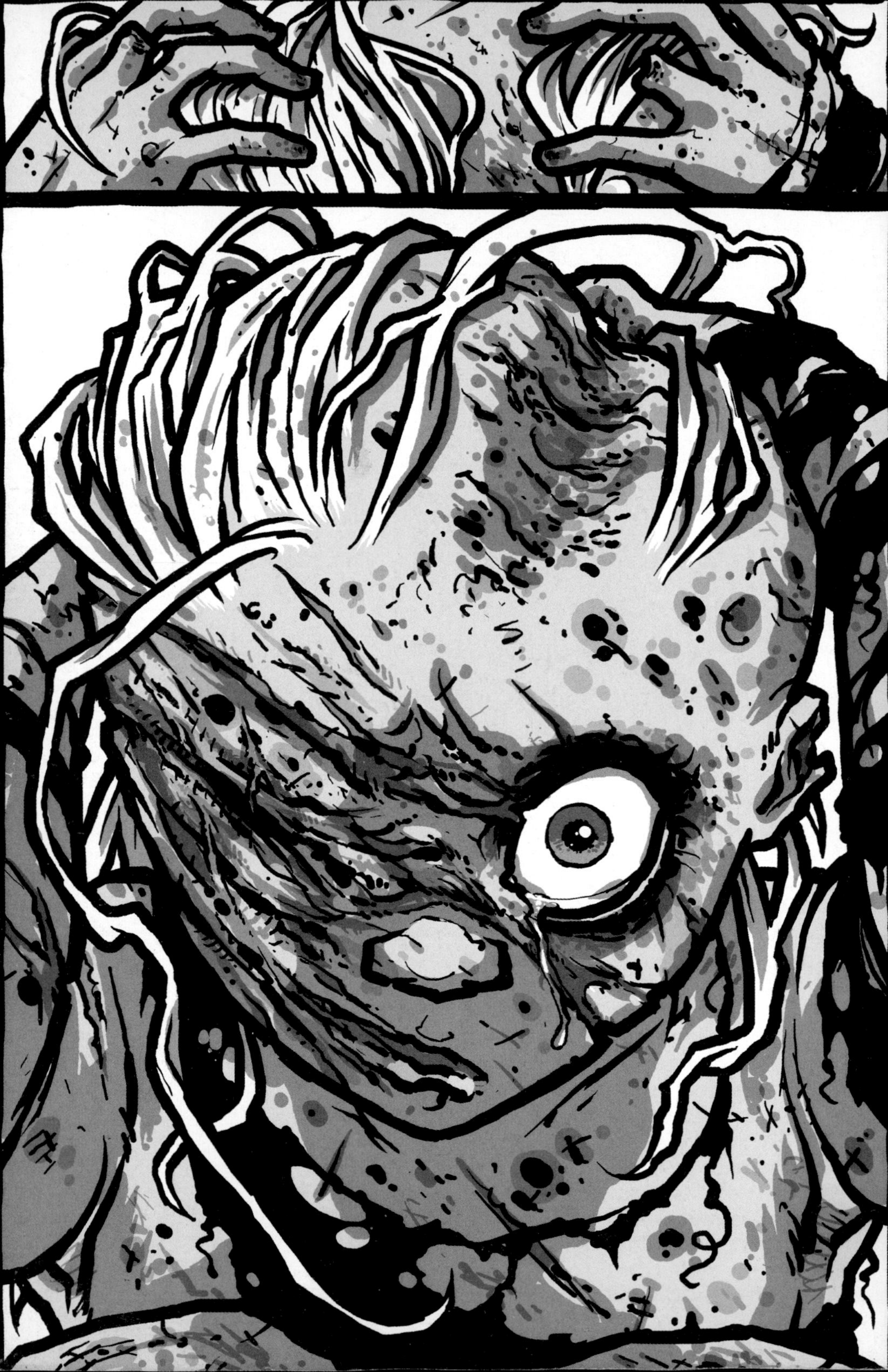